Orth

A novel by
Milton Bolzendahl

Fideli
Publishing

© Copyright 2009, Milton Bolzendahl

All Rights Reserved.

No part of this book may be reproduced, stored in a retrieval system, or transmitted by any means, electronic, mechanical, photocopying, recording, or otherwise, without written permission from the author.

ISBN: 978-1-60414-155-9

Orth

Prologue

I was introduced to Orth Schilling Volzenkoff by a lady that called upon me while I was an Adjunct Professor of Accountancy at Carnegie-Mellon Graduate School of Economics and Management. She said she learned of me through a mutual acquaintance of ours, the Reverend Michael P. Wilinda, Pastor, United Methodist Church, New Hesse, Wisconsin. She understood that I was proficient in the literary arts, to which I warned her that I do write prose with a marginal amount of success. In any event, she asked me to help her in documenting the life of her friend, and departed true love, Orth.

That gentlewoman's name is Catherine Irene Zimmerman. She supplied me with the material contained in this treatise. I wrote what she disclosed to me. The military and other life experiences of this man were derived from personal diaries and scrapbooks of the deceased which had been supplied to her by Dr. Volzenkoff's sons, John Schilling and Bertram Orth. I have disclosed the information and have written in the format and style requested by Mrs. Zimmerman. There could be errors or miscalculations in this manuscript of which I humbly caution the reader. I have merely attempted to tell the story as truthfully and accurately as my mind would allow. Possibly a lot more could be said, or a lot less could be said. I have stated it in the best manner I felt necessary to tell this remarkable tale of a man, a soldier, a scholar, a father and above all else, a Christian.

—M.B.
1999, New Haven, Connecticut

CHAPTER I

> *And when the Pharisees saw it, they said to His disciples, "Why does your Teacher eat with tax collectors and sinners?" When Jesus heard that He said to them, "Those who are well have no need of a physician, but those who are sick. But, go and learn what this means: I desire mercy and not sacrifice! For I did not come to call the righteous, but sinners to repentance."*
>
> Matthew 9:11-13

It's pleasantly warm this evening beside Lake Michigan. Inside an old decorative German tavern in central Milwaukee several customers have gathered together.

"How come the baseball strike?" asks Eddie Aiteanwealer, lamenting on the strike, sitting in his favorite haunt, tipping his fifth tankard of ale. "Those no good galoots!"

"Who?" asks his tavern friend, Barnabus Blitzgreez.

"Those lousy ballplayers – asking for more money. Heck, they are wallowing in dough!"

"Really?" replies Barnabus Blitzgreez, his always stalwart companion of the tavern and cups.

"Yeah, those d**mned slobs get over a million bucks a year while I get a stinking ten bucks an hour, after taxes, fuel, tires and all that other stuff."

Eddie downs another gulp of suds, wipes his mouth on his leather jacket and stares acidly at Blitzgreez. "Well, Eddie, maybe it's part your fault."

Eddie slams his mug down on the table top – his muscles stiffen on his fat, fleshy face, "I ought'a punch you out fer that, Blitzy!"

"Hold on, Eddie!" cautions Blitzy. "I remember somethin' from an article I read last night by this economics guy. He said somethin' about inflation – demand and stuff like that."

Eddie takes another hefty drag of ale from his mug and blurts, "Well, those bookworm guys are full of manure – that's what's wrong with this country – too much edeekashun."

Eddie continues, "We need more guys like Crush Rimboss – guys that don't eat broccoli... real men that eat double bacon cheeseburgers and fries. Too many of those queers goin' around screwing things up!"

Blitzy muses, sipping his favorite lager then asks, "You go to a lot of ball games?"

"You bet!" retorts Eddie.

"Well," Blitzy continues, "Would you go to a lot of games if the team never won?"

Eddie looks at Blitzy bleary-eyed, then gutturally spouts, "Are you kidding? I want my team to be right up there, man!"

"Then I guess you are pretty much like a lot of fans, huh, Eddie?" Blitzy remarks.

"Howszzat?" Eddie blurts.

"Well, you only show up if the team is winning – which means the owners have to keep winning or go down the tubes."

At this point Eddie's girl friend, Libby Latouche (sometime mud wrestler) joined them at the bar. Libby's youth had left her some time ago, and she endeavors to fill the vacancy with an abundance of perfume, cosmetics and assorted ornaments.

"It's sort of like this," Blitzy continues, "as I remember the demand for something pulls the price up, or if the cost of something goes up – then it pushes up the price." Blitzy thinks a moment, as Libby adjusts her bra straps. "Ya – that's it, Eddie, like push-pull economics. I think that's the term that Professor Milton somebody, used in the article."

The astute reader will by now surmise that Eddie Aiteanwealer would not attain to a very lofty height on a standard IQ exam. Barney Blitzgreez, one may conclude would score considerably above Eddie! Libby remains an enigma, as all of those of her gender seem to.

Eddie, it may appear, has reached close to the limit of his patience with Blitzy by now. So Eddie feels an urge to lighten the load in his bladder, which seems to have been exacerbated by the comments of Blitzy. Eddie returns and Libby is feeling an urge to be more noticed.

"What's all this talk about demand mean?"

"Oh, I was trying to explain something about the cause of inflation that I read last night to Eddie," Barney replies.

"Well, what of it?" Libby asks indifferently, as she examines her makeup in her hand mirror, trying to cover a slight yawn.

"It's like this, Libby, if nobody gives a hoot about watching dames mud wrestle, how much would the tavern owners be willing to pay them?"

"Oh, that's simple, Barney – not very much, if anything."

"Exactly!" Barney exclaims.

The door to the tavern swings open to admit our hero, Orth Schilling Volzenkoff. He views quietly the variety of the patrons – then walks slowly over to take a seat at a small table in a corner of the tavern. As he sits down he places his somewhat tattered briefcase by his feet and pulls from it a small brown volume and begins to read from it. Orth is a tall, lean man in his late middle years. He wears glasses and has a noble, studious, learned countenance. His dress is very modest and his bearing is such that one would expect that he has more important things on his mind than personal adornments and worldly pleasures. His hair is light brown, but graying at the temples and his facial features are Saxon-like, but with a kindly sparkle in his eyes. Orth's mouth is broad, but seems to express a calm, peaceful, joyful expression of the heart. While he is perusing the book a waitress saunters up to take his order.

"What'll it be, Ortie? Same ol' thing?"

"I believe so, Bertha," replies Orth.

Bertha jots down on her order tablet, 'vegetable plate, coffee, two hard rolls.' "Don't you get tired of the same ol' thing, Ortie?" Bertha asks.

Orth shifts his tall, angular frame, smiles and looks into Bertha's Aryan eyes and answers, "I try to keep things simple and ordinary."

The waitress shrugs, turns and hurries off, remarking over her shoulders, "You're an odd one, Ortie."

Orth grins.

Meanwhile, Eddie, Barney and Libby continue their discussion over baseball salaries and economics. "Do you begin to get the point, Eddie?" Barney asks.

"I dunno, Blitzy. I can't buy the idea that fans can push up the price of the ballplayers' paychecks yet. It just looks like those galoots are a greedy bunch, looking for a fast, easy way to a rich, lazy life."

Libby sips her glass of beer at the same time glancing around the tavern. She finds Orth sitting hunched over his supper and reading. "Hey, there's Ortie over there."

"Yeah," cries Blitzy, "let's go over and see Ortie. He's a real smart guy..."

Eddie gulps another swig of his ale and eyes Orth with his half-closed, glassy eyes, and utters disdainfully, "Ortie is just another of those d***m, religious freaks. What does he know about ballplayers and stuff like that? You guys can go over there, but not me."

So, with that Blitzy and Libby amble over to Orth's small table. "How's it with you, Ortie?" Barney opens.

"hiyah, Ortie," Libby joins.

"Oh, hello Libby and Barnabus. Nice to see you. Please, join me," Orth replies. Barney grabs a chair from a nearby table and they sit down.

"You don't eat very much, do you, Ortie?" Libby observes.

"I try to be moderate, as in all things, Libby," Orth replies.

"Speaking of moderation, we were just discussing the high prices of baseball players' salaries," Barney comments.

"Yes, I've heard there are cases where some players are getting several millions," Orth observes.

Libby joins, "Barney was trying to explain the causes to Eddie, but I don't think much sank in."

Barney asks, "What do you think, Ortie?"

"Well, sadly, a person's sense of moral values is often diminished by a zeal for economic gain. There is nothing wrong, that I can see about earning as much as you can, but money is often a trap," Ortie observes.

Libby says, "You use such big words, but I love to hear you talk, Ortie."

"Me, too," Barney joins.

"To put it plainly," Orth says, "the love of money, or economic gain leads one to many sorrows, because it crowds out faith, unselfish love for others, patience and gentleness; it's human nature. Corporations and business executives often allow greed and avarice to warp their ideals or values. God sees nothing wrong in seeing His people earn a living, but He does become angry when excessive gains are taken to the disadvantage of others and in an evil manner. Money is a trap too. It leads one away from God. Jesus said that it is easier to pass a camel through the eye of a needle than for a rich man to enter Heaven. Which means that too much money will push God out of your mind. He is replaced by worry and fretfulness over money and the things that are immaterial as far as one's soul is concerned. The greatest gifts are love and peace of mind, freely given by God, but sadly, most generally rejected by the world. I've seen a lot of wealthy people who are constantly searching for ways to bring them peace and love by acquiring new gadgets, bigger houses and so forth. It's the grand deception by the devil. God is the answer, not the things of the world."

"Now you're coming in with that God thing again, Ortie," says Barney.

Orth takes a sip of his coffee and retorts, "He's my life, Blitzy, I owe Him too much, after all He is truth and knowledge, all in one package."

Orth takes a portion of his meal into his mouth, pauses a moment, then adds, "Baseball is an art, Barney. Art is a talent and talent is a gift of God. Talent cannot be bought. You cannot go to K-Mart and pluck it off the shelf. Salaries are an aside from talent, an appreciation of talent. Excessive money does not increase talent, but it often has an adverse effect. Lavish living, an excess of food, drink and sensuality can crowd out talent. A hungry artist does better than a gluttony Falstaffian one. Talent, being from God is an expression of his love, and love is not a glutton to seek its own way, not avaricious, nor selfish."

Barney shifts uneasily in his chair and glances at Libby, who eyes Orth intently. "Well, what if you were a baseball player, Ortie, and were offered two million bucks, would you take it?"

Orth considered the question and replied, "Two million dollars based upon the economy of a baseball team is absurd. A worker is entitled to a fair wage. A person of talent is no different than a carpenter. Twenty-five percent of a product is about all one may expect, I think, in salary."

Libby's eyebrows knitted at this point and she asked, "Could that mean that for every dollar this place takes in, twenty-five cents could be expected to be doled out in paychecks?"

"That's kind of it, Libby," Orth replies. Then adds, "A big league team takes in about twenty-five million, excluding television and radio receipts, which means that, in my opinion, a fair salary would be a maximum of $200,000."

Barney asks after taking a hefty gulp of his brew, "Where does the rest go after twenty-five percent for salaries, Ortie?"

"Good question, Barney. About ten percent goes to the owners. The rest, sixty-five percent is for fixed costs, travel and overhead. To put it plainly, to operate the plant."

"Man, Ortie, you seem to know a lot about money and stuff like that. Here, I always thought you were just a religious freak, no offense intended," Barney remarks.

"Oh, I don't mind. As a matter of fact, if I can be subjected to any manner of abuse for doing my job as a Christian, I feel it is a reward. After all, my Master suffered many and violent ways to save my soul and yours, Barney," replies Orth.

"To return to your question, Barney," Orth continues, "my first act would be to ask God in prayer, then ponder a while, perhaps a day or two, being patient for His answer to come to me. This is sometimes a strong, emotional thing, or else very subtle. He expects me to stand up like a man and decide things in the best manner that my Christian faith will allow me. John Wesley did things in that manner. There are many examples where noble men have refused riches because they considered it may jeopardize their freedom and moral standards. Money can, and often does result in rapacious, inordinate greed if the recipient lacks scrupulous restraint. Oliver Cromwell refused the crown of England, and, of course, our Lord, Jesus Christ repudiated worldly riches when He was enticed to declare His allegiance to Satan and thereby deny His Father in Heaven."

"So, what would you do, Ortie?" Libby asks.

"If I said I would take the two million, you would say I was greedy, or would your estimation of my Christian living be diminished in your eyes, Libby?" Orth comments.

Barney joins in, "If you didn't take it, I would think you were nuts!"

"In other words, Barney, any guy here in the world in your estimation, in his right mind, would accept the money and run, is that right?" Orth replies.

"Yeah, that's right," Barnabus answers.

"That being the case, then, I would be inclined to deny the salary offer, because, in your eyes, Barney, I would be like any other guy, grabbing the money and running. My bearing as a Christian would suffer, and you may be inclined to say to your buddies, 'Well, Ortie took the two million like any other greedy slob, and he calls himself a Christian'," Orth concludes.

Libby adds, "You are really weird, Ortie."

Orth leans back in his chair, puts his hands behind his head, and resoundly laughs. He has a broad grin and well-formed bright teeth. "Hah! Of course,

I'm eccentric, or as you say, 'weird', Libby. A faithful and working disciple of Christ is always considered strange based upon the standards of the world."

Barnabus, attempting to get the conversation back to baseball and economics observes, "Well, where, or what do you think will happen to baseball with all this money thing, Ortie?"

"Barney," Orth adds, "greed, envy, strife in baseball all spell out a philosophy of 'get all you can, while you can', and that is wrong because it will result in somebody suffering as a result of it. The love of money will bring destruction. Did it not for Rome? And result in revolutions throughout the world in France, England, Russia, Babylon and so forth? One reaps what they sow, Barney."

Libby excuses herself and heads for the ladies' room. The noise of the tavern crowd starts to increase as the patrons dance to the small German band. Barney glances over to the dance floor and notices Eddie lumbering about grasping a young lady in an ungraceful manner, then asks, "Where did you go to school, Ortie? You seem to know a lot about different things."

"I started to learn when I became a Christian, but to satiate your inquisitiveness, I obtained by bachelor's degree from San Francisco State University, my master's – an MBA from the University of Missouri and my doctorate from the University of Utah, while I was teaching there."

Barney's eyes lit up and his face emitted amazement, and he blurts, "Man, Ortie! You did all that?"

"Yup," replies Orth as he adds, "don't admire me, Barney. God helped me and I have been much blessed."

The revelers in the tavern are getting quite animated by now and given to boisterous outcries resulting no doubt from the degree of their libations. Libby, having returned from the restroom, seems disturbed as she asks, "why do you come to a joint like this, Ortie? You don't even drink and this mob is always a rowdy mess."

Orth glances around the crowd slowly. Some young people are congregated around tables, a few older men are either hunched over on bar stools or simply standing idly by, and the rest a variety of middle agers are either dancing or talking in groups at the tables surrounding the dance floor.

"The food's good, it's close by and I feel the Lord wants me to help some people," Orth replies.

"What! Help these idiots?" Barney cries out, and he notices Bertha, the waitress passing and calls, "Hey, Bertha, could you bring me another brew, and one for Libby, too?"

Libby thanks Barney in an absent-minded manner, as she seems to have something deeply troubling her. She observes, "You always seem so peaceful and happy, Ortie."

"It's God's blessing to me, Libby," Orth replies. "I was like many others you see here and elsewhere, who have yet to experience that resounding gift, something electrical, telling one the truth about Jesus Christ."

Libby takes a sip from her glass, then says, "My name is not really Libby Latouche. It's Catherine – Catherine Irene Zimmerman ... I changed it because the places where I entertain thought I needed a more showy and sexy name." Tears seemed to form in her eyes as she spoke. "My life has really been a wretched mess, Ortie."

"I'm sorry, Libby ... er, I mean Catherine," Orth said.

"Oh, that's okay, Ortie. You can continue to call me Libby. I'm so used to it now," she replies. At this, Libby turns in her chair, gets up and hurries off to join Eddie and the others at the bar. Orth notices that Libby has been visibly shaken by what has been said or what she had been thinking.

Barney glances at Libby and vacuously asks Orth, "What's with her?"

Orth pauses a minute then admits that he is uncertain, but he has some inkling inwardly. Barney grunts, "Uh ... those females ... I just cannot understand," adding, "Ortie, could we get back to this baseball thing and the salaries?"

Orth replies, "Okay, Barney, shoot."

Barney pauses a moment then says, "Those high salaries are not all caused by greed, are they?"

"It's like this, Barney, based upon my limited knowledge of economics, as my major field of study was primarily accounting, finance and management, the law or premises of economics deals with costs, demands and prices. The price of something goes up because either the demand for it exceeds the production rate or the costs of producing the thing increases, therefore, pushing the price up. It's what economists term, 'push-pull, cost push', and then this whole thing is affected by the money supply, as the monetarists term it – too much money chases too few goods."

Barney leans back in his chair and eyes the ceiling for a moment. Orth continues, "So you see, Barney, when people have sufficient to meet their needs, they desire more to satisfy their appetites for ease and pleasure, symptoms of selfishness. And ... of course, greed is a form of selfishness. When the economy gets out of hand and prices go wacky, then the government steps in and people's greed results in the loss of freedom when they rely on government to run things."

"Huh, Ortie, what you say makes sense to me, now, considering what I read last night." Barney says.

"And," Orth continues, "the cost of ballplayers goes up because of the greed of the fans, always wanting a winner, the insatiable desire to be a legend of glory, forces them up. There just are not that many hot hitters and twenty game starting pitchers to go around, unless, of course, the supply increases."

"How could that happen, Ortie?" Barney asks.

"If a lot of other countries have baseball programs. We are starting to see that now in Europe, Asia, Latin America and so forth," Orth observes. "And, if the money bag of the owners experiences a drought, that will bring down the price also." He adds, "The market has a way of correcting itself, sometimes the correction is quite abrupt, harsh and cruel, like the crash of the stock markets. Baseball will correct itself. Some will suffer, but one reaps what they sow – selfishness breeds selfishness."

Orth pauses a moment, shifts his tall, lean frame on his chair, then adds, "Barney, God is not against success. In fact He wants His people to be successful, but on His terms, not on your own terms. That means if you use your money and position to satisfy your own selfish appetites, like expensive cars, houses, lavish parties, sensual excessive sexual activities, drugs and so forth, that is not on God's terms. He expects His people to live modestly and to use excess monies to help people. God's successful people are happy – happy with a devoted appreciation with what God has given them. Worldly, self-centered people are never – or rarely happy – they are ever in quest of more and more money, fancy gee-gaws, town houses, castles in the country. Louis XVI of France experienced this sort of thing before the Revolution. His wife, Marie Antoinette, had an insatiable appetite for the gaudy, lavish, luxurious things of the world. Well, things ended up in a wretched mess. The poor citizens got fed up paying for all this and they sent the King and a lot of others to the gallows. True success is not measured in gold and silver. True success is measured by the love you hold in your heart – a warm, unselfish, God-centered life. A lot of people commit suicide every year who are successful if measured by worldly patterns. A dean at the University where I was teaching was one of the archetypes. He had a good education, money, lived in an expensive apartment, had a fine position, a boat, and so forth. Yet he did not have love in his heart. He felt vacant. He could not buy happiness and as a solution to his 'no win' situation, he thought the gun was the answer. If only he had reached out to grasp the hand of the man from Galilee, Jesus, for his solution."

Orth stops, looks down and slowly shakes his head. Barney sits in silence, and in a pensive mood.

Barney glances over to the ornamental bar where a noisy and rowdy discussion has commenced. Eddie seems to be in the center of it all – waving his hands animatedly and yelling in a sottish, angry fashion. Libby is seen absenting herself from the rowdy, raucous gathering and walks in a concerned manner back to Orth and Barney at their table.

Barney asks, "What's all the arguing about, Libby?"

Libby sits down, places her hands in her lap and replies disinterestedly, "It's that darn baseball thing again ... Eddie is arguing with Archie Airehorn. It's getting pretty bad. I don't think either one knows anything about anything. The big bozos have always hated each other. Eddie has picked up on your idea Blitzy that the high salaries are caused by the fans and Archie says he's full of cr*p adding that it's caused by the television companies. But, now it's gotten around to just yelling and name-calling at about anything."

Barney interjects, "The dumb clowns, someday somebody is going to get hurt between those two."

At this moment, the crowd at the bar became silent and it was apparent that Eddie and his antagonist, Archie were squaring off to defend their opinions in physical combat. Barney exclaims to Orth, "Say, Ortie, I do believe violence is about to erupt over there."

Orth slowly gets up and in a determined fashion, strides over to the place where the two combatants are facing each other, hurling abusive, rude and vindictive epithets against each other. Orth's tall angular frame towers over both.

Just as Orth arrives at the spot a few steps from the field of battle, Eddie bursts forth towards Archie with his bulk, fists flailing. Orth instinctively lowers his shoulders and knocks Eddie against the bar and to the floor. For a moment Eddie sits, stunned. Then tottering up unsteadily says menacingly through bloodied teeth, "Ortie, you Bible bashing b*****d, stay out of this!"

Orth replies calmly, "Sorry, Eddie, but I abhor violence and seeing people getting hurt over insignificant details."

About this time, Archie grasps at the opportunity, seeing Eddie confused and weakened by Orth's blow and strikes Eddie a blow to the side of his head and another to his stomach. Eddie doubles up and staggers back. Orth, who had turned to walk away, and taken by surprise, springs with cat-like dexterity and delivers a stunning judo blow to Archie, who immediately crumbles up and collapses in a heap. Eddie, to finish matters, steps over to a now kneeling Archie and lets fly a terrific blow to his left ear. Orth quickly delivers another lightning fast, karate blow to Eddie, who also melts down into a heap of sodden flesh next to Archie. Both fighters are now in various stages of battered repose on the floor. Then they surprisingly glance up to Orth, who says, "Peace between you, my friends, or else you will again reap the harvest of the evil you sow. Now shake hands and forgive each other. Brothers should not fight each other."

Both men, in their faint and wounded manner, reluctantly extend to each other their hands. Archie softens and also clasps his arm around Eddie's shoulders. Orth smiles and quietly walks back to his table.

"Boy, Ortie, where did you learn that judo stuff?"

"Various places, but I guess it started in the Army," Orth said.

"I thought you were supposed to turn the other cheek," Libby adds.

"Well, sometimes to teach discipline, one has to resort to harsh and abrupt measures and because I love those men as brothers, I felt the Lord wanted me to drive the point home, as I did with a certain potency." Orth concludes.

The crowd disperses amongst a series of muted conversations, as the door swings open and in strides two police officers. They approach the bar, whereupon the tavern keeper, Otto, a large middle-aged man of a fair complexion, addresses them. They converse for several moments while one officer makes notes. They terminate their conversation and amble over to the table occupied by Orth, Barney and Libby.

"Hello, Orth," says one of the officers.

"Oh, greetings, Paul," Orth replies. They both exchange mutual phrases of minor significance, then Paul comments. "I hear you were instrumental in breaking up a brawl in here."

"I did what I thought appropriate, Paul, just a couple of confused beings, whose good judgment had been clouded by their imbibings. No harm done, Paul. I believe they have reconciled their differences."

Paul glances over to the bar where Eddie and Archie are quietly sitting, talking between themselves and others, then adds, "Looks peaceful enough. Well, let's get going, then Al," addressing his partner. "See you later, Orth," Paul concludes as he turns and walks out.

FREDERICK'S... AN OLD MILWAUKEE LANDMARK TAVERN EMITS AN AIR OF ANCIENT GERMAN ANCESTRY...

"God bless you, Paul. Say hello to your wife for me," Orth says.

"Will do, Orth," Paul says as he opens the door to exit the tavern.

"Where did you meet the cop?" Barney inquires as he tips his glass.

"He's a member of the Methodist Church I attend," Orth replies as he gathers his book and notes he had been preparing into his satchel.

"Cops go to church? Well, I'll be darned," Barney comments in a playful bantering manner.

"All people need God, Barney, the rich, the poor, police ... everybody," Orth said as he gathers his long, tall, boney frame up from the chair, pausing for a moment to glance at both Libby and Barney sitting there. "Hope to see you again soon."

Both Libby and Barney join together in bidding good-byes to Orth, as he walks slowly over to the bar, pulling his wallet from his faded jeans to pay the bartender for his meal.

Back at the table, Libby is eyeing the floor and Barney empties his glass and gazes at Libby, asking, "Penny for your thoughts?"

Libby lifts her head and pushes back a few errant brown locks from her forehead, staring blankly at Barney for a moment. Tears are welling up in her eyes and beginning to tumble down her middle-aged cheeks, as she utters with difficulty, "He's some kind of neat guy … always polite and courteous to me, even to me, a no-good slut…" She gets up quickly and walks off toward the ladies' room.

Barney empties the contents of his tankard of beer and departs the table to rejoin Eddie and the others at the bar.

Orth opens the door, takes a few steps outside the tavern and pauses for a moment, pulling on his heavy pull-over sweater. The tavern is named 'Frederick's', and is a landmark of sorts, being in the center of the downtown district of Milwaukee for many years, on North Fourth Street, close to the Milwaukee River, just slightly south of Juneau Avenue. The decor is older and emits an air of German ancestry and quiet eloquence of past eras. The bar is a massive wooden structure with a backdrop of mirrors, Falstaffian type oil paintings and an abundance of carved wood ornamentation. The interior of the tavern consists of a plain wooden floor, heavy wooden tables and an open space where the patrons danced Wednesday and Friday evenings to a small band comprised of mostly older men, except the long-haired drummer, who appears to be in his late twenties or early thirties. The music is primarily polkas and country-western, with an occasional nostalgic 40's or 50's tune. The Saxon food is plain and wholesome – tending toward the Prussian of heaviness. Orth especially enjoys the German method of preparing potatoes and vegetables. The dinner rolls are fresh and plentiful – the coffee being stout and with a hearty flavor. The tavern keeper, Otto Lufthaven, one of several great-grandchildren of the original owner, Frederick Hauptman. Employees are selected upon the basis of their Junker features and Germanic backgrounds in an effort to retain the original Prussian atmosphere. Patrons who enjoy the casual, rustic, yet efficient manner of the place, are a mixture of commercial workers and it is not unusual to see some middle and higher executives in attendance from the surrounding business buildings of Michigan Avenue and the Civic Center.

Orth pauses and breathes in the crisp, cool evening air of early spring, turns and starts walking briskly towards the parking lot.

CHAPTER II

"But I say to you, love your enemies, bless those who curse you, do good to those who hate you and pray for those who spitefully use you and persecute you..."

Matthew 5:44

    His strides are long – his keen blue eyes deep set amongst his chiseled features view the various features of the buildings. Some structures are old, cowering below those bold new towers of glass and steel that house a polyglot of offices along Fourth Street. He surprises a group of pigeons gorging along the sidewalk who express their disapproval by a whirl of wings and squawks ... On he strides, lights in the offices twinkle on – like missing teeth in a gigantic man. He becomes lost in his thoughts. His eyes focus on the pavement as he muses to himself, "How could I have done more to help those people in the tavern tonight? Would I really have the guts and Christian faith and fortitude to turn down a two-million dollar salary offer? How could I become a more effective and efficacious worker for God and Christ? Am I beginning to lose my marbles?" And so on. In a low whisper he begins to murmur a prayer, "Father help me; thou knowest all things...give me those things I lack in wisdom and intellect to bring others to know thy Son the Christ; eliminate pride and selfishness from my mind – let me be more concerned about my neighbor's well-being before my own..." and on he prays.

    "hold on there, old man!" Orth stops abruptly. He looks startled at the five youths facing him. He also senses the presence of more persons coming up behind him, but is uncertain of the number. The gang looks sinister, rags are their attire. They hold an assorted number and kinds of weapons in their hands; chains, knives, pistols. The gang emerged from the dark recesses between the buildings on State Street and have threatened Orth in the center part of the parking lot, just a few yards from his somewhat weathered and aged small pickup truck.

"I'm unarmed, boys ... and if it's my money you want, you shall have it," Orth says as he lifts his lean, sinewy arms level with is belt.

One of the gang members responds in a sarcastic tone, "Well, if it isn't 'Goody-Two-Shoes', Orth Volzenkoff." Orth stiffens and looks toward the voice. The voice continues ... "saving any souls lately, Ortie?" Orth now recognizes the person, pauses a minute, then replies. "What a surprise, Bob! I haven't seen you round church for a long time and I wondered why you haven't been coming."

The gang member is Robert (Bob) Scapegrace, the son of a well-known attorney in a community north of Milwaukee. Bob had done badly in school because of his inability to read. The attorney's wife had pleaded with his teachers and principals for special help ... but the scholars felt they could not tolerate Bob's ill temper and reprehensible disposition. It seems that Bob's poor scholastic results and his terrible manners were a defense against his inability to distinguish alphabetical letters and grammatical symbols. In his younger years Bob had been quite active in the Methodist Church youth groups and that is where Orth had met him. Lately, however, Bob has fallen victim to drugs and alcohol, and as a result has fallen away from anything approaching decency or moral virtue. His father, Alfred Worthy Scrapegrace, III, has avoided any fatherly contacts and regards Bob as a worthless wretch, reprehensible and good for the social scrapheap. Bob's mother, Mary Ann, has remained loyal and loving to him in a remarkably odd way, almost tacitly condoning Bob's activities and supplying him money, much to the chagrin of Alfred.

In his youth, Bob was mild mannered, shy, tall for his age. Now, his demeanor and personality have changed to one of resentment, antagonistic and anger. He has abruptly turned his back on anything decent and seems to see society as a phony moralistic fraud. Ragged clothes and abject disregard of his appearance now dominate Bob's disposition. His hair is long and shaggy. His face a motley mess of beard and lip hair. His long rangy tall body looks like a scarecrow plucked from a corn field. Deep set large brown eyes peer out at

Orth in a hazy, gloomy manner as he speaks.

"I've given up on all of that ... my friends are now these guys..." Bob spreads out his arms and hands, gesturing to the assembly of an angry bunch of warlike street rogues – about a dozen in number, who now surrounded Orth. Orth replies, "God is patient and He waits for your return, Bob. He is always easy to give you His help and love. He is ..." As Orth tried to continue his comments, a thundering blow was delivered to his head from behind and he crumpled to the parking lot pavement.

His mind whirled, a pool of muddled visions and thoughts. A cascade of words and ideas burst through the rills of his brain ... He is suddenly in thirteenth century England armed with a small broadsword, enlisted into the aid of Richard I (the Lionhearted)), fending off blows from Prince John's rebels – his thoughts compare the modern day street gangs to the outlaws of the forest during the days of Ivanhoe. His head aches ... he staggers ... the ground looms to gobble him up ... his mind whirls again ... vertigo ... a senseless mess ... He now finds himself humming and then singing hymns as he cavorts the green hills of the countryside. Sun splashes onto the green pasture, patches of trees are here and there like huddled peasants gossiping together, the hymns continue to occupy his mind – control his thoughts:

> "Amazing grace; how sweet the sound that saved a wretch like me! I once was lost, but now am found, was blind, but now I see."

Orth reflects upon his past life and how such a lecherous wretch he was until his mind was turned topsy-turvy by Christ ... Amazing grace! The utterly marvelous ineffable love of God received by people and not appreciated! The gift of Jesus the Christ by God the Father ... taken for granted – commonplace! How astonishing. Orth ... a complete personality change – instantly, when he was "born again" while serving as a Methodist youth leader. Like lightning zapping his brain ... yet in an almost subtle way. Amazing grace! "How can I repay God?" Orth muses. "Let me handle things," God seems to be saying ... More inexplicable images and thoughts rush into and extricate themselves from Orth's mind as he lies motionless on the cold night pavement. What about life and death? A clear voice rings in Orth's ears. The voice is baritone – firm, yet pleasing and tempered with wisdom and intellect.

"You are born from earthly dust or matter ... God the everlasting gives you a mind spirit or soul, whatever you choose to call it. The marvelous gift of life. We are born into it by the hand of the Master Builder – God..."

Extraneous voices are heard – shouts, loud banging noises. Then the pleasant deep resonant voice returns.

"Death is not for the children of Israel, Christ is the leader of Israel – live ye Christians ... believe that the true offspring of Jacob are those that accept the love of God and hold to the faith in His Son Jesus the Christ."

The voice fades away ... quiet invades his brain. Then alien voices call him, "Orth, Orth, Orth ... do you hear?"

He struggles to open his eyes. Pain – sharp knives thrust into his head, stomach and seemingly every part of his aching carcass. His eyes flicker open – his eyelids are heavy. Everything seems vague and white. The voice returns. "Mr. Volzenkoff, this is Doctor Fairweather ... do you hear me?" Orth manages a weak, "Yes." "You have taken a real beating and we are going to have to take you into surgery to try to mend you up and straighten some broken bones," the Doctor explains.

Orth's thoughts are unclear – he can only think about the pain that seems to poke at him from every direction – like some curious elf from the land of Lilliputian poking his diminutive spear into him He manages a muffled, "Okay ... I ache so blasted much ... ugh ... oh" Then he lapses back into the world of darkness. Doctor Fairweather turns to the nurse in attendance.

"Get him ready ... we have to get him into surgery right away. He is hemorrhaging very badly."

"Yes, Doctor," the nurse routinely replies.

The hours click by. Orth is under anesthetics. His mind sinks and swims again. Army days – basic training in California, the eternal fog creeping over the sand dunes while he is instructed in combat routines. His buddy in the lower bunk next to his ... Tom Tolliver – a tall, lanky red-haired guy, freckles that splotched over his whole childlike face. Always a silly little smile, rarely had to shave – his uniform never seemed to fit correctly – hair always a confused jumble. Assigned to a platoon in the 24th Division in Japan. Later to give up his life on a muddy Korean hillside. Always a shy, quiet kid ... accounts heard by Orth were that he became a real tiger in combat. Received the Silver Star for his gallantry; before he was gunned down in a hail of fire, he launched himself against the oncoming hoards of Chinese regulars with his BAR (Browning Automatic Rifle) blazing away while he told his squad to retreat while he diverted the enemy attention to himself.

THE ARMY...WHERE EVERYTHING IS REGULATIONS AND RULES UNTIL COMBAT... THEN IT IS A WRETCHED MESS - HELL ON EARTH WHERE LOGIC AND REASON ARE ABANDONED...

The blasted steel helmet weighs a ton ... run, dig foxholes, drill practice – non-coms carping at the dog recruits. "Get the lead out, Orth, faster, no chow tonight unless you guys get this place clean," etc., etc. The Army, where everything is regulations – rules, until combat ... then it is a wretched mess, yelling, pain – anger, crying – moaning. "Why, war?" muses Orth ... Let the diplomats live in the mud – slug it out, defecating on a hillside while fright stings your bowels. Yet the Army is where there is nothing left to coyness. Brave men and cowards are sorted out in the hot furnaces of desperation. Personalities are suddenly and abruptly altered. The bullies are often the ones sinking to despair. The clerks storm up slopes taking bullets into their guts.

Orth thinks on while under the influence of the anesthetics. His mind passes into and out of rooms of light and darkness. War ... no love in war. Brother gores, shoots, cooks, bayonets and grenades brother. But yet, there is sacrifice in war and sacrifice is the height of love. So one may suppose that the love in war is often an illusion. Men deluded into thinking that what they are doing is justified – is morally correct. Love is a treasure given to men by God. A treasure to be given away. He expects you and demands that devoted Christians give freely His gifts of love and charity. Orth had witnessed sacrifice on the hills of Korea. Abject sacrifice. Men suffering through cold, wet, running to help their buddies who had been the victims of gunfire.

But, what about war? Orth recalls that God punished those who attacked or misused His chosen – Moses, Joshua, David are the examples he recalls from the Bible. God protects His faithful and causes His witnesses to defend themselves against abuse. Yes! Then there were other times more recent when the early settlers in America were defended by God to fulfill His desire to let the "New Jerusalem" come forth and flourish starting with Columbus and continuing into a prosperous land of bountiful crops and wildlife ... Yes – just wars are those conflicts directed by God to defend His workers ... Christendom bursts forward protected by the umbrella of Jesus the Christ. Worldly rulers constantly repeat their same mistakes during history when they become self righteous – putting God away in a closet. Then the inevitable mistakes of trying to cure a nation's sickness by treating the symptoms.

The only just wars are those that defend God's freedom given to mankind – to freely live by His word and to worship Him. Despotism that denies men to these Heavenly gifts should be opposed because it places a barrier between men and their God ... Wars like the Revolutionary War are noble endeavors. The righteous Pilgrims, the Puritans, the Patriots who desired to live and rule this grand nation, these United States of America were denied their God given rights and freedom by King George III of England. God raised His hand in defense of His followers and children in New England. The British were astonishingly defeated by an outnumbered and out-gunned mixture of country folks and militiamen. God provides. The best soldiers that Britain could proffer were thwarted – frustrated and vanquished by a motley group of patriotic faithful men and women.

Lights flicker – people in white, vague shadows pass before his eyes. Orth struggles ... he becomes conscious – voices become clearer, but the pain is there from the operation.

"Would you like me to prop you up?" a nurse asks. Orth thinks in a confused manner, "No, just let me be for a while." He hears soft murmurs out in the hall – then quick, short, feminine steps. He closes his eyes and darkness envelopes his mind. Somehow hours – days, moments are abstract ... all running together like rice and vegetable soup. He opens his eyes slightly and glances at the ceiling ... nothing has changed ... the light fixtures, yet, he feels pressure on his hand. Orth weakly glances over to a female form sitting in a chair by his bedside. Her head is lowered almost to her lap. Orth is now conscious that the lady is Libby and manages a subdued and burdened, "Hiya, Libby. Nice to see you." She remains silent for a few moments, then slowly raises her head. Her face is flushed and her eyes are swollen ... tears are streaming down her cheeks. Orth notices a dramatic change in her appearance. She does not look like the street tramp he usually sees at the tavern. She is wearing a plain dress and a light sweater. Hardly any makeup, with her hair combed back. Orth notices her true beauty – without the gaudy adornments she usually has on. "You know, Ortie, I was so afraid for you ..." she tries to hold back the tears that burst forth. "Darn ... I'm such a sentimental old hag."

"I don't think so," Orth murmurs lowly ... "I think you're a princess." A long period of silence follows as they continue to sense each other's warmth. Then the door opens quietly and in strides the Doctor, Fairweather with a nurse.

"Well, welcome back to the land of reality, Mr. Volzenkoff," Doctor Fairweather cheerily announces.

"Orth is fine, Doctor, I'm not used to be addressed in such formal tones."

"Sorry Orth, but seriously, you came out quite fine ... I was more than moderately concerned there for a while." Allworth says, "We expect you to be up doing some light walking in a few days," he adds. Doctor Fairweather glances at the nurse who readies some equipment and medicine. "I apologize Miss Zimmerman, but we have to do some work. You can return tomorrow if you wish," Doctor Fairweather says to Libby. She rises and slowly presses her lips against the bandaged head of Orth. "Goodbye, Ortie, is there anything I can do for you?" Orth manages a wry smile through the bandages, "Yes ...

Libby, er, I mean Catherine, you can pray for me, as I will for you."

She stands still for a moment ... then quickly turns and walks out trying to hold back her emotions.

Several days pass. Orth gains in strength. It is now late in the afternoon, and he is propped up in bed reading a biography about Lafayette and the Revolutionary War period. A nurse strides in, "Are you up to talking to some police officers, Orth?" she asks.

"I suppose," Orth replies in a vague manner. The nurse walks out and several minutes later several police officers enter. One is wearing a suit, the other is in a uniform.

"Could we ask you some questions about what happened, Mr. Volzenkoff?" the officer asks. Orth thinks for a few moments. His thoughts keep going to Jesus as he asks himself, "What would the Master do in this situation?" He visualizes Christ on the Cross. "Forgive them, Father, for they know not what they do."

Orth replies, "I was walking to the parking lot after having supper and was accosted by a band of men, all in their late tens or early twenties."

"Could you describe them, Mr. Volzenkoff ... any distinguishing marks, mannerisms, color hair, dress, so forth?" the Sergeant asks.

Orth thinks for a second. "Well, in all honesty, I could probably supply you with quite a few details, but Sergeant, I know personally the leader and I would prefer not to press charges."

"This is a serious matter, Mr. Volzenkoff," the Sergeant counters, and adds, "these same hoodlums could very well wreak some more havoc on many more innocent victims because of your decision."

"If it were your son who beat you up on the street, would you like to see him put behind bars for ten years or so, keeping company with hardened criminals in prison, or would you give him a chance?" Orth asks.

At this moment, a hospital attendant comes in and declares, "Lunch time, Mr. Volzenkoff."

Orth tries to sit up ... with much difficulty, while the young lady places the tray on the bed and assists Orth in becoming more comfortable before attempting to dine. He pauses a moment to give thanks to God for his afternoon repast. The police sergeant is heard speaking to his partner in a hushed tone. Orth opens his eyes and glances at the tray ... mashed potatoes, diced carrots and a small helping of baked fish. Jello, a soft roll, relishes and coffee are also part of the meal.

The sergeant asks, "Is your mind set on this, Orth?"

Orth looks at the sergeant then over to his uniformed partner, then replies, "I'm a Christian, Sergeant, and certain things are expected of me, if I am expected to wear that badge with merit. My life was a wretched mess before Christ pulled me from the trash heaps of degradation. He did not give up on me. He watched over me while I slid up and down the muddy hills of Korea. He watched over me as I stumbled through life in school, a marriage that collapsed, my sons ... too many blasted things. I owe a lot to Him and I don't want to let Him down."

"How would you let Him down, Orth, if you cooperated with us?" the Sergeant inquires.

"It's like this," Orth says, "If God forgives, who am I not to forgive? Or, if God always gives people a second, third, fourth or seventh chance...shouldn't I?"

The Sergeant looks at Orth in silence for a moment. "If we don't come down hard on these no-good bas***ds, a lot of people are going to get hurt," he says. "You do not know that, Sergeant, you suppose that based upon some of the past cases you have no doubt witnessed.. I just do not see how more police, more jails, more courts, more guns have helped us much in the past. In fact, things are more screwed up now than they were forty years ago when I was those young persons' age.. If we would spend time and money teaching God to our young people, in my opinion, we would be heading in the right direction. LIFE IS FULL OF RISKS. The chance to save one soul from hell is worth the risk in my opinion. I am willing to give it a try."

The Sergeant closes his note pad, motions to his partner, then hands Orth a business card.

"Well, Orth, if you should have a change of attitude, call me up. Here is where you can reach me," he adds.

With this, the two officers bid Orth farewell and slowly depart. Orth follows them out and watches the door slowly close. He then reaches into his night stand by his bed and takes out his Bible, reading,

> "...love your enemies, pray for those who persecute you..."
> — Matthew 5:44-48

He slowly closes the Sacred History, places it back in the drawer with his other belongings and picks up his fork. He slowly places the fork into the piece of baked fish and recalls how the Savior told the Apostle Peter, "I shall make you a fisher of men..."

CHAPTER III

He does not forget the cry of the humble. Have mercy on me, O Lord! Consider my trouble from those who hate me. You lift me up from the gates of death that I may tell of all your praise in the gates of the daughter or Zion. I will rejoice in your salvation.

Psalms 9:12-14

At this point in the history of Orth Schilling Volzenkoff, we will treat his recovery and his unfortunate experience from the gang attack and his return to his home in the country some distance from the city confines of Milwaukee. Orth has sufficiently recovered from his injuries, according to Doctor Fairweather, to return to his home and has just finished his breakfast. He sips at his black coffee and sits up in bed.

"Ready to face the outside world, Orth?" Doctor Fairweather inquires as he abruptly enters.

"You bet!" Orth replies earnestly and adds, "My legs are still a bit sore."

"Well, it will take a little while. I'll get you a cane to help you along," Doctor Fairweather says as a nurse enters with a wheelchair.

"Do I need that?" Orth exclaims.

"It's routine," Doctor Fairweather answers. "We'll take you downstairs as soon as you are ready," he adds.

"That's fine, but how am I supposed to get home?" Orth asks.

"That's all taken care of by your friends," the nurse interjects.

"Well, I'm looking forward to this," Orth concludes as he painfully lifts his boney frame from the bed with effort and heads for the bathroom to shower and shave. Orth bathes himself and dresses, assisted by the nurse. After a stop at the hospital administrative offices where he settles his account, mainly through the auspices of his Army retirement, the nurse returns to wheel him out the front entrance where he is surprised to see Libby and Barnabus waiting to greet him and take him home.

Orth smiles and inwardly feels warm and peaceful after greeting Barnabus and Libby, who exchange niceties with him during the drive to Orth's house in the pastoral Wisconsin countryside. Orth and Libby exchange glances and smiles. He senses Libby desires to talk to him, as they pull into the drive where there is a sign swinging on a post saying "VOLZENKOFF" in chiseled wooden letters. The old sign says, "Squeak-squeak" as it yields to the wafting zephyrs. The air is warm and scented with red clover and vetch that abound in the surrounding pastures. The gravel road is about three hundred yards and winds slightly up to the house that sits on a knoll. Orth's faithful companion, "Mutnik", a small mongrel sheep dog runs up to the approaching car excitedly – tail whirling.

"Hi, old buddy," he yells to Mutnik, as Orth emerges from Barney's car. Libby aids Orth in walking into the house while Barney slowly walks behind.

They enter the front door. Libby eyes the wide expansive front porch, a swing, an assortment of plastic and wooden lawn chairs, a white metal garden table.

"Do you use the porch often, Ortie?" Libby asks.

"Well, yes, especially during the hot summer days. I like to have my morning coffee out here and listen to the sounds of the birds," Orth rejoins, then adds, "I also enjoy reading out here at the dusk hours." Mutnik stops abruptly at the front door with a shy look, his tail wagging rapidly.

"Does he come in?" Barney questions as he pets Mutnik several times.

"No, he's an outside dog ... stays out the year round – sleeps in the pump house. It's warm in there in the winter. I believe dogs belong outside so Mutnik and I have an understanding. He's a real buddy to me," Orth concludes.

Orth leads them into the foyer, then into the large parlor. Lined with bookshelves from floor to ceiling, the parlor emits a cheerful, peaceful, masculine familiarity. One wall is adorned with a massive stone fireplace. The furniture is a mixture of aged styled chairs, tables and sofas. A large low table sits in the center – cluttered with books, a large carved chess set, several jars of

ORTH SETTLES INTO HIS FAVORITE ARMCHAIR — AFTER BARNEY AND LIBBY DRIVE HIM HOME FROM THE HOSPITAL...

hard candy and clusters of pencils and pens protruding from tin cans. Spaced between the bookshelves are an assortment of framed photographs and oil paintings. Off to one side several flags are hanging from poles.

"Sorry about this mess," Orth admits in a low, offhanded tone. They stand for a brief moment in the parlor as the large grandfather clock in the corner sounds its deep resonant "tick-tock, tick-tock", and chimes the half hour note.

"Man, you sure have a lot of books, Ortie; have you read 'em all?" Barney comments.

Orth lightly smiles and chuckles slightly replying, "Oh, I've read a goodly portion of them, however, most of them are useful for my research and reference." He then reaches for a large leather-bound volume on the low table ... its black cover has that ancient look and the pages appear often leafed.

"This is my friend ... it is my 'work manual' – my daily bread," Orth says as Libby interjects in a low tone, "I'll bet it's the Bible."

"Yup!" Orth tersely says as he places the volume back down amid the other books, coffee cup, pencils and other assorted items.

Orth settles his rangy frame into a massive leather arm chair, places his legs on a footstool and motions to Barney and Libby to be seated on a long overstuffed divan adding, "Sit down if you like ... but, I know you are busy and have other things to do. I do appreciate your bringing me home. I do not want to be a burden to you."

Barney replies, "Well, I really should be going – getting back to the job, the boss is fidgety about time off."

Orth replies, "I understand, Barney. I do thank you again."

Libby is quiet, then adds, "Do you want me to stay with you tonight to help you get around? I will be decent – not seduce you." She smiles slightly.

Orth snickers, then says, "That's nice of you Libby ... I'll be okay. God will help me, and I know you've got things to do. Danny will be wondering about you. Love him, Libby. He so needs love and patience."

Libby stares at Orth for a brief moment, slowly turns and softly mentions to Barney, "Okay, well, let's be off then."

Barney and Libby bid goodbye to Orth and walk out onto the porch and down to Barney's car. The dust follows the car down the drive and out onto the road back to town.

Orth sits silently for a moment thinking, "My main job, Lord Jesus, is to work for you in saving souls ... help me." He gets up and kneels at the large table laden with books ... he bows his head and clasps his hands behind his back, raising his face skyward. Pain pierces those places on his body that have been badly bruised or cut. He remains silent for a few moments ... his eyes closed ... perspiration appears on his tanned forehead and on his sinewy arms as he prays:

"My Holy God, my Father in Heaven, I thank thee for Thy merciful kindness, Thy clemency ... grateful for helping me endure the rigors of the injuries that I have sustained at the hands of those ruffians. Have patience and mercy with them, my Father ... they so need Thee. Show those young men the errors of their ways. Open their minds to the Truth, to Christ, Thy glorious Son. Plant the seeds of Christian love in the soil of their minds ... in the name of Thy Holy Son, Jesus, the Messiah, I ask these things, amen, and amen."

He concludes his prayer and wanders into the kitchen through the dining room. The dining room table and furniture are of the old style, large carved wooden chairs and table. The table has an assortment of books on it along with two red candles set in wooden holders. The woven place mats are dusty. The walls are lined with oil paintings of seascapes and some prints of Rembrandts. Orth has a distinct like for Rembrandt Van Rijn's works – deep rich browns, reds and golds and how the artist made ample use of the contrasts of light and shade to lend a subtle genius to the works – a master craftsman.

He stands a moment in the kitchen wondering about what to prepare for himself. Hunger strikes a cord in his brain, yet he cannot bring himself to prepare anything. He pulls down a box of soda crackers, ripping it open and pulling out a packet. He places the box upon the kitchen table and walks back to the parlor mounting the stairs leading to his bedroom. There are three large bedrooms upstairs and an ample bathroom with a large bathtub mounted upon wrought iron ornate legs.

Walking into his bedroom, he places his crackers on his night stand and removing his shoes, eases himself upon the bed. He nonchalantly reaches over and grasps a volume of Tolstoy's writings and starts to read. A few moments later he reaches over to flip on his tape player ... and the Brahm's Symphony Number Four begins ... continuing to read and munching on some crackers, he feels his eyelids become heavy. The melodious strains of the music enter his ears like a whispering fountain of comfort and peace. He meditates about how God has blessed him with an appreciation of good music and literature, and recalls in his youth how he was such a rebellious rascal. He hears the country sounds outside his window – the chirp of the incessant crickets, the twitter of birds and a far off bark of the neighbor's dog down the road. The air is sweet with the smell of honeysuckle that abounds along his backyard fence. He hears Mutnik answer the bark of the neighbor's dog. Mutnik ... his faithful companion – a perfect "buddy" ... never demanding much, always giving his love, a cheerful countenance. Orth silently thanks God for Mutnik...

Orth drops off into a deep sleep as the gentle spring breezes waft through the open window by his bed and the birds add their choral assistance to the airs of the Brahma's Symphony. He dreams of Korea ... a hill southeast of

Pyongtaek, the North Koreans have butchered the green American troops badly. After enlisting and basic training, he had been assigned to the Twenty-Fourth Infantry Division stationed in Japan. His motives of enlisting were to take advantage of the GI Bill of Rights, an opportunity to attend college, to get away from home apron strings and, of course, the vaingloriousness of every young male – to prove his masculinity – a chance to become a hero in the eyes of the provincials. The early Army days were easy. The thrill of wearing a uniform – drinking beer – carousing with sluttish females and so forth. Garrison life in Japan was a country club existence – strawberries and cream on an English cricket green compared to the eternal red mud and wretched conditions he was subjected to in Korea.

He dreams – he is walking on muddied roads, boots sticking to the stuff like contact cement. Helmet heavy – crunching down on his sweaty head – clothing stinking – field rations, cans of scrambled eggs and ham, soda crackers. Of course, there was the occasional treat of a chocolate bar. He was slugged into reality one evening when his Company Commander, Captain Horace Philpot, announced at a hastily assembled formation that their unit was going to be flown over to Korea to halt the advance of the North Koreans who had decided to invade South Korea. It was termed a "Police Action" and was a farcical ploy to what was to become a nightmare of mud, blood and confusion. Over to Korea – from Pusan they were transported north. It was soon apparent that they were dreadfully ill-trained, ill-equipped, ill-lead and woefully out-gunned. The North Koreans were open for business. The Americans thought it would be a summer stroll through the park with a picnic basket...

Well, the first few weeks of combat were a rout – a comical parody of the United States Army. The North sent tanks, artillery and lots of crew-served weapons. Mortars, machine guns, etc. The Americans had nothing to stop them – they abandoned their gear in the field – helmets, boots, ammo and retreated. Orth's platoon under Second Lieutenant Treat were detailed to delay while the Company made their way on muddied roads, rice paddies, and endless foothills. Lt. Teat was soon a corpse – he was kneeling beside a Korean burial mound and received almost a direct hit from a mortar shell, his head severed substantially from his torso ... Sergeant Collins had the platoon dig in. Orth's squad – headed by Sergeant Gonzalez was to guard the western flank. As morning approached, the enemy came with armor, and it seemed to Orth, every weapon imaginable. The platoon was forced to lower themselves into the foxholes that were half-filled with water from the rain ... the water mixed with the fine red clay to form a mushy quagmire. The air was chill and the drizzle from above combined with the water in the foxhole gave Orth a sickening cold feeling. Mortar shells were bursting all around now. The Platoon returned the fire with a meager effort – many of the troops did not fire – purportedly because their weapons malfunctioned. Orth guessed about one out of seven soldiers were using their rifles. Sergeant First Class Collins ordered a retreat that was not heard by Orth's squad. Soon Orth's squad was firing almost point blank now.

Then it happened. A sudden blast hit the squad area – a shell had found the spot. Orth lost consciousness. When he came to, he was splattered with mud and debris and half out of the foxhole ... as he managed a glance about, he surmised all the squad was either dead or close to it ... the scene was a nightmare – too hideous – his stomach convulsed and he vomited wretchedly. As he lay motionless gazing upward, he felt a sharp pain pierce his left leg. Managing a glance, he pulled his legs from the ooze of the foxhole and discovered a nasty hole in his calf – blood was gushing out. He vomited again ... then lapsed into a dream world.

After a short while he regained consciousness and heard Korean voices. He lay still thinking that perhaps the enemy swine will take him for dead and move on.

Orth tries to position himself under a nearby corpse ... and is partially successful. Now he remains still as he hears the enemy soldiers stripping the dead and either firing bullets into the wounded or using bayonets. The cries of moaning buddies fill his numb ears. Soon he feels something hard jab at him ... he stifles a cry – he now feels hands jerking at his uniform and field gear. The hand tears at his filthy fatigue blouse, then there is a pause. He feels a sense of warmth, yet he thinks this impossible!

"How can I feel a sudden sensation of peace under these despicable conditions?" he asks himself.

He manages to tweak open one eye. To his astonishment, he sees a North Korean sergeant gazing down upon him ... his eyes are filled with tears! "Am I hopelessly going mad?" he muses. The enemy soldier fondles Orth's gold chain around his neck with the Christian cross attached. He had been given the necklace by his mother, Bertha, at his last visit home before he was sent overseas to Japan. Orth was not a devout believer and only wore the necklace as a manifestation of his love for his mother.

"Me Christian, too!" the enemy sergeant murmurs in a subdued tone.

Orth is overwhelmed ... but remains quiet as the sergeant motions with his index finger to his lips. At this the sergeant straightens up abruptly and calls loudly to the other enemy soldiers in the area. He hears the rustling of feet and clank of infantry accouterments – and he realizes that the sergeant has called an order to his troops to move out. As things quiet down ... the sergeant says ... "Here take," as he shoves some Koran food packages under Orth's battered uniform shirt. The sergeant then douses Orth's wounded leg with a white powder – and finishing with a hasty olive drab bandage which he ties over the wound. Then the sergeant silently rises and fires several rounds from his automatic pistol as a ploy to he troops that he has finished off the last of the remaining Americans on the hill.

Orth awakens from his slumber in his bed ... the Brahms Symphony has long since ended ... it has turned to evening and the afternoon breeze has abated, leaving the curtains limp like exhausted waterfalls. The "chirp-chirp" of crickets have taken up their place in nature's choir loft. Orth reaches over to turn on the light on one of his night stands. He recalls now how Christ had come to his rescue in Korea, by the symbol of the Cross. His parents had always been so kind and patient with him – insisting on Sunday School. How he rebelled! How absurdly ridiculous he always thought church was as a youth. Ah ... his youth. My young years were an embarrassment. Orth recalls the parable of the prodigal son (Luke 15); and he feels the peace of God in his bones and mind. How grateful he is to God for His patience with him. At this point in the history of Orth, we will turn to his early life. We will tell of his tussle with the problems of growing up, the seeds of morality planted by some people in his early life. The struggles of his parents – the difficult life on a small farm in northern Wisconsin. But first this brief digression.

* * *

Upon departing from the hospital, her visit with Orth, Libby returned to her apartment in a suburb of Milwaukee. On her way home, she stopped at a thrift store operated by a Presbyterian Church. There she purchased an old tattered Bible, a large, well-leafed dictionary, a historical novel about Saint Paul and a bright green and yellow cotton frock with white flowers along the hem line and shoulders. She arrived at her apartment late in the afternoon and found her son, Daniel, watching television.

"Turn that darn thing off, Danny. I have repeatedly asked you to watch that thing only for one hour after supper and while I am here!"

At that, young Daniel tosses down his peanut butter sandwich and storms off to his bedroom in an irritable mood, as he says over his shoulders before slamming the door, "Oh, Mom, you're always on my case."

Libby gazes at the closed door for a second then dejectedly slowly walks to the small table in the kitchenette. She places her packages on the table and vacuously commences to prepare supper. Her mind is a series of confused and bewildered ideas and thoughts. She reaches into the refrigerator and removes various articles of food, including a bottle of white wine, which she uses to fill a stem glass with.

She places the glass of wine to her lips and pauses a minute. She thinks of Orth and says to herself, "Nice guy – but an unrealistic romantic – but then he has such a hold on me, how could I ever turn around and become decent again?" She gazes out the window and sets the glass down on the counter without taking a sip. Her mind wanders back to her youth, and how her parents used to insist upon her always going to Sunday School and church. She thinks how repulsive she felt and disrespectful towards her parents … especially her mother, Adelaide.

"What a dope I have been," she thinks, then she remembers something from the Bible about how one reaps what they sow … But then that's all past, she muses. "I just could not fit in with all that 'churchy' stuff now … stiff collared, prissy, prim, church by the numbers – get out of line and they show you the door," she ponders to herself. But yet …

She turns from the window and sits at the table, burying her head in her arms as tears start to well in her eyes. "Why can't church be like the Sermon on the Mount – people sitting on the hillside, surely they didn't dress up and Christ loved them," she thinks. After a short time, she meditates.

"Golly, God, if you are there, help me … my life is such a miserable mess … I'm a slut … a drunkard … but I recall how you were always a friend to the outcasts, the whores and the flotsam of society's sewers." She remembers during one of the Sunday School lessons they talked about faith and how the woman had only to reach out and touch the hem of Jesus' robe to become well again, and how Jesus had compassion on Mary, a worthless, slovenly trollop who washed and anointed His feet, drying them with her hair. Perhaps … maybe there is hope … She continues her prayer …

"I'm like Mary, Holy Father, let me, help me to reach out and touch the robe of Christ … help me God … the miserable slut that I am … to come back to a decent clean life ... If what I remember from Sunday School is truth, God, then let me bathe the feet of the Savior with my tears and dry them with my hair, let me pick up the scraps from His table."

She feels the dampness of tears against her cheeks and lifts up her head. Her eyes meet her son's.

"What are you doing, Mom?"

Startled, Libby stammers for a moment and replies with red, tear-swollen eyes ... "Oh, thinking about a special guy in my life whom I have forgotten about."

"I was thinking, Mom ... er ... I'm sorry the way I acted ... didn't mean to make you cry," Daniel says. More tears return to Libby's eyes as she hugs Daniel adding, "When I was a little girl your age, my parents used to take me on picnics to a place called Griffith Park. Why don't we do that right now for our supper?"

"Super!" replies Daniel. "I'll just get my baseball glove and you can throw me a few," he added.

Libby hugs him again and says, "I'll make some sandwiches and get things ready."

Libby and Danny drive out to Griffith Park about seven miles from her apartment. The late afternoon is bright and warm – beams of sun are bursting through the tall elm and locust trees as they walk across the freshly mown green grass to an old wooden table a short way from a small pond where some white geese are cavorting – occasionally spraying themselves with water as they douse their long necks under the cool water of the pond. It is a pleasant spot under an elm tree – a shelter from the hot afternoon sun, quiet and peaceful. Libby feels a calm "release" from her cares and sorrows as she places the hamper on top of the table and begins to arrange things for their picnic supper. In the distance some young people are tossing a Frisbee, while a dog tries to interfere. The sound of frogs and the chirp of crickets, the squawk of geese interrupt the solitude.

Danny and Libby sit down and partake of their supper. Libby pours a tumbler of cool milk for Danny, who says, "I'm glad we came, Mom ... and I'm glad you're not drinking, too ... I don't like it when you're drunk."

Libby's hand shakes as she searches for a reasonable reply. "I'm sorry, Danny ... I'm sorry. Let's eat," she says as she manages a kindly small smile and chokes back her emotions. They complete their meal in relative silence. Libby slices Danny a piece of chocolate cake and pours herself a glass of iced tea. The shadows begin to creep across the warm grass as a slight breeze wafts through the branches above.

"Mom, why don't you and Grandpa get along?" Danny asks as he picks up his baseball glove and tosses the baseball up and down in it.

Libby picks up the other glove, getting up from the table and answers curtly, "It was something about my marrying your Daddy ... Grandpa thinks Catholics are enemies or something like that ... let's see how good I am with this thing."

They slowly walk out onto the grassy area and begin tossing the baseball back and forth. Libby remembers a passage from the Psalms she had read before her divorce from Joe ... let's see how did it go, something about parents, yes ... that's it ...

"When my father and my mother forsake me, then the Lord will take care of me." Psalms 27

She continues to think to herself as she tosses the ball back and forth (with a greater degree of accuracy than she had imagined she would have). "How I wanted Dad to like Joe, and I thought Mom would come around, after all Joe was not very Orthodox."

She misses a toss from Danny and it rolls down the slope into the water at the edge of the pond. She walks down and retrieves it and on the way back says to Danny, "How about you and me heading home. I've got some things I want to do before I call it a day." They pack up the picnic items and head for the car. The sun has headed down and the sky is a lovely bright red. Libby feels happy because of the opportunity to do things with Danny ... she feels that boys urgently need the companionship of a "buddy", a Dad, and she again feels the remorseful pain of the divorce.

CHAPTER IV

The kingdom of God is like this. A man scatters seed on the land: he goes to bed at night and gets up in the morning, and the seed sprouts and grows – how, he does not know.

Mark 4:26-28

Orth's parents were not church goes. However, they did insist on their children attending Sunday School. So, as a result of this, on Sunday mornings, Orth and his older brother, Fritz, either walked or were driven to Sunday School by neighbors. The church was Congregationalist and well attended by the local community ... however, the largest was the Lutheran Church across the park in the center of town. The Lutheran Church was a substantial structure of rough hewn stone and massive doors. The Congregational Church was a white frame building of modest size with a meeting hall attached to the main chapel. They attended the Congregationalist Church because Orth's mother, Bertha, insisted that they join a church that her parents had. There were other churches in town, the Baptist, Catholic, Presbyterian and so forth which often puzzled Orth as he asked himself, "Why so many churches? Isn't God the same for all people?" He was also concerned when people asked what church he went to and after he replied, and if the other person went to a different church, they would acquire a prudish air of resentment and hustled off with an annoyed disdainful aura about them.

The neighbors, Eddie Burran and Bessie Ordway often drove into the driveway to give Orth and Fritz rides on Sunday. Bertha would see them to the car and offer the usual salutations with an embarrassed glance – as she would not be going herself. The seeds were planted, however, into Orth's tender, youthful mind. The mighty seeds of Christ!

Orth often pondered upon the reason his parents did not attend Church … they were people of the soil and always seemed honest and trustworthy. Perhaps he thought to himself that they felt unworthy to attend because they often imbibed heavily in beer, especially his father, Frederick. And then he seemed to recall how his mother, Bertha, lacked decent "Sunday" clothes. Her attire around the farm was always ordinary – rough, simple clothes. Bertha did not drink excessively, but enough that people noticed in town at the grocery store and so forth. She was emphatic that both boys said the Lord's Prayer before bedtime and this stayed with Orth and became an automatic thing … until later in life when he realized that those prayers did work for him and saw him safely through many trials and hazardous experiences during his lifetime. Bertha always seemed to manage to come into the bedroom shared with his brother and kiss her sons goodnight – proffering a few words of comfort and love before turning out the light.

Life was harsh on the dairy – always living on the biting edge of poverty. Cold weather was a constant threat to the young calves. Orth usually fed the calves in the morning before school – lining up the buckets, filling the grain troughs with corn and wheat – ascertaining if any were sick and weekly cleaning out the individual pens. The stench of dairies was always present – manure with the occasional sweet odor of corn silage and freshly milled grain. Upon opening a new bag of grain for the calves, he used to run his fingers through the top portion – scoop up a handful and breathe in the smells. Out in the barns where the cows were housed during the harsh weather, there were long rows of mangers where the large heads of Holstein cows were thrust through with their nostrils in the hay or munching great gulps of forage and indifferently eyeing anyone who may enter with gigantic brown eyes displaying a deep sense of melancholy.

There were the wet seasons when rain drops used to find their way down Orth's neck as he did his chores in the barn. Outside the water formed lakes of manure where the herd assembled to be milked and fed. One's hands were never clean and were always hard and cracked – sometimes blood issued forth if one was not attentive to apply mom's special hand formula that stank of rancid animal lard and camphor. It worked – but the odor caused Orth consternation.

The farm was 320 acres with rolling pasture and some tillable where silage was grown. About twenty acres were wooded, including a ten acre pond. It was a pretty place when the weather was warm and the hay and forage crops were bursting forth from their deep soil winter hideaway.

Then there was rich Uncle Humphrey who always was the personification of a gentleman in the eyes of Orth. Uncle Humphrey seemed to be always wearing a tie – well-groomed and prudishly proper. Orth feared Uncle Humphrey because he felt insufficient to the task of bearing the proper manners to satisfy Uncle Humphrey – therefore Orth always felt a "coldness" between them. Uncle Humphrey would drive up to the dairy farm from Milwaukee for infrequent visits in his new large expensive Packard automobiles. The visits had an atmosphere of frigid cold – the adults sat in the small living room. Orth's dad was forlorn because he felt he was obliged to abstain from his beer in the presence of Humphrey, and the conversation was solemn. Uncle Humphrey was a lay leader in his Congregational Church – a consummate abstinent and the opinion hovered over the Volzenkoff dairy that Bertha had made a sad choice in her matrimonial alliance. Nevertheless, there it was. Humphrey had the good sense to choose a mate with considerable means. Aunt Mae (as she was called) was the only daughter of a wealthy farm implement dealer in Wisconsin. A substantial estate was left to Mae – held in trust by a bank in Milwaukee.

Although Uncle Humphrey seemed distant and not approachable to Orth, he always appeared cheerful and was indeed quite generous with his money towards Bertha. He would always send an envelope full of money on the holidays and request that it be used to buy something nice for each member of the family. Orth frequently thought he would like to be like Uncle Humphrey, always a proper Christian gentleman, never swearing, nor drinking, always composed, not gauche like the Volzenkoffs.

Fritz, Orth's older brother seemed to do everything right around the dairy, and at athletics in high school. Orth tried to follow in his footsteps but fell miserably short. Fritz was a star football player, a rugged lineman, well built with brutal force on the playing field.. Fritz' blond hair – crew cut and large shoulders made him the Saxon image of Valhalla to the young high school maidens. Orth was skinny and shy – terribly nearsighted and awkward around the farm and school. However, Orth excelled in academics over Fritz. Fritz could not be concerned about books – his interest was sports – baseball, football and basketball in that order. Fred, Orth's father, favored Fritz. The table

THEN THERE WAS RICH UNCLE HUMPHREY—WELL GROOMED—
WHO DROVE UP TO VISIT THE FARM FROM MILWAUKEE.....

top conversation always seemed to be dominated by Fred and Fritz embroiled in discussions about who is best at that position on the field – the coaches, New York Yankees and on into infinity ... Bertha would try to interject with some other topic, but she was generally either subtly or rudely informed to "shut-up". Orth felt sorry for Bertha. She was denied a "female" point of view around the house and a feminine companion to share the light claptrap that women like to partake in.

Orth studied a curriculum in high school he hoped would prepare him for college. Fritz could not be bothered and pursued courses in shop, auto mechanics and so forth. Orth tried out for the football team during his Junior and Senior years. The head coach's name was Ernie Swartz, who took a liking to Orth. Orth made the squad after session after session of bone jarring, slam-bang, bombastic training scrimmages. However, he rarely entered a game – and then only at the waning moments when the outcome had already been decided. Orth remembered how often he had been lambasted during football practice to the extent of almost being senseless and more than once seeing himself headed in the wrong direction on the field after absorbing a severe whollop. Once a huge senior right end, Olaf Larson, after slamming Orth into the turf – shoved him back to his own side after he started in the wrong direction. Larson was later to become an art teacher after college and service as a Navy pilot. Then there was the "Gus Hakeem" incident. Orth practiced with unreasonable dedication. He was slightly near-sighted so when he was on the football field, it was without glasses. If he penetrated the opposite team's backfield he tackled the first thing that looked like it was carrying a football. The whole world was a kind of blurred mess. Well, on a particular day before the annual big game against their arch rival, the Notkcot Tigers, the team was drilling in a manner to defend and thwart the Tigers' star fullback, Gus Hakeem. Gus was a giant kid and bulldozed his way through the line, usually between the tackle and end. The key to stopping him was to hit him low, behind the line, before he penetrated. Orth, as a third string left tackle, was successful in tackling a running back who was playing the role of Hakeem during practice. Coach Swartz was impressed and allowed Orth into the big game at mid-point. Orth found it difficult to believe when Ernie boomed out, "Orth! Go in for Crunchcroft." Orth leapt off the bench and into the game. Mentally, he was rehearsing his actions. "Okay, Ortie, relax – hit 'em hard and low." Well, the moment came. Out of the huddle came the Tigers and Orth eyed Hakeem in a set stance at the fullback position. Down into his lineman crouch Orth went. He felt the grass cool and damp – his nerves were almost bursting through his skin, and his ears were throbbing beneath his helmet. Then his heart sank. He eyed the offensive lineman across from him, who was an ape twice the size of Orth, so large that his helmet barely squeezed over his head and his fat belly button was visible when his jersey did not meet his trousers by six inches. No time to cower now – be tough and hit the lard ass low and jar him off his fat knees …

The Tiger quarterback, Isaacson, called the play from his crouched position behind the center … "forty, thirty-five, ten set, Hike!" Orth thrust forward with all he had! "Thud, plunk, crack…" then silence. Orth could not see a thing ... his nose smelled dirt, grass crept up his nose ... the fat ape had simply plopped his gross blubber down onto Orth and buried him. Orth was mortified, humiliated, his big chance snuffed out in a second. Gus Hakeem had run his usual play and gained respectful yardage while Orth was on the bottom of a breathing pile of fat hog flesh.

Coach Swartz pulled Orth out of the game after that, and Orth resumed his bench warming post permanently afterwards, seeing brief rare action forevermore. Ends the "Gus Hakeem epic".

Frederick and Bertha loved their sons. Oh yes, Orth recalls how he and Fritz were always critical of their parents because of their poverty, drinking problems and lack of cultural refinements. Now, Orth recalls that they gave their sons something much more than material wealth – they continually lavished them with their gifts of love! Frederick was never remiss to plant a kiss of love on the cheek or neck of his sons daily. And, of course, Bertha was there when there was a flu or cold to be ministered to with her "Home" remedies, and numberless other times. She always seemed to be present to love and encourage her sons. Yes, Uncle Humphrey had his large elegant home and expensive accouterments, but he was cold, indifferent, stiff and punctilious, lacking in cheerfulness and that warmth that one senses in certain people who are comfortable to be with.

> *If I had the gift of prophecy and knew all about what is going to happen in the future, knew everything about everything, but didn't love others, what good would it do? Even if I had the gift of faith so that I could speak to a mountain and make it move, I would still be worth nothing at all without love.*
>
> I Cor. 13:2

Orth was shy to the extreme when it came to females. He was awkward as a youth – tall, pimples, glasses, a long skinny frame and facial features that seemed too large for his skull. His long nose – deep set eyes and large ears always made him self conscious. He mouth was large – his skinny long neck was interrupted half way with an adam's apple the size of a peach. Fellow students often ridiculed him and called him "moose" because of his ears and elongated nose. He was gentle as a kid – gentle and shy as a dove – but when challenged or abused he could erupt like a courageous lion.

On a particular evening during Orth's Junior year in high school, the football team was riding home from an out of town game with Glen Oaks. The bus was a typical school bus with seats like iron cots. Orth was tired and snoozing while the rest of the team was doing the same or reveling because of the whopping victory achieved. Coach Swartz had distributed the "supper" money, fifty cents, to each player. Orth was immersed in reverie, thinking of going to the "Waffle Shop" on Main Street with his brother and some others, where they would order two waffles apiece, flood them in butter and syrup and with a mug of steaming hot chocolate, talk about the game, girls and other teenage claptrap. Then it came; "Whap!" From someone behind him, Orth received a jolting blow to the back of his head – termed a "rabbit blow" in idiomatic high school jargon.

Up bolted Orth. "Angow did it," hollered one of the players – Anderson, the large right end. Orth leapt back and grabbed Angow by the collar like an inflamed hungry lion let loose from his den. Angow was dozing and awakened with startled amazement as Orth delivered to him a shattering blow to the back of his skull – a like "rabbit" blow. Then an enormous barrage of words flowed from Angow's mouth as both he and Orth engaged in mortal combat. Players sprang from their seats to contain Orth, and attempt to calm him. Coach Swartz inquired as to the cause and ordered Orth to a seat in the front next to him. After the team arrived back at the high school gym, Orth's brother, Fritz, sheepishly said,, "Angow didn't do it." Orth was mortified – shocked, because he thought a lot of Declan Angow. He was a quiet, friendly guy, smallish in size, but built solidly. He was the second string right end who always saw a lot of action in the games because of his temerity and ability to catch passes. Declan Angow was one of three brothers who lived on the farm next to Orth's.

Orth thought after this wretched, detestable act that someone had sprung upon him, how deceitful and sick some minds are to commit a violent act and foist the blame upon someone else – ironically, an innocent mild type like Angow. Years afterward Orth would remember this event in his life and surmise that it is normal and to be expected that teenagers and those in their early twenties are inclined towards animosity, mischievousness and naturally are rebellious, resisting authority and abhorring the established systems. They are politically discontented and often scheme to incite unrest. Their only hope is to outgrow these repugnant and illogical tendencies and discover the wisdom of Christianity – solace in a lake of turmoil and self-centered egotism.

Incidentally, reader, Orth was never privy to the information as to who the culprit was who mysteriously delivered the fierce "rabbit" blow to him on the team bus. He was sheltered by the rest of the members who saw him. However, Orth always suspected afterwards that it was a kid by the name of Easton – an overgrown hulk that played first team right tackle and was always thinking up pranks, when if successful, would giggle in a silly ridiculous way.

At this point, Orth acquired a growth on his neck – in the vicinity of his "Adam's Apple" or thyroid. It became quite large and a subject of dejected mortification. Students jeered and taunted him. The growth eventually became suppurated. Various local doctors were consulted, but none seemed to have an answer. So, a specialist in Madison was recommended, Doctor Bullins – a kindly man who was also a professor of medicine at the University of Wisconsin Medical School.

Bertha bundled up Orth one wintry day and they took a train to Madison from Oesterich. This was exciting to Orth for he had never ridden on a train before – but often saw it passing, as the tracks were visible from the farm. The northbound train passed in the evening at eleven thirty and the southbound train to Milwaukee and Chicago passed in the morning at nine o'clock. The train seldom ran on time, therefore Orth counted it fortunate to see it, as he imagined how the people rode or ate their supper or breakfast in the diner. In the evenings he could see the lights shine out from the coaches and sleeping cars.

Well, the day arrived and Orth and Bertha boarded the train with wild anticipation. They rode in the coaches ... the seats were upholstered but stiff and hard. The smell of smoke was ever present mixed with an assorted whiff of aftershave lotion, foodstuffs and tobacco. Orth felt excited and grown up! Going to the "big city".

Upon arrival in Madison, they checked into a downtown hotel, not luxurious, but considered a moderate "commercial" hostelry. The room had an ancient double bed of metal tubing and the furniture was plain and obviously built to withstand the rigors of hotel types. All-in-all, it was plain but comfortable and clean. There was a restaurant off the main lobby that emitted a plethora of wonderful table delights. Bertha and Orth took their meals always in the hotel restaurant. Orth recalls the hotcakes – huge with plenty of butter and syrup. His first cup of coffee was in this restaurant – it tasted strange, but tasty as Orth added cream and several teaspoons of sugar. Bertha and Orth took the streetcar to the University of Wisconsin Hospital.

Doctor Bullins examined Orth's throat growth in the company of several medical students. As he pushed and stabbed at the nodule (Orth twitched and felt knives of pain), he explained to the students. Bertha remained by the side of Orth – holding his hand. Doctor Bullins turned to Bertha after a few moments and eyed her through his spectacles which were partly obscured by a lock of his gray hair.

"Mrs. Volzenkoff, your son has a thyrol glossal cyst," he announced, then added, "It requires surgery. They sometimes require several operations ... it depends."

Bertha and Orth were told to make arrangements at a Catholic Hospital – Saint Mary's, not far from the University Hospital.

Orth felt dejected and abhorred the thought of people cutting into his throat. Bertha attempted to comfort, "It's okay, darling, it will turn out all right." Frederick could not afford the cost of the operation, therefore, Bertha was forced to seek the help of her brother, Humphrey. Humphrey supplied the funds with his usual rigid formality.

Bertha and Orth sat at a desk at Saint Mary's while a nun filled out papers to admit the patient. The nun was perfunctory and prudish, Orth recalls – white cowl, stiffly starched collar and a long black gown with an overly large crucifix around her neck, coupled with the usual rosary beads. When she walked all was silent, except the "clank-clank, tinkle-tinkle" of the accouterments and a set of keys which hung from her waist on a gray cord. All was mysterious to Orth. "These women are so plain and indifferent," he thought to himself.

The nun completed the necessary papers and Bertha and Orth were accompanied to the elevator and to a room on the seventh floor. The room was occupied by two other patients – both elderly, who were listening to the radio and engaged in light conversation concerning the coffee commercial as Orth entered with Bertha and two nurses (also nuns).

CHAPTER V

Wine is a mocker, strong drink is a brawler, and whoever is led astray by it is not wise...

Proverbs 20:1

"Drink Folger's Coffee" the radio blurts out as Orth is dressed in his hospital gown and rid of his "civilian" clothes. He feels embarrassed because the back of his gown is open and the "chill" of the room embraces his buttocks. He reaches around and tries to tie the gown – but fumbling and awkward, he gives up as Bertha says, "Here, I'll do that darling." The old men in the room mimic the coffee commercial and lightly chuckle to each other as they continue their arcane, woodsy chit-chat.

"Do you drink Bolger's coffee, John?" one elderly patient asks the other.

"Naw," he replies, "I like Maxwell House and I make it strong, so as I can float a horse shoe in it."

The other continues, then both chuckle and continue to talk. Orth feels alien because of the vast age differences. He recalls from his Sunday School class, "Cease listening to instruction, my son, and you will stray from the words of knowledge." (Proverbs 19:27)

Hospitals are cold, white places. Orth feels chills as he lies in bed. Bertha chats with him for a while, ends and then kisses him on the cheek and departs. Nurses come and go – their starched dresses and gowns giving off a silent "swish-swish-swish-crackle-snap." Orth stares at the white ceiling. Minutes

- hours pass and the men in the other beds call over to him in an effort to console and succor him. Soon Orth learns their names and he feels a warm friendship developing.

The old men and Orth chat about things – the oldsters feel gratified that Orth asks them questions.

The following morning - early - a nurse comes in and Orth is prepared for the operating room. Onto a gurney – wheeled hurriedly down the hall. Orth stares at the ceiling as it rushes by – medical people with instruments dangling about their necks and protruding from their white coats – most mysterious. Suddenly the gurney stops.

"Hello," a nurse enveloped in a gown and face mask says to Orth. "I'm going to give you an injection that will make you drowsy…just a slight little prick in your arm…" she concludes.

"Okay," Orth weakly replies in a voice filled with trepidation.

* * *

Into the operating room, someone places a mask over his face and comments, "Just breathe normally." Orth sees lights gleaming down – he starts to breathe – then the world and consciousness stops. Orth awakens, pain stabs at his throat. He feels sick to his stomach. He vomits. He is semi-conscious. Voices call to him, "Hello, Orth, can you hear me?" He senses slaps to his cheeks, again and again voices sound with senseless pithy phrases.

"Hello, Orth, it's all over. Can you hear me? Hello – Hello – Hello."

Orth vomits again – again and again. His stomach cannot yield anymore, just a painful wretching in his abdomen. He passes out – regains consciousness – hearing voices. The world is spinning. Pain comes and goes. The voices murmur, "Change the dressings." Other phrases are heard, everything is confused.

* * *

Consciousness is present in young Orth's mind now. He is swathed in bandages, but is able to eat a moderate amount. Bertha came often. Orth notices she usually had the odor of alcoholic beverages on her breath which was so discordant with the cheap perfume she wore. One particular morning a Catholic priest entered the room and performed ministrations over Orth. The priest was accompanied by two nuns in starched immaculate white garments. Chanting words in Latin, Orth was given the emblems of the Eucharist while the nuns busied themselves with mysterious activities.

Young master Orth was perplexed and confused.

"What is all of this?" he mused to himself. "Is this some kind of hospital routine?" he asked himself. Finally, he could contain himself no longer and asked the priest. "What is this for?"

The priest was aghast!

"Are you not Catholic?" the priest anxiously blurted out.

"No, I'm a Congregationalist," replied Orth, sheepishly and embarrassed.

This resulted in an explosion of activity as the nuns in attendance yanked away the ritual accouterment and utensils. The Priest commenced a long tirade in Latin over Orth's head, tried to compose himself and withdrew from the room without another word uttered.

"Bam!" went the door as priest and nuns hurried off in a bustle of activity absent of words.

Silence followed. Orth lay still and silent in his bed staring at the blank white ceiling trying to think how he had annoyed the priest. The two other older gentlemen in the room broke the silence a few minutes later with gay laughter! John and Bill, Orth's two elderly room mates, both Catholics, are having a merry good time, chatting about how mortified the priest was, and how he was trying to be officious but was failing in his clumsy, punctilious maneuvers, and how the nuns were nonplussed how to correct the situation.

"Don't worry about it, son," John yells to Orth. "Those priests are always so supercilious with we poor parishioners. It's humorous to see them get a little of their own medicine," he adds.

Bill remains silent, but emits several more muted laughs, then says, "Did you see the looks on the nuns' faces? They looked like they had both swallowed a cat. They didn't know what the heck to do – it was great!"

After this episode, evening came, and things in the hospital room fell into the usual dull routines.

The meals in the hospital seem so bland and ordinary to Orth. Home cooking by Bertha was heavy, spicy German victuals. Food that was meant to "stick to your ribs" according to Orth's parents. In the hospital, the heavy plates and plate covers always seemed to belie the sparse repast.

"Why can't they bring pie a la mode instead of this blinking runny tapioca pudding?" Orth often said to himself.

Doctor Bullins comes in early one morning and examines Orth. Bertha is present along with a nurse. Orth likes Doctor Bullins. He is not aloof to Orth and chats with him about school and sports. On this particular occasion he is serious and after removing the bandages from Orth and several "ums" and "ahs", he turns to Bertha and announces, "Everything seems fine, however, I want him to stay several more days to be certain. Sometimes we have to perform a second operation to insure that all the growth was removed."

Those words of Doctor Bullins' struck Orth deep in his heart. He trembled and shook. After the doctor departed floods of tears came into young Orth's eyes. Bertha tried to console him with small talk, but Orth was shaken terribly! The thought of going through all that again, the pain, sickness simply destroyed Orth's confidence. He had been reduced to a sodden mess. Bertha departed in the late afternoon. After supper, Orth was still in a stage of constant remorse, weeping uncontrollably. He muttered to himself a prayer.

"God, my father, hallowed be Thy name – Thy kingdom come, Thy will be done, on earth as it is in Heaven. Give me this day my daily bread and forgive me my trespasses as I forgive those who trespass against me and lead me from temptation, but deliver me from evil, for Thine is the Kingdom and the power and the glory forever…God, please make it so that they will not have to operate on me again, please - please - please!"

Orth's prayer words were clumsy, but effective as he was not led again to the operating room. Bertha had taught her boys the Lord's Prayer and insisted that they said it every night before they slept. Orth recalled many times when Bertha would look into their darkened bedroom on the farm and ask that familiar question, "Did you say your prayers?" If the boys said "yes", she would come in and kiss them and bid them "good night". It would be many years later in his life that Orth would remember the importance of those events – and their impact upon his close relationship with Jesus Christ.

The day finally arrives when Orth is released from the hospital. He is so weak that it is difficult for him to walk. However, he and Bertha leave the hospital and take a return train back to Oesterich where Frederick awaits their arrival.

"Grandmother Ida would like to have you come to visit with her for a few days," Frederick says to Orth, as the ancient old red Dodge pickup truck pulls away from the train depot. "She has sent the money so you can take the train to Milwaukee as soon as you can make arrangements," Frederick adds.

Ida, Orth's paternal grandmother, met him at the train station in Milwaukee. The train arrived in the morning and the station was a bustle of activity. Orth's eyes picked out Grandma Ida in the crowd. She was waving frantically. Orth was still heavily bandaged from the operation and was extremely thin and weak. His tall frame boasted a feeble 130 pounds and his clothes hung from his bones. Grandma Ida warmly embraced him and Orth was engulfed in a smother of costly perfume. Ida wore expensive clothes and usually was well adorned with jewelry which was quite at home with her black dresses and furs.

"How thin you are...well, we will just have to fatten you up," Grandma Ida exclaimed as they headed toward the train depot exit.

The crowds waiting for taxis were enormous as people were often coming or going to Chicago to shop, work or play. The situation looked woefully sad, however, Ida quickly solved the dilemma by explaining to the cab dispatcher that her grandson was weak from an illness and that they needed a taxi immediately. All this was done in a sly, clandestine manner while she also pressed a ten dollar bill into the palm of the dispatcher. Presto! A cab immediately came to the fore and Ida and Orth were off in a puff. Orth felt embarrassed to think that there were many other people who were obviously waiting much longer than they had, who were more deserving. But, such is the voice of money and greed...

The apartment was small, but well furnished with expensive rugs, tables and other items, and was located in a fine building off Wisconsin Avenue and across from a Jewish Synagogue. Ida felt comfortable living amongst the Jews because they seemed to place the same amount of value on material possessions as she. And, she often commented on the well dressed Yiddish who drove up to the Synagogue on Saturday mornings in their expensive Buicks and so forth. The owner of the apartment building was Mr. Stillmann, who was a huge, heavy-set Jew who was always cheerful and took a liking to Orth.

Orth was bored staying with Grandma Ida. She dwelled on minor details around the apartment and nettled him about picking up his clothes. Don't make marks on the carpet with his dirty shoes. Dress nice with a tie and so forth. Ida took Orth around the neighborhood to meet her cronies. One lady was Hazel. An enormous woman who had an extremely likeable personality. Hazel couldn't be bothered with minor details and always defended Orth when Ida would attack him about blowing his nose, combing his hair, keeping his fingernails clean and so forth. Hazel liked chocolates and kept open boxes of them around her apartment for Orth to help himself to (which she encouraged). Once in a while Hazel would take bus rides with him downtown to shop while Grandma Ida would go somewhere else. Hazel would buy things for Orth and treat him to sumptuous lunches with plenty of desserts and good tasty treats.

Another of Ida's friends was Evelyn who was a very devout and religious person who was always hopeful that she could convince Ida that her life of smoking, drinking and heavy eating was not good for her health and would destroy her. (which it did later on!)

Evelyn was always pleasant and friendly, quiet and listened intently as Ida would control the conversation with wordy gossip and odious, foul, repulsive words. This is why Orth supposed that Ida liked Evelyn. She was always courteous and polite. "Clean" as Orth would think to himself. In later life, he would realize that Evelyn was a perfect Christian lady. Not stiff and prudish, but just loving and kind. She was a vegetarian which was thought odd by Orth, who would remember years later as he became one also, which contributed to his health and mental outlook.

Ida frequently ridiculed and poked fun at Evelyn for being such a devoted church goer and vegetarian. Ida would drink her Manhattan cocktails before dinner while Evelyn would sip her lemonade or apple juice. Evelyn later left Milwaukee and moved to Honolulu, Hawaii, where she located an excellent position with a large department store.

Grandma Ida usually took Orth to do the daily shopping at the neighborhood food stores. The frequent stops were at the butcher shop, bakery and drug store. These were unique little stores that had a bevy of regular customers. And, orfcourse, there was the stop at the green grocer's for melons, fruits and vegetables. Ida entertained a great deal, when beer and spirits were well supplied.

Orth took long walks in the afternoon along Wisconsin Avenue, stopping occasionally to watch a local baseball game in the City Park.

The visit ended after about two weeks and Orth took the train back to reality and the harsh bucolic life of the farm outside of Oesterich.

* * * * * * * * *

Orth tried out for the American Legion baseball team in town. His first year he was a miserable flop. He was sixteen years old, awkward and clumsy. He liked first base because Lou Gehrig of New York Yankee fame played that position, and after seeing the movie, "Pride of the Yankees", wherein Gary Cooper played the part of Gehrig, Orth came to idolize Gehrig. Try as he would, Orth could not hit the ball while at bat, and his fielding was an exhibit that would amuse a circus audience. He got into one game as a pinch hitter and he struck out, or as the players chided him - he "K'ed", the letter "K" is used in baseball score keeping to indicate a strike-out. And, Orth was dubbed the "K-King". The situation did not remain static, however, and Orth improved enormously the next year.

The following year, Orth tried out for his usual position and was his usual inept self. However, one day during batting practice, the coach, Phillip McDurmott, announced that they were in need of a catcher, as the regular batting practice player, Doug Nicely, could not attend practice that day. Coach McDurmott asked Orth to try and catch this time – as he was just extra baggage as a second string first baseman. Orth was elated at the thought that Coach McDurmott even noticed him!

A word about Coach McDurmott at this point. He was a short, stocky man in his mid-thirties. He had seen action in France during World War I, and following the war he came home and had a short career with professional baseball, rising to the "A" level with Elmira, New York of the Eastern League. He was a catcher and sometime outfielder. Following his professional baseball career, he returned to Oesterich where he obtained a job as an equipment salesman with the local John Deere farm equipment dealer. Phillip had a drinking problem. He was a notorious heavy drinker who frequently stayed out until the early morning hours. Yet, his drinking did not seem to hamper his ability to coach nor handle his position as an equipment salesman. Coach McDurmott was well liked by all and the boys on the American Legion team performed well under his direction. The boys called him "Mr. Mack". Mack had an assistant - who also enjoyed his booze. His name was also Scottish... Mr. Ted MacIntosh. Ted wore thick glasses and worked as a clerk in the local lumber yard. United Lumber Yard was a sizable place and Orth had a brief stint there hauling lumber for 75 cents per hour. It was hard work and Orth's muscles were just not capable to handle it. Anyway, Ted MacIntosh did not know much about baseball, but all liked him. He was valuable to Mr. Mack because he handled all of the financial details, something that Mr. Mack found repugnant. Ted was the subject of many puns by the boys who often were amused at Ted's alcoholic large red nose and his "ash-tray" glasses.

Now, back to Orth and his baptism into the catcher position. He took to it like a duck to water! He loved it! He thought to himself, "Why didn't I do this sooner?"

The afternoon was hot – the heavy protective gear, termed by baseball players as the "tools of ignorance" were clumsy and burdensome at first, but soon he mastered how to shift his weight, endure the perspiration and throw the ball with ease. Coach "Mack" was impressed! He encouraged Orth and gave him some tips on his stance and calling for the various types of pitches that he may expect, the curve, slider, change-up, and so forth. His battery mate was an Italian boy, John Galileo, whose dad had a rather large farm outside of town. John was short and stocky - strong and muscular. His motions were mechanical and not rhythmic, but he got the job done. Players called him "Iron Arm" because of his awkward pitching motion and his ability to withstand long innings without having to be replaced. Galileo's fast ball was okay, but his curve lacked the emphatic snap to be effective.

All things considered, John Galileo and Orth worked efficiently and effacious to bring about a successful season. The Legion team won their sectional pennant - but were defeated in the area finals by a team from Madison who had superior pitching. The Oesterich squad only had one relief pitcher – an awkward left-hander who never seemed to be able to get his hat on straight. This boy was tall and skinny – having a good motion, but that was about it. He lacked a fast ball and about everything else. As a result, during the area championships, when he came in to spell Galileo, he was hit unmercifully. Coach Mac just sat there and let the blood spill all over the diamond. Galileo (Old Iron Arm) could only do so much and was pulled out of a game only if at the point of total exhaustion.

Orth suffered from the Wisconsin hot summer and the physical demands of the heavy equipment placed on the catcher. His frame was skinny – he never seemed to gain much weight after the operation and for the remainder of his life he remained slender, even to the point of being almost a walking ghost during his Army days losing so much weight in Korea that his battle gear hung on him like a dilapidated coat hanger. The added handicap of having to wear glasses exacerbated the problem. His glasses often became smeared with sweat and dirt – but he was persistent. He became self-conscious at times when opposing players yelled annoying cat-calls like, "Hey, four-eyes, what's the matter?" or "What's the matter, four-eyes, can't you see the ball?" Orth would recall later in life how unkind and ridiculous youth are inclined to be and how a grounding in the teachings of Christ would have eased the pain.

The Legion baseball days ended and young Orth enters his senior year at Oesterich High School. Because the family was not prosperous, Orth needed money for clothes and other things. He looked around for a job, and because

ORTH TOOK TO THE CATCHER POSITION— LIKE A DUCK TAKES TO WATER.....

of his baseball success became known to the owner of the local minor league baseball team, from the Class "C" Oesterich Reds - a farm team for the Milwaukee Brewers of the then Class AAA International League.

Word got around that the Reds were looking for a grounds keeper to maintain the park, so Orth asked for the position. The owner, a man of doubtful scruples, yet friendly enough, gave Orth the job and a free rein to run the place. With this job, it meant that he had to do the farm chores early in the morning - then hustle off to town on his antiquated bicycle to keep the grounds at the antiquated ball park. You may recall, reader, that the Volzenkoff dairy farm was roughly ten miles from Oesterich so it took Orth about an hour and a half to trek the distance. The ten miles were not level, so he peddled furiously down the hills in order to ease himself over the opposite peaks. Ah, yes! The energy and zeal of the youth!

Orth did an outstanding job keeping the old park – and he became friends with most of the ball players – many of whom managed to climb the summit into the Major Leagues.

Orth's "office" was underneath the center grandstand and was a room that was cluttered with grass mowers and garden equipment, huge watering hoses and other items, including gigantic burlap bags of peanuts stored there by the vending operator. Orth was given permission to make himself at home and help himself to as many peanuts as he liked (which he did often). Orth later recalled how he enjoyed the "smells" of the old park. The fresh cut grass, the roasted peanuts, cigars and so forth. Orth terminated his employment with the owner in the winter of 1947 and remembered that he was never paid for his final month's duties. He let this be known to his dad and was informed that the Red's owner had a tendency to overlook debts to people if it were convenient to do so. Orth's repeated appeal to receive his back pay were met with feeble excuses and promises unfulfilled. He eventually gave up.

The final year in High School was one of great expectations mixed with sadness. Orth thought of going to Milwaukee and living in the excitement of the big city. His mind was occupied with these thoughts. He would visit Grandma Ida and stay with her until he located a job or gone to college. He did not know what he wanted to do except to get out of the provincial stagnation of the Oesterich air and to see and living in the city. His friends did not think such thoughts - most of them would remain on the farm or with their parents in the stores or shops. When Frederick learned of his son's ambitions he was saddened, but understood that there was little of a worthy nature awaiting him on the farm where they were barely able to squeak by - milk prices were low in comparison to everything else. Orth's dad would just have to find other means to fill the gap. Orth was relied upon the help around the place and his brother Fritz was forever complaining that he just could not handle it all by himself. Fritz often erupted with his violent temper - yelling at times, "Why didn't I stay in the Army? At least I had some time off there."

Fritz was always reminding Orth how great a war hero he was as a paratrooper in the 82nd Airborne Division, and mocked and ridiculed Orth as a feckless weakling. This hurt Orth and he would always remember it through his lifetime - even after his hair raising experiences in combat in Korea. Orth revered his brother, but the heckling and pestering against him would continue. Later in life the chasm of differences would widen until Orth simply could not see himself seeking the company of Fritz. The final blow came over supper one evening when the two were in Milwaukee visiting. Orth offered a blessing upon the food before they began. Fritz replied in an amiable mood so Orth prayed a simple beautiful little supplication:

"Our Father, in Heaven, we they humble servants and children thank Thee for this food and for Thy bounteous blessings. Strengthen and guide us that we may remain steadfast in our faith to Thee. We ask these things, and thank Thee our Father, in the name of Jesus Christ, Thy glorious Son and our blessed Redeemer – Amen, and Amen."

Orth glanced across the table after the entreaty to see a smirkish smile on Fritz's face. He was mortified and also burned down to his bowels to think that Fritz would stoop so low as to rail and jeer him during such a sacred moment. To make matters worse, Fritz frowned and with a contemptuous air and sarcastic, condescending way, announced proudly that the prayer was incorrect and should follow the pattern of the Catholics, whereupon he pompously blared out what he thought should have been offered to God as a thanksgiving. Orth restrained himself, but his guts and spleen were erupting in a holocaust! The supper was finished in silence. However, Fritz did not give up. He sent some more barbs against Orth when he ostentatiously proclaimed that he thought golf was a more difficult and tiring game than tennis. This was an affront to Orth who was a tennis fan and player. Fritz had tossed down the gauntlet. Orth immediately went to his own defense and declared that, "Well, I have played both and I tell you frankly that I was more physically fatigued after playing several sets of tennis than I was after plodding over an 18-hole golf course."

That lit the fire under the pride of Fritz and he commenced to launch into a fusillade of abusive words and a lengthy tirade of comments! Orth was embarrassed and kept quiet hoping that this would quiet his brother down, but, alas, to little avail. Finally, in desperation, Orth simply announced, "Okay, Fritz, I think you are correct. Golf *is* more demanding and difficult than tennis."

Fritz glanced at Orth with wide-eyed amazement! He was totally disarmed by Orth's refusal to keep up the preposterous argument. Fritz, with his blunt rustic mind somehow realized that his brother had won the debate by ironically giving in! Orth would remember this as part of his Gospel and Ecumenical training. The power of love includes not arguing over frivolous things. One wins an argument by removing the barrier. You disarm your opponent by agreeing with him. Love wins over darkness and ignorance. However, if the argument is over Gospel principles - the Christian defends them to the end. Not in violent exchanges, but by silently and faithfully remaining calm and steadfast in the storm. To know that Truth wins over error and doubt. That Christ is the way. That Christ is the beginning of wisdom and knowledge. Christ showed by His example of majestic nobleness how to defend against ignorance.

And that is how the schism developed between Orth and Fritz. After that encounter they never met again as you will learn later in this volume.

During his high school days, Orth associated with the minority students primarily. His closest buddies were those students whose families were non-Lutherans, farmers, the common folks. The "other" students, or as they were called by Orth and his cohorts, "The 500's" were students from the wealthy town folks - doctors, politicos, lawyers, store owners, and the like. These guys and gals wore a style of clothes that symbolized their station; white buckskin shoes, clean pressed corduroy trousers, starched dress shirts, etc. The name "The 500's" had remained a mystery to Orth, and nobody seemed to have a clue as to its origin, other than it seemed to "fit".

So, Orth's close circle of friends included, of course, John Galileo, a Negro lad named oddly enough Bob O'Kelly, and Louis (Louie) Gonzalo. John, I have mentioned previously, was of an Italian family and they were generally considered less than worthy by the 500's who termed them "Whops" or "grease balls" or some other ignoble slurring name. Bob O'Kelly was a small boy - a Negro - but who was from a family that had money. Blacks were not allowed to live in the decent part of town where the 500's dwelled, so O'Kelly's family lived amongst the common folks of Oesterich - yet their home was modern and large. Bob dressed well and always had a cheerful countenance which Orth enjoyed. Bob did not partake in school sports, but was well versed in the professional teams. Bob's mother, whom Orth met once, was a beautiful black woman with an attractive figure - well dressed and with expensive jewelry. Bob was a bright boy who did well in school. He went on to become an M.D. in Los Angeles where blacks were more accepted.

Then there was Louis Gonzalo - a lad from a Mexican family. Louie's family also lived in the "wrong" part of town. Mexicans, along with the other minorities were detested by the 500's. Louie's dad worked as a common laborer at one of the town's grain elevator companies, and his mother was a large, fat lady who had a grin seemingly permanently fixed upon her broad cheerful face. She would chide Orth on his being too skinny and that she would fatten him up with some of her home-cooked corn cheese Mexican table delights - which she never seemed to be able to do. Orth remained his youthful tall gawky skinny self during his high school days.

The Gonzalo house was too small for the numerous items of furniture. Orth enjoyed sitting in the kitchen, where he and Louie often sat discussing baseball or other things. Louie would mock and goad "Momma" Gonzalo in a good natured way and she would rear back and laugh, saying, "Oh, Louie, you are such a bad and nasty son." Then both Louie and Momma would laugh unceasingly. Life in the Gonzalo home was always joyful. They did not have much, but they were always happy. Louie had two older brothers and one younger sister (born much later) who tottered about the small house. In the winter times, the Gonzalo house was always offensively overheated and poorly ventilated, with the smell of cooking forever present. Orth had many other friends who I shall mention later, but these are some of the primary ones. Oh, by the way, Louie played on the same baseball teams as Orth - high school and American Legion. He played the outfield mainly - with a few stints at third base. He completed high school, was drafted into the Army and returned to Oesterich to open a gasoline station on the edge of town. He never had an intention to enter college and his primary ambition was to foster a local semi-pro baseball team comprised of those men who lived on the "wrong" side of town and were the blue collar simple folks. Louie was quite successful at doing this and became, the sort of, Casey Stengel of Oesterich's Sunday afternoon baseball locals who enjoyed playing the game as well as the accompanying revelry.

* * *

This note is to remind my honorable reader that as all authors of biographies or autobiographies will readily admit, it is beyond the scope of a treatise or a person's life to include all the scraps and pieces of a person's experiences. At best, the writer will include those events and characters that made a significant dent in the person's personality and added to the totality of his being. Orth's life was an ocean of variety, specked with islands of important epochs to which interest will be drawn to the reader's attention. His youthful life was chock full of humorous as well as serious events. Cardboard was frequently used to plug holes in his shoes – his brown bag lunches were routine and sparse. Holes were often in his socks and he was embarrassed when he had to remove his shoes to dress for football or baseball and display his emblems of poverty. His underwear was saggy and shot with holes. One five-cent candy bar a week was all he was generally allowed. His first bicycle was a worn-out old blue hulk that he acquired during his junior year at high school. And it continues. I, as author will make a strong effort to enlighten the reader with the poignant stuff and hope to avoid becoming distressingly tedious in detail.

* * *

Now we continue to observe the ending of our hero's high school days. The formula for Christian living is:

$X + Y = 360$
This is explained by:
X = Knowledge
Y = Experience
360 = Total, all knowing profound sagacity. The complete circle, 360 degrees eternal life and continual learning.

Obviously, 360 is *never* attainable. And, God comes first, knowledge second and all else third. The more one knows, the wonderful world - as created and nurtured by God, through his Son Christ, the more wonderful it seems. And the greater the power, glory and perfection of God become evident.

As a youth, Orth has embarked upon a life which will gain in the appreciation of God. The seeds were planted by various loveable Christians. He will remember his horse, "Nylon", a gelding, that he kept on the farm, and how the horse was a source of fidelity and would allow Orth to prod him on until he would drop dead in his track, if need be. Loyalty and love - fidelity, attributes of the Lord Jesus Christ who expects His own to exhibit the same characteristics. and God manifests His love through Nature. The loyal horse who will be driven to the limit by his master, the rider. The loving hound dog who will remain by the side of his boss through all situations - good and bad. Christ showed His love by walking to the cross to save mankind. "I will be with you always, even unto death," our Master proclaimed. Orth will remember these memorable words throughout his existence - words he learned in Sunday School during childhood - and recalled later as he faced old age and the grave.

Memories of the cold stiff, perfunctory, almost prudery of the Congregational Church in Oesterich remained with Orth a long time. He never felt comfortable until later on when he realized that his feelings were manufactured by false opinions and ignorance. His mental impressions were not factual. Christ is not a grumpy old man. Christ is not a stiff, cold, punctilious, self-pious monster. Rather is a smiling, loveable, warm hearted amiable clement older brother. Always holding out his arms to give an assist - a shelter to His storm tossed brethren.

Christ does not close the gates to select a few. Wide He swings open His doors to receive those repentant souls lost and mired down in the vomit of their own sins. False misconceptions fallacious generalizations are delusions conjured up by evil spirits. Jesus is the light to brighten the corners of fear, doubt, worry, fretfulness and self pity.

Christ is our Big Brother in Heaven. He loves us but He also rebukes and punishes us if we deny Him or do harm to our neighbors, so that we will learn. How else will we know when we screw up?

The rod and rebuke give wisdom, but a son left to himself brings shame to his mother...

(Proverbs 29:15)

The time draws near for Orth's graduation from high school. It is springtime 1947. His hopes of the future are buoyed by the folly of youth. He is elected to the class Presidency and is quite popular around campus. Ida Tross is his algebra teacher. She is youthful - dark haired and attractive. She likes Orth and Orth performs well under her tutelage. Mrs. Tross wears a particular perfume that Orth finds pleasant and she has that warm soft feminine charm that men seek.

Then there is Larry Parkinson (Parky) his high school baseball coach. Parky is a short wiry man - middle aged whose idol is the past diamond great Ty Cobb. Parky was not a friendly type and goaded Orth into taking more risks in base running. Orth was slow running and was mortified when he tried stealing a base and was cut down effortlessly. His buddies on the team would banter him with such phrases as, "Hey, Orth, what ya' dragging behind - an anchor?" or "Get the lead out of your a–, Orth."

Parky was not well liked by the boys, but he was an excellent teacher who knew the game. In later years, Orth went to visit him. Parky was ailing at the time and received Orth in his robe and pajamas. Parky chatted with Orth briefly, then parted. Parky died soon afterwards of cancer. But, up until his death he remained cheerful and straight (as best he could) as a ramrod.

Mr. Francis Hutchinson, ("Hutchy") was Orth's chemistry teacher. He was a moderately built man who "looked" like a teacher. He was the typical teacher, wearing metal framed glasses that kept slipping down his nose, a tie that was always the wrong color and dreadfully out of style. Baggy trousers that seemed to be always filled with too many things in the pockets.

Hutchy wore an apron (spotted) when he taught. Chemistry was divided into a class session, then laboratory time. The period was after lunch break and as a result was met with a warm and drowsy feeling. Orth did well in Chemistry and he enjoyed Hutchy who was humorous in the way he taught. One of Orth's friends in class was Joe Gariotta — a lad of Italian heritage, so obviously a non-member of the 500's. Orth nick-named Gariotta "Joe Atomic" because it was the time subsequent to the development of nuclear power and the name seemed to fit.

During one afternoon session in the laboratory a near catastrophe came about. Hutchy had assigned the task in the workbook to isolate chlorine gas (Cl) from hydrochloric acid. Things went well, except a leak developed in Orth's tubing resulting in the green chlorine gas escaping. Hutch had warned that the gas was extremely dangerous so Orth informed him of his accident, whereupon Hutchy exclaimed as best he could with a calm teacher's decorum that all students should exit the lab immediately.

And they did! The students poured out of the lab into the sun drenched patio next to the classroom all giggly and gaily pointing fingers at Orth and "Joe Atomic" because Joe was next to Orth during the fiasco and seemed to be guilty by association. This tale of a near explosion, etc., spread throughout the school and Orth and Joe Atomic soon became notorious and the epitome of the bungling scientists.

Another favorite teacher was Jim Brancis, the assistant football coach, physical education instructor and history teacher. Jim was a large hulky type that had the appearance of a plow horse farmer. His huge hands fumbled through the book and mashed chalk against the board. His voice was resonant and he pronounced words with a thick guttural sound, that student mocked. For example, "book" came out "booooch". Grades came easy in Mr. Brancis' class, especially if you played on the school teams that Jim coached. As a result, Orth earned A's in Mr. Brancis's class with very little learning taking place. Rather tragic, because Orth would learn later how important history was to one's education.

Next, we have the school principal, Mr. Schultz. Nobody knew Mr. Schultz's Christian name because one would never dare utter it, for fear of being expelled or put in prison. Mr. Schultz was the "Adolph Hitler" of the school. He wore the nickname of "Bullet Head", because of the shape of his almost hairless skull. Mr. Schultz was the absolute. At assemblies he sat on the stage in his dark suit with a pompous air, white shirt dark tie and collar that was always too tight for his fat neck. He wore glasses that also seemed too small for his thick face and had the style of Heinrich Himmler, the German Nazi SS Chief of ill fame.

That does it for Orth's teachers. We mentioned his coaches in previous pages. The reader may note that the author at times identifies himself in the first person, "I", and other times in the plural "we". If this is irksome, then apologies are deeply rendered. But I humbly remind my audience that I believe being conventional is boring and unimaginative. Editors and those tending to have meager minds dwell in trivial matters and will delight in discovering this one fault of mine, amongst many, to which I respectfully bow and announce..."tut-tut".

High school graduations in Oesterich are conducted usually at the Central Wisconsin Methodist College, south of Kenosha. Mr. Schultz (Bullet Head) favors this locale because this is the school where he received his Bachelor's and

Master's degrees, and because his brother-in-law is the President, who hopes that a fair percentage of the graduating seniors will be favorably impressed with the college and select it as their choice to further their education. The ceremonies are held in the Amphitheater, a colorful garden setting. Should it rain, the event is held in the Chapel, a majestic old Gothic style structure with beautiful craftsmanship abounding.

It was a warm June 17 evening when Orth accompanied with almost two hundred of his fellow students assembled under the sycamore trees outside the entrance. Girls wore white gowns, boys black. The boys gathered in groups, the 500's more or less off by themselves. Some boys exchanged off color jokes, swearing and cursing a great deal in an attempt to prove their manliness. The girls were mainly giggly and coy, exchanging glances at the boys in a flirtatious manner.

Ah, yes! God's gift of memory. Orth remembered those days. Bertha came to the graduation - Frederick did not. Fritz also avoided much social contact. Bertha sat in back of the theatre, because she was probably sensitive about her dress. Uncle Humphrey did not come, but sent a fifty dollar check to Orth with a card wishing him well. Orth would recall how he always loved and admired Uncle Humphrey, but close social encounters with him tended to give Orth fiery attacks of diarrhea because of nervousness.

The school band played "Pomp and Circumstance" by Elgar, which added to Orth's sad feelings. The missed notes by the violins did not cause him mirth, as it did some of his buddies who always found the band a source of many jokes. Orth glanced out at the large audience from the stage and noticed the Catholic families sitting in the rear with their many children sitting like rows of organ pipes.

Mr. Schultz sat next to the rostrum, in his doctoral robe and hood, gazing out at the motley assemblage with a pompous air. Orth would recall how many Army officers would display this same ostentatious presence with their medals, stars, beautiful uniforms. Yet, how the Lord Jesus Christ had no need of fancy, flashy accoutrements to impress upon people His power and intellect. They just <u>knew</u> when they glanced into His eyes! They would <u>melt</u> when they saw the Son of God, His presence convinced you that he is the <u>Truth</u>!

The valediction was given by two - a boy and a girl both members of the 500. The boy was Dick Harvis, the star quarterback on the football team, whose dad was a mechanical engineer for a large Chicago-based steel fabrication company. The girl was Mellisa Hyatt, a tall pretty girl whose father was a local dentist. Mellisa had a pretty face, but a mouthful of braces so that when she smiled, her mouth looked like a tool box. Orth could not remember what they said other than the words were lofty and empty of reality and reason. Harvis' pop had given him a spanking new convertible Ford for graduation and he would sport it about town during the summer filled with giggly gals of the 500.

Orth often thought poverty as the worst kind of slavery. He would like to date girls, but he was without means to impress them with transportation, meals and so forth. Later in life he would remember that when one is of the world, freedom is an economic thing. Money gave you freedom to enjoy life's pleasures, clothes, homes, cars, etc.

But wisdom slapped him in the face through faith in Christ! Life's greatest treasures are not bought with money. Love, a cheerful countenance, health are God's gifts. Christ came as a lowly carpenter's son to mock and ridicule the phony wealth of the world. Christ's standards are eternal. He holds out His hands, "Come unto Me...and be ye comforted." The wealth of the world is lost at the grave. Christ's wealth is ongoing.

CHAPTER VI

After Jesus rose from the dead, He stood in the midst of His disciples and Apostles...and said, "Peace to you." But they were terrified and frightened, and supposed they had seen a spirit. And he said to them, "Why are you troubled? And why do doubts arise in your hearts? Behold My hands and My feet that it is I Myself. Handle Me and see, for a spirit does not have flesh and bones and you see I have." When he had said this, He showed them His hands and His feet.

Luke 24:36-40

Orth is recovering from his injuries from the gang attack referred to in Chapter II. His life is beginning to settle back into his usual routine. However, he still struggles with the pain and inconveniences of his injuries. He reads the Scriptures and other Christian literature in the morning in the large kitchen while he sips his morning coffee and munches on an apple. He ponders on the miracle of the resurrection of Jesus and admits to himself that it is natural of man to doubt Christ rising from the dead with a physical body, and that it is only by the Holy Spirit telling you the Truth that one is able to believe. Man, given his evil inklings will be skeptical and, of course, unbelief is nurtured and grows through the forces of darkness, the devil and his hosts. But the resurrection of the body to eternal life is the kernel of Christianity! The whole sales pitch of Christ is simply that! "I am the Way, the Truth and the Life." Else,

THE LOCAL FARMERS KNOW ORTH, EITHER BY SIGHT OR PERSONAL ACQUAINTANCE... EACH WAVE TO EACH OTHER AS THEY PASS ON THE ROADS...

why should a person bother believing?

Many people place a limit upon God. They feel it preposterous to believe in a life after death. Is anything impossible to God? Why do people fail to believe? Their noses are too close to the pages. They revel in their sins. They want to cling to their absurd life style of worldly things. They do not wish to give up pleasures of the flesh, money, fancy, gaudy trappings of society.

"Ponder Luke, Chapter 24," Orth urges himself. Think when the Master says, "Why do doubts arise?", or "Why are you troubled?" He seems to be saying, "Let go – do not worry my friend – just sign on the dotted line and I will carry the ball for you." To nurse himself back to full strength, Orth struggles with his daily walks around the country side. He takes Mutnik, occasionally, who tails alongside faithfully eyeing his master. The country roads are full of the verve of Nature. Insects whirl about Orth's ears, robins flit about, the blackbirds line up on the overhead power and telephone lines, clacking to each other like a large assemblage of black gowned academics in a baccalaureate Procession.

The local farmers know Orth either by sight or personal acquaintance. When they pass him on the roads with tractors or trucks, each wave to each other. Orth loves the old farmers who tussle with God's weather to bring forth crops at a meager return on their investments. The country folk are delightfully simple. City people turn inward, become defensive, clutching to their one bedroom apartments as their lifeline of survival. Farm people have space to stretch out. They have a chance to see seeds pop through the rich midwestern soil, to witness the eternal marvelous miracles of God's hand upon the earth. And, they often suffer severely during hail storms, floods and droughts. But, they have that pioneering ilk, that great American tenacity to bounce back. Some do not survive the harsh realities of crop failures or disasters, but most do. Orth has compassion for the much maligned farmer who is often the target of ridicule and mockery by the pseudo intellectuals dwelling in the cities who wolf down their morning toast without thinking where it comes from and what it takes to get it to the table.

Prior to his daily constitutionals, Orth usually does a series of gymnastic exercises, pushups, sit-ups, and so forth. However, since his attack, his routine has been one of going slow and doing just as many calisthenics as his mind and body would dictate before his injuries would become painful. His morning walks completed, he would work on writing, reading, and other housekeeping necessities before dinner, which he tried to complete at noontime. His desk was usually cluttered, but he had an inkling where things were. Orth recalled how his departed wife, Donna, used to nettle him about his seemingly lack of order. Orth loved Donna devotedly and felt that few women live happily with saints and he supposed that is why they agreed with each other most of the time. If women do not have a man to carp at they are thwarted and become Lady MacBeths – shrewish hags that forever find minor faults of their mates to become irritated over. Of course, there are blazon exceptions, like Martha Washington and others that remain constant without becoming a nagging magpie.

Afternoons are times to attack the chores to do about "Home Port", like roof repairs, mowing the grass and so forth. If snow and other types of weather curtail outside activities, Orth writes, reads, does research or other types of inside tasks. Housework is low on the list of priorities. Shopping is usually done in New Hesse, a town seven miles distant. For larger items, Orth travels to Milwaukee about 27 miles southeast.

Several boats are stored in the large old barn behind the house. One, a twenty-one foot fixed keel sloop named "Nob-Nob", another, twelve-foot aluminum skiff named "Red Baron" that Orth painted a Snoopy on the side, decked out in his flying helmet and scarf, sitting on top of his doghouse. The remaining boat is a fourteen foot sailing dinghy named "Donna" after his late wife. He enjoys sailing on the numerous small lakes around Wisconsin, and Mutnik would sit in the bow and bark at the noisy water skiers or speedboats. Orth did not name Nob-Nob. He had purchased the boat second hand and as sailing lore has it, it is bad luck to re-name a boat. He never had discovered where or how the name came about.

Orth discovered sailing while on a visit to Australia, during his Army days, and the fascination stayed with him. Then, he added to his sailing experience while attending college in San Francisco, becoming a crew member for an elderly gentleman named Les Masterson, who owned an ancient 28 foot wooden yawl. He raced and crewed with Les for five years on the San Francisco Bay. Saturdays were race days and things around the Saint Francis Yacht Club buzzed with activity on that day. All members and crews racing were expected to wear white, by tradition, and the racing fleets were divided into classes by size and type of craft. The club was a beautiful place and Orth enjoyed the opportunity to mix with such enthusiastic yachtsmen. By a stroke of luck, Orth had been admitted to membership in the Club. He had a friend, a Jewish buddy named Bruce Namyah, whom he met at San Francisco State. Bruce was a lawyer that was teaching a class in Business Law. He had obtained his law degree from Bolt Hall, University of California, and was a brilliant mind, having passed the C.P.A. (Certified Public Accountant) examinations as well as the California Bar examinations. Orth was slightly older than Bruce. Bruce had joined the Air Force as an enlisted man to escape the draft and spent six months on active duty with an obligation to remain in the Reserves for another four years after his release. He detested the military and once made the comment to Orth, "I wouldn't remain in the Air Force even if they made me a general." The irony was that Bruce had a brilliant brain and could easily have had a direct commission if he had elected to do so. He often commented to Orth how he used to manipulate the officers in order to gain certain favors. He loathed K.P. (Kitchen Police), where the lower enlisted slobs are assigned to slave labor to do the more base jobs, for example, clean the grease traps, scrub the heavy kettles and run the "Clipper" as the automatic steam dish washer was called.

Orth later discovered that there are many "Bruce" types in the military. Well-educated chaps that had to go in because of the law and hated every moment. They refused commissions for one reason or another, usually because they felt it would mean they would have to remain in the military more than the basic requirement. So, you would often encounter the lowly private reading Shakespeare or Homer in the barracks and who articulated as a man of culture and manners, while often some officers who read comic books and had the language of a backwoodsman. But, such is the way of war and the military life where logic, reason and good manners are not rewarded, but looked upon frequently as a plague. Orders are expected to be followed in an inexorable way. Non-coms yell and spit at their charges. Blind obedience is expected. Individual freedoms are plowed under and the dolts surface as heroes shouting into the ears of the civil soldiers – "booze – broads – and promotions."

This afternoon, after he had completed his morning routine, Orth drives Whitey into Milwaukee, to do some shopping and his laundry. After completing his tasks and chores, it is six p.m. and he drives to Frederick's, the downtown tavern that he enjoys as a place to partake of his evening repast.

As he enters Frederick's, his eyes quickly glance about, and he notices several of the usual customers in attendance. Otto, the host, yells exuberantly in his resonant voice, "Well, look who has just entered! Orth! By golly, it is nice to see you have recovered!" Otto thrusts his large beefy hand into Orth's rangy, boney one and shakes vigorously. Orth winces. "Still ache, do you, Orth?," Otto asks.

"Howdy, Otto," Orth answers quietly, then adds, "Yes, still have aches and pains pretty much all over, like I was run over by Eddie's truck."

Otto and Orth chat momentarily, then Otto seats him in his usual small table close to the fire place. The fire is not going as it is mid-summer. Orth hums quietly to himself Martin Luther's Battle Hymn as he eyes the patrons:

> *"A mighty fortress is our God...the body they may kill; God's truth abideth still; His Kingdom is forever!"*

Bertha, the waitress saunters up and catches Orth in his moment of reverie.

"Well, I do believe it is Ortie back from the dead!" she exclaims.

Orth pauses, smiles wanly and replies, "Yes, Bertha, my friend, they can kill the flesh, but the soul lives on."

Bertha hands Orth a menu absent-mindedly, then retracts it saying, "Golly, Ortie, it sure is nice to see you! Can I get the usual for you?"

Orth nods, "Yes, please Bertha, if you would be so kind." Bertha jots down on her order tablet – "vegetable plate, coffee, two hard rolls," then darts off across the dance floor and through the swinging kitchen doors as they sound "clomp-dee-clomp", closing behind her.

Orth reaches into his brief case and retracts a volume, a biographical novel about John Calvin, and places it on the table, and begins to read. A short period elapses until his thoughts are interrupted by Barney Blitzgreez.

"Hi, Ortie!" Barney enthusiastically bursts forth, adding, "My gosh, it is nice to see ya' back!"

Orth glances up and replies, "Greeting, Barney, my valued friend, yes, I am recovering and I thank God for His mercy."

Barney helps himself to a seat. "A lot has happened since you have been gone," Barney says.

"Oh, yes?" Orth replies adding, "Well, tell me...please."

Barney changes position in his chair and crosses his legs and comments.

"Libby has not been around, she has stopped her mud wrestling and has a job with a bank now...punching some kind of machine. She also has written off Eddie...says he's too ill mannered and rude."

"Well, that is a turn around, Barney," Orth says.

Barney nods, then explains at length how Libby has, "cleaned up her life" and her appearance, and that she even admits to going to church occasionally.

"She still live in the same apartment with Danny?" Orth inquires.

"Yes," Barney replies, "I've been over to see her. She doesn't even booze it up any more. She and Danny take walks together and do a lot of bicycling. Strange ... such a turn around," Barney states.

Orth pauses and looks reflectedly at his hands resting on the table, saying to himself, "God wroughts miracles." He looks up at Barney and asks, "So, what else has happened around here?"

Barney looks over at the bar then back to Orth. "Let me go get my beer, Ortie, then I will tell you about Eddie."

Barney clops off to the bar while Bertha walks silently up to the table with a tray full of Orth's supper. She places dishes down carefully and stands for a moment wiping her hands on her apron.

"Barney tell you about Libby?" she asks quietly.

"Yes", Orth replies as he starts to adjust his plates around. "She said it was a sudden thing that changed her mind and life, Ortie. She said that she was reading a passage in the Bible at her kitchen table when she felt a strange sensation...a rush of peaceful emotions overcame her. She said all of a sudden, she felt that nothing really mattered much in her life except to know about God and Christ. I was amazed at the way Libby changed...she has become a real lady again," Bertha concludes.

Orth glances at Bertha, smiles and gestures with a thumbs up. "God works in strange and wondrous ways, Bertha."

"He sure does," Bertha answers as she heads back to the kitchen.

Barney returns from the bar holding his glass in one hand and a bottle in the other. He seats himself and takes a gulp from the bottle.

"Eddie lost his truck...couldn't make the payments and his uncle has refused to help him," Barney asserts. Then Barney explains that Eddie could not manage his money and lost a great deal on frivolous purchases of expensive clothes and an automobile. He even went so far as to add fanciful gadgets to his truck and purchased another new trailer (which he did not need), rationalizing all these acquisitions with such trite and hackneyed phrases as, "Well, you only live once," and "You have to get big in this business or get out."

"What is he doing now?" Orth asks Barney.

"Oh, he goes from job to job – relying on his old friends ...he comes in here now and then. The last I heard he was driving a delivery truck for Seven-Up Bottling. One of his old high school buddies owns the plant, that is, his dad does, and they took pity on Eddie. He asks about you, Ortie."

Orth shakes his head adding, "Poor Eddie will never grow up, I suppose."

Orth finishes his supper and bids goodbye to Barney and the others. His thoughts are about Libby, and he concludes that it may be appropriate to call upon her. On the way to the parking lot he stops at a pay phone to call her up. He fumbles for his change and grabs the directory. His glasses hinder his ability to see up close and he annoyingly jerks them off and places the wire framed old pair in his right shirt pocket as he glances down the list of names... muttering to himself, "Latouche, Latouche..." nothing listed under "Libby Latouche", trying Catherine Irene Zimmerman, he spots a listing, and dials the number.

"Hello?" he hears Libby say. "Greetings, Libby, or Catherine, it's Ortie."

"How nice to hear from you, Ortie, how are you getting on?" Libby asks.

"Splendidly...I understand you have discovered our Savior?"

"Something happened rather suddenly," Libby says. Libby asks Orth to come over and visit, so he jumps into Whitey and motors on to her apartment. He feels that he has an obligation to comfort Libby and encourage her after her conversion, and to perhaps aid her to understand certain things that may be confusing her about the Gospel. After all, he thinks, "That's my job... to teach, preach and witness for the Lord Jesus Christ.

Orth drives Whitey onto the freeway north towards the suburban town where Libby's apartment is. Orth is a defensive and conservative driver – trying to stay within speed limits. He shudders at the way the "sharks" zip in and out in close quarters in front of him, rarely bothering to signal. After a twenty minute ordeal on Interstate 43, he pulls off and onto the ramp leading to Green Bend, a small bedroom community. Libby's apartment is in an attractive building, modern and contemporary. Orth wonders how people can live in a cluttered up situation. Children's tricycles and assorted toys litter the area around the building.

Orth sounds the door bell at the second floor apartment and waits, he hears the sounds of voices and the patter of feet. Danny answers, "Hi, Mr. Volzenkoff," he says stiffly as he opens the door widely. Libby remarks loudly from somewhere inside.

"Come on in, Ortie, excuse me, I'm trying to get some things done before supper time."

"Take your time, Libby," Orth says as he sits down on a chair in the living room. Danny walks off into the bedroom. A short while later, Libby comes in from the kitchen, still attired in her waitress uniform, she wipes her hands on a towel she is carrying. She stands still in the middle of the room eyeing Orth who has risen from the chair. Tears trickle from Libby's eyes. They each say nothing for a few moments, just staring at each other.

"Why the uniform?" Orth says.

"Oh," Libby comes back from her moment of reverie, "I've taken a job as a waitress here in town...I just could not bring myself to mud wrestle any more. Things have changed in the last several weeks, Ortie."

"Yes, you look different, Libby...tell me about it."

Libby takes Orth's hand and they sit down on the couch. She tells of her experience of being born again. She explains how her mind was somehow altered...how her values suddenly changed – what a peaceful feeling she felt as she sat at the kitchen table reading the book of James in the Bible. Orth understands because his conversion was the same sudden burst of cosmic energy from God. Like Paul on the road to Damascus explained in the book of Acts. Suddenly one's mind sees a burst of light, the Truth comes down and crushes you.

"When's supper?" Danny inquires as he comes from the bedroom. Danny is a quiet boy and well mannered. Orth remains for a cup of coffee, having previously supped at Frederick's.

"Please join us and have something," Libby says.

"No, thank you, I've had ample at Frederick's," Orth replies. Supper is finished and they sit at the table. Danny, being impatient retires to his bedroom after asking his mother to be excused.

"It just happened," Libby says to Orth about her instant conversion, gesturing with her hands and a slight smile.

"The same with me, Libby, we were lucky, with some it takes quite a while before they are 'born again'," Orth replies.

"Explain 'born again'", Libby asks as she starts to clear away the dishes.

Orth sips his coffee and leans back in his chair. Libby rejoins him at the table.

"John Wesley cleared it up for me in one of his sermons he wrote which I happened to read. 'Born again' is a change in your mental attitude, an alteration of your values. Things that once seemed vitally important now seem trivial. To some it comes suddenly, like to Paul in the New Testament, and, of course, to you and me."

Libby nods reflectively adding, "I have so much to learn, Ortie. I...I...I," and tears trickle down her cheeks. Orth understands, she is feeling joy and at the same moment remorse for her past wretched mistakes.

"God understands," Orth utters after a few moments. "You now have a great commission, Libby, to carry on the work of those that have gone before us...Martin Luther, George Whitefield, John Calvin, Oliver Cromwell, those gigantic Christian leaders whom God has blessed to carry the banner into the heated battle against evil and darkness. I thought I knew combat in Korea, but it was an afternoon tea party in the park compared to what we Christians are expected to do as the time draws close. Christ will come when the situation becomes intolerable. And, I feel we are very close now."

"I'm so dumb," Libby inserts. "Can you help me to learn enough to get started?"

"That's my job, Libby. He calls me to help in many different quarters," Orth says.

Orth then discusses how it is essential for her to keep reading the Bible with the appetite of a hungry shark – then to read other authors of worthy character, Tolstoy, etc. He then reminds her how prayer should become an obsession and that she should attend church out of God's gratitude.

"It will seem so strange going to church again," Libby adds as she gazes at her hands in her lap.

"Never you give a fig, Libby – you just remember that if God be for you, who can be against you?" Orth states, as he begins to get up from the table. He pauses then says, "Before I go, let me sketch a brief outline of the history of the Christian church for you. It will get you started thinking about the tremendous army you have been inducted into. You will become a veritable Joan of Arc for Christ." Follows is the outline Orth left for Libby:

Roman Empire

Christ crucified

Caesar Nero A.D. 64

Christians persecuted - Mass murders - Catacombs, etc.

Constantine Augustus — first Christian Roman Emperor 300 A.D.

Rome falls to the Visigoths 410 A.D.

Eastern Roman Empire moves to Constantinople

Patrick convertsheathen in Ireland 461 A.D.

Bishops; Ignatius fed to wild beasts -
Polycarp burned at the stake by the Romans circa 107 A.D.

Saxons invade Britain defeating the Romans

Pope Gregory converts the Saxons in Britain

Boniface sent to Europe to convert the heathens in Germany, etc.

Boniface murdered by pagans in Germany

Mohammed denied Christ dies 632 A.D.

Charles Martel "The Hammer" King of the Franks defeats The Moslems at Poitier 732 A.D.

Charles I King of the Franks (Charlemagne) 799 A.D. first Emperor of the Holy Roman Empire

Pope Urban II inspires Crusades 1095 A.D.

Crusades battle the Moslems for control of Jerusalem

Pope Innocent III, 1198

Saint Francis from Assisi begins his mission, 1201

Saint Thomas of Aquinas of noble birth but chooses to be Dominican Friar becomes great scholar, 1250

Pope Innocent III begins Inquisition 133 A.D. Heretics tortured and murdered by courts of Dominicans

John Wycliffe (England) b. 1328 revolts against the Pope and Catholic Church

Wycliffe first translator of Bible into English

John Ball led peasant revolt in England 1350

John Hus from Bohemia begins reformation work in Switzerland 1414

Hus burned at the stake by the Pope

Renaissance - Italy begins 1450

Martin Luther starts Reformation 1517

Wittenburg, Germany posts 95 points to the door

Phillip Melanchthon German professor of Greek at Wittenburg follows Luther

Erasmus 1500 Dutch writer

Diet of Worms 1521

Luther emphasized Bible reading – translated Bible into German for common folk

Erastus b. 1524 Swiss reformer

John Calvin, 1533, forms the Calvinist movement in Switzerland

Ulrich Zwingli reformer in Switzerland circa 1500

Lutheran Church grows in Germany and Europe

1540 Loyola forms the "Jesuits" - Roman Catholic priests

1563 Council of Trent denounces the Reformation

1564 Calvinists form the Presbyterian Church

It was declared a crime in Britain by the Catholics to read the Bible

The Lollards in Britain (pioneer Reformists) followers of John Wycliffe

25 Cambridge scholars executed for reading the Bible and other anti-Catholic literature

Thomas Bilney of Cambridge burned at the stake, 1531, for preaching against the Catholic Church

William Tyndale updates Wycliffe's English translation of the Bible

John Firth martyred - burned at the stake

William Tyndale executed in Holland 1536 by strangulation

King Henry VIII orders the publication of an English Bible 1538

King Henry VIII who married his brother's widow, Catherine of Aragon, desired to divorce her and marry Anne Boleyn - the Pope refuses dispensation

In 1534 England breaks with Rome

Thomas Cranmer Archbishop of Canterbury preaches the Reformation 1553

Spanish Armada defeated, 1588, sent to defeat the English Protestants

John Knox and George Wishart preach protestation in Scotland 1528

John Knox forms the Presbyterian Church in Scotland after John Calvin's methods, 1560

King James I, 1604 had King James Version of Bible authored

Puritans, 1604 opposed to Bishops and the Church of England

Puritans depart England for fear of persecution go to Holland, 1608

Navigation developed - sextant invented

1630 more Puritans go to America land in Maine John Winthrop settles in Massachusetts

King Charles succeeds King James, tries to force the Church of England on all 1633

People revolt - Presbyterians win the support of Parliament

Oliver Cromwell becomes Lord Protector of England - has King Charles beheaded for treason

Roger Williams forms the Baptist Church in Providence, Rhode Island 1635

George Fox, in England forms the Quakers, 1636

Jonathan Edwards preaches in New England, 1740

The Methodist Movement gains members under John Wesley in England, 1740

George Whitefield comes from England 1740, converts many to Methodism in America

A great American awakening

The Age of Doubt begins in 1800 - the educated doubt God using human reasoning

Baptist Missionary William Carey in 1792 is successful in India

Adroniram Judson missionary to Burma and Robert Morrison missionary to China, 1830

John Colderide Patterson missionary to the South Seas

The Greek (Eastern) Orthodox Church ruled from Russia under Czar Peter the Great 1721

Religion is deep and rich in Russia

Russian Revolution, 1917, Bolsheviks take over - Communists rule

Church suffers in Russia

Christians murdered - tortured in Russia

Falling away from Christianity in America 1920's and 1930's Christ seen as

an ordinary "do-gooder" in the USA by many, His divinity is denied
> Hitler comes to power 1933 in Germany

> Christians and Jews are tortured and murdered by Hitler

> World War II begins 1941

> 1948 World Council of Churches meet in Holland to discuss church policies and problems

> The Age of Doubt continues in America and world wide

> Present Day

Orth hands Libby his scratch notes – and carefully places his well worn "memory jog" cards in his battered brief case. Libby glances over the notes while Orth once again rises preparing to depart. Libby walks to the door with Orth while he opens the door pausing a moment. He towers over Libby. Placing his briefcase down, he embraces her with a warm hug, then quickly turns and heads down the stairs.

Libby slowly closes the door, resting her two arms on it for a moment. Danny enters the room and sits on the couch.

"What were you guys talking about?" Danny asks.

Libby crosses to the couch and sits down next to Danny.

"We were talking about Joan of Arc," Libby replies.

The evening air was cool by the time Orth got into his pickup and started towards the freeway home. His thoughts wandered as he drove and he reached down to turn on the radio to the Milwaukee Public Radio station…that Orth enjoyed listening to for the classical music.

CHAPTER VII

Wisdom is better than weapons of war...Wisdom raineth down skill and knowledge of understanding, and exalteth them to honor that hold her fast.

Eccl. 9:18

It was a warm June morning in the year 1946. Frederick, Orth's father, and Bertha, his mother, have driven him to the train depot in Oesterich. The cows had been milked and the chores had been completed. Fritz bid Orth goodbye from the breakfast table in his dirty overalls showing little emotion – while Orth fought back the tears. He had decided to leave the farm and head for Milwaukee where he hoped to find employment while temporarily staying with Grandmother Ida. He discussed it at length with Frederick and Fritz and it was tacitly agreed that the farm lacked the resources to support another family should Orth remain and marry. Orth desired to try his luck in the big city where more opportunities may exist. Our hero was a child of seventeen and he was wide-eyed at the prospects that lay ahead.

Frederick pulls the old battered red Dodge pickup truck into the train parking lot – pulling on the brake – "brrratt." Bertha looks sad. The train usually due at nine a.m. will no doubt be late they all thought as they sat in silence watching the railway workers pull the mail and baggage carts onto the ramp for loading. The train was late – fifteen minutes – which was good for the Milwaukee Southern Railway. Frederick kissed his son on the cheek, as did Bertha, then walked to the coach car with Orth. Orth carried one suitcase Frederick had given him. It was a rather expensive, but old leather case that had been in the family for years. It had two straps around the middle.

Orth climbed the steps of the railcar, located a seat next to an attractive young lady and gazed out the window where he could see Frederick and Bertha standing silently waiting for the train to leave. Orth felt deep sadness and struggled to fight back the tears unsuccessfully. The young lady, who was some years older than our hero seemed to sense Orth's remorse and attempted to find some common ground for conversation. Orth was always shy to an excessive amount – fear gripped him when he was in close association with an attractive female. He chatted off and on with the young lady who was also traveling to Milwaukee. The seat was hard and the back was broken so when he leaned back it gave way. This meant he had to sit in an strict upright position the entire way. The train was crowded and this apparently was the only open seat available – or so it seemed. The train pulled into Union Station Milwaukee about five p.m. Orth was tired of sitting in his strained position and welcomed the chance to rid himself of it. The young lady bid Orth "goodbye" with a sly seductive smile that made the blood rise in Orth's neck.

"Well," he thought, "that's that...perhaps some day I'll be able to understand women and feel comfortable in their presence."

Grandma Ida was waiting in the station that echoed with train announcements and the usual confusion of the hustle-bustle of travelers.

"Are you hungry?" Ida asked Orth after she had hugged him and smothered him with kisses. She still over-did the perfume and dressed quite stylishly.

"Yes, kind of," was Orth's answer to his appetite. They walked to the restaurant in the station and were seated at a side booth. The restaurant was large and well attended by travelers. The food was always good and Orth would remember the white linen tablecloths and shining silverware. The ceiling was high with enormous chandeliers suspended seemingly from the clouds. Along the walls were paintings of train scenes. Orth ordered hot cakes, which was odd for that time of day – but he missed breakfast before leaving Oesterich, and he remembered from the past how the hot cakes were large and fluffy – being served under a silver dish cover with genuine maple syrup and plenty of Wisconsin butter. Breakfast was served all day at the Union Station restaurant because of the variety of schedules of travelers and train people. Grandma Ida did not order anything because she had supped previously with Evelyn Lovejoy in her apartment.

Orth stayed with Grandma Ida in the apartment while he looked for a job. Living with Ida was a trying experience because she seemed to be constantly annoying Orth with trivial faults as commented previously in Chapter V. One morning while glancing through the want ads in the Milwaukee Journal, he noticed one asking for "bookkeeper trainees" at Wisconsin State Bank. He is excited and puts on his only tie and "dress" outfit. He grabs the streetcar on Wisconsin Avenue and heads downtown.

The personnel department of the Wisconsin State Bank was on the tenth floor. Orth enters and is told to fill out a questionnaire, which he does quickly, then sits and waits. Secretaries flit in and out of offices – men in their middle ages enter into and out of offices. Orth is humbled by the apparent importance of the place and the people. Telephones "brringgg" and typewriters go "clickedy-click-snap-bang". Papers are in stacks on desks and the wall pictures are unimaginative gigantic flowers or pastoral scenes of northern Wisconsin.

Orth feels self-conscious. The young and older men are wearing double-breasted or three-piece suits with nice pressed white shirts and ties. Orth has on his only old second hand sport coat and best shirt. He tries to hide his mortification in a magazine, but is not very successful.

Finally, the moment arrives. He is shown in to see Mr. Flowers, a Personnel Department Assistant Cashier. Mr. Flowers has very little paperwork on his desk and is wearing a continuous insincere sugary smile. His manner is soft and is the type that would only be slightly disturbed if it were announced that the world would collide with the star Vega in thirty minutes.

"Well–well, Orth, it is certainly nice of you to inquire at our Bank about career positions," Mr. Flowers begins, while glancing over Orth's application. At the conclusion of the interview, Orth is informed that the Bank would be in touch with him in a day or two to let him know what the decision had been. He returns to Grandma Ida's to wait.

The next day he is surprised by a phone call from Mr. Flowers who informs him that he has been accepted as a bookkeeper trainee, and is to report to a branch office at Seventh Street and Pine Avenue. The starting salary is $75.00 per month. Orth is nervous and happy – the pay isn't substantial, but he realizes it as a start.

Ida chides him in a moderate way – calling him "my banker". Grandma Ida is also quick to remind him of several of her relatives who were prominent in the banking industry in early Wisconsin. Orth reports to the branch bank earlier than required and taps on the door. A man answers who is wearing glasses that keep sliding down his nose – requiring his attention to push them back up. The gentleman announces that his name is "Bill" Williamson and directs Orth to take a seat until some other people arrive. Bill is a short person of stocky build – with most of his hair gone. He is in his mid to late thirties. His manner is punctilious while he thumbs through mounds of checks that had arrived in the early morning to be posted to customers' accounts. He scans the documents for proper endorsements, dates and so forth. Orth notices how Bill seems to be forever pushing his rimless glasses back up because they had slipped down his short, stubby nose. It was quiet - Bill talked measuredly. Orth finally learned that Bill was a teller and had come from Oklahoma where he had graduated from Oklahoma State University with a degree in English. He had taught school for a while in Wisconsin, but found out that his likes for the academic life were not realistic and decided to try a career in banking. Bill had escaped service during World War II because his left arm was slightly withered. Orth later sensed how he regretted this fact and carried it as a burden. Men who have not served in the military appear to regret it, seeing the military as a symbol of manhood – of heroics, where the brave and noble ones exist; where one earns their courage and respect. Orth can recall the returning War veterans in Oesterich and how they were the center of attraction at the barber shops or wherever "real" men gathered. To hear their tales of combat – even if they were grossly exaggerated, was a riveting experience.

As the days passed, Orth learns about bank bookkeeping and is under the tutelage of a young lady soon to depart from her position because she is with child and prefers to lead a proper life of home maker and mother. As he masters one task after another, he enjoys the independence and thrill of making his way in the big city. He still lives with Grandma Ida, but discovers that their relationship is becoming strained. Ida almost continually chides Orth with annoying and irritating barbs – "Pick up your clothes, make the bed, sweep the kitchen", and so forth. To add to Orth's uneasiness, Ida imbibes constantly and her tirades become more intolerable by the day as she baits Orth with comments that are nasty and castigating about Bertha. Ida never seemed to entertain kindly thoughts about Bertha and often inferred that she was a slovenly, lazy woman, unworthy of her son. And… on – on it went, until one day when Orth returned home from the bank in mid-September, when Ida started out with a particularly violent attack, he made a decision. She had been drinking and Orth saw that her speech was slurred and her gait unsteady. Her breath was full of the smell of whiskey and smoke. Orth could stand it no more! He stood quietly then started to pack his few belongings in his suitcase provided by his dad. Ida's censure did not cease while she watched this. She began to shout about how she continually showered him and the family with gifts and money. Finally, Orth closed the lid of the suitcase and departed, slamming the door behind him abruptly. That was the last time he ever spent with Grandma Ida as a house guest.

He did not know where to go to find a place to live, but he recalled that the YMCA in the downtown section of Milwaukee had rooms. So he hustled his bag down to the corner of Wisconsin Avenue where he had seen taxicabs waiting frequently, and hired one. His funds were scarce. The bank job paid a scanty wage, so he was forced to be parsimonious. Upon arrival at the downtown Y.M.C.A. (Young Men's Christian Association) he handed the driver the exact fare and started off.

"What's for me?" he heard over his shoulder. Embarrassed, he turned around and handed the taxi operator most of the remaining coins he had and entered the building.

The room he rented was small with a single bed, small closet and one chair, a rather barren thing…rent was seventy-five cents a day and you walked down the hall to the large open shower room, hand basins and toilets. The floor he was on also had large dormitory rooms for those who were not concerned about privacy. The building was filled with a mixture of men, young and old. There were many service men from the Army, Navy and Marine Corps who could be heard on the walk down the halls because of the "clink, clink," of their dog tags and the "clackity, clack" of their shower togs.

Orth suffered from the shock of loneliness while at the Y.M.C.A. and wrote often to Bertha, who never missed sending a warm response back soon. He soon acquired several friends that alleviated his melancholy somewhat. They frequently met for breakfast at a cheap coffee shop close by. One of the friends – a heavy set boy of about nineteen who was from a small distant town in Northern Wisconsin attended a local trade school to learn printing and generally always ordered two jelly doughnuts and coffee for his morning repast. Orth usually had a stack of three pancakes that lasted him all day until he returned from the bank in the evening. His eating habits were erratic because he was parsimonious to the extreme. His bank salary was only $75.00 per month and he was paid every two weeks. He hoarded his money like a jealous hawk over her chicks. He usually stopped by the bakery and purchased half a cake, plus a quart of milk and that was it for his supper. His weight plunged and he was soon to discover he was down to less than 140 pounds.

But – his spirits were high as he took on the tasks at the bank with a zest. The women employees at the bank felt sorry for him and suggested that he eat more or his health would suffer. This embarrassed Orth and he remained silent because of his characteristic shy nature. His only dress shirt, sport coat and slacks were wearing out fast, yet he shelved any ideas about purchasing new clothes.

Then, something changed this. Older and more worldly men came into the branch bank to help as temporary relief workers or to audit the records. These men were older than Orth, so he gazed at them with admiration. They had been to war, at least most of them, had university degrees and had "been around", that is, traveled, either in foreign countries or to other states in the U.S.A. Orth noticed that their clothes were stylish – up-to-date. They wore starched white shirts with button down collars. Their ties and other accoutrements were manly and attractive.

Orth thought…"Well, if I'm to get anywhere in the bank, I had better start looking successful and cast off the "country bumpkin look". So casting off the shackles of abject denial, he went to one of the finest stores in downtown Milwaukee, Meyer Brothers, and purchased several shirts, trousers and a handsome sweater. This buoyed his spirits and he enjoyed the feeling of wearing new clothes. In fact, it so elated him that several weeks later, he purchased a new brown double-breasted suit.

As time went on, Orth was given complete responsibility for the bookkeeping department, then assigned to junior teller after attending a teller training class at the main office. He enjoyed the teller duties, but was still a shy type and awkward with the ladies. He had never had a date with a girl and he felt a deep mystery about them. Orth was not ugly, but he lacked self-confidence because of his long, skinny frame, slender face with a rather too large nose. And above all, his glasses. These he felt made him appear like a sissy, feckless person. So he suffered.

On one trip to Oesterich, Bertha sensed her son's awkward position and one evening taught Orth how to dance. This bolstered his sense of self esteem to no end. Upon his return to Milwaukee, he began to think about asking someone out to dance and dinner.

He did not have to wait long to test his skill. The lady who replaced Orth at the bookkeeping position had a daughter who was a typist in the local F.B.I. (Federal Bureau of Investigation) office. She asked Orth, now the junior teller out of the three assigned to the branch bank, if he would accompany her daughter to the annual Christmas party. Orth found the lady quite pleasant – from the Southern states, talking with a provincial drawl, and being considerably older than he, admired her. He felt obliged to agree to the kind offer. The party was held at a very expensive hotel in the suburbs. Since his assignment as a teller, he felt inclined to purchase an automobile. The car was an ancient 1933 Ford sedan that he acquired from a used car dealer close to where Grandma Ida resided. The auto dealer was obviously without scruples because he sold the hulk to Orth for $75.00 while its condition was vastly lamentable. The black beast burned oil like a steel mill and as Orth drove along the street, his car trailed huge billows of smoke. That wasn't all. The brakes were horrible – to the extent that he had to plan his stops well in advance or he would blithely coast right through a stop light! Next, because the hulk burned so much oil, the engine fumes came up through the floor boards and saturated the innards. This condition meant that he had to leave several of the windows down while he drove or one could be overcome by effluvium.

During the warm weather, this was not severe, but during the cool days – driving was a sufferable existence. Orth would bundle up and pretend he was a World War II fighter pilot flying over the cold lands of France and Germany.

Well, back to the night of the party. The girl's name was typical southern - being from Tennessee; it was Marigold. She dressed attractively, was well mannered, but these attributes did not overshadow her lack of feminine charm. Anyway, for Orth, it was a start. He picked Marigold up at her apartment. Her mother, "Max", answered the door and was fawning over Orth, he supposed because Marigold lacked the necessary physical qualities to have a cadre of suitors. Max (short for Maxine) bid them adieu and off they went in the smoky black beast.

Orth felt embarrassed as he drove along to the party, smoke billowing up through the floorboards. Marigold did not seem to mind. She seemed content to be with her date. Things went well at the party. He danced with Marigold the sole steps Bertha had taught him, the Fox-Trot. "One-two-three-together," Orth counted to himself. Marigold glided along like a dream and Orth felt his confidence buoyed until the band commenced a Rhumba and Samba. He smartly led Marigold to their table, explaining he did not know the steps. There was another couple at the table – an agent of the F.B.I. and his wife. The agent had a "crew cut", was fairly tall and seemed the personification of what Orth deemed necessary qualities for a J. Edgar Hoover man. The agent was very pleasant and soon Orth felt at ease in his company.

The evening wore on. There was a fair amount of drinking but the party was ruly. Orth did not imbibe. His mind told him that the fruit of the vines and whisky could lead him into a trap that his parents seemed to suffer from. He discounted the fact that the German culture seemed to expect the people to consume alcohol in moderate and even at times to the extreme. So – he abstained with a vengeance! Feeling the fire water as deadly as a hand grenade with the pin pulled. At the close of the evening, he drove Marigold back to her apartment and bid her goodnight. He did not attempt to woo her – he had never kissed a girl and was frightened to death at the thought. This was soon to change.

His friend at the Y.M.C.A., Charles "Swede" Swensen, not the chap who attended the printing school; invited Orth out on a double date. That is, Swede made the arrangements and Orth had not previously had the pleasure of meeting the young lady. Her name was an odd one – that is, not frequently heard, Malvina. Swede, apparently took pity on Orth and thought him too shy – too introverted, therefore, the date to loosen him up. Become more "of-the-world". Swede had been in the Navy in the waning years of the war and had enlisted prior to graduation from high school. He was from a small Norwegian town in Minnesota – a Lutheran stronghold - yet Swede appeared not a zealot - quite the contrary.

The evening out with Malvina went marvelously well. Swede used his car - a fairly recent model Chevrolet sedan. Orth and Malvina occupied the rear seats. They commenced with supper at a spot on the outskirts of Milwaukee that served a buffet of chicken and numerous other delights, all you could stuff yourself with. And, Swede made the most of it. His girl friend seemed embarrassed because of his swine-type habits - a roll in one fist - elbows on the table - fork in the other fist - he sat there and kept shoveling down the grub. Talking all the while, he urged Orth to "finish up - there's plenty more."

Orth ate sparingly because he desired to make a good impression on Malvina, who had a horrible complexion with blotches of pimples, but was endowed with an attractive figure and a pleasing warm personality. Orth felt "comfortable" with Malvina. She was bolder than Marigold, which pleased Orth because he considered girls almost as items made of porcelain that were easily affronted.

After supper, the two couples drove to downtown Milwaukee to watch the New Year's Day Parade. The affair was usually so well attended that space

THE BANK ASSIGNED ORTH AS A RELIEF TELLER - TRAVELING TO VARIOUS BRANCH OFFICES AS HELP WAS NEEDED... HE REPORTED TO MR. FLOWERS AT THE MAIN OFFICE.

at the viewing side would be difficult to obtain. Swede thought that because the parade commenced at eight in the morning and by the time they finished supper it would be a prudent idea to park close to the parade route and sleep in the car all night - therefore, having a premium location at parade time.

So they slept, or attempted to. Swede had blankets, Orth placed his arm about Malvina and he smelled her hair which had the pleasant aroma of "sweet female". About six in the morning Orth had his first kiss. It took him by surprise, but he was pleased that she took the initiative. Then the two wooed each other continually. Orth was not in love with Malvina, but he appreciated her as a friend and warm female companion. He dated her several times later, then their closeness ended as Orth began to have other female companions.

The bank assigned Orth as a "Relief Teller", at his request. He felt that he wanted to leave the Branch – see the city and become more knowledgeable. Mr. Flowers at the Main Office assigned Orth to various places to report where he would spend one day, or perhaps a week. The Bank reimbursed him for mileage, as he drove the "Black Beast", his 1933 Ford to various locations. He salary was continually increased and he was able to set some aside for his estate. He recalled how Uncle Humphrey was always thrifty and businesslike, plus, he was a Bank Director for a Bank in Milwaukee, Milwaukee First Savings Bank, a fairly good-sized bank, and Orth continually admired Uncle Humphrey for his virtuous life and his respectful community standing.

Orth traversed throughout Milwaukee and the suburbs in his assignments, becoming well known with the various Branch and Main Office officers. His skill as a teller was admired and he could handle currency very well and usually had no trouble balancing at the day's end. A teller had to total debits and credits so they equaled. This usually resulted in an equation such as:

Beginning cash, plus deposits, minus checks cashed equals ending cash.

Of course, there are a multitude of documents that constitute debits and credits. Well, so it was that Orth was introduced into the financial world and how well he adapted to it. His frequent trips back to Oesterich met with Brother Fritz's jeering..."Well, here's the 'Banker' again...don't get your hands dirty, Orth." Orth did not mind and laughed because he felt that Fritz was jealous because he was so shackled to the dairy farm. Fred, Orth's father was becoming a worse problem as he began to drink more heavily and squander his few dollars on entertaining his drinking cronies.

Bertha suffered. She loved Fred and she also despised his bad habits. She made do as best she could, working long hours about the farm, scraping up enough funds to have a fine table ready for Orth when he came home. And, of course, at Christmas time, Bertha always had to have it a special time. She would buy used clothing items and nuts from neighbors – wrapping them up carefully for "her boys", Fritz, Orth and, of course, "dad" Fred.

These times were sad for Orth. His dad was failing, Bertha was growing older and having difficulty getting about and Fritz was struggling with endless hours milking and field work. Soon there would come an abrupt change in Orth's life and the family's.

CHAPTER VIII

Then the Lord turned to him and said, "I will make you strong! Go and save Israel from the Midianites! I am sending you!" But Gideon replied, "Sir, how can I save Israel? My family is the poorest in the whole tribe of Manasseh, and I am the least thought of in the entire family!" Whereupon the Lord said to him, "But, I, Jehovah, will be with you..."

Judges 6:14-16

It was a warm Wednesday afternoon at Homeport as Orth prepared to drive to the Methodist Church in New Hesse, about seven miles, to direct the Youth Group who met at five in the assembly hall. There were roughly fifteen students, two girls, of which were the minister's daughters. As Orth ambles out to the garage, Mutnik sidles up to him with his tail wagging and with his usual broad warm smile across his muzzle.

"Hiyah, Mutnik, my ol' buddy," Orth says as he walks and rubs Mutnik under his chin occasionally. He thanks God for Mutnik and for many other things in his life that have made it enjoyable for him. He recalls how Saint Paul and John Wesley always had a prayer of thanksgiving to God on their tongues as they sojourned through life.

He climbs into Whitey and his faithful pickup barks into life as he edges down the lane to the main county road. Mutnik remains sitting on the back lawn and watches as Orth moves away. Orth knows that his trusted companion will remain close to Homeport to keep watch on things.

The birds twitter in the monstrous cottonwood tree out back and the forever "caw-caw" of the ravens sound in the distant fields. He ponders the ravens - always detested by the farmers, but appointed by God to be a clean up detail as they feast upon the corpses of dead animals who have been victims of trucks and automobiles along the roads and highways. God's marvelous ways of nature – each animal and insect doing their predetermined task and chores to help mankind.

As he opens the double doors to the church assembly hall, he is met with the usual ruckus of the teenagers. They greet Orth with a mixture of greetings and he bids them to assemble the chairs in a circle as he commences a lesson by having the students take turns reading from their Bibles. Orth requests that they bring their own Bibles and to make frequent use of marginal notes. Today they are discussing a sermon given by John Wesley termed, "The Almost Christian." Orth likes to have a lively discussion with the youth and abhors the use of "institutional lesson plans" authored by career ecclesiastics as being tasteless prattle not geared to prepare Christ's own people to become evangelists. After all, he concludes, "Is not that our main business – to endeavor to bring the truth about Christ Jesus to people?"

Most of the pupils like the style and mien of Orth's teaching methods. He brings the discussion to a close reminding the group that if you do not love God, and love your neighbor as yourself, you are among the many "almost Christians" who do many of the things expected of them but fail in the most important.

They break after about an hour of study for refreshments. The elder ladies from the church usually supplied the goodies and soft drinks. Orth took several cookies and a glass of ice tea and wandered off to a table where Minister Paul was sitting with several others of the youth group.

"Greetings, Ortie. How are the injuries healing?"

"Hello, Paul," Orth replied and they entered into light conversation. Orth enjoyed Paul, but felt that he lacked the spark of enthusiasm so necessary to be an efficacious witness for the Lord Jesus Christ. Paul had been a Baptist preacher for many years, but changed his loyalty to Methodism when he discovered that the Baptist preachers lack a decent means of retirement and medical insurance. He was well educated – holding a doctorate in education from the University of Wisconsin. Paul was ponderous in his sermons, quite accurate and profound in scriptural depth, humorous at the right moments and enjoyable and educational to listen to.

Orth generally sat on the front bench during the worship services and made notes as Paul spoke. He mentioned to some, that to sit in church and not take notes is missing a choice opportunity to garner some choice tidbits from the Holy Spirit.

Paul had spent two years in the Army during the Korean War as a draftee. He often remarked that his Army days doing clerical tasks were not exactly inspiring, as a soldier is usually thought of as a hero of sorts.

"Clifton here is going into the Navy, Ortie," Paul reflects. Clifton glances down at the table in a semi-embarrassed posture.

"Oh? That so? Well, you will gain from the experience I'm sure, Clifton," Orth concludes.

"Ah, yes, I recall my first days and weeks in the Army," Paul adds. "They were filled with fear, doubts and anxiety."

"Basic training is a time of violent adjustments," Orth says as Clifton eyes him with questions in his eyes.

"Tell me what it's like, Ortie, I mean, what was it like for you?" Clifton asks with a weak voice.

Orth looks down into his glass of iced tea and puts his cookie down on the plate.

* * *

The author cannot recall the exact wording in the newspaper article that Orth noticed with interest one Sunday morning while relaxing in his small Y.M.C.A. room, but it progressed along these lines:

> *"Enlist in the Army – one or two years and earn the G.I. Bill for your college education...Contact Captain, etc."*

Orth thought about this and ripped the advertisement out of the Milwaukee Journal. He was still working as a relief teller for the Wisconsin State Bank and enjoying it. However, he noticed that the young men who had come back from military service and who had attended college or university at the expense of the G.I. Bill were selected for officer positions in the bank much sooner than chaps like Orth who were the plodding high school Philistines, uncultured and crude, who were the yeoman tradesman types. This irritated

Orth and he carried this resentment with him as he witnessed the puppies fresh from college being assigned as loan or other bank officers with ample responsibilities.

So, it was decided that he would enlist for two years. On the following Saturday, he drove the Black Beast out to the Milwaukee Airport where he located a low building wherein was housed the Army Recruiting Office. He entered and discovered several men in uniform and he was bid by one to have a seat for a moment – he was a sergeant with many accoutrements on his uniform which seemed to be mysteriously exciting to Orth who was instantly impressed. The sergeant was fawningly friendly and introduced Orth into a private office wherein sat an overweight Captain wearing glasses and with plump jowls.

Orth felt the bottom fall out of his stomach as he answered a series of questions asked by the officer. Soon he raised his right hand and was part of the U.S. Army – Private E-1!

He returned to the Y.M.C.A. He was told to await further instructions as to where to report for basic training, traveling orders and so forth. His head was awhirl as he made mental notes as to what he should do before departure. In several days, he received a form letter from the Army telling him to report to a downtown address for a physical examination – it was in a window envelope and looked quite official. The room where the physical was given was uptown Milwaukee – upstairs over a variety of stores. The room had subdivisions with desks scattered here and there. An Army medic in a white coat bid Orth to have a seat in the next room until called. He was in the company of about twenty or thirty other recruits. All sat around on the benches in a morose fashion eyeing their hands or fumbling with papers or chatting idly with those sitting close by. Soon the same Army medic came in handing out medical forms that he requested be completed and handed back to him. The questions were numerous, lengthy and trite...such as "Do you wet the bed? Yes, No, Occasionally; Have you had any of the following: smallpox, scarlet fever, etc." Orth struggled through the maze and handed them back to the medic who shuffled through them then grunted, "Go into the next room there and take off your clothes. You can leave your underwear on, but take your socks off."

After this he sat along the wall with the rest of the unfortunates – it was chilly, and the doctors who were performing the examination did not exactly exude exultation, and went about their duties in a disinterested manner.

The Army gave the recruits a "meal ticket" for a nearby restaurant limited to $1.50. The young men crowded in and ate with a vengeance. After lunch all reported back upstairs at 1300 (1:00 p.m.). Then there was a series of tests to ascertain how stupid one was. About 1700 (5:00 p.m.) all was over and Orth collected the Black Beast and drove back to the YMCA. It was raining slightly and he felt gloomy like the day. He phoned Bertha to give her the news about his decision to enter the Army. She was overcome with emotion and wept over the phone. Orth said that he would be up to visit before he left (he hoped). He spoke briefly with Fritz, who had come in after completing milking. Fritz met Orth with his usual berating remarks, "…Well, Orth, the peacetime Army is sure not like the real Army of World War II, and especially the Airborne. You straightlegs are soft palmed garrison types." Orth did not speak to Frederick.

He gave his termination notice to the Bank. Mr. Flowers in the Personnel Department was his usual calm, unruffled self and commented that he was surprised by Orth's action, but bid him good luck and that he would be welcome upon his return from the service, conditions permitting. Orth continued on working at his relief teller position awaiting notice from the Army. He did not have long to wait. A window envelope was awaiting him upon his return from work one evening with the address labeled "Pvt. Orth Schilling Volzenkoff," with the Department of the Army printing in the left hand corner. Orth swallowed hard as he went upstairs to open the envelope. It related in an officious tone that he was to report to the location where he took his physical examination next week at Tuesday morning 17 May 1950, 0800 to proceed to Basic Training, Fort Ord, California.

* * *

Orth visited home before departing, leaving the Black Beast and other things there that he thought he would not need. He took the train back to Milwaukee and stayed with Grandma Ida the night before he was due to depart. Ida was declining and her imbibing accelerated her deterioration. Orth caught the city bus on West Wisconsin Avenue and hustled it to the appointed spot. There were about thirty other young recruits like himself waiting in the upstairs hall. They were given a set of instructions and meal passes for the train. All would be going to California. Then they were loaded onto an Army bus and driven to the Union Station whereupon they waited the arrival of a local train to Chicago where they would change trains to the Union Pacific – "City of San Francisco". Orth thought it fortunate that they had upper and lower berth sleepers, and did not have to endure the long journey sitting in a coach seat.

This indeed was a real adventure. The trip to Oakland, California, took two and one-half days and upon arrival at the station, there was a sergeant waiting there and they were directed to board a chartered Greyhound for fort Ord, some eighty miles southwest. Before we head for wind-swept, foggy Fort Ord, I shall briefly comment upon how the Army master-minded the train journey.

Orth had an upper berth – below him was Tom Tolliver, who would remain as one of his stalwart, steadfast buddies until killed in Korea (Chapter II). There was one man (a recruit also) who had experience in High School ROTC (Reserve Officer's Training Corps). This young man of about eighteen or twenty years of age was short and stockily built and had a brusque personality. The author cannot recall his name. Anyway, the Army deigned to appoint this roughneck in charge – and needless to say, he let it be known continually. Oddly, it turned out that his was the only behavior that could be termed "Philistine". He managed to find the means to acquire alcoholic beverages and most of the time, came rolicking back to his berth feeling his cups late at night.

The group went to the diner en-masse. They were not given a menu, the waiter usually asked the simple question, "Army?" Whereupon each man nodded sheepishly and received the standard fare. The food was reasonably good – Orth was not one to complain. Tom Tolliver and he usually sat together. One thing occurred on the train that the author is compelled to comment upon. Orth was sitting in the lounge car reading a magazine. Not many people were in the car at this time, however, directly across from him sat an elderly Negro lady dressed in all white – humming quietly and reading. Orth thought it curious that she be dressed entirely in white. After a short while she and Orth exchanged pleasantries and she confessed that she was returning to California after visiting St. Louis where she led a revival evangelical meeting. She professed to be a minister for the Lord Jesus Christ and headed her own church in Oakland. Her name she said was "Mother". She continued to chat with Orth about God, Christ and the Holy Spirit. Orth felt a calm feeling as he conversed with her – she had an exciting fervor as she spoke about Christ, so absent from the ministers he had sat and listened to at the Congregational Church in Oesterich. Her life was a wretched mess of sin and lustfulness before she came to know Christ. She was interested in Orth's adventure to join the Army and he liked being listened to when he spoke. So often people are interested in their own selves and do not make an effort to listen with patient attention when others speak, and he told her this. She said, "God listens always," and urged Orth to cling to his faith. Orth would remember this lady throughout his lifetime. She was not wealthy by worldly standards, but she exhibited a "golden" heart – a heart and soul that exuded the love of Christ. She was like sitting under a shady tree by a murmuring brook on a hot afternoon.

Fort Ord is an enormous place set on the beach of California – extending inland covering about 20,000 acres. It lies roughly one hundred miles due south of San Francisco. Orth recalls that the climate was always damp, windy, foggy and chilly. Soldiers crossed the road to the beach and trained on the sand beaches. The land was originally owned by a German family - Giggling, and acquired sometime after 1937 by the Army, naming it Fort Ord after a Civil War General – Major General Edward Cresap Ord.

In 1940 the "sand pit" was home to the Seventh Infantry Division – they left in 1943 to fight in the Aleutian Islands. Upon the departure of the Seventh ID, a series of units came and left. During Orth's days, Fort Ord housed the Fourth Replacement Training Center, which became the Fourth Infantry Division, under the Command of the Sixth Army headquartered at the Presidio in San Francisco.

The bus ride to Fort Ord took about three hours. They pulled into the fort about 1700 (5:00 p.m.) and off loaded whereupon a sergeant came up and formed them into three ranks, each man placing his bags in front of him. The sergeant had three stripes and wore a "Smoky, the Bear" type of hat ... one Orth was to learn later that all "D-I's", drill instructors wear. Kind of symbols of fear. A soldier, a servile follower of the rules...given honors and medals to attempt to heal the mental and physical wounds. In peacetime soldiers are unemployed killers, not bright, with the morals of a Billy goat and the life of a priest, because of the lack of female companions. In war, soldiers are mobs of men against mobs of men where guts erupt telling one it is all a mistake – being sent away to a foreign place to spill your blood and be forgotten. Not a life for anyone with a fair amount of wisdom or intellect. Well...on with our story.

After the initial formation the group was shunted off to a barracks – two floors of wood and covered with black tar paper. The sergeant split up the group and made bunk assignments. The bunks were lined up in rows – two high with a wooden "footlocker" at the foot and a series of metal lockers along the walls. There were no window coverings and the toilet facilities were on the lower floor at one end. A row of toilets, a row of wash basins and a common shower room of about eight spigots. It was a barren building – gloomy – made for utilitarian purposes only. At the end of each floor was a private room where the "platoon" sergeant and his assistant were housed.

Some men went upstairs, some down. Orth was fortunate to get an upper bunk – across from him was Tom Tolliver. There was no bedding – they had to march off and "draw" it at a distant location. The present time was used to familiarize the recruits with the building and unload their personal items. The author begs the forgiveness of his readers if he is either too detailed or has omitted critical cogent items in his narrative. One simply endeavors to paint a vivid picture of what it was like. Additionally, it could very well be that there will also possibly occur inaccuracies for which the author pleads guilty – not out of a purposeful desire to mislead or evade the truth – rather an honest lack of adequate recall and historical data.

Living in a barracks demands time to adjust. If one has been used to privacy in civilian life…well, now you are tossed headlong into a system of organized confusion and cacophony. After a while, however, things do settle down and one adjusts, or goes absolutely insane. Officially, Orth was assigned to the first Platoon, Delta Company, Sixth Battalion, Third Brigade – the rest does not matter, but it was all under the Fourth Infantry Division, Sixth Army. This had been noted on his orders to report – but had been overlooked as being too complicated at the moment to decipher.

So, now we have Private E-1 Orth Schilling Volzenkoff, Serial Number RA (standing for Regular Army, as opposed to U.S. which later signified draftees) 19-375-236. The duration of Basic Training at this time was seven weeks, commencing at the Reception Center where one completed a series of forms which took roughly four hours. MOS (Military Occupational Specialties) were assigned, then you were sent off to follow red arrows on the floor. Orth soon learned about the ubiquitous military "lines". One stood in line for a haircut, immunization shots, clothing, etc. Haircuts were ugly messes and the shots were painful. The recruits drew (were given) four sets (pairs) of fatigues (the Army term for play clothes), jackets, boots and so forth.

* * *

"Hey, Ortie! What are you guys talking about?" one of the youth clambered up to where Orth, Paul and Clifton were sitting.

> AT BASIC TRAINING IN THE ARMY EVERYTHING IS PLANNED SO THAT YOU HAVE FEW HOURS TO YOURSELF - YOU MARCH - YOU GO TO CLASSES, ETC.....

"Oh, just about some of my Army experiences," Orth replies.

"How about shooting the basketball around, Ortie?" another of the youth asks.

"In a second, but first we have to work on that singing we will be doing during the Educational Week Sunday service," Orth adds.

Then several of the young men join the table where Orth and the others are sitting. Orth pushes back from the table, pushes the glasses back on his nose and crosses his long, bony legs as he thinks about his Army Basic Training days. He continues to answer questions from the young boys about military life.

On with our story of our hero and back to Fort Ord.

The first week was in getting adjusted to the Army way of life. For example:

1. SOP's - Standard Operating Procedures – Army Regulations, Field Manuals, etc. Everything is in writing ... one was expected to "go by the book".
2. Wearing of the Uniform - Class A's (dress) polishing boots, shoes, etc.

3. Army History - Units, etc.
4. Physical Training - in fatigues and "T" shirt - pushups, running, obstacle courses.
5. Guard Duty - memorizing the eternal "General Order"... "I will walk my post, etc."
6. Religious Services.
7. Drills - how to march, handling the M-1 rifle, etc.

The troops marched, sat in classrooms, stood guard duty, read Army literature, took tests and became accustomed to Army apparel. Time careened past, everything was planned so that one had few hours to yourself. The barracks were cleaned, latrines (toilets) scrubbed. The Bulletin Board on the first level posted by the Platoon Sergeant showing who were those selected for "KP" (Kitchen Police), Guard duty ... and so it went on. There blossomed forth the usual complainers, the rowdies, the quiet types. But the Platoon was beginning to look like a military organization.

Orth became fearful of "noncoms", non-commissioned officers, corporals and above. Commissioned officers were fire-eating dragons, especially Second Lieutenants. They walked on water! Orth would walk miles to avoid them!

During the second week of training they went into a gas chamber, cleaned rifles, dismantled them, reassembled them, attended classes on military justice and, of course, more marching, drilling and physical training. Orth had difficulty fitting his mask properly, and this resulted in his getting a slight whiff of tear gas. It stung his nostrils like a knife jab, and his eyes watered. A captain led the chemical demonstration, nicknamed "Captain Gas" by the platoon because of his odd, even demented enthusiasm about the lethality of poison gas. He was a pudgy, overweight short man who wore thick glasses that were grossly too small for his fat round face. This resulted in giving him a comical air – more bizarre because he tried to be so serious and punctilious.

Tom Tolliver never seemed to acquire a soldierly appearance, looking like a scarecrow, his fatigues loose around his tall, bony body, his hair always tousled and his freckles seemed to grow more pronounced by the day. He and Orth lost a good deal of weight and seemed to acquire an ever present cough and sniffle because of the damp weather.

Week Three. The platoon moved into "the field", which meant they went into the back country of fort Ord and lived in tents with frequent forays to the firing range. The tents were heavy critters of canvas, designed to house eight to twelve men, termed "squad tents". They had minute holes in them that Orth soon discovered leaked rain onto his folding wooden bunk. Wooden pallets were put down as "floors". Orth acquired a "friend" during this week. His name was "Larry, the Lizard."

Larry took up residence under Orth's bunk and came out on occasion scooting across the tent area to the glee and amusement of the tent troopers. These tents were a mass of confusion to try to put up and demanded at least six to eight men to manhandle the poles and lines. Two and one-half ton trucks, "duce-and-a-halves", as the Army called them, moved the Platoon. Meals were sent out on a truck and Orth was introduced to mess kits and Army style "camp outs". One cleaned his mess kit by immersing it into garbage cans full of steaming hot water, and if you were not quick and careful, you could receive a scalding. Often soldiers had the misfortune of dropping articles into these cauldrons of Hades only to be lost forever...There were times when the meal trucks did not show up, whereupon "C" rations were distributed. Ingenious devices – cardboard boxes with cans inside of comestibles such as scrambled eggs and ham, beef hash, sliced peaches. Also, included were small packages of "essentials", such as cigarettes, chewing gum, toilet paper, matches, etc. The soldiers soon established a bartering system.

Orth enjoyed the scrambled eggs and ham, so he would trade his canned chocolate cookies for them, and so it went throughout the Platoon. Fruit cocktail was a "low item" on the demand list. Many of the troops smoked the cigarettes as they deemed it "smart", or socially desirable, a filthy health denying habit they would learn later.

Things on the firing range did not progress well for Orth. The author forgets the length, but a figure of 300 yards seems close. Well, they were issued a certain number of bullets (rounds) for various positions of firing – standing, prone, squatting, kneeling. The first several rounds out of Orth's rifle, he blasted into the soldier's target next to his. This meant, he had to score high on the remaining shots, which he did not. His sights were not adjusted correctly and he kept firing low, kicking up dust. This all resulted in his not "qualifying" upon the first time out. However, this changed later, when he exchanged rifles with a friend of his, a mountaineer type, who said, "Here, Ortie, this time out use mine." He did and scored "Marksman"...one of the highest marks under "Expert".

It all worked out. Target detail was something worth talking about. A squad is twelve soldiers – therefore a Platoon is roughly three squads – thirty-six men. While two squads were on the firing line, one was sent to the "pits" to man the targets. These were massive wooden things that were hoisted up with strength, springs and weights. you had to paste on a new target for each new group sent to fire. You marked the hits and they were relayed back to the firing line to record or to let them know how bad the result was, aiming too high, low, etc.

It was cold, damp and chilly in the "pits", the troopers hunkered down until the squad leader would tell them to pull down the targets and mark them. The squad leader was a recruit assigned to lead. Orth was a squad leader on one "Pit" trip. They had a telephone in the pit to communicate with the firing line. Orth would remember how the sound of the thirty caliber bullets deluded one into thinking they were harmless as they went "ping", "zing" or "twang", careening off the sand or targets. How Korea did teach one how these weapons could wreak devastation to the delicate body tissues!

During the fourth week they were shuttled off and out to the ranges to learn the hand grenades – tactical methods of crawling, camouflage, machine guns and recoilless rifles. The fifth week saw the platoon move out to the field again into a "bivouac" situation, where defensive techniques were instructed and moving during the night, etc. During this time they were on 100% alert. Guards were posted, defense perimeters were set up, the digging of entrenchments and so forth. Orth thought it was kind of fun "playing" combat, like the movies he had often seen of John Wayne and other film heroes of battle pictures.

There was a series of "forced" marches carrying your pack, six to fifteen miles. All went relatively well –- and upon return from the exercises, they were rewarded with a weekend pass. I should mention something about the bivouac exercise. Each squad had a tent … and the Drill Sergeant thought to put a spark of fun amongst the "dogfaces" held a tent naming contest. The tent that won the contest would receive an extra 24 hour pass.

Well, behold! Orth's tent won – their name was "Home of the Rich and Famous".

Tom Tolliver, Orth and some of the others took a bus ride into Monterey and Carmel, but did not tarry long, as they did not have a lot of money, their pay being only $75.00 per month, and they had not yet had their first "pay-call".

Week six. Back out on the rifle range. More rifle cleaning, Orth was sent back several times to clean again after a speck of carbon had been discovered here or there. And again, they ran a hand grenade assault course. Destructive little critters – one pulled the pin – waited and tossed – "Ka-Pow!" The problem was how does one get close enough to toss them? Another weekend pass after week six and then on to graduation week.

Week Seven: This was a fun week, compared to the rest! There were volleyball games and flag football between the squads and platoons. Out processing consumed several days – and all the troops received orders for further schools and training. There were anxious moments. Tom Tolliver was going to advanced Infantry training at Fort Dix, Texas; Orth was going to Artillery School at Fort Sill, Oklahoma. Others were going to armored schools, Airborne training at Fort Benning, Georgia, and so forth. Graduation was held on the parade ground and the men worked hours getting ready. Shoes were polished, uniforms pressed. Orth's stomach was tight as a drum...almost to the point of vomiting, but all went well. What a relief after passing in review before the Company Commander, the Battalion Major, and the Brigade Lieutenant Colonel. Orth estimated there must have been about fifteen hundred men.

Onto another train for Fort Sill, Oklahoma. Orth gathered his belongings and stuffed them into two "barracks" bags – canvas bags – round and cavernous. He placed locks on the tops and tossed a few essentials into a small carrying case. He then called at the Company Headquarters Building to receive his orders, pay and travel tickets. He was wearing his heavy woolen "OD's" and looked quite smart as a soldier. Several others were also accompanying him to Fort Sill for artillery school. They were loaded onto a truck and carted to the Greyhound stop, outside the Main Gate. It was chilly as the men stood in the early morning air awaiting the bus. Orth was thinking about things back in Wisconsin. About Bertha, his dad and, of course, cantankerous Fritz, his brother. It seemed like ages ago when he saw them last. Bertha replied to Orth's letters, and his dad occasionally, but Fritz never wrote, which manifested his rude, boorish attitude, Orth thought.

Yet, he mused, he must try to be more tolerant of others' mistakes. In the pit of his bowels he still remembered the Christian principles planted there by his past Sunday School teachers, and, of course, faithful Bertha.

CHAPTER IX

Put on all of God's armor so that you will be able to stand safe against all strategies and tricks of Satan. For we are not fighting against persons made of flesh and blood, but against persons without bodies – the evil rulers of the unseen world...resist the enemy...you will need the strong belt of truth and the breastplate of God's approval...In every battle you will need faith as your shield to stop the fiery arrows aimed at you by Satan.

Eph. 6:10-16

Driving home from the youth meeting, Orth thinks about Clifton going into the Navy, and ponders on what topic he should cover at their next get together, Wednesday. He concludes that he would lead the discussion along the lines of how great and powerful is God – and how the futile efforts of man are so puny in comparison. Also, how ridiculous war weapons are in mankind's attempts to resolve political and social differences. He also thinks about Libby and considers inviting her and Danny to the next youth meeting.

He pulls Whitey up next to the rural mailbox, rolls down the window and pulls out the mail – he tosses it down on the seat beside him, thinking, it must be 80% junk mail – another 10% stuff to be casually considered and 10% serious correspondence that requires his immediate attention. Turning up onto the long lane to Home Port, he once again hears the familiar sound of the wooden sign "Volzenkoff" saying, "squeak-squeak", as it yields to the early afternoon breeze. Up he drives the gravel road and notices that the white picket fence around Home port could use a fresh coat of paint. Orth enjoys doing projects about the house and considers Home Port as a faithful, noble lady who has served him well. After all he thinks to himself, "all gallant elderly ladies need and deserve constant tender loving care.

He stops at the back gate to drop off several packages as Mutnik ambles up smiling – tail wagging like an excited windmill. "Hiyah, old buddy," he says as he scratches under his chin. He deposits Whitey into the garage and walks into the house, sitting down at his desk in the front office. He dials the number for Libby. The office is in the front of the first floor and has a large sliding door. An enormous antique desk fills most of the office – the walls on all four sides are filled with an assortment of book cases – several are the older "glass front" types . As usual, the corners of the office and desk are dusty – and an assortment of pencils, books and other objects are scattered about on top of the desk.

"Hello," comes a man's voice over the phone from Libby's apartment. Orth was immediately infused with a sense of cheap jealousy – yet, he was aghast at himself! Who was he to think that he had any sort of claim upon Libby? He chastised himself because of these childish self-centered thoughts. He paused then answered, "Oh, excuse me, I'm calling Mrs. Zimmerman."

"Hiyah, Ortie!" the voice echoes, then adds, "this is Barney. I came over to see Libby as I was in the area on my way home." There ensues a brief conversation between the two, and Barney concludes, "I'll get Libby – she's in the kitchen...hold on, Ortie." Orth hears the domestic sounds in the background then the soft voice of Libby, "Hello, Ortie." Orth explains that he thought she may enjoy an evening out with Danny next Wednesday with the Methodist Youth. Libby accepts with gratitude and Orth concludes with a remark that he would drop by to pick them up about six thirty p.m. as the meeting starts at seven thirty and he needs the extra time to prepare some things.

Libby invites Orth to supper before the meeting and he agrees heartily because he becomes bored with his own menu and tends to prepare the "same old thing". This is why he looks forward to his evenings in Milwaukee at Frederick's. Besides, he has a warm feeling about Libby. He realizes he lacks female companionship and has not had very much of it since the death of his wife, Donna. Of course, there are a few women friends he has and whom he uses as confidants. One is Nancy Steinmann, whom he met at the University of Utah, while he was teaching there.

Nancy was a plump jovial - lively Jewish lady in her middle life. She was a Teaching Assistant at the University of Utah, where she was a Doctoral Candidate – School of Health Sciences, specializing in psychology. Orth met her at a University social gathering at Fort Douglas. They dated on and off for ten years. you shall learn more of her later.

Upon arrival at Libby's apartment, he is invited in to sit in the living room while Libby excuses herself and returns to the kitchen to finish the preparation of supper. Danny has the television on and is watching a movie about the Second World War. In the film is one of Orth's favorite actors, Glenn Ford, who is playing the part of a sergeant, who impersonates a Major General in order to rally his troops who have become wearied, disheartened and shaken by the trials of battle. Danny turns the set off and he and Orth talk about the Army and the routines of combat. Orth feels uncomfortable talking of these things because he has been through the horrors and hell of combat. "Battles are not as depicted by Hollywood," Orth explains.

Danny sits pensive and melancholy expecting Orth to explain and describe his experiences. Orth tells Danny that the military life is often not a heroic event and that the soldiers life a life often of dissolution – drinking heavily, swearing and just existing to live more days at lechery. Orth does not admit to yielding to a life like that, but his mind quickly reflects how he had few scruples before he became a Christian and that his Army life consisted of many days of carousing and being ribald, lustful and loose morally. In later life, he greatly regretted these actions – and how he as a soldier mocked and ridiculed those few hearty Christians in the military who held to their standards and principles.

Libby begins to set the table and the three seat themselves. Orth provides the blessing:

"Our Father in Heaven, we thank thee for this food and for the joy of our companionship. Please help us to rely upon you for all of our temporal and spiritual needs and not to be as a ship upon the water without a rudder – running and going hither and yon without any direction. Give us faith and courage during the times of our trials and misfortunes – and love in our hearts toward all beings. Correct and alter those things in our lives and spirits that displease thee and hinder our opportunities to witness for thee and the Lord Jesus Christ, our Savior. In gratitude and with humility, we ask these things, in the name of thy Holy Son Christ Jesus.

They had held each other's hands during the prayer and this made lasting impressions upon Libby's and Danny's minds. They concluded the supper and drove to the meeting at the Church. Danny seemed to enjoy the company of the boys in the group. Orth gave a short class upon the resurrection of Jesus Christ and admonished the young people to read the Bible daily – especially the New Testament to equip them to meet the challenges that await them in college and young adulthood.

"The Army teaches you to know your enemy – unfortunately, in Korea we fell far short of that and paid a dear price for it. I urge you to realize that the Devil is your foe – and he is a battle hardened wily veteran. So keep the scriptures slung on your shoulders ready for combat. As Sir Walter Raleigh said, 'Praise God, my lads and keep your powder dry! You will struggle and fall, but Christ is your Buddy in the foxhole – he knows how tough the battle is and will not let you down. Give the Devil volleys of prayers and watch him quiver under the name of Jesus the Christ…"

After the class – the young people adjourn to play basketball, chess or some other favorite pastime. Danny is a little small and young for the group, but enjoys playing basketball anyway. Libby sits quietly listening to Orth during the class and chats with Orth while the activities are taking place.

"You have been through so much, Ortie," Libby states, as she casually thumbs through a church magazine trying not to be emotional – yet, she has a warm feeling for Orth, something she has seldom felt toward any man.

"I feel embarrassed, Libby," says Orth, adding, "I do not enjoy the feeling of being the center of attention – I am nobody unusual – just a common, ordinary clumsy old man."

Libby takes his hand and Orth notices how soft and moist it is. He had almost forgotten the feel of the fair sex. "I'm glad you brought us, Ortie – I am always embraced with a feeling of warmth when I am with you, and I can talk with you in a way I find difficult with Eddie or Barney, or anyone else. They all seem to be so dumb!"

Orth jerks back in his chair and laughs out loudly. "Libby!" he blurts out.

"Well…it's the truth – the men I have been around seem to think of such stupid shallow things – football, duck hunting on Lake Superior, or discussing their ex-wives, or latest feminine conquest."

"It is dangerous to leap to conclusions or to generalize, Libby," Orth chuckles, "but I must admit, I feel this is a sad reflection not too distant from fact. Education teaches one to endure injustice and overcome weariness and vulgarities... and many people we associate with are infidels lacking intellect and wisdom. Their tongues soon betray them. But, we must as Christians bear with them, Libby. I learned from the Army that there is a deadly foe more frightful that the bloodthirsty enemy or an errant artillery shell – or an aimed bullet – and that no weapon is effective against and it is boredom..."

Libby lets loose of Orth's hand and she sits with her eyes looking out at the basketball court where Danny is still playing. "Yes, I've got to understand to have patience with people and being so harsh and judgmental with them..." Libby says quietly. "I think Saint Augustine said it so clearly when he said to 'Love – and do what you like'."

Orth adds after a pause, "Our Lord said, 'I am the Way, the Truth, and the Life,' Orth says, adding, "I try to follow the teachings of Paul as best I can – because my life has been kind of a Paul – I became a real Christian late in life similar to Paul. We Christians are the world's Gospel, Libby. We have to live exemplary lives, to exude our love and forgiveness."

At this point, Danny bursts through the open door – panting and tossing himself down upon an empty chair..."Man! That was fun – I scored four points!" he wheezes out. Libby wipes his moist forehead and concludes, "Well, we must be going, Ortie – I've got to be at the restaurant early tomorrow."

Orth drives Libby and Danny home and sees them to the door. Danny rushes into the apartment while Libby turns quickly and hugs Orth then adds as she enters, "Thanks, Ortie – Call me soon."

Orth returns to Whitey and drives home. He thinks to himself how in one way he is crushed by loneliness – yet he clings to Christ as his lifetime "buddy". And he thinks how Christ was a man often lonely and saddened by people He loved then deserted Him... And he, Orth, is a follower of Christ and he must harden himself to overcome feelings of loneliness. After all, it is sinful to turn inward and to be self-centered, squirming in your own stew of self pity. One thing about the Army and the University, was you always had a vast horde to talk to, he thinks to himself as he heads north towards New Hesse and Home Port. He swings up the lane to homeport and his headlights pick up Mutnik coming toward him. Putting Whitey in the garage, he pats Mutnik goodnight and goes into the kitchen to open a can of fruit and have a cool glass of iced tea before bed time. The house is dark and he heads up the staircase to his bedroom with his bowl of fruit and glass of tea balanced upon his large, bony hands. He flips on the radio to hear the weather forecast ... "partly cloudy, forty percent chance of rain showers ... highs in the mid-seven-ties and lows in the sixties" ... he turns the radio off, gets into his pajamas and lies reading... "Two Years Before the Mast," by Dana.

Soon his eyes become weary and he closes the book, places it upon the night stand and clicks off the light. He stares into the dark thinking about Libby – the Army and other unconnected events. A cool breeze enters the bedroom along with the night sounds of rustling trees and crickets.

* * *

At this point we shall return to Orth's days in the Army.

"Hissssss-shisssss," the big Greyhound bus comes to a loud stop outside Fort Ord, and the waiting soldiers, including Orth sling their barracks bags in the baggage compartment and climb in. The bus is full, but he locates a slot next to a young woman holding a baby. Little is said as they travel on to San Francisco where our hero will board a train to Kansas City, then on to Artillery School at Fort Sill, Oklahoma. The woman with the baby asks the usual mundane questions, "Where are you going?" "Where are you from?" and so on. She explains that her husband is a pilot in the Navy and is stationed on an aircraft carrier. Orth lets his mind drift and remembers how he always wanted to be a pilot, however, his near-sightedness would prevent him as the Navy and Army Air Corps (as it was called then) required 20/20 vision. And Orth's eyes were considerably below that standard – Fritz often called him "blind" and described his thick glasses as "ash trays". The Army infantry was more tolerant – warm, eager young bodies with or without glasses were agreeable to them. After all, in war and combat all that is required is to pour out as much ammo as possible. The foot soldier is spoiled if they are educated. The best are those that are like the barbarian Goths and Franks – uneducated heathens that lunge into it.

Orth also had a desire to be a Navy man, but, as things are now all that seems so very distant. Yet he recalled how sparkling were those Naval officers in their white uniforms and stripes of gold. Now – the Army was for him – olive drab field gear, mud, bitter cold and those dreaded "C" rations.

The bus pulled into the terminal in the center of San Francisco and Orth along with three other soldiers located their duffel bags and they all shared a taxi to the train station where they boarded an evening train to Los Angeles, then changed to a train going East that would take them to Oklahoma City. The train ride was terribly long for Orth because it did not afford him the opportunity to exercise.

When they finally arrived in Oklahoma City, they had to wait about two hours for a shuttle bus that would take them to Fort Sill. The Fort was a huge rambling mess hacked out of the sage brush and tumbleweeds of North Central Oklahoma. Nothing was beautiful about the place and to Orth, the Army seemed to take extraordinary measures to locate the most uncomfortable spot on the face of the earth to train officers and enlisted bums to shoot canons and howitzers. The whole stinking totality was begun in 1910 and was called the "School of Fire for Field Artillery". From then on it grew into the center to train gunners, artillery men – "red legs".

A lot can be said about the sixteen weeks Orth spent at Fort Sill. However, it will have to be left to some other essayist as this one deems it a bit tedious to delve that deeply into this idiocratic area. Let me say, however, that the course was intense and comprehensive. Orth was selected to train as a Targeting Specialist rather than a cannoneer. As a Targeting Specialist he would normally be assigned duty in a Fire Direction Center of a Field Artillery Battalion. Here he would receive information on targets and communicate the requested firing to the gun batteries. Orth had to train on maps, artillery, plotting and a vast amount of concepts and systems. He also was trained on the guns to a limited extent – learning how to set fuses – shell and explosive types and so forth.

Orth had fun out "on the hill" as it was termed, where he trained for two days getting hands-on experience as a Forward Artillery Observer. About twelve men would go "on the hill" at a time in jeeps and trucks where they would spend several days directing shots from the guns to targets out on the prairie – which were old junked Army tanks and trucks. The days were beastly hot and the evenings were bone jarring cold. The tents were drafty and would fill with red Oklahoma dust when a blast of wind would come ripping out of the west.

It was a twenty-four hour operation while the team would have eight hour shifts. One of the men in Orth's shift was a Private Durfy – a chubby short jolly chap that Orth enjoyed talking to. Durfy was a draftee from a wealthy family in Utah and he detested the military and made a mockery out of it. "Durf", he was known as – actually his first name was Michael, but in the Army, hardly anyone went by their given names. Orth was "Ortie", Tom Tolliver was "Red" and so on. Instead of subsisting on the "C" Rations, Durf filled his field jacket pockets with goodies he had acquired from the Post Exchange (PX) and he and Orth would sit under a truck and tell stories while they feasted on chocolate bars and an assortment of cookies. Well, the end of

FORT SILL OKLAHOMA, U.S. ARMY CENTER TO TRAIN "RED LEGS"- ARTILLERY- MEN - IN THE USE OF CANONS AND HOWITZERS....

the course came and Orth was assigned to the Twenty-Fourth Infantry Division stationed in Japan. Actually, his orders were that he was assigned to the Division Artillery as a Targeting Specialist.

The Twenty-Fourth had four Artillery Battalions as follows:

Division Artillery Headquarters

155 mm BN   105 mm BN   105 mm BN   155 mm BN

All of these guns were towed behind trucks and were difficult to wield about as they would woefully learn later in Korea.

But, let us look back at the graduation of Orth from Artillery School. A hefty tall Lieutenant Colonel gave a boring talk...leaning heavily upon the speaker's stand. He blurted out "Wars of the future will be decided by artillery. Troops can be replaced in case of need – but big guns will decide the issue."

Orth would remember these comments and how the artillery units were ill-equipped and handled in Korea – becoming in many instances useless because of the obstacles of the terrain. In many cases battles were decided by the smaller mortars that could be easily moved and rapidly deployed. But then Korea was a strange war – not clearly defined battle lines – difficult terrain and climate – often the enemy would infiltrate and hit you in the ass as well as in the front.

Orth was treated to an airplane ride to Japan. From Fort Sill, he and some other troops were packed off into a C-46 cargo plane that would take them to an airfield in California. Fort Sill has an "airport" that at that time was a long, lonely windy strip of ground far south of the main post. The ancient C-46 had seats along the side and two engines that roared incessantly during the flight so that by the time they landed at Travis Air Base in California, Orth's ears were ringing and he had a splitting headache. Meals were provided in white boxes... cheese sandwiches - white bread, an apple and banana, a small carton of milk and that was it, not fancy, but ample and nourishing.

The plane made a fuel stop at some windswept field in New Mexico where the troops got off for a minute – then off to Travis Air Force Base which is in the vicinity of San Francisco. here they changed planes after a lengthened wait in a hastily built "waiting room" which held a mixture of military people awaiting flights for various places overseas and here stateside. Men were trying to rest or sleep – draped over wooden benches. Bags were lying casually about every which way. Officers and enlisted men mixed in an aloof manner.

Orth was still fearful of officers and treated them with a dreaded respect because he had been taught that military punishment for disrespect of officers could be severe and often was in disproportion to the offense. "Yes sir, no sir, thank you, sir" were words to follow. Be obedient – do what you are told – avoid volunteering and so forth.

Eventually, at about 0600 in the morning following a sergeant announced that in two hours a chartered Pan American airplane would be ready to board and take those destined for Hawaii and Japan. Orth thought about Fritz and how at this hour he would be beginning milking the cows and the chilly morning dew covering the rich green Wisconsin countryside. Ah! The peace and serenity of the country life now seemed so distant, he thought, and how the really worthwhile things of life are so subtle that one easily overlooks them.

The airplane was huge – a four engine monster that swallowed all those waiting with quite a few seats remaining. Out, to the edge of the runway, trundled the plane where it paused to test the engines – "ROAR" the engines sounded one after the other. Orth glanced out the window and thought, "how can this thing hold together – look at the way the wings vibrate and jerk about as the engines pound away?" Eventually, the plane thundered down the long runway and labored into the sky. Orth glanced about as the airplane passed over the expanse of the San Francisco Bay and out across the Pacific Ocean – over the orange painted Golden Gate Bridge.

It was a dreadfully long flight – first landing in Honolulu.. The meals were served by attractive young women who were attired in smart uniforms. They smiled constantly and Orth enjoyed their friendly attitude, and thought about how wonderful the life of a pilot would be – carefree, dashing about in airplanes to interesting places around the globe. They were allowed to get off in Honolulu and stretch in a small building during refueling. Then off they went again. Orth's heavy woolen uniform was uncomfortable in the heat of Hawaii. But upon arrival in Japan, he discovered the air cool – almost chilly.

Yet, there was another fuel stop before Japan at some small island that this author believes was named Wake. It was a small place and the ocean seemed not more than a few feet from the plane. They were allowed to get off and walk about. Several of the men walked down to the shoreline and collected pieces of coral.

It was dusk when they landed at Yakota Air Force Base. Orth collected his bags and he and the other Army people were transported to their posts on an Army bus. Orth reported into the 24th Infantry Division Artillery Headquarters at Sasebo where he encounters a second lieutenant who orders him to button several unbuttoned pockets on his uniform "Ike" jacket that he had left undone during the long flight. Orth muses to himself, "I suppose they will always be lurking behind every bush and building those ubiquitous second lieutenants who feel it is their main objective in life to ambush hapless privates who may have a button undone or tie askance." But, then he thinks the junior officers have been taught that their job is to lead and enforce discipline. The problem is how they go about it.

Later in his Army life, Orth would recall how during a lull in combat when he is standing in a line to receive a Red Cross doughnut and coffee, a full colonel berated him for not wearing his steel helmet and how he felt that this abuse was unjustified and did more to damage morale than raise it.

Orth is assigned to a barracks where the Headquarters Battery is housed and he unpacks and attempts to settle in. Other people are sleeping or lying in bed trying to read. Into the bunk he goes and tries to sleep which became fitful because he was overly fatigued.

Orth's life in Japan was brief prior to being shipped off to Korea. There was the usual life in the barracks, some time off – sojourns into Tokyo and so forth. During this time, he acquired the nasty habit of smoking, being encouraged to do it by his friends, and the prevalence of the addiction in the Army. Additionally he commenced to imbibe. The Enlisted Men's Club there at Camp York was a popular place during off hours and Orth joined the mob and shared pitchers of beer and conversation there. The dialogue amongst soldiers is usually quite plebeian consisting primarily of women, money, promotions and jibes against non-commissioned officers. It was not uncommon for Orth to consume too much beer and he would stumble back to the barracks.

The sergeants occupied separate rooms at the ends of the buildings where Orth often heard them returning from a night on the town with loud and animated talking. Morning inspections were frequent. The Battery Commander and First Sergeant would walk solemnly through looking at this and that – inspecting clothes and things. The "old man" or Commander, would make comments while the "top" or First Sergeant would be jotting down on pieces of ruled paper on a clip board.

Orth was often detailed for various duties such as cleaning the latrine, "KP" or mess hall, etc. The First Sergeant would post the duty roster to the Orderly Room Bulletin Board – and you had better read it…or "your ass would be had"…or in civilian terms, there would be harsh recriminations from your superiors. We shall now get on to the jump from Japan to the Korean scene.

* * *

It was evening after "chow", or supper…about 1745, or 5:45 p.m. civilian time. They were assembled in the street outside the barracks, first day of July 1950. Captain Philpot, the "old man" was solemn, as was the First Sergeant Smith. They announced that the Division Commander had placed the unit on alert because of the movement of North Korean Communist troops across the border, 38th parallel, into South Korea and that he was sending a Battalion from the 34th Regiment by ship over to Pusan to assist in the "Police Action". The Division Headquarters Battery had been assigned to fill in vacancies in the First Battalion caused by peace time manpower shortages.

"You are now in the infantry," announced Captain Philpot, adding that a

Battery of Artillery had been sent previously, who had set up their guns in a defensive perimeter at Ansong. Captain Philpot related that he doubted that there would be any shooting and that the United States troops were being sent over to display a show of force. He further said that intelligence information was that the North Koreans were ill-trained and without adequate numbers or types of weapons.

The Company was dismissed and directed to draw their field gear from supply for the trip to Korea. In the line to the supply room was a lot of laughter and joking amongst the men. The air was filled with a sense of over confidence. Orth did not like it. He felt that there was a forboding or ominous atmosphere present – like when baseball teams think they can walk over an opponent and suddenly find themselves with egg on their faces trying to overcome a ten run deficit.

The troops drew full field gear – rifles (MI) or carbines, sleeping bags, back packs and so forth. Orth had not seen some of this stuff since basic training. It seemed strange to put on a steel helmet again. In the barracks, the jesting continued, "those gooks will probably shit in their pants when they see a US uniform," "They'll probably drop their bamboo spears and run," "I'll bet we are back before football season," and on and on.

On the morning of the second of July, 1950, the assigned troops were put onto trucks or buses and driven to the port of embarkation, Kyushu and loaded onto Landing Ships run by the Navy. Orth and his buddies spent the time lounging about the deck across the Sea of Japan to Pusan, South Korea.

CHAPTER X

And the Philistine looked and saw David, he disdained him for he was but a youth ... And the Philistine cursed David ... The Philistine said to David, "Come to me and I will give your flesh to the birds of the air and to beasts of the field" ... Then David said to the Philistine, ... "This day the Lord will deliver you into my hand" ... David ran quickly toward the battle line to meet the Philistine. And David put his hand in his bag and took out a stone, and slung it, and struck the Philistine on his forehead. The stone sank into his forehead and he fell on his face to the ground.

1 Samuel 17:41-49

The above quotation depicts a situation wherein overconfidence and underestimation led to the demise of the boastful braggart. Similar circumstances prevailed over the United States Army troops that were selected to move to South Korea to stem the flow of North Korean Armies south, as alluded to in the last chapter, Orth and his buddies in the Twenty-Fourth Division. There was much joking about how the "yellow bastards" would drop their rice bowls and run back north as soon as they saw an American uniform. Well ... Orth would soon discover what a harsh lesson it was when they realized how vastly incorrect the intelligence reports were. The North Koreans came south with a bone in their teeth. Their tactics were similar to the German Panzer attacks during World War II.

Infantry were led by heavy tanks. The North made heavy use of highly mobile mortar fire. The US forces had little to halt the armored units. It was a rout in the early days. The US troops were ill equipped and trained. Even their clothing could not stand up to the cold, wet, muddy conditions that prevailed during the early days of the War.

The trip across the Sea of Japan was choppy and wet. Most of the men were dreadfully seasick or on the verge. Few of the men took the trouble to check their weapons or equipment. They would discover that the wet Korean summers would take a high toll in jammed rifle bolts and malfunctioning machine guns. It was so ridiculous. Orth was questioned by one man – a finance clerk, about how to put the bolt in his M1 carbine and load it.

So ... our hero, is tossed out of the Navy LST at the port city of Pusan in the lower eastern part of the country of South Korea. Pusan is a rather scenic place – but the buildings are primitive – small low hovels – narrow winding dirt roads and the ubiquitous small children clamoring about the streets with beaming grins – oblivious to the seriousness of the situation.

It was an overcast gloomy day. Rain was lightly falling. Sergeant Smith assembled the Battery and informed them that it would be several days before they would be put onto trains to the Seoul area, they would be unloading the LST and checking equipment in the meantime. Orth was depressed ... the rest of the men were no help. There was much griping and morale was low.

Sergeant Smith, in his inimitable southern dialect barks, "Listen up, maggots ... look sharp and be a good example of US soldiers, your ass is had if I catch anyone not pulling his weight." Orth thinks how the Army has its own language, crude, harsh, but a few well chosen words seem to prevail against an army of disorganized clap-trap. The men understood Smith's intoning phrases. Captain Philpot was not about. The men wondered where he had retreated to. But then, the men relied more upon First Sergeant Smith than any other of the officers. There were other officers in the battery, but they did not have command responsibility. Of course, there was the Communication Platoon, who had a Second Lieutenant in charge. The remaining officers were specialists in artillery, personnel and so forth.

On 4 July 1950, troops, including Orth's Battery, were loaded onto trains, beastly plain uncomfortable rail coaches for the three hundred odd miles to the defense positions at Ansong. The seats were wooden and close together. The soldier had his barracks bags carried separately on a baggage car. In the passenger cars he carried his field back pack plus his rifle. The officers mainly carried hand pistols or the familiar "45" automatic. Orth was issued a 30 caliber carbine and several magazines of spare ammunition which he stuffed into pockets on his webbed belt. A lot of other items needed for combat were also carried on the webbing, like canteens, first aid kits, hand grenades, etc., which made the sitting for a long ride almost unbearable.

But the men were young, and they endured the detestable ride by playing cards, eating or sleeping. The train pulled into Ansong in the early evening after a nine hour ride from Pusan. It was still raining while the troops wearily got off. They were handed "C" rations and told to get into a sheltered area and rest for a while. More ammunition was issued now and each man had about 80 to 100 rounds each. Orth's Battery, which was actually now a Company, as it had no artillery guns, assembled between two old buildings that had a corrugated roof overhang. It was a motley group. The soldiers in the weapon platoon sat off to one side trying to decide how to carry the 60 millimeter mortars and recoilless rifles, but someone had neglected to ship the ammunition for them. Well, there they sat for several hours.

At about midnight Lieutenant Colonel Smith drove up in a jeep. Nobody bothered to come to attention. He called into an assembly the officers and senior non-commissioned men for a briefing. Everything seemed so muddled to Orth and his buddies. Rumors flew like wild pigeons. It was now made known that the group was known as "Task Force Smith", part of the Twenty-First Infantry Regiment and their job was to stop the flow of North Korean Army south. It was further discovered that there were six guns of field artillery due to arrive soon to support them. These guns were 155 millimeter towed Howitzers, range about 15 miles maximum.

Most of the men thought these guns would probably not be needed as the North Koreans were thought to possess little more than pea shooters and bamboo sticks. They would sadly soon realize how wrong this was!

The rain hit the metal roof ... "twang-de-tink-twank", and holes in the roof let rain in on the troops. Orth sat slumped against a wall — the water trickled down his back because his poncho had holes a plenty. He was chilled and it seemed to get clear into his bones now. He pried open a can of scrambled eggs and ham and endeavored to cram it down his throat. It was not that he was hungry, it was an effort to take his mind off of things.

Brigadier General Barth, the commanding officer of the 24th Division's Artillery was there also. It was learned how he was there to stem his boredom of barracks life in Japan, but he came in the pretense to lead the battery of artillery and direct them to Osan. What Orth saw of Barth, he liked. General Barth was a West Point man, but he was likable, a true "soldier's man". He never tucked in his fatigue jacket and was stockily built. He gave the appearance of rolling as he walked. During training exercises in Japan, he would show up at the odd moments at the Division "TOC" – Tactical Operations

Center and scan the maps, never saying a whole lot, but when he did say something it meant a great deal of sense.

So, here it was, still raining and Orth tired and disheartened. This was war? Hollywood never mentioned the uncomfortable wet, cold mud. The canned cold food, the interminable weight of the rifle and back packs…Up they lifted themselves at the bark of Sergeant Smith. Forming a column of twos they began to march northward – one column on each side of the muddy road. The red dirt when wet formed into a sea of gluey mush that clung to the boots. At times, Orth could hardly lift his feet until he knocked off some of the mud with his rifle but. Some of the men took off their boots and carried them slung around their necks.

Still the rain came. The artillery trucks with their towed guns passed them on their way north to Osan. Orth thought about Bertha and home a great deal. March – March – March … The weight of the packs and equipment began to take their toll. Some of the men began to discard canteens, ammo packs, helmets and many other items. Orth managed to keep all of his issue, but it was a tussle to trudge along. The weapons platoon men had a difficult time carrying the machine guns. Trucks carrying the field tents, stoves, etc., had gone on ahead with the idea that they would have things pretty well set up by the time the troops arrived. This was not the case, however. By the time the Company had arrived at the bivouac area, not much had been done. Much confusion arose about how to set up the defense positions, etc. Discipline was also seen to be lacking. Some of the officers carped about others and the enlisted men thought most of the officers inept and too proud to get their hands dirty setting up positions.

They passed through many small villages which had narrow dirty streets. The bivouac area was in the hills, of course, most of Korea is hills, very mountainous the further north one traveled. They set up defensive positions and dug in. The automatic weapons were positioned to be able to sweep the entire Company area. It was difficult to dig foxholes, because the red clay dirt was heavy, wet and sticky. As soon as the holes were dug, they started to fill with water. Orth's boots were saturated and his feet were cold. The men had no idea where the rest of the Battalion was, but they supposed they were further on ahead. The nights were wet and the tents leaked. For the most part, the meals were cold "C" rations. Although at times some hot meals were sent up from Battalion Headquarters by truck.

Sanitation was a problem. When you felt a need to urinate or defecate, a near spot was it. The men did not take the trouble to walk to the "latrine area" or the slit trenches. Washing of the body and hands were neglected, as well as shaving and brushing your teeth. As a result of this, disease was always present. Almost all the men coughed and had colds in various stages. Orth was beset with a terrible case of nausea and flu. His appetite failed and he could hardly manage to go to his post. Sergeant Peterson, his Platoon Sergeant, gave him some aspirin and told him to stay in his cot a while. The fever was alarming, and he was very weak. "Try some of these peanuts, Ortie," Sergeant Peterson said. The thought seemed bright to Orth, and he ate them with a vengeance. "Thanks, Pete," Orth replied…They worked…along with coffee and Seven-Up that Sergeant Peterson acquired from some troops that brought up some supplies from Battalion.

He was back on his feet now and able to do his assigned duties. The rain still came and the red mud oozed as he trudged from tent to field position – back and forth – all hours. The men coughed. There is a close relationship between war and disease, Orth thought. Rotting corpses – sanitation neglected – emotions cause field soldiers to forget precautions of washing, etc. In Korea, disease seemed more crippling than gun shot wounds … Men were constantly being shoved off to the rear for 'sick call'. There was a medical detachment at the Battalion CP (Command Post). They lived in an eight-man 'squad tent'. There was no doctor (MD). A nurse second lieutenant was in charge with two assistants. The attitude of the medics was distant indifference. They looked at you with cod fish eyes then shoved 'APC' pills in your hand. Told you to "drink lots of fluids and rest."

How this was possible under the present conditions was difficult to believe. But, there you were … serving your country … protecting the innocent people twelve thousand miles away who could care less about your discomforts and many did not know where Korea was or cared a fig about what went on there. Most people remain committed to their own ambitions than to the public interest. It's kind of a "cover your own ass" world. Opposing social forces – the arrogant wealthy buy their license to abuse the unfortunates, either directly, or abject disassociation.

The real heroes lack material treasures and worldly riches. The Korean War was filled with incidents of lowly privates or corporals fighting under terrific odds and 'buying the mortgage' in the end … a spent corpse lying head down under a truck or foxhole. And back home the soldiers' parents spent with grief asking "Why?"

Orth is puzzled when he returns home from Korea, he recalls. Civilians have a great deal of interest in military matters of which they have very little knowledge ... and they talk and argue about wars with a John Wayne Hollywood movie mentality. Little do they realize how wrong they are. Wars are confused messes. They stink of evil. The glory given to war is done by misdirected, deluded or sick minds.

Well, back to Orth's health. He is recovering from the flu ... his weight dropped to 140 pounds. His field gear almost weighed as much as he did.

The news of the North Korean avalanche filtered back to Orth's unit. Soldiers from the artillery battery and other support units from the 21st Infantry Regiment came straggling back in a disheveled, disheartened mess. Many were wounded. They were sent back to shelter tents. The able bodied were kept and Captain Philpot had them set up in Orth's area.

"What happened?" Orth asked a buck sergeant gunnery section chief he knew. Sergeant Smith sat with his elbows upon his knees, shaking his head and mumbled, "It was a rout... a joke. Charlie came in the night. First mortar rounds, then tanks, followed by ground soldiers. We had nothing to stop them. Men slung their rifles in the mud and ran." Smith paused and coughed. He crossed his legs as he sat on the cot in Orth's tent, then continued.

"Our guns could not stop those damned tanks. Shells just bounced off them. It was a confused mess. The machine guns were firing, but were soon blown to pieces by the tanks and mortar rounds. The C.O. was an early casualty. A piece of shrapnel went right through his helmet."

"So, that's it, Ortie. I doubt if we can do much to stop them unless we get some help."

Sergeant Smith staggered outside the tent to urinate, then returned. Soon it was time to take up positions on the line and Orth headed up the hill to his dug-in spot. Smith stayed behind and slept in Orth's cot. "The lucky sot," Orth thought, as he trudged up the slope. He was following several other soldiers when he lost his footing in the mud and slid down a steep embankment about fifty feet. His buddies above him kept up their constant chatter, unaware of Orth's misfortune. Orth recovered himself, uttering several words of vilifying nature, and once more mounted his route to his assigned post. His carbine and outer gear were covered with wet red clay as he sat disconsolate. His buddy in the foxhole, a Chinese chap from San Francisco, Private Chang asked, "What happened to you?" Whereupon Orth started to reply when they heard sounds.

ORTH'S COMPANY COULD HEAR THE NORTH KOREAN TANKS COMING — MORTAR SHELLS WERE BURSTING ALL ABOUT... THE U.S. HAD NOTHING TO STOP THEM....

It was pitch dark, but they thought they saw shapes moving. The North Koreans blew whistles and then set off flares, trying to cause confusion. They succeeded in that.

Men in other positions started to fire at anything that made sounds, or even looked suspicious. Soon to their surprise, they heard American voices! It seems that some of the troops ahead of them had been overrun and had abandoned their artillery and started south, similar to Sergeant Smith.

"Rumble - Clank - Rumble," Orth's Company could hear the tanks in the distance. The Koreans started to send mortar shells into the area and Orth ducked down his head as the noise was deafening. Orth could hear men yelling and groaning from being hit by shrapnel. Chang, who was nicknamed "Chopsticks" asked Orth, "What should we do, Ortie?"

"Stay put – you'll get your yellow ass blown off if you try to run for it," Orth replies.

Chopsticks was the son of a wealthy Chinese banker in San Francisco's Chinatown District. Robert Stimson Chang was his full name. He was very intelligent, quiet and seemed always to be deep in thought. Holding a Bachelor's degree from the University of California - Berkeley, Chopsticks was frequently the object of bantering remarks from his fellow GIs which he shrugged off with a nonchalant air.

The reader will recall from Chapter III how Orth's platoon leader, Lieutenant Treat was an early casualty. Explosions were everywhere. One mortar shell lit close to Orth's foxhole and he felt a severe sting in his right leg. Soon it began to throb, yet he could not see, because it was so black ... no moonlight. He felt where the pain was and his hand became sticky. He knew he had been hit. He yanked off his bandanna he had around his neck to keep the dust off and tied it around his leg ... the calf. He called to Chang, but there was no reply. Dimly he saw through the smoke and flare light that Chang was a crumbled mass. He shook him and yelled, but there was no response. Orth could see he was badly hit and he called out for a medic.

The scene was noise and confusion. It seemed as if fire was coming from all directions. Soon a voice yelled out, "Get the hell out of here — pull back!"

"Who's that?" Orth asked.

"It's me, Ortie... Provert." John Provert, nicknamed 'Pervert' was the Platoon Sergeant for the Second Platoon. Orth told him he had been hit and could only move with difficulty. There was no reply from Provert as more explosions and machine gun fire poured into the area. Orth heard more voices saying, "Pull back! They've got us on all sides," and similar remarks. But, that is combat.

They battled for six hours. Orth had depleted all of his ammunition. They had been overrun as explained in Chapter III. After he had been left for dead by the North Koreans, he had to find a way to make it back to friendly forces. Pulling himself out of the hole, he gazed again at the still and lifeless body of Bob Chang, "Chopsticks." "Such a waste," Orth tells himself. It is light now and he gazes at the area. Other dead troopers were here and there. He hobbles down to the road with a makeshift crutch ... a tent pole that had been blown into a manageable length.

He is lucky. As he sat by the road, dejected and thinking he hears the roar of a vehicle in the distance, he hugs the ground behind a clump of brush. He soon discovers that it is a US truck, full of wounded GIs heading south. It seems that some of Colonel Smith's men had been bypassed, so they gathered the wounded and started south after abandoning their artillery pieces.

Orth flags them down and lifts himself in the rear. It is a five ton, ten wheeled heavy truck used for towing 155 millimeter guns. He learns from those able to speak in the back that all US troops are retreating rapidly and intend to try and hold at the Kum River. The truck driver drives slowly, for fear of an ambush or mines. They forge several streams where bridges had been blown in attempts to halt the tanks. The truck has one mounted 50 caliber machine gun on top and any rifles the men had inside. Ammunition was low. After dark the truck still moved. As daylight came, they came under fire from the hills and some of the wounded would not need to worry any more. A second lieutenant who was sitting in front manned the machine gun and started firing in all directions.

As the truck sped down the road, the lieutenant kept up the fire and they made it into friendly territory. The lieutenant kept up the fire, even though wounded several times and some of the wounded fired rifle bursts into the hills in a haphazard way.

All in all, it was a miraculous escape and the troops they met, also from the 24th Infantry Division, were amazed.

The truck was filled with shot holes and leaking oil badly. But the old faithful Detroit Diesel engine just continued to "Ka-bang Ka-bang" along.

It seems that General Dean had sent those other troops of the 34th and 19th Regiments to try to stem the flood of North Koreans southward. They were now somewhere south of the Kum River. Orth was sent in the rear to a field hospital to recover from his wound. It was a luxury to be in the rear. His head still ached from the noise, but he had the comfort of a warm cot. He had lost a lot of blood, but because of his youth and farm background, his recovery was rapid. Other wounded suffered gravely as a second lieutenant nurse from Wyoming admitted, they were sadly short of all supplies, bandages and morphine.

Orth thinks to himself how many unknown heroes are recorded in history. Those privates who shed their lives on a bleak hillside. The high ranking officers will receive the laurels, but the battles are decided by the many privates slugging it out with indescribable determination. Orth meditates, "Perhaps it is religion that gives the spark and zeal. How about the lieutenant in the truck who kept firing the machine gun after being hit several times mortally by enemy fire?"

CHAPTER XI

And Jesus said to him, "Today salvation has come to this house, because he also is a son of Abraham; For the son of Man has come to seek and to save that which was lost."

Luke 19:9-10

It is a warm late summer Saturday morning in Wisconsin as Orth sips his coffee and enjoys his dish of apples and mixed fruit on the front porch. He has read his Scriptures and works at a math problem from a textbook on finite mathematics for economics and the social studies. He feels inner peace as he props up his long legs on an adjoining chair. Mutnik saunters up onto the porch and sits with his eyes upon his master.

"Hiyah, ol' boy. Any gophers out there this morning?" Mutnik smiles and wags his tail excitedly. The crickets and grasshoppers abound and Orth eyes the distant fields and notices God's plans being fulfilled. The corn is grown to the limit and the ears are fully developed. In another two months or so the country roads will be buzzing with harvesting equipment – combines and grain trucks.

He finishes his fruit and coffee, answers some letters, then dons his white tennis shoes for his daily morning walk in the countryside. It's a warm day so he prepares by wearing just a "T" shirt and jeans. Of course, he also has his trademark, a battered old white spinnaker hat. Mutnik joins him down the lane but stops at the road. Orth knows his buddy will maintain his sentinel around Home Port. On occasion Orth takes him on his constitutionals, but likes to keep him close to the house for security reasons. Of late city rogues have been combing the farming areas and stealing whatever they can get their hands on to finance a drug or alcohol addiction. People in the country seem prime targets as they are often alone, or elderly or both and are distant from police protection. The county sheriff does the best he can on limited funds. Orth realizes that a God-less community is beset often with a variety of pesky crimes.

He finishes his walk and prepares his dinner of porridge - reading between mouthfuls. He thinks of Libby and Danny and reaches for the phone next to the bed on the night stand cluttered with back issues of newspapers and magazines to be read.

"Hello, Danny," Orth says as Libby's son answered the phone. "What are your plans for Sunday?" he asks.

"Well, I'm not sure what Mom has in mind, she's at work now, but I'll have her phone you," Danny concludes.

Orth hangs up the phone and goes down to the lane to collect the mail. As he pauses to glance at the mail, his friend, Don Nitalag drives by and they exchange the wave of hands.

Don is a fairly well-to-do retired farmer. His wife died several years ago and now he lives alone on the farm in a white ranch style home. He was in the Navy during World War II and witnessed the bombing of Pearl Harbor first hand. Orth enjoys talking to Don about his war experiences. He was a gunnery petty officer in the Navy, but was transferred to the Marine Corps as his ship was sunk and they needed gunnery sergeants during the Guadacanal invasion.

Don enjoys buying new sports cars. His family is grown – the oldest son being a medical doctor in Racine – specializing in neurology. This eldest son flies in to see Don at times and lands his classical antique Navy biplane on a grass strip that Don had made by neighbor farmer friend Bill Rice.

About eight p.m. Libby phoned Orth back and he invited her and Danny to a picnic lunch and sail up at Lake Ehai after church Sunday. Libby accepted the invitation with warm enthusiasm. And Orth felt excited about having company up at the Lake. Orth picks up Libby and Danny early Sunday morning and they attend Church services at the Methodist Church in New Hesse. Orth excuses himself to go to the choir room to practice before the service and Libby and Danny sit near the rear of the sanctuary – still feeling rather intimidated by the "churchy" atmosphere, even though they are warmly welcomed by the members they encounter.

The members of the choir are wandering into the room to rehearse. The Director is a youngish brunette, slender speaking with a southern accent. She is Bernadette Lore – knows music well and helps Orth over difficult parts of the music. The choir is small usually six or seven ladies and three or four men. Orth is often troubled with thoughts as to why there are not more – especially men and he thinks, "Perhaps it is the heathenistic influence – how the Devil preys upon men telling them that music is feministic and that 'real men' do not do that sissy stuff."

Paul Semirg, the minister comes into the choir room and leads them in prayer before the service. Paul preaches this morning on the "Children of Promise". His topic emphasizes the fact that Abraham was blessed by God and that Jesus Christ was the "Promise". So as Christians we are children or offspring of Christ because we have been "born again". New persons with the blood of Abraham, Isaac and Jacob in our veins. Who can deny that? Paul said, "The Christian religion is the world's oldest, as recounted in the first chapter of John,

> *"In the beginning was the Word, and the Word was with God, and the Word was God. He was in the beginning with God, all things were made through Him, and without Him was not anything made that was made. In him was life and the life was the Light of Men."*

"Think upon this!" Paul continues. "Before anything was Christ – the 'Word' of God his Father. Christ was the person in the Old Testament that taught and led the Prophets of ancient times."

After the service Orth, Libby and Danny motor to the Lake. Libby was moved by the words spoken by Paul at the service and asked Orth several questions during the day.

"I always used to get things confused Ortie about God. Nobody seemed to help me in my younger days. Some said 'God' was all three, the Father, the Son and the Holy Ghost combined – things of religion were so mixed up – the different sects and their doctrines," Libby laments.

Orth nods to himself and understands. He then tells Libby, "God, His Son, Jesus Christ, and the Holy Ghost all three separate and distinct persons. Many theologians and church groups do not follow the scriptures accurately.

THEY SAIL FOR SEVERAL HOURS - DANNY TAKES A TRICK ON THE TILLER, LIBBY AND DANNY ENJOY THE TIME ON THE WATER AT LAKE EHAI WITH ORTH...

It is a sad thing, Libby."

They chat together for a while at the picnic table while Danny sits silently listening.

The details of the love story are tedious to tell and this writer will leave them up to the hack pulp writers of sensuous fiction who fashion them for the vacuous young females who delight in such prattle. Let it be said that Libby and Orth had a unique and warm relationship beginning.

After lunch the three drove to the lot that Orth owned in a small cove. It was a short distance from the picnic park area and down a tree lined beautiful lane. The lot sloped gently down to a neat little dock where a small sailing dinghy was tied up. The area was shaded by tall oak, maple and hickory trees – the grass was closely mowed and trimmed. Orth tossed several bags and boating equipment from the rear of Whitey and the three meander down to the dock.

"Meet 'Donna' Danny", Orth remarks as he points to the fourteen foot Capri sloop. Danny seems excited as he scans the boat and fondles the spars and gear.

"Why are sail boats named with female names, Ortie?" Danny asks.

"Because they demand a lot of attention, are difficult to handle sometimes and must be treated in a tender, loving manner." Orth replies as he sneaks a side glance to Libby, who manages a wry smile. After a short, pregnant pause passes, they all begin to laugh together.

Orth teaches Danny how to rig Donna and all three get into the boat as Orth casts off and they head out into the main channel of the lake. The wind is brisk from the south and Donna responds well as she enjoys the romp, healing over considerably at times and water slops over the gunnels. Libby and Danny exclaim surprise and excitement, but Orth remains calm and assures them that all is well – that it is only the lake "saying hello."

They sail for several hours under the warm sun and Orth lets Danny handle the sheet lines and the tiller for a trick. Libby smiles approval and seems to enjoy the sailing as much as Danny. They maneuver back to the dock, tuck Donna away and fold the sails preparing to head home.

"It's my ritual to take a swim before heading home," Orth exclaims.

"Well, we'll have to change – where do we do that?" Libby answers as Orth points to the trees and bushes bordering the property. They enjoy a brief swim in the warm water, dry off and head home.

Orth pulls up in front of Libby's apartment building and Libby invites him in. However, Orth politely refuses saying he has quite a few thing to take care of before Monday. Danny dashes inside while Orth helps Libby unload some of the picnic relics. They pause for a while and gaze into each other's eyes holding hands.

"The day was special, Ortie," Libby says softly.

"For me, too," Orth replies and he hugs her closely. Libby then quickly raises up on her toes and kisses Orth on the cheek and abruptly spins and hurriedly walks up to her apartment.

Orth stands for a moment and watches Libby, then he slowly turns and gets into Whitey for the drive to Home Port. His mind is filled with thoughts about Libby, Donna and other women he has known during his somewhat turbulent life. He cannot tolerate thoughts of another marriage because of his experiences after the loss of Donna after twenty years. As he turns onto the freeway that leads him to New Hesse, he thinks to himself, "Our grief and sorrows seem so great, but actually, last briefly – for they are small ... Time heals the weeping heart. We are ficklc...loves are gained and lost. There is no 'right' woman...The only solid thing one can cling to is Christ Jesus. Unchangeable, steadfast, solid granite Truth. A friend always – the Master is always there when needed. Poor folks marry for love and the wealthy marry for money – ah, yes!

The follies of humankind! He drives to Home Port, puts Whitey in the garage and unloads the sails and gear that he stores in a back room off the rear porch that he calls his "sail locker". Mutnik greets him as usual and Orth scratches him under the chin as he smiles back. "Hiyah, ol' pal – catch any gophers?" Mutnik shakes all over – tail wagging as he seems to understand undisputedly the question.

Orth goes into the kitchen, prepares his vegetarian supper and prepares to take a shower before having his meal bedside. He usually eats in bed while reading, listening to the local classical music station, KXER, that he can pick up from Milwaukee. This station also provides him with news of the performing arts being done in the area. He enjoys repertory theater and a variety of other theater and musical events and feels them an escape from the sometime burdens of living a reclusive life out in the country. Alas! The wonderful merits of a rural bucolic life must be punctuated on occasion with sojourns into the glamorous existence of the city. He thirsts for good conversation, which he sometimes finds at Frederick's – if the German band is not playing. Good conversation is frequently discovered also while traveling where he often meets well-traveled educated people – mild in temperament willing to talk and discuss a variety of subjects. Nancy Steinmann was like this at the University – and he enjoyed lengthy conversations with her.

The phone is at bedside – Orth puts down his book and answers. "Orth Volzenkoff". He always answers in a formal manner identifying himself clearly – and is irritated at people who answer in a dull uninterested way – such as "um - ya - hello" and so forth.

"Hi – how's it goin'?" the voice replies and Orth immediately knows it as his younger son, Bertram. Bert chats with his father for a brief spell and they exchange friendly gibes at each other spelled with frequent laughs. Bert phones Orth at irregular intervals to talk about light matters. Orth enjoys these moments and he feels closer to his sons in these later years.

As his sons grow older, he feels they acquire wisdom that dispels those hotspur silly antagonistic thoughts that youth hold against their parents, especially sons against fathers.

"What are you doing for Christmas?" Bert asks.

"Well, I've got to be here to sing in a church cantata, then I've got to give a Christmas Eve thing at the Nursing Home in New Hesse, it looks like I'm kind of tied up, Bert... maybe, I can make it out the first of spring." They continue to talk for a while. Orth hangs up after the usual 'good-byes' and settles back in bed, thinking to himself how men foster children – bring them up with a nice home and the comforts the parents did not enjoy. Soon the children demand more and more and they receive all the attention – the father considered excess baggage. How things do change. The American "Youth Culture" spurns the old folks' advice. People over fifty are led to pasture to rot – to be distantly, disdainfully tolerated. Other cultures, the Oriental, seem to engender a continued love and respect for the elderly.

"Well, Ortie, you have your books and your memories, but at times I am bloody lonely," Orth thinks to himself.

* * *

It was now the fourteenth of July, 1950, and Orth was awakened early in the morning by one of the enlisted medics who came into the tent and noisily announced that they were pulling out because the North Koreans had penetrated the defense lines that the U.S. 19th and 34th Infantry Regiments had set up along the Kum River.

"We have about two hours to get out of here," the sergeant yelled as men came in and started to load the wounded into trucks. The trucks soon started to move out and Orth could see that much equipment had been abandoned in efforts to hasten the move.

After a slow move down muddy roads, Orth's truck stopped and it was learned that the enemy had infiltrated past the U.S. positions and had set up road blocks ahead. Orth could hear rifle and heavy weapons firing. They waited for several hours, then they started moving south again and sometime during the night, they stopped and set up camp in the Taejon area. The rumors were fast coming as men from other units came past and left their wounded at the field hospital. Some men said the U.S. troops were being chewed up badly...no fire power to stop the North ... there were too few eight-inch and 155 mm and no 175 mm artillery guns. Ammo and supplies were critically low. They remained at Taejon for several days and Orth was almost totally recovered. Orth learned that the Second Infantry Division had been sent by General Walker from the 8th Army to replace the 24th Division, who were sent back to Sasebo, Japan – what was left of them. The wonderful 24th division – the "Victory" Division who saw action during World War II in New Guinea, Leyte, Corregidor, Verde Island and Mindanao had suffered gravely in Korea and would not return.

Names of his lost comrades spun around in Orth's head, and of Charlie Company – he would see no more of those who served with him on the rain soaked hills. First shirt Smith, PFC Tom Tolliver, SSG John Provert, SFC Collins, Captain Philpot, Second Lieutenant Treat – they had all evidently been killed the night they were overrun. He shed tears – he felt remorse for being spared. Dear readers, I might fill volumes with tales of Orth's experiences in the War and other life systems, were I so minded, but at this rate, my recital would not be brought to conclusion for years, and who knows how soon my God will call upon me to stop?

Now that he was able to move about relatively easily, Orth helped with duties about the hospital and they moved again to some point behind the Naktong River. Here they remained until sometime in August. This was the so-called Pusan Perimeter. There were a lot more units sent into battles along the Naktong River lines. General Kean led his 25th Infantry Division into the fray and General Reiser marched his Second Division in. Marines were there, South Korean (ROK) forces and Orth even met several soldiers from a British unit. Tons of material and men were being dumped into the Pusan area.

Orth was anxious about where he would be assigned. Sent home? back to the front? Waiting is part of the Army system. It was now the middle of September 1950. He moved about the hospital helping the wounded write letters, cleaning latrines and other menial tasks. He did not mind nor complain – as long as he kept busy time moved faster. Now he was completely recovered from his wounds. Soon one of the medics came into his tent and handed him an envelope from Headquarters Twenty-Fourth Division. He sat on the edge of the bed for a few moments holding the envelope in his lap, almost afraid to open it. He lit a cigarette – a habit he had unfortunately acquired a few months earlier while he was in deep pain and misery.

After a few minutes he garnered sufficient strength to tear open the letter and read ... Army orders are the epitome of dryness. They are mimeographed and sent in at least four copies. he read down through the names until he found his...

> "...PFC Orth S. Volzenkoff, RA472-31-2785, Assigned Duty, B75, Artillery Targeting Specialist, HQ, I Corps Artillery, Sector XRay. Report NLT, 0800 12 September, 1950.

His heart plunged as he stuffed the orders back into the large envelope and stuffed it into his locker at the foot of his bunk.

He had entertained high hopes of being sent back home on leave or at least to Japan. He was sick of war – mud and the world of olive drab. About noontime the same medic corporal that had delivered the orders came in to announce that Orth was to pack up, ready to depart the Hospital Camp at 1300 (one p.m.) directly after "chow" or noonday meal.

His mind was awhirl as he got into the rear of a two-and-a-half-ton truck. He was driven to the tent area that housed the Headquarters Battery of I Corps. He reported in to the First Sergeant who was a stockily built sandy-haired man in his mid-thirties, Orth guessed. They were positioned about seventy five miles east of Mokpo, and the Communist forces were giving it everything they had he learned. Pusan was the prize the North Koreans desired and if they were successful, there would be a disaster, because the U.S. forces were bottled up with their backs to the Sea of Japan.

CHAPTER XII

For though we live in the world we are not carrying on a worldly war, for the weapons of our warfare are not worldly, but have divine power to destroy strongholds.

2 Corinthians 10:3-4

Orth was later to understand God's will and the power he holds, and how puny are mankind's weapons of destruction compared to the Divine. History tells a dreaded story. Works of history should inculcate moral lessons. But, alas not! Men continue to flaunt God's intent to love one's neighbor as one loves himself. Enormous sums of money are spent by politicians and monarchs to force their ideals or beliefs upon others. Treasuries are drained. In the Seventeenth Century King Phillip of Spain was defeated in his efforts to expand the Roman Catholic doctrines. The Catholic Church in Rome tapped many kings' and noblemen's coffers to finance wars against the Protestants – only to fail because God's plan would not be thwarted! Queen Isabella failed to force people and the Spanish Inquisition failed.

Violence will never replace love and respect as a means to convince people of a superior way of life. God has his hand continually in the destiny of mankind. He has an unfailing hope that many souls will realize the futility of trying to resolve differences by means of force and violence.

Lime is an essential ingredient of mortar, plaster and cement. It is soft. Love is soft. The flesh of the precious young infant, Jesus the Christ, was soft.

Yet, paradoxically powerfully strong! The young soft flesh of Christ became the strength and massive force to topple nations – Rome, Greece, etc. The soft, sweet tones of the Gospel pierce stone walls, penetrate steel doors, topple over fortresses. The soft, peaceful words of Christ are the means that God warns those who dare to place obstacles in its way. Those words will lazer their way through anything mankind may have the audacity to design. And, the Devil knows this.

Western civilization was born with pistols in their brains it almost seems. Logic and supernatural truth (Christ) have been substituted with gunpowder and bayonets...Oh! When will they ever learn?, Orth laments to himself in later life. A soldier gives up his blood for his country, but never his honor. A politician gives up his honor for his country, but never his blood.

There has been a romance of war born out of the age of feudalism. Kings and noble lords rode into battle as their ambition. Killing their neighbors over petty arguments, differing philosophical viewpoints, or a plot of ground. Liberty, equality, fraternity. God gave these to mankind to preserve and protect. Freedom from despotic rule, from bondage, freedom to choose. But, if Christ is left out, then it ceases to work. The United States has been successful in wars to defend her shores against tyranny. When America goes to war to further her interest economically, or when the motives are moot...example, Viet Nam, Korea, etc., then the outcome will be questionable even if a victory is achieved. God will insure success if the question is to defend freedom to worship Christ and God's desire to have His faithful live and work in an unselfish loving manner.

Early Christians defeated the heathen hordes by using love as a weapon. Wretched Rome soon after the downfall of Nero was converted to the Christian center of the world by the examples they set when smilingly they accepted their fates as they were burned at the stake or fed to wild beasts because they valued their freedom to worship Jesus Christ greater than yield to those demands that they deny their Master and pay homage only to their Roman "gods".

Saint Boniface in the Seventh Century was faced by a mob of pagans in Germany he was attempting to teach the Truth. They demanded his life and before they murdered him, he prayed for them. Not long thereafter, all Germany became a stronghold of Christian culture – enormous churches were erected and many stand today as living manifestations of the German people's devotion to Christ. All early missionaries to Europe and elsewhere faced the

WESTERN CIVILIZATION WAS BORN WITH PISTOLS IN THEIR BRAINS – THERE HAS BEEN A ROMANCE OF WAR BORN OUT OF THE AGE OF FEUDALISM ...

terrors of robbers, heathen mobs, pagan idol worshippers and rogues who would mock and revile them.

Christ will win. Deceptive lawyers and politicians frequently flaunt liberty in front of ideologues and simpletons forgetting that the solid truth of liberty is attainable only if it is based upon a firm foundation of moral virtue – of the "Truth" – of Christianity. Moralistic values based upon the precepts of mankind are soon to shatter and fall at the behest of self-centeredness and avarice.

"Lord save us ...we perish," as recited in Matthew, Chapter 8, verse 23-25. Heard from the mouths of the deceived when they realize that there is no "ideal" or "utopia" from the hall of Washington, D.C., or elsewhere. God's Holy Spirit keeps up His battle against the Devil's plan to lead the sheep to slaughter. Is it any wonder that God is often angered and woeful when He sees His children running helter-skelter for answers? A triumph of military might brings momentary pride and enjoyment when is soon ended by reason and fact. The general who wins a battle is joyful until he surveys the cost – heaps of rotting flesh – a multitude of ideas lay lifeless on the ground. The cost of the general's laurels is too great!

* * *

"Get yourself squared away, Orth – then report to Eye Corps Artillery, they are over on the western side of the TOC. They will give you the low down. The Commies are blasting our asses and we've got to get hopping," First Sergeant Ibsen told Orth.

Orth eyed the pieces of paper thrust into his hand by Van Ibsen.

"Captain Dillbert is the 'Old Man'. You'll see him later," Van added as Orth hoisted his duffel bags onto his shoulders and trudged out of the tent.

His tent was close by and it was the usual eight-man affair. Only one man was there, although there were eight bunks – all centered around an oil heater that was belching out heat like a dragon with heart burn. The one man was sleeping and did not stir as Orth entered. The one unoccupied bunk, that is one without any gear around it, Orth took command of and sat down upon it to collect his thoughts. Soon he started to unpack and looked for places to place things.

Soldiers are soon to acquire a knack for improvising. They use cans, old discarded boxes and various odds and ends to try to make a home out of otherwise plain and drab surroundings. Orth went to the mess tent and was successful in obtaining a large coffee can to wash his socks and perform his daily toilets in, and an orange crate to use as a bedside table.

The outside of the tent had a hand-painted sign that read, "Home of the Rich and Famous I Corps, FSE." Later it was explained that his tent won a naming contest in the camp – thus, the sign. The troops occupying the tent were all from the Fire Support Element of Corps Artillery – mostly sergeants with several corporals and privates. One – a corporal was of Mexican blood and was a radio operator assigned to the section – name of Joe Rosales. Nice chap, but rather brainless who enjoyed his beer and food and thought the army was a thing to be ignored. Joe's name was "Rosie" for all intents. Joe would play a key role later in the Orth drama.

Next to Orth in the tent was buck sergeant Steven Iversen – a large, jolly Swede from Minnesota, who had a quick wit and always a jovial answer for most situations. About half of the men were assigned for air support and the others, ground support guns. Orth was in the close-ground support section. The whole FSE Section was run around the clock which meant that some men had to sleep and live at odd hours. To begin, Orth was assigned to the night shift of twelve hours from six p.m. or 1800 to 0600 the following day. Each shift had two enlisted men and one officer, a Captain. Orth's shift had a Captain named Marvin Funkweiler.

Captain Funkweiler was a short, fat punctilious person who graduated from Brigham Young University, Provo, Utah. He wanted everyone to be aware that he was a college graduate and gained his commission through the rigorous ROTC program. Marvin was a Mormon, or a member of the Church of Latter-Day Saints, therefore, he was abstemious of alcoholic beverages, coffee, tobacco and other stimulants. Orth admired Marvin for his gentlemanly presence, but felt him too stiff and not warm.

Captain Funkweiler did not grasp the idea of artillery easily and had extreme difficulty in sizing up the battle situation readily. Therefore, Orth and Steve Iverson had to tactfully remind him of the situations that demanded his immediate attention. There was another officer named William Snowbert who wandered about the Tactical Operations Center and was supposed to be an expert at Engineering and his job was to advise the high ranking officers of problems concerning highways - bridges - defilement's and so forth. This he rarely did and he spent most of his time joking with the enlisted men and cleaning his M-1 carbine rifle. In fact, he spent hours cleaning his rifle, scrubbing it with a toothbrush and so forth. Bill Snow Snowbert was short, but well-structured. His manner was jovial and easy-going, therefore all the enlisted men enjoyed him which made the officers rather ill-disposed toward him. This, no doubt, resulted in Second Lieutenant Snowbert's assignment to the "Jump" TOC, kind of like being given the black death.

The "Jump" TOC is the alternative, Tactical Operations Center. Its function is to serve as the Artillery Coordinator if the Main TOC is flattened by a shell or overrun by the enemy. In this instance, the Jump TOC was located in an old building about five miles to the south west near a village called Yamping. The building was empty and littered with stinking and rotting vegetation that First Sergeant Ibsen called "shit", but the genteel name would be human offal.

Something must be said now about the General in charge of Corps Artillery. Brigadier General W. Herbert Schuler was a recalled World War Two Army Reserve Officer. His civilian job was a high school principal in a small California town named Lodi. General Schuler was friendly and knew what to do, he was not ostentatious – but mildly humble about his education and experience. He did not see combat in the war, but he had extensive training in military schools and courses. His commission was direct – a field commission as a second lieutenant – he rose rapidly, probably because he had a pleasant personality and got along well with people.

Orth liked General Schuler – what he saw of him. When he visited Orth's section, he usually sat in a chair, leaning back and joking with all – officers and enlisted. But, Captain Funkweiler confessed to Orth that the General was a changed man during strategic meetings with the high ranking officers, given once daily in the Corps Headquarters tent. Actually, because of the fluid situation of the war, the TOC was comprised of several ten-wheeled trucks which had expandable sides. These were placed together to form a sort of mobile building. These had electrical wires running between them and there was a constant high-pitched soprano sound from the generators that supplied the "juice" to the lights and radio equipment. The whole area was kept secure by sentries of Military Police but the enemy still found means to infiltrate. Some times the TOC received mortar bursts from all sides.

* * * * * * * * * * * *

Now it happens. A strange set of circumstances. The TOC of the Corps came under a severe mortar attack about 1000 hours on Monday morning, 3 October 1950. The Corps had recently moved forward because the Second Division had been successful in pushing the Chinese and North Koreans back and the First Marine Division and the U.S. Seventh Division had made a beach landing at Inchon further north that had weakened the enemy's attempts to push the U.S. into the sea at Pusan.

Orth was in the Jump TOC when the radio operator, Joe Rosales came running in.

"Hell, Ortie! All hell's broken loose!"

Rosie was wide-eyed and in shock. Orth tried to calm him down and finally received the news that the Main TOC had been demolished – truck parts and bodies were lying about – nothing was left. Both Generals Schuler and White had been killed. The whole place was in a state of confusion. The enemy had infiltrated and hit from the rear. Litter bearing helicopters were arriving and carrying out the wounded. Rosie had managed to send out a radio message early in the attack for aid.

Staff Sergeant Steve Iversen was talking to Lieutenant Snowbert. It was a heated exchange, Orth could tell. Steve came over to Orth and said, "I don't know a damn thing about running this section, Ortie. I was a gun-bunny, red leg and that shity Snowbert has gone to pieces and thinks we should get the hell out of here and beat it back to Chonan."

Orth went over to the desk where Lieutenant Snowbert was sitting hunched over, head in his hands and crying. He was, as the Army terms it, "gone ape", or emotionally uncontrollable. Orth tried to console him, when suddenly Snowbert got to his feet and blurted out, "I can't do it! I can't do it!" Then he again sat down in a bent over crumpled heap.

Orth went over to Sergeant Iverson, "Steve, we've got to carry on, the Commies will sure as hell take over as soon as they learn we have no commanders."

Iverson gazed intently at Orth then said, "Okay Orth, let's do it, you run the damn battle and I'll give what help I can. That milksop Snowbert's no use to us."

Just then Lieutenant Snowbert sprang up and ran to Sergeant Iverson and Orth yelling, "Let's get out – I order you – Run for it – It's all over – Leave everything!"

It was clear that Lieutenant William Snowbert was temporarily or permanently insane. Orth hit him squarely on the side of his head and he fell to the tent dirt floor. "Glad you did that, Ortie. I would have done the same. Let's move him over to one of the cots there and tie him down." They tied Lieutenant Snowbert to a cot and placed a stand up peg board in front of it. Just then a jeep came roaring up and a British officer jumped out and came in. "A bloody mess up front – whole TOC area is a shambles, confused mumble jumble." He gazed about briefly, then added, "What's up?"

Sergeant Iverson answered tersely, "We've got command now. 'general' Volzenkoff here is running the Corps now."

Reginald "Reggie" Arnold-Berkmister, was a Don at Oxford before he joined the Army. He was from a wealthy family and he obtained his officer's commission after a brief sixteen weeks at the Sandhurst Military Academy in England. Reggie went into the military to please his father who was a retired Colonel in His Majesty's 44th Fusiliers – and served with distinction in both World Wars. Reggie was not of a soldiering ilk – he was fun-loving soft spoken and would rather read a book than play rugby.

"Well, I'll help out the best I can," replied Reggie, then added, "Jolly good to meet you, sir," as he eyed Orth suspiciously. Steve Iverson grabbed Reggie by the sleeve and told him to sit down. He then explained the situation and Captain Arnold-Berkmister nodded finally and replied, "Well, Yank, we will bloody well have to make the most of it. You'd best get Corporal Orth here a new uniform in case we have visitors. Orth had agreed to carry on the battle and to do whatever was needed until replacement officers came. The four men now sat down and devised a plan.

CHAPTER XIII

God, who has saved us and called us with a holy calling, not according to our works, but according to His own purpose and grace which was given to us in Christ Jesus before time began.

I Timothy 1:8-9

Later, when Orth reflects upon these events, he sheds tears to think that God spared him and gave him the wisdom and courage to do those things that he would have thought impossible before the shelling and destruction of the I Corps Tactical Operations Center. Now, four men huddled together in a tent on a chilly evening of 4 October 1950. Those present were: Orth, Staff Sergeant Steve Iverson, British Captain Reginald Arnold-Berkmister, and Radio Operator Corporal Joseph "Rosie" Rosales.

They devised a plan. Under ordinary circumstances if the Corps Commander is killed or unable to perform his duties then command is passed to the general in charge of Corps Artillery, then to one of the Division Commanders in order of seniority. However, in the present case, General "Shoe" Schuler was at the Main TOC when it was shelled and was killed along with the Corps Commander.

The four decided not to disturb the Division Commanders as they had their hands full – and to carry on until they could notify Army Pacific Area Command - General MacArthur and await his decision. Army Headquarters-Pacific Command was in Sasebo, Japan. Captain Arnold Berkmister agreed to drive Lieutenant Snowbert to a field hospital and have him committed as a "shell-shock" case. So, Lieutenant Snowbert departed the area yelling hysterically at the men that they would all be court martialed and face a firing squad.

Orth acted fast. As a soldier one forgets the impending disaster and expects it to happen to the other fellow and not you. He called in Joe Rosales.

"Rosie, get hold of the Division CP's and tell them that the Corps TOC has been hit and that 'General Orth' has been sent in by chopper from Japan to take over. Then hop over to the TOC area and see if you can get me a general's uniform, or something close," Orth tells Rosales.

"Also, I need all the updated intelligence data you can get hold of from the Divisions. I've got to update the maps," Orth adds as he starts to work.

Both Steve Iverson and Orth work feverishly at getting things up to date. Rosales brings in the uniform of General Schuler which Orth fits into rather nicely – plus Rosie brought in the radio and teletype dispatches that he had been receiving constantly since the Main TOC had been hit. The tenor of the battle had changed.

The First Marines and Seventh Army Divisions had been halted in their advance north by severe and massive counter offensives all along the 38th Parallel. Ammunition and artillery shortages are reported. The Chinese had launched frantic suicide charges. Things did not look good.

Reggie Arnold Berkmister returned from his journey to the field hospital and was helping to sort things out.

"Those bloody medics were difficult to deal with!" Reggie announces to Orth and the others. He then goes on to explain that Lieutenant Snowbert had been placed in a separate tent and put under sedatives, however, he related that when they finally realize that the whole scene is a ruse, they would be up to their "billy-bongs" in trouble.

All men agreed that the main objective now is not to fret over court martials, but to keep fighting to survive. War is, after all, drudgery, boredom, delay, waste, heartlessness, disappointment, cruelty, stupidity, destruction, death, misery and everything else that is bad. So...what if they were sent off to prison. At least they are doing their job as best they can and injustices in war are all too common, almost normal. The only security is in a tranquil, peaceful mind and that cannot be had at the cost of condoning cowardice or injustice.

Lieutenant Snowbert was all for abandoning his post, forgetting those that depended upon him. Orth and the others did not feel they could stand the thought of running away while those up front needed their support and help. Best death with honor than saving your ass with cowardice.

Reports are now coming in fast and furious. Marine and Division officers are coming into the Jump TOC to talk with Orth and the others. The cover-up is going well and Orth manages to convince visitors that his is "real". Word is that the Chinese have more than 300,000 men pouring down from the north and that the artillery units are firing at point blank range in some areas.

Some communication problems from the Main TOC before it had been hit led to heavy losses on our side. Stories keep coming in that the Chinese are punching at the front from Panmunjon to Million Dollar Hill, right across to the Sea of Japan. Orth had Rosie send messages to Eighth Army and Tenth Corps on the eastern side to ascertain what their situations were. Japan was also barking at First Corps for information and Iverson and Captain Reggie were successful in remitting replies that seemed to satisfy MacArthur that the western section was holding. Actually, it was not, it was starting to sag southward like a wet sack of marshmallows.

The Chinese were getting close to Seoul. Their units were using deceptive tactics of blowing whistles and setting off flares to confuse the U.S. troops. Rosie was receiving messages that said morale was weakening - shortages were reported of medical people and supplies. Some field hospitals reported no bandages nor morphine.

Orth thinks about things and people as he works on the map boards with Steve Iverson and Captain Reggie.

"I'm so damned confused and worried, Reggie," Orth confesses.

"Don't fret, Mate," Reggie answers, adding, "Oliver Cromwell said, 'A man never rises so high as to when he knows not whither he is going' –you have need to wonder, Ortie – a need to feel free – God wants man not to worry about failures."

"I did not know you were religious, Reggie," Orth says offhandedly.

"If it's being a Christian you mean, old boy, I confess readily I jolly well am, but I sometimes wonder at my behavior, when I'm out here bloody well killing people."

The men chat amongst themselves as they toil with the battle progress. Orth says softly. "My old buddy Bob Chang used to say that water was the symbol of humility, of strength. It is quiet, soft, yet penetrates rock and metal. It is pretty, yet knocks down buildings and bridges. It is quiet, yet can deafen your ears by a hurricane. The use of force represents weakness and real strength comes from meekness and softness."

The men remain quiet for a moment. Rosie, who was sitting over in a corner sifting through messages, after a moment quietly adds, "An old priest in my home town told me when I was leaving for the Army that soldiers are weapons of evil. Now I know what he meant."

Steve Iverson, working on the map boards says, "In my home town, which was only 85 people, in Northern Iowa, there was a little old man named, 'Guy'. He was 87 years old and never owned a car, so we would see him tottering around town bent over with a cane. The kids in town always made fun of him, called him the 'Pig Man', because he always seemed to stop at least one youngster in town and tell them a poem about a pig that was actually a parable about a Bible character. Let's see if I can remember one...oh - ya, here's one:

> The pig is an animal that loves the mud...
> He sputters and rudds with his head in the flood...
> His whole life is spent to eat to get fat -whereat
> Upon the dinner table he lies flat.
> Now this is no artifice to entice.
> It shows simply some die to sacrifice.
> Their lives are love to be precise.

"I memorized that poem as I rode in the bus after being drafted into the Army. Old Guy saw me off at the bus station and handed it to me as I boarded," Steve concludes.

Orth and the others laugh slightly. Then Steve continues his story.

"The 'Pig Man' was self-educated. Never went beyond the sixth grade. He is the one great thing I remember about the stinking little town of mine. Guy was always smiling and talking to the youngsters in town. He was the School Superintendent, and a lawyer. Taught himself law reading and passed the State of Iowa Bar Exams at the first sitting. Even though he did all these things and was such a damned nice man, most of those town brats still made fun of him. Life is just shitty, sometimes," Steve concludes.

"When did you last see him, Steve?" Captain Reggie asks.

"Oh, I went on leave after basic and he was there in town, walking as usual. He had been elected Circuit Judge. He invited me over to his house for cake and coffee before I left for Japan. It was a small, dilapidated house on the edge of town – looked humble – just like Mr. Guy. One bedroom was stacked with books and one whole wall was nothing but books on theology. You know, church stuff. We talked about church. One thing for certain, Mr. Guy was all Christian – not stuffy, just friendly and hard working."

Rosie added, "My Catholic memories do not include a 'Mr. Guy'. Oh, we had friendly people, but I never understood much about all the bell-ringing and robes and stuff."

"Mom wrote me," Steve says, and adds, "she said Guy was in a Nursing Home now, had a stroke, but he is still cheerful and reads a lot."

"Whop - Whop" - the building housing the Jump TOC is rocked by several close blasts. One piece of shrapnel rips through and strikes Steve Iverson in the leg. Orth yells, "We have to move out of here – the chinks have us zeroed in."

Things moved fast. The wound to Iverson's leg was not serious, he found an available jeep and started driving south towards Chongu and was successful in locating a Field Hospital about three miles south of that town.

Orth and the others loaded all the maps and equipment of the TOC into a ten-wheel diesel truck and headed towards Suwon. They stopped a short distance from the town and set up the TOC as best they could in an abandoned school house. Corporal Rosales sent out radio messages to the Division Command Posts for the First Cavalry, Third and Twenty-Fifth Infantry Divisions. Messages were coming in relating stories of heavy losses because of confusion. Orth calls for a conference with the Division Commanders in an effort to discover how bad things are going. Orth was nervous, but all went reasonably well. The news was that the Chinese were launching massive attacks along the front.

Supplies were low and frozen hands and feet were common. Some units had disintegrated and there were a mixture of units. Morale was low, but there were pockets of heroism. Some walking wounded went fighting on. The Chinese were using waves of soldiers. Some not even with weapons. Some U.S. units were falling apart when their leaders were killed or wounded. The Commander of the 25th Division reported that several times friendly planes had dropped Napalm on his troops. During a break in the meeting, Major General Luther T. Odem, C.O. of the First Cavalry Division was plying Orth with questions endeavoring to ascertain his background because of his young appearance. Orth did look older than his age of twenty, because he had allowed his beard to grow and he sat off in the corner during the briefing shaded by the muted light. Orth fended off the questions and finally was rescued by

SUPPLIES WERE LOW—FROZEN HANDS AND FEET WERE COMMON... MORALE WAS MINUS—BUT THERE WERE POCKETS OF HEROISM...

Captain Arnold Berkmister, who came over and said, "General Volzenkoff, excuse me, but I must see you about an urgent dispatch we just received from Ninth Corps."

Orth jumped up and walked out of the building with Reggie.

"I think that old fart suspects something, Reggie," Orth whispers.

"Do not worry, Ortie, the meeting is just about over and you've got to give them a word of encouragement. Chin up, old boy."

They went back into the meeting. Orth had his general's helmet on, his general's field jacket on and he told the commanders that he would soon be up front to visit. Meanwhile, they should try to hold at all costs. The commanders seemed cheered up and were in agreement that a visit may help morale and rally the forces.

The next day after the meeting Orth, Reggie and a private from a replacement detail set out to visit the front. They left behind Rosales on the radio and two field artillery captains that the Division Commanders had left behind to man the TOC because of its under strength. Orth and Reggie conferred the night before on the strategy they would use during the visit.

Their main objective would be to boost morale and gather information useful to direct operations back at the TOC until replacement officers arrived from Eighth Army. They agreed to carry on the deception so that the troops would not be discouraged by the loss of leadership and that direction was sorely needed during this critical period when the Chinese regulars were pouring south of the 38th Parallel. Reggie and Orth pondered how best to rally the forces.

They drove north in two jeeps. The private and Orth were in the rear one and Reggie and a corporeal were in the lead vehicle. The corporeal had been clerk typist for the 25th Division and had been "volunteered" to the Operations Center to help with the paper work.

Captain Arnold Berkmister equipped the lead jeep with a mounted 50 caliber machine gun plus a 57 MM recoilless rifle and some small arms in case they should run into trouble. Infiltrators were a constant threat.

So north they started towards the First Cavalry Division's area. On the road to Kaesong, they passed many 2-1/2 ton trucks laden with wounded. The wounded were stacked two deep and some soldiers were hanging on to the sides. Orth and the others stopped frequently visiting. They finally located the Command Post for the First Cavalry Division, which was located in an abandoned farm house - straw roof. The stories that they heard sounded pathetic. Machine guns were jamming because of the cold. Orth told them to fire them every fifteen minutes to keep the heat up. He also called back to the TOC and ordered some close air support from carrier based navy planes.

He noticed the Commander of the Division speaking in a doubting manner and contradicting Orth's commands. Orth yelled to the general, "If you do not change your white assed West Point tactics, you are soon going to see a hell-of-a lot more dead bodies lying around here!"

The tenor of Orth's voice seemed to work and the general began to issue orders at the behest of Orth.

"If your men are freezing their balls off, use warm up tents or trucks and send them there in intervals. At night if the gooks start blowing whistles, order your men to counter by hooting and banging their mess kits. Anything to get those chinks guessing."

Orth and Reggie eyed the maps and soon ordered changes in positions to give the advantage to crew based weapons and artillery. He also sent a radio request to Tenth Corps for needed ammunition and medical help. Reggie and Orth continued their tour of the front line positions gathering information and attempting to bolster morale. The rides in the jeeps were bitterly cold, but they kept moving. The U.S. lines were falling back. Faulty radio reception causes confusion and needed "C" rations and ammo were discovered to have been air dropped into Chinese hands.

Orth informs the battalion and other unit commanders to relay radio messages by L-5 spotter planes. At one point on the road to the 25th Division positions they came under small arms fire. Bullets hit near and they pulled off to cover. Orth takes out his carbine, but it jams because of some frozen mud it accumulated. Reggie mans the .50 caliber machine gun and rakes the area. They wait until it seems calm – then continue on.

They reach positions close to the Han River where they find part of the 24th Division mixed with the 25th. The ground was so cold that the troops could not dig in, but huddled behind trucks and clumps of rocks, anything to shelter from the cold and mortar bursts. They walked about and at several points, the men slid down the frozen hillsides. One could hear the Chinese burp gun blasts and the 3.5 bazookas being used against armored vehicles.

Orth kept in touch with the Jump TOC by radio, ordering in napalm and rockets upon suspected enemy concentrations. The lines were still collapsing and incidents of heroism flooded in. One case heard was when a private had his legs blown off by a grenade and he kept firing his BAR (Browning Automatic Rifle) until he was hit again by a grenade – then he fell silent in the arms of God.

Orth learns of a French Battalion who had been held in reserve because of a language problem and he orders it forward to bolster the 2nd Division who were experiencing difficulty holding out in the Chipyong-ni sector.

They learn that General Almond of the X Corps had radioed the "Eye" Corps TOC and asked about the situation, having heard that the main TOC had been torn up by enemy mortars. Rosales had radioed an answer that Major Volzenkoff had taken command and the reply from General Ed Almond was, "Who is he and where did he come from?"

Well, now the news is out and Orth and the others still carry on in their efforts to perform their duties, until there is a new command sent from Japan. Orth continues to visit the front. He orders Corps Artillery units to adjust their positions in order for the 175 MM and 8-inch guns to reach enemy units. He also orders harassing fire and illumination rounds every five minutes to keep the Chinese guessing. He locates some hand crank sirens in an abandoned fire station and gives them to forward units to use at night when the Chinese start their hand grenade attacks.

ORTH CONTINUED THEIR TOUR OF THE FRONT LINE POSITIONS GATHERING INFORMATION AND ATTEMPTING TO BOLSTER WEAKENING MORALE....

Around the Chipyong-hi sector and Hill 397, they encounter some U.S. soldiers running down a hill, with a lieutenant after them shouting and grabbing them by their clothing and cursing them. It seems the unit came under mortar attack and started running.

Orth, the lieutenant, Reggie and the others rallied the troops and they retook Hill 397 by hand to hand combat. One of the jeep drivers, the Corporal Clerk Typist received a bullet through his left eye and yelled, "I'm hit, I'm hit!"

Orth reeled about and pumped several rounds from his carbine into some running Chinese. The Lieutenant received a bad leg wound from a Chinese "ink bottle" grenade, but he kept fighting with his 45 caliber pistol. The radio in the rear jeep an SCR-536 was hit by a stray bullet and some friendly unit artillery fire was falling on U.S. troops. Orth was aghast at the confusion.

Orth and the others departed Hill 397 and borrowed several GIs to help them in their travels. The wounded Corporal was air lifted out by helicopter. The Chinese attacked in the night blowing bugles, etc., then were quiet during the day.

Orth and the others abandon their visits and start driving back to the TOC. Upon their arrival, they learn that the Chinese have suffered their first defeat since entering the war at Chipyong-ni and that the lines are generally holding. Orth ordered another radio from the 2nd Division and they started updating their battle maps.

At this time, a series of helicopters began to arrive and several generals and high ranking officers arrived accompanied by a squad of Military Police. And to top it all off, Second Lieutenant Snowbert finally stumbled in uttering accusing remarks to the other officers.

The officers announced that Orth was under arrest for impersonating an officer

. The others were released. Captain Arnold Berkmister was told to return to his Brigade. Reggie demurred and went to the defense of Orth in a vehement manner. But, Orth was finally taken away and sent to Japan on a flight from Pusan. Others heard of this event and also defended Orth and praised him for his courage and action. Colonel Firth of the 31st Infantry Regiment was so angry that when he was presented the Silver Star by General Barth, he ripped it off and tossed it into the snow.

General Keiser assumed command of Eye Corps.

CHAPTER XIV

> *Let every soul be subject to the governing authorities. For there is no authority except from God, and the authorities that exist are appointed by God. Therefore whoever resists the authority resists the ordinance of God, and those who resist will bring judgment on themselves.*
>
> (Romans 13:1-2)

The flight from Pusan to Tokyo was about one hour in a beat up old C-119 cargo plane. There were two military policemen who accompanied Orth. The airplane was cold and noisy. Once in Japan they went by jeep to a disciplinary barracks at a location called Camp Lovejoy. The place was surrounded by barbed wire – bleak and chilly. The barracks were wooden covered with tar paper. So, there we have it. Orth was crestfallen. He thinks about people in the Army who are aimless and feel happy and secure because everything is regulated by strict rules and they rarely have to think about what to do next. But, this was not the mind of Orth Schilling Volzenkoff. Orth matured rapidly and he did what he did in Korea because he thought it best in the circumstances, regardless of rigid rules or sanctimonious rituals. He had been in combat and experienced the abject horror of it and he acted to benefit his buddies – those who wear mud on their fatigues – those men who are thrust into the worst of conditions to placate the generals and politicians who create and worship war. Orth was a quiet type who thought and meditated about things. But he was also with a soft heart. He shed tears easily when he thought about his buddies – Bob Chang, Tom Tolliver and all the others who had "bought it" – killed in combat. Met death at an early age in the senseless struggle of men pitted against men over ideologies. "Which or who is right?" he thinks to himself.

His beloved mother, Bertha, his neighbors back home who took him and his brother, Fritz, to church. "Is it a grand hoax – this Christianity?" Orth ponders, "Or is it the right way? What sparks people like Eddie Burran and Bessie Ordway to go to church, to read the Bible and be career 'do gooders'?"

As he sits in his room he hears a tap on the door. Standing in the doorway is a tall lean officer, a Captain. "Hi, Orth – I'm Captain Carl Scholder - Chaplain for the Disciplinary Barracks."

They sit and chat for about an hour about Orth's experiences and about hope and God. Orth feels comfortable with Chaplain Scholder, who calls himself "Captain Sinbuster". He tells laughable stories about religion and seems to cheer Orth up in this moment of despair.

"All is not lost Corporal Orth, try to cheer up. I'll pop back in to see you from time to time."

Orth devotes a lot of time to thinking during these hours awaiting trial. He thinks about the farce of law – lawyers quoting the letter of the code when justice lies bleeding at your feet in the nightmare of combat. He reads how Alfred Nobel, the venerated Peace advocate who fostered the Nobel Peace Prize was in fact the inventor of smokeless gun powder, ballistite, that started all the artillery slaughtering. Hah! What delusion it all is this military fantasy! The Prussian officers, proud of their medals and polished monocles, who loved war, who fertilized their women between battles wearing their shining jack boots during the act of love. Well, at least the Prussians by custom require the field soldier to be honored first. Seemingly, in the U.S. Army, the enlisted man was seen as trash. Orth was becoming bitter – he had to fight off these illogical generalizations. He even thought about the politicians back home who promise to punish the fortunate and soak the rich in order to gain the popular vote. Well, so there you are. Freedom – justice – hollow words unless they are defined. And even if defined they become distorted by the use of self-centered people to gain economic advantages.

After several days passed, a Jewish Second Lieutenant came to see Orth in the Judge Advocate's Offices. He announced that he had been assigned to the case as defense attorney. Orth sat uneasily in the stark office as Abraham S. Rapaport, Esquire, sat opposite Orth gazing through stacks of papers. "Abe" was a small man, slight build, dark hair and a long beak-like nose. He sat hunched over and spoke to Orth without looking directly at him.

"Orth, I'm Abe Rapaport. I've been asked to defend you. Probably because I'm a Jew and the Army does not like Jews, and secondly because the Army thinks what you did stinks – regardless what others may perceive as an act of heroic magnitude."

"Well, I don't like the Army either – so if you like, I will accept to defend you."

Orth sat amazed, then after a pause added, "Lieutenant, I would be happy to have your help – my actions in Korea were done because I thought it my duty and not for any damn hero awards. If the Army wants to can my ass for it, let them, at least I think I helped to save some lives and the battle."

"Noble thoughts, Ortie, but the Army has some brass asses with oatmeal brains that do not think kindly to situations where an enlisted man proves that he can run a war as well as they can. Also, you physically assaulted an officer, which looks black," Abe replies.

Both Abe and Orth talk a great deal about the situation and conclude late in the afternoon. Several other meetings took place and then the trial commenced. A good many of the men who were with Orth during combat, plus Captain Arnold Berkmister, Corporal Joe Rosales and Sergeant Steve Iverson came. An evening before the trial Orth was visited in his barracks by Rosie Rosales and Steve Iverson. They were not supposed to be there, but they used stealth to gain entry.

The three men sat and talked like all GIs...on the edge of bunks.

"Remember Charlie Prince, Ortie? Steve asks. Prince was a black PFC. in the 24th Infantry Division Artillery who joined the Army to escape from a small Texas town where the mentality of the populous deemed the abolishment of slavery was a disaster wrought upon the South. Charlie Prince used to tell stories about his life and how during Saturday nights it was accepted social protocol to drag Main Street up to the Dairy Queen drive-in then turn around and start the round robin again. Charlie felt it was a boring idiotic existence so he enlisted.

"Yah, I remember Charlie. What happened to him?" Orth replies.

"Well, he bought it...He was coming back off the hill from the 24th's TOC and was ambushed by infiltrators. He managed to fight them off, but a grenade blew his legs off. He died quickly. Always liked Charlie, and that damned saxophone he used to play in the barracks," Steve related.

Rosie adds, "Charlie told me once that in combat one sometimes acquires the strength of an ant who carries off the body of an insect ten times his size – and how bravery was fearing what one ought and not that which one ought not. That's Charlie. Can't forget the time we were positioning a 155 Howitzer at Sill and he just picked up those stabilizers and swung that gun around like it was a toy – just laughing all the time."

"Damn, what a waste," Steve said, and added, "I seem to recall that the Prussian way of discipline in the 1800's was to sink and degrade all intellectual faculties and reduce the enlisted men nearly as possible to mere machinery, which was I suppose effective on slobs who are weird, non-patriotic, desperate low lifes. I see maybe why they are hot to have your ass, Ortie."

They all laughed. Later on Regie came in, "Cheerio, Chaps."

"How did you get in Captain?" Orth asked.

"Well, I just sort of informed the guard that I was part of the prosecuting team for the Judge Advocate, and the lad snapped to attention and that was that," Regie replied.

They sat and talked some more. Regie adding, "It seems a bloody shame, Ortie, ol' boy, if you had not taken over and word got out that the General had bought it, well, morale all along the front would have received a jolly-good jolt. That has been seen throughout history."

They all agreed, then Regie added, "In the British Army, officers don't have to know very much because the enlisted lads run things for them and it works quite well. The sergeants and officers have this tacit agreement and stay out of each other's way."

"I must run along, Chaps," Regie announced, "I have a meeting with Lieutenant Rapaport in a few minutes. He will pummel me with a lot of questions, and I'll tell him my summary thought that you did the right thing as nothing will ever be attempted if all possible objectives must be overcome. Time in combat is crucial. Well, cheerio, lads!"

With that Regie smiled and departed.

* * *

It is Saturday morning at home port and Orth usually mows the lawn at this time. It is also late October and some leaves have fallen and Orth thinks to himself that only a few more mowings will be needed before winter starts his thundering Wisconsin blitzkrieg. He has had his three cups of black coffee

SECOND LIEUTENANT ABE RAPAPORT, ORTH'S DEFENSE ATTORNEY – TALKED A GREAT DEAL ABOUT THE CASE AND TRIAL....

and fruit and he pulls his old Army field jacket off the kitchen hook and heads out the back door. The farmers are roaring about the fields harvesting corn and soybeans. Mutnik comes out from his shelter in the barn and greets Orth with tail wagging a mile a minute.

"Baa-rat-Baa-rat," the mower starts after several pulls and Orth starts the task of cutting the nearly one-third acre of lawn under the shade trees. It usually takes him about three hours with his push mower. He favors the push mower because it gives him needed exercise. He will not walk today on the country roads because this is "Yard Duty" day.

He finishes the mowing and heads indoors to prepare himself dinner, consisting of cooked wheat and oat cereals. He sits down and eats while reading a biography of the Krupp industrial dynasty of Germany. The phone rings and it is Nancy Steinmann.

"Can I come and live with you?" Nancy jokingly asks.

"You know the answer to that – you couldn't stand me – I'm too much of an independent introverted beast. Besides you're a Jew and I'm a Christian," Orth chides.

"I'll become a Christian if you let me come," Nancy says. Orth laughs and they talk for a short while and Orth ends it by giving his usual light-hearted reply to Nancy's plea for him to come and visit her in Salt Lake City.

"I'll see – perhaps in March."

His thoughts wander after the phone call and go back to Abe Rapaport, the Jewish Army lawyer who successfully defended him in Japan. Abe had a way of discussing things that made him interesting to sit and listen to. He once commented that most wars involve money as well as religion and how the Spanish under Queen Isabella fought the Moors and persecuted all non-Catholics during the Inquisition. Hitler's blood bath against the Jews and Communists. Muslims killing Christians – and how the Communist doctrine endeavored to eliminate religion and anything metaphysical as bourgeois claptrap. How God must laugh at these puny mortals! Orth thinks about the trial.

*　*　*

The Military Court was convened in a one-story building. It was stark bare. The presiding officers sat at a long table with a Colonel in the center – he being the power. It was a cloudy overcast day – chilly as Orth sat next to Abe Rapaport listening to stories of witnesses and the rhetorical legal phrases of the attorneys. The prosecuting attorney's name cannot be recalled by this writer, but he was a major – stockily built in a clean, neat officer's dress uniform. He was slightly bald headed with a sharp narrow nose and deep set dark eyes. His mouth was wide and turned down at the corners. His whole appearance gave one the impression that he seldom smiled and had a bad case of irritating hemorrhoids. He seemed to gloat when he gained the advantage during the case. Abe Rapaport was calm and calculating - he spurned intimidation by the major. Abe's uniform was the common OD type – looking rather rumpled, and his tie seemed never straight – shirt collar was upturned at the corners, that gave the appearance of wings. Despite his appearance, Abe spoke brilliantly and one could easily perceive of his intellectual acuity.

The major opened the assault upon Orth.

"Gentlemen of the Court, I intend to show how under Articles 76, 89 and 90, Corporal Orth Schilling Volzenkoff on the day of the third of October, 1950, did physically strike a commissioned officer of the United States Army and did willfully disobey said officer's orders. Further, that Corporal Volzenkoff harbored latent desires of disrespect towards said officer and verbally abused him using abject and crude disrespectful language."

Orth moved uneasily in his chair.

Abe under his breath whispered, "Hold on, Ortie. It is a long ride yet."

"And furthermore, Gentlemen of the Court, said Corporal Volzenkoff did willfully and with designs to ennoble himself, and in a shameful and disrespectful manner, brought dishonor upon the U. S. Army and himself by assuming command of First Corps by impersonating an officer – the Corps commander, who had been mortally wounded in action."

The major continued for a while, then Abe Rapaport came out of his chair slowly and presented his opening comments.

"Gentlemen of the Court. You have all seen combat and have experienced the horror and confusion of it all. It is my intention to try to convince the Court that the actions of Corporal Volzenkoff were done without regard to self aggrandizement – rather done in the interests to aid his fellow soldiers in war. Corporal Volzenkoff, in an unselfish act, did those things he was trained to do. Those are to maintain his post, aid in the mission of the Army and perform those tasks he was trained to do in an efficient and timely manner. Gentlemen, I will further attempt to prove that the acts of Corporal Volzenkoff were indeed beyond the realm of normal activities and were indeed those of heroic dimensions, done above and beyond the call of duty." Abe resumed his seat and the trial commenced in the hearing of evidence and the calling of witnesses.

A series of witnesses were called including Lieutenant William Snowbert, who brought the action. Rosie Gonzales told how Orth, while visiting the front lines, successfully stopped a charge of North Koreans by leading a company of GI's in a phalanx with bayonets fixed. The Americans were out of ammo, so it was the only way they could repel the enemy. He further related how Orth advised some of the units to harass and confuse the enemy by using false frontal attacks, then moving around on the flanks to ambush from the rear and encircle which proved highly successful in several battles for Hills 362 and 574 in the Chanan Valley.

Steve Iverson was grilled intensely, but Orth remained calm. Steve told how once when he was driving Orth up to visit the 32nd Infantry Regiment south of Naktang he had told the officers to use scare tactics at night by making loud noises with horns – banging on buckets and so forth to delude and confuse the enemy. Which proved to be effective. And how he rallied the demoralized troops by his words and appearance.

"I think his youthful appearance inspired the young troops – all seemed to sit up and listen, even the older officers," Iverson said.

"Did you see Corporal Volzenkoff strike Lieutenant Snowbert?" the Major asked.

"Yes, and he had it coming. He had gone berserk. He wanted to run..." Iverson was stopped. The Presiding Officer instructed the witnesses to answer a simple "yes or no" to the questions. And so it continued.

Captain Reginald Arnold-Berkmister was called to the stand. Regie looked resplendent in his British dress uniform. His breast beheld many medals. He related how Orth had done a "bloody good job" of keeping the Corps operating and how in his opinion, as a combat veteran, Orth acted unselfishly and devoted to defend the Corps' position and acted in the best interests of the Army – nobody else being capable and available. Regie stated how Orth had used unusual perceptiveness in his job. For example the time he had ordered fires around front positions to deceive the enemy on thinking there were more troops there that there actually were.

"He was always concerned for the troops – ordered added helicopters and medical aid from Eighth Army and so forth," Regie added. "Corporal Volzenkoff's valor would probably compare to the courage of the early Christian disciples – giving his all to save his friends and buddies," Regie further said.

The Major objected, "I plead, Sir, that those remarks be stricken from the record, as they are the opinions of the witness and not fact."

Abe rose abruptly and interjected, "Sir! We are here assembled to decide if under combat conditions where the issues to be dealt with are vital to the war, if the accused acted in a dishonorable manner, or, to the contrary, acted for the best interests of the U.S. Army. Also, if Lieutenant Snowbert did, under Articles 99, 84 and 85B did, in fact, misbehave before the enemy, acted in a manner unbecoming an officer and gentleman, and did indeed intend to dessert with intentions to avoid hazardous duty. Therefore, I plead to you combat-seasoned officers to consider all of these remarks as vital and circumstantial to the welfare of the Army as well as the accused."

"Objection overruled. You may proceed Lieutenant Rapaport," the Colonel announced.

And the trial went on.

The Commander for the Third Division, General William "Iron Pants" Casebolt, had some kind remarks to say about Orth.

"Well, I had some doubts about Corporal Volzenkoff being the 'Eye' Corps commander, but I was desperate and needed a hell of a lot of help. The Chinese were pouring down out of the north. Corporal Volzenkoff had me set traps and using old vehicle parts to line the perimeters to slow down the enemy – and it worked beautifully. At night when we were running low on ammo, the Chinese came at us by the droves. They were stunned when they discovered many of their comrades falling into holes filled with sharp metal and some were impaled upon spears that we set in the barbed wire we laid. Morale was helped by Corporal Volzenkoff. The men seemed to have new heart. I remember another time when Corporal Volzenkoff and I were driving along in my jeep to visit some of the line positions south of Nantak when we came under fire from enemy rifles. We stopped under some cover and Corporal Volzenkoff got on the radio and called an artillery unit of the First Cavalry Division he knew was in the area by his maps. The artillery unit replied that it was out of their sector, whereupon the Corporal yelled back, 'I know it's out of your area – this is the Corps Commander and those sons of bitches are firing at me and I want to flatten their asses."

The courtroom erupted into laughter and the Colonel called for, "Order in the Court." The trial continued for several days.

Finally Lieutenant Snowbert took the stand. He lied repeatedly stating that he was calm after the blitz of the Main TOC, and that Corporal Volzenkoff and the other enlisted trash had mauled him when he attempted to perform his duties. Lieutenant Rapaport saw through his ploy and commenced to reduce him to a babbling nincompoop.

"Did you or did you not tell Sergeant Iverson that they should abandon the Jump TOC?"

"Why, of course not. I told him to stand fast and we would set things up to run it as the Main TOC," Snowbert replied.

"Mmm," Abe hummed. "Were you or were you not hunched over your desk, head in your hands and uncontrollably weeping?" Abe continued.

Smirking, Lieutenant Snowbert rolled his eyes replying, "That is an absurd lie. I was calmly pondering the situation, preparing plans."

The questioning continued. Finally at the conclusion of the trial, Snowbert was placed on the witness stand.

"Can you describe what happened at the Field Hospital, after Captain Arnold-Berkmister took you there?" Abe inquired.

Lieutenant Snowbert replied, "I was placed in a separate tent where I rested …tha-tha-that's all I can recall."

"Is it not true, that the doctors there had to treat you for a mental condition described in their records as 'Extreme shock and schizophrenia – unable to function in a rational manner'?"

Lieutenant Snowbert sat visibly shaken – examining his hands – then blurted out, "That's all a lie – those damn medics don't know their ass from a hole in the ground!"

"If it pleases the Court, I request that Doctor Morrison and Sergeant Kohler be flown over from Korea. They are at the 745th Field Hospital in the Eye Corps Sector somewhere north of Placu."

Lieutenant Snowbert vehemently protested, saying, "Now that's not necessary...those galoots will lie to save their own asses...this whole thing stinks... I, I, I..."

Lieutenant Snowbert was led from the Courtroom shaking and trembling, his head hunched down on his chest. The room sat in stunned silence for a while. The Judges dismissed themselves to consider the verdict.

"The Court finds the Defendant not guilty of those charges he was accused of. The Court finds Second Lieutenant William A. Snowbert guilty of the charges of intent to dessert his post to avoid hazardous duty; conduct unbecoming an officer of the United States Army; and committing an act of misbehavior before the enemy. However, in light of his medical condition, sentence has been mitigated. He is to be admitted to the Army Medical Hospital, Walter Reed, Denver, Colorado, for treatment and upon release, to be returned to civilian life. Those men who assisted Corporal Volzenkoff in the duties he assumed as Eye Corps Commander are exonerated from all charges and are to be returned to their units." The Colonel announced in a rigid and stern manner.

The Colonel then added, "This Court further declares that the acts of Corporal Volzenkoff in the discharge of his duties in the heat of battle and combat, commendable and laudable. The Court recalls a similar case in 1870 during an artillery duel between France and Prussia, wherein a Prussian Sergeant assumed command over a Corps upon the demise of his commander. The Court noted that Corporal Volzenkoff did not deny the facts and seemed ready to accept the consequences of his actions. A person who denies anything either does it because he condemns it or considers it detestable, or is unable to or unworthy to admit the truth, or good of it. This Court, convened under Article 19 of the Uniform Code of Military Justice is hereby adjourned."

With that, the Colonel slammed down the gavel, "Crack!", raised his tall, lean frame up and snappily walked from the Courtroom followed by the other presiding officers.

Abe and Orth shook hands. "Thanks, Sir, for your help…" Orth quietly said, while tears welled in his eyes.

"I would not have taken the case if I had not believed that you were being unjustly accused…It was my honor and joy to act as your lawyer, Orth," Abe warmly recited. They stood for a few moments while Captain Regie, Rosie and Steve came up to Orth and smiled and hugged each other. Somehow, all knew that this would be the last time they would meet and it was an emotional quiet time.

Soldiers are taught through experience that friendships here on earth are but brief fleeting moments. And they expect that somewhere on the other side of mortality they will assemble again through the grace of God, and be members of a loving, peaceful community not governed by gunpowder and silly nationalistic philosophical pride. Brothers will be brothers, rather than enemy facing enemy. Praise be to Christ Jesus and the blood he shed to save the wretched world – and the love of His Father – yea, even the immortal God in Heaven, the Master of the Universe and space beyond – Author and Master Economist of Love and Wisdom infinite and faultless!!

CHAPTER XV

And I will pray to the Father and He will give you another Helper, that He may abide with you forever...

(John 14:16)

After the trial Orth received orders to report to the Replacement Depot, Fort MacArthur, Seattle, Washington. He was packing his barracks bags in his upstairs room when a knock on his door announced the entrance of Captain (Chaplain) Scholder.

"Greetings, Ortie. Hope I'm not interrupting."

"No, not at all, Chaplain...I am just getting things together. I pull out early tomorrow for the States," Orth replies.

"Well, that is good news, is it not?" Chaplain Scholder asks.

"You bet! Can hardly contain my enthusiasm." Orth cheerily states as he locks shut one bag and starts to fill another. But he stops and sits on the edge of the bunk. Chaplain Scholder sits on the opposite one facing Orth. They talk about the trial, luck, religion and life's tribulations.

"You know, I prayed for you Orth. I prayed that the Holy Spirit visit you and give you peace and calmness during the trial...Did you feel it?"

"Actually, I guess I did...I felt sort of a warm settling notion inside me... like I did not care *how* the trial turned out. I did what I thought best and that's that." Orth says.

They talk further. Orth still feels fidgety about religion, yet has a deep sense that there is something there and he holds admiration and respect for the Protestant Christian believers and the men of the cloth.

"Good luck to you, Orth," Chaplain Scholder says as he turns to depart.

As he is about to step outside Orth runs to the door and says, "Oh, say, Chaplain – could you kind of pray for Lieutenant Snowbert? He's in a sad shape and I always liked him before our difference, and oh, yeah, tell him I'm sorry I hit him."

Captain Scholder smiles, saying, "I already did," hugs Orth and walks out.

Orth stands for a moment in the doorway and looks up into the clear night sky. The stars seem to be winking at him saying, "All is well my son... God has things well in hand."

The trip back to the U.S. was by troop transport that landed in Seattle. The ship was full and Orth was crammed into a small spot with bunks four high. It was a miserable journey, most men were seasick and underweight. Orth was spared the awful task of "KP", but was detailed for mess check. Mess check consisted of sitting at a small table and making certain each man presented a small white card that had an officer's signature. This was a "Class 'A' Rations Card" and it had a Form Number. The Army numbers everything and writes volumes of Regulations making it a system of highly organized confusion and inefficiency. For example, a can opener you used opening "C" rations, which is canned food is called a P-38. If you go temporarily insane because a shell burst lands close to you and you shit in your drawers and cry out, then you are "Section Eight". And so it goes. Form 10 is your Pay Record. Your military history is Form 214.

The ship docks and Orth finds himself awaiting further orders. He is given a "Class-A" pass which means he can leave the Base after 1700 hours daily and does not have to report back until the following morning at 0600. He enjoys this momentary casual life, especially after the hell of combat. Upon several occasions he visits Seattle and watches the ships and sailboats traversing the locks. He has always been fascinated by the sea and ships and supposes that all men harbor similar desires...to sail off into the vast oceans of the world – men carving their destiny, pitting their wits against Triton and his wrathful ocean storms and tides. Ah! The romance of it all as he leans on the railing along the port and sees men working on the boats – repairing, painting or simply exchanging stories.

He enjoys Seattle but laments that it seems to be raining constantly. When he gets up in the morning and goes walking amongst the tall evergreens, the air is clear and crisp...then around mid-day it clouds over and rain is accompanied with a chill wind from the northwest. He recalls life in rural Wisconsin this time of the year, late spring. The sun would peep over the hills and into the dairy barn in the morning. Fritz would be about through milking and the calves and heifers would be yelping for the feed. Fritz would be ill-tempered and be chiding Orth to "get on with it", and so forth. He thinks about home, Eddie Burran, Bessie Ordway, going to Sunday School with them, seems like ages ago.

The Army arranges for the soldiers to go on tours...the Coors Brewery, Seattle Rainers Baseball games. He went on several of these. All the GI's were in uniform and Orth did not feel at ease when he wore his. He spurned attention and did not want to be treated as a hero. After all, he thought, "there were plenty of World War II men out there in civilian life that probably endured as much pain and hell as he had." He further guesses, "those men who have been in battle do not seek accolades, they just seek quiet and peace. They remember their buddies and how they 'bought it', spilling their blood on some foreign hillside, rice paddy, or forest. And they felt like they should be there with them." After all, Orth thought, is he any better than the buddies he had known who had their bodies maimed and are dead over there; Lieutenant Treat, Tom Tolliver, Bob "Chopsticks" Chang, and the names went on and on.

"My God!" He aches so inside, thinking about the politicians and high rolling officers who use words such as "freedom, bread, security" in a cavalier, supercilious and trite manner. All empty catchall mottoes to delude the simple minded population!

"Am I becoming a commie?" Orth thinks to himself, "There's got to be a better way." Then somewhere off in the distance he hears the mournful, yet beautifully serene sound of church bells.

"Golly, that's pretty," he says to himself.

The Red Cross sent word that Frederick was ill and that he should phone home immediately.

"Your father is in the hospital here in Oesterich," Bertha haltingly says over the phone. They talk briefly and Orth says he will apply for emergency leave, and will phone her back tomorrow. Orth is saddened. He loves his father immensely in spite of his drinking problem and lack of attention to details around the farm. Fred loves his sons, and Orth recalls how he always kissed his sons in the old German style. Fritz never had anything good to say about Fred...usually speaking to him in a derisive, disrespectful manner. But his dad absorbed the verbal abuse quietly and kept up a cheerful demeanor through it all.

Frederick died before Orth reached his bedside. The funeral was held in a parlor in Oesterich. Fritz, Orth and Bertha sat together in a side room during the service. There was no Church service. Orth was in uniform and cut a handsome figure. Fred was lowered into his grave in a small cemetery close to the farm. Bertha was not taking it well. She seemed to be detached from reality thinking that Fred was still here. She started to drink, heavily at times. Orth supposed she wanted to numb her sadness. She had no interest in life anymore. Fritz was no help. He mocked and ridiculed her as much as he did Fred, his father.

A good many of Orth's old school mates were at the funeral; Declan Anglow Joe Gariotta, Louie Gonzalo and so forth. Uncle Humphrey was not there as he never had a great amount of respect for Fred, however, he did send a large spray of flowers.

Orth returned to Fort MacArthur after a three day visit. Upon his return and report in to the Replacement Company Headquarters, he was greeted with his awaited assignment from First Corps.

> "Special Orders 19-046…Volzenkoff, Orth Schilling, RA 19-375-236 Cpl, E4, PMOS, 74B is hereby promoted to the rank of SGT, E5…SMAP, Sgt. Volzenkoff is further assigned to Training Detachment Echo, Fort Benjamin Harrison, Indianapolis, for training and is to report nlt, 0600 hours 1 Feb. 1953…"

Orth was elated! He had been assigned to the Finance School to train as a Finance and Accounting Clerk, something he had applied for recently, but thought the Army had summarily disposed of his request in a waste basket. He was to retain is Primary MOS (Military Occupational Specialty) as an Artillery Targeting Clerk, but this new opportunity meant a respite, at least, from a front-line, mud-slogging dogface.

Other orders soon followed in rapid succession awarding him the following medals:

Distinguished Service Cross
Silver Star
Purple Heart
Presidential Unit Citation, awarded the 24th Infantry Division.

These awards were presented formally during a parade at the Post. Several other soldiers received similar medals and they stood beside the Commanding Officer, as the troops passed in review. The band came by, "thump-thump-thump," and Orth was embarrassed, started to cry. He tried to hold back but his whole body shook. He was so happy and proud because someone had taken the time to recognize his unselfish efforts to help others. "But..." he thought to himself, "these are not my medals, but belong to all those buddies, dead and alive, who gave it all to help...the Bob Changs, Tom Tollivers, Steve Iversons, etc."

Then he thought of his Dad, Fred, recently deceased, and down deep in his bosom, he said to himself, "Hi, Dad, it's for you...thanks for your devoted love. I'll miss you, wish you could have been here." And with that he seemed to hear a distant voice calling quietly in his ear, "I was with you, Ortie."

* * *

"How about Church Sunday?" Orth asks Libby over the phone. "Then we can do brunch afterwards at the Lodge at the Lake, bring Danny along." Libby has a lot of things planned that she has to do, but she enjoys Orth's companionship and feels Danny needs a man's friendship.

"Sounds lovely, Ortie, do I need to bring anything?" Libby cheerily replies.

"Nothing, just your smiling, charming self. I'll swing on by about nine thirty. I need to be there early to practice singing in the choir."

It is late summer at Home Port and the Sunday morning of 7 September 87 is bright and cheerful to Orth as he backs Whitey out of the garage to head for Libby's apartment then to the Methodist Church in New Hesse. Deer hunters are out and roaming the fields much to the chagrin of Orth, who feels the deer have the disadvantage and he feels sorry for them.

"Why not issue the deer bloody M-16's and make it a jolly bang-up war?" he thinks to himself. "Ah–well, Ortie, ol' boy, you're getting to be a puritanical ass – an old fart," he further thinks. "Did I turn off the coffee maker and the stove? That's the thing about old age, your memory seems to take a vacation." He turns around and heads back up the hill. Mutnik is there wagging his tail as Orth enters the back door to check things. Then, once again, he heads down the lane for Libby's place.

Libby and Danny are waiting as Orth pulls up to the apartment building.

They drive off. Libby has a colorful dress on and Orth notices how she has an attractive figure in spite of her advancing middle age. Her breasts are firm and she has a pretty face. In the Army she would be described as a real "looker" or "nice chick". Orth does feel emotionally drawn to her. Yet he is fighting the loss of Donna, his wife, and he is defensive.

"How would his sons react to him getting married again, and worse to a woman almost thirty years younger," he ponders. "Yes, I'm 62 years old, but I believe I can still perform my tasks as a bed partner. Heck! I'm lonely for the smell and touch of a female!"

Libby places her hand upon Orth's as they drive towards New Hesse. Danny sitting on the outside doesn't seem to notice as he gazes out the window at the passing traffic. Danny *is* well mannered and Libby is concerned that he not adapt to the wretched ways of the modern teens.

"Paul isn't preaching today," Orth says.

"Oh?" Libby replies. "Who is?"

"A chap recently retired from the Navy, as a Navy Chaplain, name of Mike Wilinda. Haven't met him, so I don't know what to expect. Paul's getting along in years and maybe Wilinda will take over after Paul is put to pasture," Orth concludes as they pull into the Church parking lot. The choir was led, as usual, by Bernadette and after singing the Processional sang as the Anthem, "How Great Thou Art."

> *Oh Lord my God! When I in awesome wonder*
> *Consider all the works Thy hands have made,*
> *I see the stars, I hear the mighty thunder,*
> *Thy power throughout the universe displayed.*
> *Then sings my soul, my Savior God to Thee:*
> *How great Thou art! How great Thou art!*
> *Then sings my soul, my Savior God to Thee:*
> *How great Thou art! How great Thou art!...*

Orth gazed out into the congregation and perceived a ray of sunlight that peeped through a side window fall upon Libby, and she looked serene as their eyes seemed to meet. She looked so fresh, hands in her lap. Libby gazed at Orth in the choir loft, tall upright, a young man by all standards. Although he wore glasses, his features were finely chiseled and his frame was lean and sturdy.

"It was easy to be with him, he seemed to understand my hurts and needs," Libby thought.

Reverend "Mike", as he called himself was a warm, humorous, deeply intellectual man. He was like Orth in physical appearance, tall, lean, angular. He had thin balding blond hair with deep set blue eyes that seemed to hide under dark thick eyebrows. He was in his Navy uniform as he had a month more till retirement, and as he put it, "was still on active duty." He wore sleeve lace as a Commander and set a striking handsome figure from the provincial pulpit of New Hesse. Yet he was not stiff nor sanctimonious – to the contrary – his manner was easy and he inferred that he was against "big church gimmickry and pompous tapestry." This delighted Orth, as he thought there was too much of the stiff organizational traditionalism, wooden pew stuff in the Methodist Church – not the down to earth evangelical Wesleyan spirit.

When the choir sang, Mike popped right up from the pulpit chair and joined in with them. He had a beautiful tenor voice and added needed vitality to the choir. Later in the service, he sang a duet with his pretty brunette wife, Linda.

"What a Christian couple!" Orth mused. "God has blessed them enormously."

Mike spoke about "Eternity." His scriptural reference was from Matthew 25: 31-46:

> ...Then the righteous will answer Him saying 'Lord, when did we see You hungry and feed you, or thirsty and give You drink? When did we see You a stranger and take You in, or naked and clothe You? Or, when did we see You sick, or in prison and come to you?' And the King (Christ Jesus) will answer and say to them, 'Assuredly, I say to you, inasmuch as you did it to one of the least of these My brethren, you did it to Me!"

"You can learn from old people and humble people," Reverend Mike continued. "There was an old man in my home town, named Arthur Plate – when I knew him in 1972 he lived on the edge of town in a small, yet neatly kept home. Eighty-seven years old, self-taught, his school education ended at the sixth grade. Yet through determination, he became the local School Superintendent and a Circuit Judge. He felt he had a special calling from God to

"REVEREND MIKE – A SOON TO BE RETIRED NAVY CHAPLAIN GAVE HIS FIRST SERMON IN UNIFORM AS HE WAS STILL ON ACTIVE DUTY...."

serve Christ, and this he did by placing signs on the sidewalk, on walls, and he handed small cards to people. All had the same wording – one word. And that was 'Eternity'. People asked him, 'Why do you do it?' and he replied, 'God told me to do it.'"

Orth enjoyed Mike's warm enthusiastic nature. After the service, Orth,

Libby and Danny met briefly with Reverend Mike in the Reception Hall where coffee was being served, and the congregation had an opportunity to meet Commander Wilinda. Mike was interested to discover that Orth was retired from the Army and he tried to press him about his experiences. However, Orth has always been extremely reluctant to discuss his Army life with anyone. Libby has been an exception. Later, a few months, it was announced that Reverend Paul would be moving to another Church in another town and that Mike Wilinda would be the new Pastor at New Hesse.

Orth, Libby and Danny drove to the Lodge at Lake Ehai where on Sundays it was a ritual to enjoy a large sumptuous buffet brunch. The Lodge was a beautiful rustic type building with an enormous stone fireplace at one end. There were large windows that overlooked the lake and a dock area where boat owners could pull up – secure their boats and walk the long, sloping lawn up to the Lodge for dinner. They were lucky – the young blond waitress assigned them to a splendid table overlooking the Lake.

Danny, twelve years old now and curious about cars asks, "Orth, why do you drive a Japanese truck?"

Orth responds, "Well, you see, in the early twentieth century, Japanese engineers were trained in Germany. Essen, in the Rhur Valley, and were schooled in the Krupp industrial methods of building machinery. They learned well and took the knowledge back with them to Japan. The airplanes, trucks, ships, guns and so forth, that they used during World War II were designed almost by Germans and proved excellent weapons, unfortunately for the U.S. After the war that German know-how was used by the Japanese to build Toyota, Mazda and other makes of cars and ship them worldwide. Their road records proved vastly superior to those of the United States – and forced the United States to enforce more efficient quality standards. They were simply losing the edge in the markets. So, that's it, Danny. My light weight pickup serves me well and is reliable. I will trade her in after 100,000 miles for another like her."

"MMMM," Danny replies and adds, "I think I'll have some more waffles and strawberries."

"You didn't have much to say to Reverend Mike about the Army," Libby quietly chides Orth.

"You know the reason, Libby. I've already told you too much – I want to bury the whole mess." Orth does not look at her but through the window out upon the Lake. "Mike's an officer, once more a Naval one. There is a vast gap between us. I cannot find words to effectively describe the battle field." Orth continues, "you know, once I saw a fellow GI robbing some dead corpses of our soldiers for their few coins, watches and so forth. I became so damned enraged that I rushed over, ripped off his helmet and hit him in the head with my rifle butt. He fell over stunned and I left him in the red mud. I walked away and puked. He lived because I saw him later at Fort MacArthur. But I tell you one thing, he will remember that blow."

"Sorry, Ortie," Libby says.

"That's okay, you understand me," Orth concludes. Danny returns to the table.

They finish brunch and Orth drives Libby and Danny home where Libby invites Orth in for coffee. They sit and chat.

"Play chess, Danny?" Orth asks.

"Not really, some of the kids at school play in the Library at noon time. I just watch," Danny says.

"Let's play. I see you have a set there on the bookshelf," Orth relates.

They play while Libby busies herself in the kitchen. Orth explains the moves to Danny who is an alert and perceptive young man. The game is finished quickly and Orth and Danny go outside to a small park across the street where they toss a baseball back and forth. Libby watches them out the window after she has placed the week's laundry in the dryer.

"Brrrrr-Ring," goes the phone. "Libby?"

"Yes."

"It's Barney – What's up?" Barney Blitzgreez calls Libby often and shares the local gossip with the crowd at Frederick's. It is a friendly relationship – platonic. "All the gang miss you, Libby. We see Ortie on his regular visits to town, but not you."

"Well, I've been busy, Barney. Work, Danny and all that," Libby relates.

"Eddie got into another brawl Friday night during the dancing. Yah, some big football player type knocked him down. The police hauled him off... That galoot will never learn. Otto is becoming fed up with the fool," Barney laments. They talk some more.

"Got to run, Barney," Libby concludes.

"Okay, Libby. Say 'hi' to Ortie. He's getting to be a regular with you, hay?" Barney chides.

"He is a true friend and has helped me more than anyone in my sordid life. Cheerio, Barney," Libby concludes.

Danny and Orth return from the park and sit at the kitchen table while

Libby pours them iced tea. Libby joins them.

"I did enjoy Mike's sermon – he has a simple, down to earth nature. And his sense of humor delighted me," Libby says.

"I'm glad you did," Orth says, adding, "While I am sitting there in the choir loft, I kept thinking about what Lafayette said during the Revolutionary War...it was something like, 'The time has come to rally to the cross of Christ! The standards of love, liberty, equality and order....it is this alone –that it is our Christ a duty to defend against encroachments from abroad and against infringements at home. The incurable delusion that ideas can be gotten rid of by the use of force...that thought can be conquered by fisticuffs.' I think Mike's comments about big business – big institutionalism in the Protestant Churches is similar. The cross of Jesus – that is, the primary job is to spread the word of Christ, by whatever means it takes. I get the distinct feeling that the Methodist Church is suffering from administrative constipation. Too concerned about the minor details instead of keeping their eyes on the goal – the cross of Christ. The Master said, 'Go ye and preach to the nations,' he didn't say 'Go ye and build brick buildings, hold ice cream socials, monthly committee meetings, write Sunday School manuals, etc.' I suppose I'm overly critical, but they sit in Sunday School classes following some booklet invented by a career theologian in Nashville. That's reinventing the wheel."

Orth sits silently for a while, then looks at his watch. "Got to dash off – sorry to have been such a boor," he concludes. Orth heads for Whitey holding hands with Libby. Danny stays behind and gazes at the instruction booklet for the chess set.

"Thanks for brunch, church and everything. Danny said he really likes it when you come around," Libby quietly says as she gazes up into Orth's eyes. They hug, and Orth says, "You are a treasure in my life – call you later?"

"Make it often," Libby says and with that Orth gathers his long lean frame into Whitey and heads off to Home Port.

***

Indianapolis in February is cold. When Orth stepped off the train the wind was blowing and with the chill factor, the locals said it was about minus twenty, and Orth felt it. He had packed his winter gear in his barracks bags that had been checked through. Fort Benjamin Harrison was a beautiful old Army Post, but the Finance School was in a four story modern structure. Life was easy here compared to the Artillery and Infantry. You fell out in the morning at 0600, had breakfast (or "chow" in Army jargon) then classes from 0700 until noon; classes from 1300 (or 1:00 p.m.) until 1600 (4:00 p.m.), then you were released until the following day.

Orth was senior man in "E" (Echo) Detachment and as a sergeant with combat experience, was assigned Detachment Leader. There were three squads of twelve men each. Duties were as usual around barracks life – cleaning, KP (or Kitchen Scullion) and so forth. The First Sergeant of the Training Company was an older man who had seen action in World War II. He was white haired, plump, and was always with a cigar in his mouth, when not outside. He hailed from Alabama and spoke with a slow deep southern drawl. His name was Albert Casebolt, "Case" to the troops. All the men liked Case – he was easy going but stern when required. Orth enjoyed listening to his yarns about home, and Case liked Orth and tended to show more sympathy toward him because of his Korean experiences. School was sixteen weeks. It passed rapidly for Orth. After graduation he had a pass to go home before reporting to Sixth Army Headquarters, Presidio, San Francisco.

So, our hero, takes a greyhound bus back home to Oesterich, a dreadful six hour stint. Orth read and slumbered. No one met him at the bus station and he thought something must be wrong. It was. Bertha was in the hospital, and Fritz was carrying on at the farm by himself. He sat for a while in the small depot, thinking. Then the ticket agent, who closes for lunch said, "Ortie, I'm going out your way and would be happy to drop you off."

"Thanks, Pops," he knew him from school days in Oesterich. Pops was a regular at the football games. He was one of the officials.

"Mom is bad off," Fritz says as he sits at the kitchen table eating a late breakfast. "Doc Collins doesn't think she will make it. Kidney problems, and there just isn't the technical ability to solve them. And besides, she is old and overweight."

Orth stayed three days – visiting Bertha daily. She hardly recognized him. She seemed to be in a semi-conscious state. A few days later she passed away while Orth was on his way to San Francisco. The Army granted him emergency leave and he attended the funeral. This experience really hit Orth emotionally. He shook for hours. Could not seem to control the flow of tearful remorse. He thought, "Combat was nothing to this!!"

Well youngsters expect their parents and especially mothers to be immortal, beyond the grips of death.

He recalls as he travels back to San Francisco on the Union Pacific's "City of San Francisco" that there was a great release. "Bertha has been taken by God. She will be in the bosom of Abraham. No longer to suffer the life she had experienced here at the farm." Her's had been a hard life, yet she stood up, fought the pangs of poverty. A terrible blow to her was the loss of Fred. She seemed to lose all interest in life after that. Now, Fred did not name Fritz "Junior" or some such other appendage to distinguish between the two because he was adamant against the nature of the thing. It is felt the author has been cautious in his rhetoric so the reader may easily ascertain who is who.

Orth reports in at the Presidio and soon settles in at the Finance Office where he is assigned to the Disbursement Section. His enlistment terminated and he reenlisted for another four years. The readers may feel this madness. Perhaps it was, but Orth was young and enjoyed the chance of travel and the steady nature of the Army. So another four years to 17 May 1957. It will make his total Army time of seven years. Note, his initial enlistment from 17 May 1950 to 17 May 1952 had been extended by Presidential declaration.

In his duties as a Disbursement Clerk, he rises rapidly in position. He remains at the Presidio Headquarters Sixth Army for two years, then is assigned to Fort Bliss, Texas. In Texas he is promoted to Sergeant First Class E-7. He was promoted to Staff Sergeant E-6 in San Francisco. At Fort Bliss he is placed in charge of the Accounting Section, which was comprised of twelve men. Orth liked the assignment, but not the dry southern Texas area around El Paso. He had a separate room in the barracks and enjoyed the special privileges of a senior non-commissioned officer. The NCO Club was a large spacious edifice and Orth was a frequent customer. After the work day he would meet with others to exchange stories over pitchers of beer. He smoked, laughed and enjoyed the company. On Friday and Saturday nights there was a dance band. Orth liked to dance, after Bertha's patient instruction, and he sat there over drinks, dancing waltzes, rhumbas and fox trots with the women who came from town or lived on Post. One, petite brunette was a favorite of Orth's. She was medium height, had a nice figure and pretty face. Unfortunately, she was married, but her husband never came to the dance with her for reasons unknown. The writer cannot recall her name. She liked Orth, he felt, because she always came and rarely danced with anyone else. Orth held her close and liked her smell and feel the warmth of her body and her breasts upon his chest. Ah, yes! The female mystique – the beguiling and coyful character of the creatures!

Then disaster took hold. Her husband was transferred to Germany and Orth had to bid her "goodbye". He missed her, and she him. But that is life's hazards. Actually he supposed he had fornicated because he had a deep lust for her, but God spared him and led him from a possible catastrophe. How could he "love his brother" and then go to bed with his wife? His Sunday School instructions had given scruples, however loose they may be now. Certainly Bertha had kept him in her prayers – perhaps even Fred, his Dad.

CHAPTER XVI

Get wisdom! Get understanding! Do not forget, nor turn away from the work of my mouth. Do not forsake her, and she will preserve you; love her and she will keep you. Wisdom is the principal thing; therefore get wisdom. And in all your getting, get understanding.

Proverbs 4:5-7

Our hero completes his stint at Fort Bliss, and he receives orders to report to Fort Riley, Kansas – west of Kansas City. He is now forty years old, but has managed to retain his tall lean stature. However, he is still smoking, both cigarettes and cigars, plus enjoying his evening bouts with the troops at the Non-Commissioned Officers Clubs. His dress uniform is a wonderful array of medals, service stripes and overseas (Hershey) bars. He cuts a bold figure – young troops and officers respect and ogle at him. Yet humility has not abandoned him. He is still quiet and thoughtful of others. "Get wisdom", indeed! God has mysteriously blessed him with a voracious appetite to read. Yet his religious life, as yet, is vacuous. He begins to read light novels, then moves swiftly to more serious works by classical authors of the 17th, 18th and 19th centuries. Names like Tolstoy, Samuel Johnson, James Boswell, Cromwell, Thackeray came into his vocabulary. He had read earlier in life, but not at his present pace. And, his interests spanned wide fields, history, biographical and autobiographical works, science, arts, performing and fine, philosophy, religion.

He read several volumes by the Chinese author and philologist, Lin Yutang and gained new insights into eastern and western philosophies and the real treasure of the Christian faith. I suppose his favorite author was Leo Tolstoy because he saw his own life sort of parallel to his. Of course, he had many authors that he enjoyed. Mostly whose works he could learn from, who mastered the art of rhetoric and used a variety of words in an artful, intellectual and virtuous way. Oddly, he was repulsed by the modern pulp hacks who had to resort to off-color, lewd and street slang words and phrases to sell their trash. The public ate up cheap heroic, sexy and violent laced novels. The black arts, occult also irked Orth. God was earmarking him in His silent benevolent way for better things.

Thoughts about past friends flood his memories. He recalls how some were much more educated and culturally refined than he was and he learned from this. He began to see how intellect and wisdom are not closely coordinated with social or professional status. Friends he knew in the Army who were of lower rank than he seemed quite contented to read, play chess or tennis, or chat over a cup of coffee at the EM Club, (a club for those lower than a corporal - "EM", standing for Enlisted Men.) While he was at the NCO Club drinking too much, and smoking too much and using bad abusive language with his fellow buddy sergeants. Hah! The light seems to start to flicker into a small flame. Orth, deep down, begins to believe that wisdom and intellect are constantly the target of blockheads.

"Is this why officers, who discover one of their subalterns to be intellectually superior, are fearful and exert unusual unjust cuts toward them, because they feel inadequate?" Orth ponders.

He recalls reading somewhere, "the object of a higher education is to learn to endure boredom and injustice." Seems like a witty platitude – but is it? Men in the barracks alone reading seemed at peace – not bored like many GI's.

Fort Riley is on the plains of Kansas – flat country – cold that knocks the fillings out of your teeth and heat in the summer that makes Hades seem like an ocean breeze. The Finance Office was a one-story wooden building nestled under the Armpits of Post Headquarters, which was an impressive brick building. His duties at this office was to head the Travel and Commercial Accounts Sections. The Post is Headquarters for the 11th Airborne Division, plus several Air Cavalry Regiments. It is a busy place, having a large airport where it buzzed with helicopters and large cargo planes. Plus, an occasional lumbering C-119, or C-46 or C-47, planes he came to know plenty about in Korea and Japan. The old reliable C-47 (Civilian DC-3) was the favorite of the troops. Christened "Gooney Bird", they chugged along at 125 mph. One pilot remarked, "You could take a shower, lay down and snooze, and the old ladies would fly by themselves."

Orth remained at Fort Riley until 7 September 1960, then was transferred to Fort Leonard Wood, Missouri. He was kind of happy for the change. He had spent two years at Fort Riley and had "itchy feet" to go somewhere else. He phoned Fritz frequently and learned that he was carrying on, but is thinking about selling the farm, as it was too much to do on his own and the money wasn't there to install needed improvements, let alone keep up the repairs. Fritz seemed to be more understanding of Orth, but he still let forth an occasional barrage of mocking remarks. "Ah, well – forgive and forget," Orth thought.

His arrival at Fort Leonard Wood was accompanied by a pleasant array of Ozark Mountain scenery. The Fort is large and has a huge artillery range at the south end where one's ears are met with the frequent "thump-da-thump" of the 175MM and 8-inch guns being fired for practice.

Also, the Fort is home for the Army Engineer School, which trains Army, Marine and Navy personnel. Orth was surprised to be met with a gigantic Navy anchor placed on a hill as you enter the Fort. It was a memorial - given by the Navy to the Fort - a symbol of pride, gratitude and of course, the ever present "service jealousy". But when Orth saw the overpowering hunk of iron, he thought, "what's this? Is Missouri sinking?"

The Finance Office here was in a two story long brick building next to the hospital. Orth was placed in charge of the large Accounting and Disbursement Section. His new MOS (Army Specialty Code) was 70270, "Finance Supervisor". He didn't have to do much, but had plenty of headache cases to solve, error corrections, reports to edit, payrolls to audit, etc. There were many "WACs" in the office. Women in the Army. Some were attractive, some were there because their success in landing a husband had been less than expected.

Missouri was a pretty place, north were vast undulating fertile farm lands, south were the beautiful gentle rolling low hills of the Ozark Mountains. Not really "mountains" from what he had experienced in Korea, California (Sierras and Coastal Ranges) or the Rockies – majestically high monsters forming the Continental Divide. Lofty in Canada and gently lowering to New Mexico and Arizona.

Nevertheless, the Ozarks had their own beautiful personality. Lakes, streams, rivers dotted the area. Orth was not a fisherman. He tried fly casting, but woefully failed...Fritz was an expert at it and (as usual) mocked and

ORTH VISITED THE UNIVERSITY OF MISSOURI CAMPUS - HE DREW THE ATTENTION OF THE YOUNG COEDS BY HIS UNIFORM.....

ridiculed Orth's ridiculous attempts. Orth made frequent trips to many of the points of interest around the place. Charming, quaint farm towns, moderate sized cities – Jefferson City (Capitol), Columbia (University of Missouri). Little did he realize at the time that he would return to the University of Missouri, Columbia, where he would be successful in obtaining a Doctorate, Ph.D., in Business Administration. The University was a pretty campus. The main administrative building was a domed classic Romanesque type and it commanded the cluster of class buildings that formed the main campus quadrangle. Off in the east from the quadrangle was the gigantic Clock Tower that was a marvelous Gothic type with ornamental carvings on the facade.

On the particular day he visited the campus, he was wearing his summer uniform and often drew the attention of the young female coeds. They coyly and coquettishly eyed him and giggled. He enjoyed it secretly, "What man doesn't?" he thought. Of course, the young men were jealously inflamed, and feigned not to notice our hero.

"Ah, so life is all a deception – the art of man is to pretend to do something, then do something else," he thought. In battle, it was all ruled by deception – feign an advance here, then hit the enemy over there. The W.W.II invasion of France from England – a deception that failed! So – there you have it. Cut away all the false deceptions and there is a kernel of fact remaining.

What is "truth"? Christ was asked by Pilate, Orth recalls from his Sunday School days in Oesterich.

"I am the way, the truth, and the life," the Lord answered.

Orth thinks, "The dictionary says 'truth is absolute, indisputable fact, honesty, integrity, precision, exactness."

Well, I have read that Einstein explained that *everything* is changing. Aristotle said, "Everything has a beginning and end.

"Perhaps the clouds over my eyes *will* be removed. That Christ is indeed the epitome, personification the *one* thing that is absolutely 'Truth', that all else is not accurate, is not reality in the unchangeable or indisputable way."

Our hero begins to attend church at the Soldiers' Memorial Chapel. He feels comfortable there because all people in the Army are moving here and there and he is not subject to the gawks of provincials that prevails in small local churches. He is welcomed into the choir. He has always enjoyed singing and Tina, the Musical Director helps him enormously. Tina Lovelace, the wife of an officer, is from Alabama and speaks with a musical air of southern belles. She has a delightful soprano voice. So, Orth manages to sing rather regularly on Sundays, with practice Wednesday evenings at 1900. His appetite for tankards of beer at the Club has been abated to some extent, as he feels he may become addicted as many in the Army are.

The Finance Officer at the Presidio, Lieutenant Colonel Lawrence P. Worth was such. Colonel Worth, it seems, was on a lifelong drunken spell. He showed up at the office in the mornings bleary eyed and by day's end he was fairly well intoxicated. Orth nicknamed him "Wait and See", because whenever he was asked a question he would reply with his standard saying of, "Well, let's wait and see." Colonel Worth would sign *any* document coming into the office that looked halfway legitimate. Orth recalled that many of the invoices coming in for the purchase of rice from Japan lacked proper documentation, Purchase Orders, Bills of Lading, or Receiving Reports and "Wait and See" would approve the payment defending his action with a milquetoast comment such as, "Well, I'm headed for Federal Penitentiary anyway, besides, the Army has tacitly been told to support the Japanese economy."

Orth discovered later that "Wait and See" had been relieved of his duties at the Presidio and sent to Fort Juachuka in the desolate nothingness of New Mexico. Perhaps this was the Army's way to dry out Colonel Worth.

Orth still smoked, not cigarettes, but small cigars. He heard cigarettes caused cancer and this was an attempt to cut back. He was deceiving himself, actually, as he discovered later. The bloody cigars had about twice the dose of nicotine and tars.

He spent one year at Fort Leonard Wood. Orders were received for Fort Leavenworth, Kansas. He was to report NLT (not later than) 1 June 1961. He had some leave time coming, so he took a flight from Kansas City to Milwaukee to visit Fritz and some of his old friends around Oesterich. Prior to departure he received the happy news that he had been promoted to Master Sergeant E-8. The plane was a TWA DC-6, four engined plane, and the flight took about two and a half hours. The airport in Kansas City was almost standing in the center of town. The runway bordered on the KAW River. Orth wore civilian clothes, tweed sport coat and tie, on his head he wore an English style country tweed chapeau. To the casual observer he was a university professor, or wealthy land baron. From Milwaukee, he took the Greyhound Bus to Oesterich. Pops was there, but was aging fast.

Orth was successful in getting the only taxi in town, operated by a person whom he did not recognize, a youngish man, dark hair and beard. The cab was a beat up old Chevrolet, 1953 or so, color of green. The driver took Orth to the farm, hardly a word was exchanged between the driver and him, but he did find out that the taxi's main business was hauling elderly persons to and from the doctor's office or the market. He was a kindly chap and did not charge Orth anything for the ride. He said, "It's on me. Pops told me about your war experiences. See ya' later." And with that, he sped off waving.

The farm looked deserted. It was later afternoon, 6 p.m. and Fritz was sitting in front of an old television set he had acquired in a farm sale. At his feet were the remains of what appeared to be his supper.

"Sold the farm, Orth," Fritz said. "Hans Roesch, next door bought it, one third down and the balance on a mortgage of 2%."

"How much?" Orth asks.

"Hundred thousand. You'll, of course, get half after I settle all the debts and crap. Probably will come to about twenty-five thousand, give or take," Fritz concludes.

They talk a long while into the night. Fritz explained that the sale stipulated that the house remains with the Volzenkoff family, and that includes the barns and other out buildings. Orth was happy for Fritz, who seemed relieved that it was all over.

"Master Sergeant, huh? Well, I'll be damned. I never got above a dog-assed PFC. Well, the Army has gone to hell when my little brother makes Master Sergeant," Fritz playfully chortles. "Hungry?"

"No, not really," Orth replies. "I could stand a cup of coffee."

"On the stove," Fritz says as he turns to a different TV channel.

Orth spent three days at the farm and Oesterich, then heads for Milwaukee for his return flight to Kansas City and Fort Leavenworth. Fritz had driven him to the airport in Milwaukee, using Fred's old Dodge pickup truck. They hugged, then parted. Orth felt a new warmth for Fritz, who was all alone now on the farm. He explained that he had acquired a job milking for another farmer, Dick Leeterson, a Swede up the road.

"Good deal, five bucks an hour, weekends off, hospital benefits, a hell of a deal compared to what I had – working night and day, no time off and going further in debt each year," Fritz relates.

Fort Leavenworth is about forty miles north of Kansas City, and is the center for officer's staff and warfare training. The place is buzzing with officers running here and there to attend classes, meetings and such. Much of the Fort is old and dotted with brick buildings of the Civil War period.

Orth is assigned a separate room in the senior NCO Quarters, west of Post Headquarters, which had the ubiquitous old cannon embedded on the front lawn. Every morning and evening a detachment would raise and lower the colors (flag) and fire off an adjacent 75MM Howitzer..."KAA-BOOM!", then a bugler would play Reveille or Taps, if it were retreat (evening). This ceremony was accompanied by the playing of the National Anthem. If you were outside, you stopped in your tracks at the sound of the bugle and faced the flag. If you could not see the flag, then you faced where the sound emanated from. You stood at "rest" – hands behind your back clasped in a military fashion – head erect – not smiling; then when the National Anthem began, you came to attention (achtung!) snappily and saluted. You held this position until the music ended, then "ordered-arms", which meant you dropped the salute and resumed on your way.

If you were caught not performing this function, that meant an abrupt dressing down, and perhaps more severe penalties. Orth had several times noticed lately how some Army people took this responsibility lightly, especially the younger scamps. He dressed down several young soldiers, and one female WAC.

Orth visited Kansas City on frequent occasions. He enjoyed Kansas City. It had a distinct atmosphere. People around Milwaukee and Chicago always thought of Kansas City as 80% stockyards and 20% brothels. Not so! Orth was pleased to discover just the opposite. The City had culture and class. Many wonderful green parks, Opera, Symphony, Shakespeare, a wonderful Art Museum, good restaurants and friendly mid-western people. He read about the City and the State of Missouri, and discovered that it has a deep German heritage. Many of the names of people and places are Germanic-Prussian sounding. This aroused the Aryan blood in Orth's veins. The Germans are a proud lot – always entertain a deep-set belief that they are the chosen. And Orth thinks, that is what helped create the disaster of the Third Reich.

"But, my gosh! What country does not foster pride in the hearts of its citizens?" he surmises. "Should all the blame be placed on Hitler and the German people? How about France and England demanding such huge ridiculous reparation payments from the 1918 fiasco. People were starving in Germany. Riots broke out, people were being shot for a loaf of bread. Mothers eating the flesh of their children!" No, Hitler, a despotic charismatic demented stepped into a vacuum. This situation in Germany was chaotic, and the Brownshirts took advantage, Orth thinks to himself. "If France and England would have been more humane, and taken the advice of President Woodrow Wilson, the outcome of World History from 1929 to 1947 would, no doubt, have been considerably different," he concludes.

Orth did not re-enlist prior to his time which was 17 May 1964, and he was discharged on that date. He did, however, remain in the Reserves. He had enough – thirteen years, and wanted out to take advantage of his GI Bill benefits. So, our hero receives his discharge from active service and packs his bags to head for a life in California.

CHAPTER XVII

> *Does not wisdom cry out, and understanding lift up her voice? ...For wisdom is better than rubies, and all the things one may desire cannot be compared with her.*
>
> Proverbs 8:1,11

Orth travels from Kansas City to San Francisco, by flying and telephones Bob "Chopsticks" Chang's mother from the airport in South San Francisco. He has a keen desire to visit with Bob's parents to let them know what a dedicated soldier Bob was and how much of an impact he had upon his life. Bob's Dad picks Orth up at the United Airlines baggage claim and they drive to Mr. Chang's home in the Russian Hill District. The house is a "typical" San Francisco type, the garage underneath and two story house above. The bottom story was rented out to Chinese friends and Mr. Chang and his wife lived on the top floor.

"Bob was a brave soldier, Mr. Chang...he fought in a manner you would be proud of," Orth relates over the supper table. Mr. Michael Chang, always with dignity and suppressing emotion in the traditional Oriental manner, nodded as he looked into Orth's eyes, then said,

"What are your plans now? Do you have a place to stay?"

"I thought I would find an apartment, then see if I can get into college or university," Orth slowly said.

"Well, I would be honored to have you stay with us until you locate something, and my brother, Roger, is the Registrar at San Francisco City College. I'll give him a call and see if he can work something up. It isn't a name school, but it will be a start. They have a good name and the tuition is practically nothing. See how it goes, then transfer your credits to Berkeley, (University of California) Stanford or whatever," Mr. Chang suggests, adding, "that's what Bob did…"

So, with that, Orth stayed at the Chang's for about two weeks, finally locating a small basement apartment in the Sunset District, on 14th Avenue. He was readily admitted to San Francisco City College, where he enrolled for four classes. Basic courses in the liberal arts. He struggled because he had been absent from the classroom for so long, but he managed not to fail. His grades were average, but improving.

He located an Army Reserve Artillery unit at the Presidio and he attended weekend drills monthly. This would help him financially and he only required seven more years to attain retired status. Of course, he discovered, before he could draw retirement pay, he would have to reach sixty years old.

"Well, I'm in my forties now. What the heck, it will not be long," he thought. His economic position was not all that plump. He applied for a position at Wells Fargo Bank and was successful to land a job as a teller. This meant that he would have to arrange his classes at College, which he did and things seemed to work out relatively well.

After completing one year's study, Orth sat for the entrance examinations at San Francisco State College (now named University) and was admitted. He neglected to apply to other top named schools because he felt he was not of the privileged few with top grades, besides money was a pestering problem. He arranged his classes so that they were in the late afternoon and evenings. This allowed him to continue working at the Bank. He studied with diligence and his grades did improve slightly. His faculty advisor, Dr. Rasher, became a friend. He supposed because he was no doubt the oldest student he dealt with and he sympathized with him. Dr. Rasher, Ph.D., was Professor of Finance. He was of medium height, glasses on the edge of his nose, and his gray hair seemed never combed, always a jumbled mess. He abandoned being fashionable and his coat and trousers never matched. The ties he wore were the sources of many jokes from the male students, who joined Orth for smokes during class breaks. Dr. Rasher did not believe in brief cases. He carried his books, lecture notes and such materials to class and about campus in a cardboard box, labeled "Del Monte Peaches", or some such name.

Now, our hero approaches a mile marker in his life's journey. He kept passing a certain young coed on the walk from the Student Union building to the College of Business building. Soon they were saying, "hi" to each other.

On a certain afternoon, Orth went into the Union to have supper, prior to an early evening class that met at seven p.m. The Union was busy and he had difficulty locating a seat. He did eye a table that had four students sitting there, one happened to be the same young lady that he often met in the walk to class.

"May I?" Orth asked her as he eyed the one empty chair.

"Oh, yes, please do," she replied.

Orth placed his tray down and leaned over to sit and catastrophe developed. His tie end happened to find a convenient landing spot in his cup of coffee. When he straightened up, the tie emptied itself of its black contents all down the front of our hero's shirt, and light colored trousers. She laughed, other students gaped as if Orth was in some kind of a drunken stupor. And he wished he was, for then there would have been an excuse for his awkward mess! He was deeply mortified! He had a tie on because he had just come from the Bank, on the streetcar, to class.

So, after he settled down, he sat quietly for several minutes consuming his chicken a la king. She sat quietly also, pretending to read. Then their minds met, and they both spoke at the same time.

Orth said awkwardly, "I'm Orth," while she attempted, "hope your tie isn't stained." They both erupted in laughter, and then they talked delightfully together until it was time for Orth to walk to class.

"May I be so bold as to ask your name?" he said.

She answered, "Donna Lue Sregor," and further remarked about being from Wisconsin, a town just north of Oesterich, Orth's home town. It turns out that she was born in the same hospital as Orth, however seventeen years later. She was twenty-five, coming to California to escape from the small provinciality of Cockhan, Wisconsin.

The bonds were there. Orth and Donna met often at school and they dated frequently, going to movies, taverns, dances, football games or just walking along the beaches of Northern California.

Orth had purchased an ancient 1953 Chevrolet Sedan and he and Donna used to drive here and there in it. Or, just park at some lonely spot, talk and kiss and fondle each other. They talked about having children, life, families, school, etc.

DR. RASHER - PROFESSOR OF FINANCE WAS AN ECCENTRIC - HIS CLOTHES AND TRAITS WERE THE SOURCE OF MANY CAMPUS JOKES....

Orth finally garnered sufficient courage to pop the question, Donna accepted.

Orth Schilling Volzenkoff and Donna Lue Sregor were married at the Church of the Wayfarer, Carmel, California, on 10 January 1964. Paul Nippep, an ex-Army buddy acted as Best Man, and his girlfriend, Joyce Nutworthy acted as Maid of Honor to Donna. Donna wore a light blue frilly dress (she was still a virgin, however) and Orth wore a neat dark blue business suit. It was a private ceremony, only the four were present and the Episcopalian Priest. Neither Donna nor Orth were of the Church of England, but they were married here at the suggestion of Mr. Chang, who said it was a quaint little chapel (it was) and that Orth should honeymoon at the Highlands Inn Lodge, which has cozy, comfortable cottages that cater especially to newlyweds. The food and amenities at the Lodge were first rate. Orth and Donna enjoyed themselves, having cocktails before supper, and after dinner sherry before the roaring fire in the Inn's lounge. Paul proceeded to get ghastly drunk after the wedding and annoyed the Inn staff when he tossed a lawn chair and table into the swimming pool. But...after a while he sobered up and he and Joyce drove back to San Mateo to Paul's apartment.

Orth and Donna rented an apartment in San Mateo. It was a moderate place. They had no furniture, except a mattress, some blankets and minor other items. They used wooden crates and cardboard boxes for tables. It was fun – they did not mind – they were young lovers and life was their oyster.

Orth graduated from San Francisco State, receiving his bachelor's degree in Finance.

The graduation ceremony was held in the Football Stadium. Orth sat on the field on wooden chairs along with the other candidates. It was a pleasant day. Donna sat in the stand with the other spectators. An exciting day for Orth. Rick Jaggar sat with Donna in the stands. He was a friend of Orth's at Wells Fargo Bank. Rick was a joker – a jolly type – laughing often, of short stature – a graduate of the University of Idaho where he was a cheerleader. Rick and Orth formed a pair. Orth liked Rick's forever lively nature, he was the personification of a cheerleader, always sort of jumping around, joking, laughing. One time, as Orth was walking down a corridor at the Bank's main office, Rick saw him from a distance and proceeded to run at full speed and jumped into Orth's arms. It was as if it had been rehearsed.

Shortly before they were married, Orth, Donna, Rick and his girlfriend, Tina Whitecastle, a registered nurse, had supper at a small Italian restaurant in the North Beach sector of San Francisco. They had enjoyed several drinks before eating, so Rick was in an extremely joyful mood, even beyond his usual. During the course of the meal, Orth said, "I really like these red-checkered table cloths."

With that, Rick took the one from an adjoining table and handed it to Orth in a stealthful manner, saying..."It's yours, Ortie – a wedding gift." All laughed – Orth stuffed the cloth into Donna's oversize purse. When the waitress returned, she nonchalantly and unconcerned replaced the "lost" tablecloth…and this even added to the merriment of all.

Rick's girlfriend, Tina, was a cheerful type and Rick related to Orth that she enjoyed sex to the extent that she frequently invited Rick to her bed. Rick called her "Series 'E' Bonds", because she was a sure bet for a joyful sexual experience without any risk. Orth lost track of Rick after Rick departed from the Bank to seek his fortunes elsewhere, and he did; becoming an executive in the marketing staff of a large paper manufacturer.

Donna conceived quickly and was deeply miserable during the first few months of her pregnancy. She still attended college and took the bus from San Mateo to San Francisco, which meant that she often had to depart the bus prematurely to vomit at some gas station rest room or another some such place. She suffered the common female disorder, "morning sickness". Donna was not gifted as a creator of kitchen delights, so husband and wife suffered together through frozen prepared dinners, etc. Donna's first attempt at baking a custard pie, because Orth indicated that this was his favorite, ended in a disaster. The pie turned out to be a hard mass of eggs, flour and so forth – that resembled a metal garbage can cover, only harder. They laughed and enjoyed it anyway. Orth had to almost cut it with a hacksaw.

Orth, had a position change at the Bank. He applied for a position with the Auditing Department and was accepted. The pay was better and it gave Orth an opportunity to gain experience in a variety of banking functions. The drawback, however, is that he had to travel up and down the state of California. Donna understood. He would be home on the weekends if he had to be out of town on an assignment.

After a series of apartment rentals, Orth purchased a small house in Walnut Creek, California. It was on a hill, about two miles from the town center. It was a pretty place of wood with a quaint fireplace and small, but comfortable rooms. Donna liked it. When Orth had audit assignments in town, Donna would drive him to the Greyhound Bus stop…And she would pick him up. On one such day, quiet little Donna announced, "I've got to go to the hospital."

John Schilling Volzenkoff was born 11 November 1964. He was a healthy boy. Soon thereafter, Donna was with child again. this time her pregnancy was not as torturous. And on 26 December 1965, John's brother, Bertram Orth Volzenkoff came into this world. Now the Volzenkoff household was ablaze with baby cries and the stench of unwashed diapers. But it was a happy home. Orth loved Donna. The sons were his blessings. His position as auditor improved steadily. His responsibilities increased. And, he felt the urge to continue his education.

On a Saturday morning, he drove to San Francisco State College to sit for the GRE (Graduate Records Examination), which was a grueling thing that lasted almost the entire day. He was nervous...and could not seem to control his bladder. He was embarrassed. But he completed the tests and was accepted into the Master's Degree program, (MBA - Master of Business Administration). Orth was surprised to find out the results, because he thought, "for certain I bilged it, especially the bloody math parts." However, his algebra held up, thanks to the efforts of Ida Tross, his old teacher back at Oesterich High School.

Donna and Orth celebrated the day he received the good news. Donna invited one of her girl friends over and Orth invited one of his auditor buddies. They had a spaghetti supper with red wine and candles adorned the dining room table. Thereafter, Saturday evenings were spaghetti night with wine and candle light. Little John and Bert could never say spaghetti, it came out..."Buggetty".

Orth, again, arranged his classes at College to fit into his work schedule. Often, the crew chief of the audit team would allow him to leave the Bank early, so that he might meet his class on time.

The boys continued to grow, however, Bert was rather frail and needed constant attention. Donna had visits from her relatives from time to time. Her father and mother journeyed out from Cockhan, Wisconsin, and stayed several days. Orth did not find this visit enjoyable. Bill Sregor was likeable enough. It was just the fact that he rarely uttered a word. He was a small man...a rustic type that chain-smoked cigarettes, and would just sit and listen. Donna's mother, Marjorie, was just the opposite. She would cackle on like a proud hen...always gossiping about the "folks" back home. Orth had the distinct feeling that Marjorie disliked him. Over the dinner, or supper table, Marjorie would continually take the opposite view of Orth's. She seemed to delight in mocking him with the use of her homespun old wives' tales and provincial axioms. Donna sympathized with Orth, admitting that she and Marjorie never were close, and that Marjorie was one of the primary reasons for her leaving home so soon after high school.

"I just had to get away," she would exclaim.

Marjorie would sit in the kitchen and cackle away as Donna was preparing a meal or attending to the boys. She was short and roundly plump. Her hair was gray and she wore a long apron that looked as if she was ready to wash down a dairy barn.

More of Donna's relatives arrived at various times. The Sregor family was large, "breed like rats," Orth would playfully ridicule Donna, who didn't mind because she agreed.

Leyland Sregor had a doctorate in Chemistry and worked for the government in Idaho, doing something with environmental research. He was quiet, like his father, but his wife, again, was the opposite, and she cackled like Marjorie.

Then came "Little Will", Donna's little brother, Bill, who helped his dad in the plumbing business. Little Will was a fun person, bright, intellectual, and Orth enjoyed his company. Little Will was an ardent reader, a self-taught lad. His interest was politics and history. Little Will wrenched himself loose from Cockhan and came to stay with Donna and Orth while he attended a two-year college. He worked part time at a local restaurant in the evenings, cleaning and doing a moderate amount of cooking.

Little Will completed one year of college, then decided to enlist in the Navy. A disastrous move, according to Orth, but youth has its eccentricities. So, off Little Will went, to basic training in San Diego. He returned on several occasions, and finally was discharged after a four year stint, whereupon he became a postmaster in a small town in Wisconsin. Orth often lamented the fact that such a bright, intellectual soul as Little Will was wasted and died away in the backwaters of rural Wisconsin. Life's odd quirks.

Donna had a younger sister named Karen Joy. Karen was lively, short like Donna, but with blond hair. She had a petite figure, small breasts, but slender and attractive legs. Her eyes seemed to always be smiling and she had a personality that delighted in vexing those that held vain and false thoughts. She seemed to toy with people who thought too highly of themselves. Orth liked Karen. She livened up the house, playing with the boys and entertained herself, never a burden.

Karen Joy was divorced from a Wisconsin farmer and now worked as a customer representative for a large bank in Cleveland, Ohio. She had a bachelor's degree from Ohio Wesleyan University. From the marriage, she had two daughters.

Donna did not complete her studies at San Francisco State. Her domestic duties and the boys consumed her time. Orth completed his Master's Degree work and was awarded the Master of Business Administration on 14 June 1966. He was still in the Army Reserve unit at the Presidio as a Senior Master Sergeant...Section Chief, Fire Support Element, Eighth Corps Artillery.

The Reserve duty was play duty. They practiced drills on the weekends, then deployed to some other place in the country for a two-week active duty tour. He was grand-dad, because he was probably the oldest person around the Reserves. Most all officers and enlisted were many years younger. He was a combat veteran – which placed him in a state of awe to most, who never saw real action.

The auditor position at the Bank was enjoyable, but the constant traveling was beginning to annoy Orth. He thought he might like to try for the CPA (Certified Public Accountant) examination. But, this meant he would have to go back to school. And the family budget was already fairly well stretched to the limit. Orth was a budget conscious person, and he religiously banked ten percent of his pay into a savings account for "rainy days" or investments. He would not want to disturb this, if possible. He and Donna discussed it, and they decided it was best for Orth to attend classes.

So, it was back to school for our hero. This time it was Golden Gate College -- a downtown college that concentrated upon commerce and accounting. They were offering specialized classes on CPA review. Orth attended evening classes and studied ardently...He worked late at night studying and every opportunity he could, while commuting on buses, hotel rooms, when he was away on out of town assignments.

The California CPA Examinations were offered twice annually; March and November. Orth applied to sit for the November one. It was held in a vast auditorium in the Masonic Building on Mason Street. There must have been three hundred candidates there. The tests came in three parts and lasted three days, an energy draining experience.

The atmosphere is electrified – the setting is almost prison like. Plain tables, steel chairs and test proctors prowling about like SS-Gestapo Death Squad soldiers, hawking one then another to make certain there is no cheating. Two parts Accounting Practice, Accounting Theory, Law, Taxation and Ethics.

At the end of the three days, Orth was exhausted and asked himself, "Why didn't I die on that bloody hill in Korea –why didn't Sergeant Kim Lok kill me, then I would not have to go through things like this!"

Of course, he was just being silly. He <u>knew</u> he had to plug on in life, now that he had a family to provide for and establish a worthwhile name for.

The results of the examination came and he passed only one part, Theory. He was saddened. However, he continued to study and take classes at Golden Gate College. He learned that many candidates take three or more attempts before they pass. In California, if you are successful in passing three parts, then you can retain them, and just take the remaining parts that you failed. Accounting Practice – comprising two parts because it had two separate sections. I hope the writer is clear in explaining this, anyway, it lends little to the overall theme of our journey with Orth.

At the next try at the Examinations, our hero passed three parts. He was happy! Now he need concentrate only upon Theory and Auditing the parts he failed. At the next attempt, he took the tests in Sacramento, because he thought a smaller crowd and less confusion may help him concentrate. He labored through the examinations and had a sinking feeling as he departed, thinking, "Surely, I failed Auditing."

Well, he did not! He passed! He and Donna hugged and kissed when the news came. And they decided to celebrate by taking a weekend up at Yosemite National Park – in the Sierra Mountains near Merced, California.

Orth had sold the old Chevrolet and had purchased a new German Volkswagen "Beetle", automobile. It was miniscule for the load – both boys, a dog named "Piddles", Donna and Orth jammed themselves in, tied the luggage onto the top on a rack, and off they went. There was not a square inch to spare! Orth purchased the car because he heard they were reasonable to operate and reliable – which turned out to be true – but one had to sacrifice. Yosemite was beautiful. They rented a cabin and hiked about. The boys had to be taken in a carriage. John could totter along some, but Bert was still not walking. So, they hauled along their bundles of diapers and off they adventured.

"I still have to have two years of practice experience in a CPA firm before they will grant me a license," Orth explained to Donna. She understood. She always accepted Orth's decisions. He discovered that the experience that he gained at the Bank practically counted as nil. He would have to find some other means to fulfill the requirement. A casual friend of his, Fernando Gonzalo, worked as a Staff Accountant for Main, LaFrenz and Company, a regional CPA firm and "Gonz" suggested that Orth apply there. Because of his banking experience, the firm may look favorably upon his application. Main, LaFrenz & Co. were the independent CPA firm that audited Wells Fargo Bank and Orth had met Fernando while assisting him doing some of the "pick and shovel" work of verification of account balances and other minor assignments. Fernando had passed the CPA examinations about a year before Orth, and was hoping to gain a partnership in the firm. He was a tall, dark Latin type, trim and had a broad smile that exploded with large white teeth. He was well thought of in the firm. He wore dapper suits with (always) a starched white shirt. He was a sharp accountant – much more militant than Orth. Orth was a "plodder" in accountancy. It took him longer to think things through. His undergraduate grades were barely good enough for him to get into graduate school at State. But he had determination. CPA firms, especially large ones like Main, LaFrenz sought top students. Orth felt his chances slim, but he asked for an interview.

He was interviewed by one of the junior partners, a small man wearing a tweed suit with gray hair and horn rimmed glasses. Orth thought he looked like the "typical" CPA, narrow minded, exacting, droll, never smiling, etc. After the interview, he was introduced to several other partners, no doubt, to size him up.

"We shall let you know," said the junior partner, as Orth departed with a dry, sour taste in his mouth. He thought for sure that he would not be accepted. In about a week's time, he received an envelope from the CPA firm saying that he had been accepted and they stipulated the starting salary, date to arrive and other details. Orth was happy, but nervous. The starting salary was slightly higher than he was earning at the bank, but it was a tentative appointment for a six month probational period. It meant going from a secure position at the bank to an uncertain one with the CPA firm. It was a risk, but the rewards seemed to overshadow the uncertainty. Orth discussed it with Donna and she agreed that Orth should try it.

"We will manage, Ortie. You've worked so hard to let the chance slip by."

CHAPTER XVIII

And you will hear of wars and rumors of wars. See that you are not troubled; for all these things must come to pass, but the end is not yet.

Matthew 24:6

Orth continues to attend his Reserve meetings in San Francisco. Many units and individuals have been called to active duty to serve in the Vietnam conflict. He shudders to think that perhaps his name will come up. He now has a position with the CPA firm, Main LaFrenz, has his wife Donna and his sons, John and Bertram, and he would be devastated with grief if he should be called once again into combat. Yet the specter looms over him. He worked for one year with the CPA firm then filed for his State License, because he later discovered that his time as an auditor with Wells Fargo Bank, and the time spent in the Army Finance Corps would count as "one year's experience" toward the two required.

His certificate arrived. He was now officially a Certified Public Accountant, State of California License Number 13709E. He was elated! After the years of study, and the hours of day and night study, it paid off. He and Donna discuss the possibility of moving out of the San Francisco Bay Area to the quiet rural atmosphere of Central California where Orth could start his own private practice. They had been impressed with the area around Merced, California. It was quiet, void of the crime, congestion and adverse elements of the now overpopulated Bay Area. Orth simply could not see staying in the San Francisco area and starting a private practice, competing with the many larger firms. He postulated that most of his clients would be cast-offs from the other CPA's, seeking a "cheap deal", or people wanting simple "bookkeeping" help. Orth was seeking to build a practice with primarily audit and systems analysis clients. A hopeful, or perhaps a pollyannish attitude.

On a weekend, Donna packed up the boys and the dog. Orth backed the VW bug from the garage and they were off to Central California to look things over in the Merced Area. They stopped in Turlock, California, for lunch in a city park and noticed a real estate office on one of the side streets. After lunch Orth looked in the window of the real estate office and noticed a forty acre farm for sale in the Hilmar vicinity. So they motored down to have a look. Hilmar was a small, primarily Swedish village, of dairy farmers. Orth was successful in locating the farm and inquired about the place from the owner, who replied, "Sold it, five days ago, sorry. Maybe you would like to look at Tony Azeredo's place just down the road, two-story white house on the left going towards town, green roof and white picket fence, he's getting old and wants to move into town – has thirty acres."

They drove up the long drive to the white house. An elderly man came to the fence gate and invited Orth and the others in. They sat around a large old kitchen table, and then Mr. Azeredo explained his story that he no longer has a dairy and his wife had died and his sons had moved away. Consequently, he felt it best to sell the farm and acquire a small house in town. "I'm thinking of $30,000," Tony said. "Think it over and let me know."

They departed and on the way back to Turlock, Orth pulled into a dairy farm to see if the price was reasonable according to local standards.

He drove into a neat looking dairy farm with a sign over the large barn "Tellborg Farms". A large hulking man emerged from the house. He wore a large grin and grasped Orth's hand and shook it heartily. "Name's Bill Tellborg, howdy." The Tellborg farm was about a mile from the Azeredo place.

Bill Tellborg and Orth chatted for a little while and commented, "Well, I've been trying to buy Tony's place so that I can have more alfalfa ground, but he won't sell it to me. I think he's just being stubborn – the Swedes and Portuguese in these parts cling together and have their own groups and church, you know how it is?" Mr. Tellborg seemed to think $30,000 was about right, not too much and not a cheap bargain.

Orth had saved diligently. He decided to buy the Azevedo place paying

$10,000 down and Mr. Azeredo would carry the balance by a mortgage. It was a big move, and Orth gulped, but Donna thought the country life better for the boys and the family. So, Orth gave his termination notice to Main, LaFrenz & Company and they prepared to move. Orth rented a "U-Haul truck and Donna drove the VW with the boys and the dog. The Hilmar house was old, but spacious. Each boy had a room upstairs. Also upstairs was the master bedroom in front – and a rear bedroom that they converted into a den-TV room. They were a happy family here on the farm. The neighbors were friendly. Bill Tellborg called from time to time to chat and Mrs. Tellborg, who had a speech problem, liked to visit with Donna and the boys.

Orth opened his CPA practice by building an office in the large downstairs bedroom that led off the rather small parlor. There was a large dining room that had a set of windows that overlooked part of the farm. There was not a great deal of furniture. Donna frequented the used furniture places in the surrounding areas to add to their vacant spaces. Orth called it "junking", when they would go in search of a bed or chair at the second hand stores. But their budget was tight. Orth had difficulty locating clients, and he mentally equipped himself that he would have to live off their savings for at least six months until he acquired some clients to add to the cash flow. It was a struggle, but they were happy.

The farm was a level thirty acres with a pipeline irrigation system. It was more or less square and the house was situated off the road on a dirt lane, about two hundred yards. It was a pretty place. Mr. Azeredo had planted it to alfalfa and had rented the land out to a local dairy farmer named Svend Peterson. Orth left the arrangement remain, he could use the rent and besides, he had no equipment nor the time to adequately work the soil. Svend was a large blond jovial Swedish type who had been a sailor during World War II. Orth enjoyed his easy going attitude.

To shore his sagging reserve, Orth hired himself out to several large CPA firms in San Francisco and Los Angeles and worked on an hourly per diem basis. He enjoyed this, it was pure audit work, his favorite. He helped and in some cases directed audits of banks in Central and Northern California. And, the money was decent. He even managed to start putting some into his "Rainy Day Fund."

* * *

On the fifteenth of August 1964, fate dealt a devastating blow to the Orth Volzenkoff household in Hilmar, California. Sixth Army mailed Orth orders recalling him to active duty, the term was "indefinite - subject to Command Authority". He was to report not later than 1 October 1964. He was stunned. He and Donna devoted many hours deciding and planning how to cope and what must be done. It was decided that Donna would remain on the farm in Hilmar where the boys would attend grammar school when they reached age. The land would continue to be rented out to Svend Peterson, and Bill Tellborg agreed to "kind of look after things."

Orth accepted the recall as inevitable. He had heard that the Army was in dire need of people to train the South Vietnamese Army (ARVN), and as a Senior Master Sergeant experienced in artillery and combat, the Pentagon acted. So, he had Donna drive him to San Francisco to report in. Mrs. Tellborg (Ethel) babysat the boys. It was a sad parting. Neither Orth nor Donna talked much, just about silly things like, "be sure you water the plants on the front porch," or "have Svend's boy, Larry mow the lawn," and so forth. Neither had an appetite as they had their last meal together in a cafeteria on Lombard. Then they parted. Orth wept. And he thought, "I don't give a damn if they see a Master Sergeant cry, I'm just glad I'm so much in love with that little gal and my sons that I can cry like this!"

The Army flew Orth and other senior non-coms and officers from California to Bien Hoa Air Base, north of Saigon. Upon arrival, they were assigned quarters in a decent building near the city. On the seventh of August, 1964, Congress approved the use of U.S. Troops in combat, by the Gulf of Tonkin Resolution. Prior to this time, U.S. troops were there to "train and advise". It was tacitly known that they *were* involved in the fighting against the North Vietnamese. There were a lot of Army people there when Orth arrived. It was said, there were about 25,000 troops stationed in Southeast Asia in October 1964. Lieutenant General Westmoreland headed the forces.

It was a strange situation. The men there were a mixture of malcontented draftees, young inexperienced officers and some "lifers", or Regular Army non-commissioned types. There was a great deal of disobedience that rocked Orth on his heels. He would see a young Private talking in a disrespectful and rude manner to a Lieutenant or Captain, or refuse to carry out an order, and think to himself, "how the Army has changed!, how can we ever expect to do anything with this mess of rabble!" Orth was of the old school of military discipline, one followed orders and kept his mouth closed. It was considered

> IT WAS A STRANGE WAR... THE ARMY IN VIETNAM WAS A MIXTURE OF MALCONTENTED DRAFTEES - YOUNG INEXPERIENCED OFFICERS AND REGULAR ARMY NON-COMS....

good form to complain, it was expected, once the troops ceased to complain, then it was time for the commanding officer to start worrying! It embarrassed Orth to see some punk youngster not even old enough to vote, berating a non-com in a rude manner, and he would often erupt into a rage of fury. More than once he had called down a young unruly soldier, and several times he had turned them about and booted them in the ass.

Orth was assigned to assist and train the ARVN (South Vietnamese) Army First ("Eye") Corps, who were located in the northern part roughly from the DMZ (Demilitarized Zone) in the north-south along the A Shau Valley through the provinces of Quang Tri, Thua Thien, Quang Nam, Quang Tin and Quang Ngai. The sector was about four hundred fifty miles long – rough terrain, heavily forested and thick underbrush. It was easy for the North Vietnamese to infiltrate then hit the friendly forces from the rear. Eye Corps had three ARVN Infantry Divisions assigned to them, the First, Second and Third. The Command Post was located at Da Nang - about half way south from the DMZ.

Orth was air lifted most of the time from his quarters near Saigon. It was totally different than World War II or Korea. Here in Vietnam, the U.S. Troops enjoyed plenty of supplies, ammunition, food and quarters. The few days that Orth did spend up at the CP were in relative comfort compared to the filth and mud in Korea. It was President Lyndon Johnson in the Whitehouse – President Kennedy had been killed by an assassin's bullet in Dallas, Texas, on 22 November 1963.

The United States was a disunited mess. The populous were about evenly divided about whether they should be sending troops to Vietnam. Mobs of demonstrators roamed the college campuses and cities decrying the shedding of United States troops' blood in a senseless struggle that the French had walked out of. The Army had little respect from the young and middle aged people back in the U.S. And, this sentiment spilled over to the young draftees and volunteer enlisted men. They resented being there – considered themselves pawns of the politicians. Which is true of any conflict. The officers had to swallow hard and endure. They had no recourse other than dishonor. Their commission was an irretrievable document. They were accessories before the fact. They were wearing the emblems of an agent of the Government and its policies. They attempted to operate using force or intimidation. How do they enforce rule and discipline to soldiers who reply, "fine, Lieutenant, court martial me – I could care little – at least I will not get my balls blown off by an NVA (North Vietnamese) grenade, or land mine."

Trying to train the Vietnamese was difficult because of the vexing language problem. The author regrets to also admit of a gnawing racial problem among the white troops – the negro troops and to some extent the Vietnamese. Truth or not, some of the blacks felt they were being manipulated by the "white pigs". This irritated Orth who had little time for those in the Army who labored under self pity. In one instance when he was setting up an advance artillery post with camouflage netting, he discovered a black Specialist-Four sitting in the cab of a GI two and a half ton truck (Army lingo – "duce-and-a-half"). He was leaning back smoking a cigarillo. It was hot and humid, and Orth had his troops stripped to the waist and they were working hard to master the gigantic nets and poles, trying to get them stretched over several large expandable Army eight-wheel vans. A big job for any group.

Orth spied this "gold-bricker" (Army slang for loafer) opened the truck door and yelled, "Get your black ass out of this truck and get to work helping with the netting or else I'll kick your buttock into a bloody mass of oatmeal!"

The soldier nonchalantly said, "Kiss my ass, Sarge, you bastards – officers and youse E-8's, and E-9's use us blacks like slaves while the white boys lounge around drinking beer and screwing women in Saigon!"

With that Orth whirled him about and booted him in the behind...he fell,

Orth continued to kick him...then the boy turned and opened a knife, lunging at Orth. Orth fended off the attempt and hit the young black a stiff blow to the stomach, followed by a swift clip upon the jaw. The boy crumpled into a heap, getting up slowly wiping the blood from his mouth, and skulked to join the others working on the netting.

Later on, one of the other black soldiers, a young private from St. Louis, Missouri, came up to Orth saying, "dat Joe Black is a bad nigger, Sarge...bad...bad...kind-o-glad you walloped him..." The private was a tall, heavy set young black who always seemed polite and timid. Orth noticed that he wore a gold chain around his neck that had a Christian Cross. Orth thought to himself, "Now there's the church in action," adding, "thanks Josiah, I'll probably have the American Civil Liberties Union on my neck for doing it, but I just don't like it when we are all in this together and seeing someone thinking he's above helping his buddies."

They were continually suffering casualties from infiltrators who would cross over and plant land mines or ambush troops at night. Finally the U.S. sent in a Marine Brigade, the 9th Amphibians, to try to stop it. More troops were being added daily to the line forces and soon the U.S. had over 25,000 troops committed to the MACV, (U.S. Military Assistance Command Vietnam).

Then it happened. While walking with two officers back from a meeting on artillery tactics in the Khe Sanh sector, they were hit with two grenades. Often these isolated attacks were launched by angered enlisted men who harbored deep resentment and contempt towards officers and senior non-commissioned officers. It was laughingly referred to as "fragging". One of the officers, a young U.S. Captain was killed instantly. A piece of shrapnel went through his left eye – he fell and that was it. The South Vietnamese officer had his foot blown off but he lived. Orth had a gash in his right arm requiring twenty-one stitches, and numberless other small fragment wounds over his body. He survived, but lost a lot of blood before they picked him up by a medic-evac helicopter and placed in a hospital in Bien Hoa.

He healed fast and was up and about walking in several days. His right arm was bandaged and in a cast. Donna wrote almost daily and he received spurts of letters, sometimes three or more daily. It was a large and well-staffed hospital and Orth enjoyed talking and harassing the nurses in a friendly way. Good news came. He was being released from active duty and would be sent home soon. It was on the fifteenth of March 1965 that Orth landed in the United States at McCord Air Force Base, near Seattle, Washington. He was then sent on an Air Force C-120 cargo plane to Travis Air Force Base near Stanislaus. His wounds were healed now.

Donna and the boys were there to meet him at the terminal. Emotions ran high. They hugged for a long time, kissed and said nothing. Little John and Bert stood tugging at Donna's red suit skirt. The little mutt dog, on a leash, was circling about in a wildly animated way. "I missed you so damn much, you silly old girl," Orth said. She didn't say anything as they collected the bags and headed to the VW Bug to drive back to Hilmar.

During the drive home, they talked about various things. Orth commented that he would start up his CPA practice again, and Donna said she would like to finish her bachelor's degree, because the California State College system was building a new four-year college in Turlock, seven miles north of Hilmar. The farm looked about the same as he had left it, Orth thought. More weeds had grown up about the barn and about, but that was understandable. Orth was always concerned about keeping the place neatly trimmed.

Donna enrolled in San Francisco State College and studied Speech Pathology. Orth opened his practice again and life commenced once more as a civilian for Orth. The going was slow, but Orth landed a part-time teaching position at Modesto Junior College. He was assigned to teach classes in the evening. One on Wednesdays and the other on Fridays. Both were in elementary accounting. The College paid him a stipend of $300 per semester. It wasn't much, but he needed the cash flow. Ethel Tellborg baby sat for Donna while she attended classes.

Donna's sister Karen Joy came to visit from Cleveland. She was her usual lively self, and played with John and Bert for hours. She would take them swimming at the Hilmar pool which was part of the High School.

"Did you know that you have family in Turlock?" Donna was astonished. She knew there were loads of Sregors about, but this news was not expected.

"Yes, it's Dad's younger sister, Evelyn May. She married an M.D., a Doctor in, I believe, Turlock," Karen said. Donna rarely heard Evelyn spoken about around the house. It seems that Evelyn had left Cockhan early in life and went to Omaha, Nebraska to take up registered nursing. She met her husband there, Dr. James Colling Wilberforce, who was enrolled in the College of Medicine, Creighton University. Evelyn had never returned to Cockhan, therefore she had never met Donna.

Donna and Karen drove into Turlock to look up Evelyn. They located her in the telephone directory.

"Here she is, Dr. James C. and Evelyn S. Wilberforce, 1195 East Lawndale Drive," Karen recited.

They hopped into the VW and off they went. Once more Ethel Tellborg had been asked to babysit John and Bert, who were nearing kindergarten age. The Wilberforce house was a large rambling ranch style place surrounded by five acres of lawn, orchard and horse paddock and stables. In the rear of the house was a large swimming pool. It was obvious that Dr. Wilberforce had money. He lived way above the standards of the Hilmar Volzenkoff's.

Evelyn answered the door and seemed to recognize Donna, intuitively, as her niece. All three women burst into a marathon of chatter like a brood of hens, animated gestures were mixed with elated laughter. It was a perfect female gossip bang. Throughout the meeting a series of children came and went. They were introduced but Donna and Karen lost track. The Wilberforce's had six children ranging in ages from nineteen to eight. Four boys and two girls. Evelyn was of average height, dark hair and a trim figure, as if she made frequent use of the swimming pool. She had a broad mouth and upturned nose. She really was rather quiet like her brother.

At about noon time, Doctor James drove into the driveway and entered the house through the dining room which had access to the front entrance way as well as the front door. He was a tall, lean man with deep set eyes and thick eyebrows. He combed his brown hair straight back and wore a white shirt, open at the collar. His air was casual. He entered the large living room where the women were seated and sort of collapsed into a large white easy chair (known to be his favorite and all had best remember that). He draped his right leg over one of the arms of the chair and said, "it's been a hell-a-va morning. Could you get me some tea?"

Evelyn rose and walked to the kitchen through the dining room. "Hi, who are you?" Doctor James said after lighting a cigarette and examining Donna and Karen. They managed introductions, and Dr. James took a noticeably immediate liking to Donna. Evelyn returned with a tray of drinks. A tall glass of iced tea for Dr. James, which he tossed numberless spoonfuls of sugar, and lemonade for the ladies. Dr. James always had his iced tea winter or summer. They talked a long time until Dr. James abruptly extricated himself from the easy chair, leaving his unfinished sandwich, and walked out to his car, bidding Donna and Karen goodbye.

This was the beginning of a long friendship. Donna, Orth and the boys frequently visited at the Wilberforce home. The boys would swim in the pool because now they could manage quite well on their own. John could swim the breast stroke masterfully. Bert just kind of bobbed around in the water like a cork. Doctor James enjoyed talking with Orth, however, it was mainly one-sided. He would corner Orth and flood him with his highly opinionated, distorted and unfactual generalizations about politics and the government and a multitude of other topics. Dr. James always felt his beliefs were infallible. Orth just sat there listening and managing a word here and there. Orth knew why Dr. James liked to talk. It was like most men in a family household. He was lonely.

Few women realize that the children and mothers form a binding clique—a clan within the walls of a man's castle. The husband often feels alienated, alone in his own abode. The children seek aid and advice from Mom, but Dad is just there to pay the bills, sign checks and to ignore. And this seemed to be the case in the Wilberforce home. The six children seemed to cling around Evelyn and ignore Dr. James. Perhaps, Orth thought, it was because he was absent so much, being an M.D., always on call and so forth.

Orth's CPA practice was slowly budding. He continued to teach, and Donna was nearing the end of her quest to complete her bachelor's degree. The country continued in turmoil over the Vietnam War, and the social climate in the country vexed both Orth and Donna. Crime was a constant threat to the peace of the citizens. There were widespread accounts of addictive drugs being used by students of all ages, even down to the grammar school level. Home break-ins, and other forms of robbery seemed rampant as addicts sought money to purchase their opiates. These things troubled Donna more than Orth, and she thought about little John and Bert being raised in such a wretched environment.

CHAPTER XIX

"Therefore I say to you do not worry about your life, what you will eat or what you will drink, nor about your body, what you will put on. Is not life more than food and the body more than clothing?"

Matthew 6:25

    Orth and Donna continue to visit with the Wilberforces. Evelyn is now called "Aunt Evelyn", by little John and Bert, and Doctor James answers all of the medical needs of the Volzenkoffs at the behest, no doubt, of Aunt Evelyn. No charges are assessed and Orth is very grateful. And, besides all the medical help, Dr. James invites the Volzenkoff's over often for supper parties and to enjoy holidays together – Christmas, the Fourth of July and so forth. They enjoy each other's company. Orth becomes a confidant to Dr. James – he tells all of his woes and problems. They have a lot in common. They both were in the Army and had seen combat, both were reasonably well educated, and both had the same traditional-fundamentalist attitude. Dr. James had been an M.D. in a forward Army field hospital in the Pacific during World War II. And, he had seen and done a good deal. He was quiet about the war, except to say that he didn't give a fig about rank, a soldier was a soldier, be it General or "buck-ass" private. All received the same attention as far as he was concerned.

    Both Dr. James, Orth, Donna and Evelyn continued to discuss the developing problems in the United States which ran the scope of government's unmovable bigness and lack of efficiency – the waste of the "Welfare State", rampant taxation, crime at all levels of ages - drug abuse, the decline in educational standards, the abysmal collapse in morals, etc. Then Evelyn started to plant the seeds of Australia into Donna's ears.

"If I were young again I would go to Australia to live. They seem to have a higher standard of living than we do, and they do not have the runaway crime problem that we do."

And so, for several months and even beyond a year Evelyn kept commenting to Donna the advantages of an Australian life.

"Jim's niece, Judy, spent two years over there and really enjoyed it. She was a teacher, received her degree from Iowa State. She's working now for Wells Fargo Bank in San Francisco as a Public Relations Officer – seems to discover the most fascinating jobs," Evelyn remarks. "She's still single – kind of a character, she should be coming down one of these weekends, and you can corner her and get some ideas from her," Evelyn continues.

Orth has his doubts about moving lock-stock-and-barrel overseas. His CPA practice was progressing nicely. He had added a staff person to handle some of the bookkeeping duties, and he opened an office in the downtown Merced in a bank building. But yet, his mind was troubled by the domestic unrest. Bobby Kennedy, President John Kennedy had been killed – gunned down by some geek, the black civil rights groups had become antagonistic, free speech groups were attacking the pillars of tradition – marches here and there by pressure cliques. It seemed like the nation was soon to erupt into something that happened in Germany during the early 1930's. Gun toting galoots were everywhere – and the police just seemed hard pressed to maintain a semblance of order.

Orth even thought of carrying a gun in his briefcase, because he spent a lot of time driving the roads at night. And, he thought, "To hell with it – if the bastards want my wallet, let them have it – I'm finished with killing, two and half years of combat taught me some pretty brutal facts."

Our hero has yet to learn that all of the troubles in the world and the United States stem from the abandonment of faith in Jesus Christ. Those treasured gems of wisdom recited in the Gospel of Christ, "I am the Way, the Truth and the Life." These words altered the course of history changed heathen nations into Christian strongholds – brought America to preeminence. Now the United States had turned their backs upon Christ. Religion became the dollar – the Christian is looked upon as a puritanical ass – a blue nosed narrow minded killjoy. Of course, there are the cherished few that Christ will not abandon. Those stalwart souls that keep trudging to church to pay homage to Our Master – the Author of Truth. Where is the Lord God of Elijah? Certainly not in mainstream America. Certainly not in public schools where you would be locked up in the hoose-gow if you mentioned Jesus Christ!

The legal profession including the Supreme Court seem to shun Our Lord Christ as a thing like the Bubonic Plague. Mention the name of Jesus Christ in public and people think – "Watch out – some more of those religious fanatics – a Jesus freak!"

Yes...Orth is searching. The seed was planted way back in Sunday School in Oesterich when Eddie Burran, and Jessie Ordway used to drive Fritz and Orth to church. Then there was Bertha who always had the boys say their prayers before climbing under the covers on their Wisconsin farm. Ah yes... Christians along Orth's path of life that seemed to add a word here or a helping hand there will add up when the time is ripe according to God the Father in Heaven.

A CPA firm in Stockton, California, named Ardenello and Jarvis learned through the California Society of Certified Public Accountants that Orth had bank auditing experience, and Bill Ardenello telephoned him. It was arranged that Orth would supervise the audit of several small Northern California banks and receive a per-diem fee. The arrangement worked well, and Bill Ardenello and Jim Jarvis thought it may be well if they merged practices to have offices in both Stockton and Merced.

It was informally agreed. So, the name of the new firm was "Ardenello, Jarvis and Volzenkoff, Certified Public Accountants". All went well. Bill helped Orth audit the banks, but Jim Jarvis remained mostly involved with his estate tax clients. Orth was not totally at ease not having a formal document drawn up to represent the partnership, but he trusted Bill Ardenello and liked working with him. Eventually, Orth was doing all of the audit assignments, with occasional help from Bill and a staff man. Orth was beginning to think that his end of the bargain was slightly uneven, he was spending an enormous amount of hours away from Donna and the boys on the road while Bill and Jim were in their comfortable offices in Stockton. Yet, he felt he was perhaps suffering from self-pity and shrugged his shoulders and carried on.

Judy Wilberforce came to spend a weekend in Turlock. She brought a girl friend who also worked at the bank. Judy was a short, chubby young lady that sort of bounced around smiling and laughing. She was likeable and contented herself by playing with little John and Bert. They would go in swimming together and Judy would read stories to them.

"You'll love Australia – they love their beer and cricket," Judy related.

They had long talks about the country and Donna seemed to be more convinced than ever that they should move there. Orth was still reticent. He had worked long hours to build up the practice and establish the home and so forth. Donna and Orth spent long hours talking about what they might do.

"Things in the United States are not conducive to raising a family," Donna would quietly relate.

Then it happened. Suddenly, Orth decided. They would move. He was getting older, and the time would have to be now or never. He was reluctant to give up all the things he had acquired – but perhaps John and Bert could lead more decent lives overseas. It was a tremendous risk – but the rewards would be worth it.

"Why should I let those dolts in the public school system harm and destroy my sons' minds?" Orth thought.

In Stockton, Orth stopped at a travel agency and inquired about ship travel to Australia. A lady attendant explained that the British shipping company, P & O Lines, (Pacific and Orient Lines) have frequent ships leaving from San Francisco or Los Angeles to Australia and other ports of call in the Pacific. She further said that in September of this year, 1972, the Orsova, a ship operated by the P & O Lines would depart San Francisco for the Pacific and Australia, and she would apply for bookings for the Volzenkoffs if he would like. She supplied Orth with several brochures. Orth departed – his heart seemed to soar at the exciting time that the family may enjoy on board ship and a new beginning in a foreign and little known place.

Things were planned and the wheels set in motion. The Orth Volzenkoffs would depart their mother land in quest of a decent environment for the raising of their sons. Orth booked passage on the Orsova for Perth, Australia, on 12 September 1972. It was now 25 April 1972 – not much time to make arrangements and to sell the farm. To relate this news to Bill Ardenello and Jim Jarvis, he would have to garner some courage. Bill Ardenello took the news sadly – Jim Jarvis was in a suppressed anger mood. Anyway – it was out there. Orth felt compassion for Bill, as he was getting older and the burdens of the practice were telling upon him. But as Aristotle said, "Everything has a beginning, middle and end," so Orth moved onward. Evelyn Wilberforce was elated. She was living vicariously – she herself – she thought, herself – leaving the U.S.A. for a new and exciting life – to rear her six offspring aloof of the wretched influences of the United States. Her life had been one restricted to childbearing and managing a large and difficult family. Dr. James was away most of the time, and she had to handle the reins of the household.

The farm was soon sold for $30,000. Orth had cash to start afresh now. They held a yard sale and sold about everything except the clothes on their backs – even the VW Bug went, which necessitated Orth to rent a car for one week before the ship departed. They moved off the farm into a small furnished apartment close to Stanislaus State College in Turlock. All was excitement. Orth phoned Fritz to give him the news, and as expected, he was dour.

"You're a fool, Orth – but wish you luck, you dumb bastard," were his parting comments.

Several days prior to departure, Evelyn Wilberforce drove the Volzenkoffs to San Francisco. They rented motel rooms at an Inn on Lombard Street and visited various spots in the city. They visited the ship that was in port, and deposited most of their luggage at a pick-up point on the wharf, then visited the ship. She was one of the older passenger vessels of the fleet. And she showed her wear. The party was partly escorted about the vessel by a sailor that called himself, "the Quartermaster". This man was noticeably drunk...and did not impress Orth with the tidiness of a ship that he was about to embark upon with his beloved family. But, all was righted when the following day they boarded the ship to embark upon the vast Pacific and other oceans to Perth, Australia.

The liner was clean and comfortable, and the ship's crew were polite and looked smart and orderly in their uniforms. They located their cabin – in the First Class Section. Evelyn, Judy and Kent (the second oldest son) accompanied the Volzenkoffs when they boarded, to have a friendly farewell in the Passenger Lounge. Judy had stealthily sneaked a large bottle of champagne under her coat and they adjourned to the Lounge for a farewell toast.

"Oh, Steward...Could you please bring five glasses for us?" Judy called out authoritatively to a passing crewman, and in a few seconds the mess steward returned with a tray of shining glasses and some party snacks. The steward smartly opened the bottle and all had several glasses of bubbly before the ship's loud speaking system announced that all visitors were to disembark.

It was a heart wrenching experience to bid farewell to Evelyn. Orth liked her enormously – she was always there when Donna needed help and she was a true friend to the boys.

The ship slowly edged away from the dock. An officer on the bridge was calling on his radio to waiting tug boats and the ship's howsers were being cast off one by one from the shore bollards. Evelyn and the others were standing on the Wharf yelling various phrases of salutations up to the Volzenkoffs who leaned over the railings. The ship supplied confetti streamers that were tossed overboard to the shore. Music was played over the public address system. Then they were parted. Tears were shed as the ship was now out in the harbor and gaining momentum under her own power. Out under the Golden Gate Bridge, the Orsova sped. Orth and the boys stood on deck and watched as the California Coastline slipped from view.

In the cabin Donna was unpacking and trying to arrange things in the tight quarters. It would take a while before they would adjust to the shipboard routine. They were assigned a table in the dining room and they soon acquired many friends on board. Some were Australian, others American and British. The seamen were primarily from Goa, a province of India, and the officers were British, Scotch or Irish. John and Bert were soon romping about the ship and enjoying the freedom of sea life. The food was excellent and plentiful.

After about two days the Orsova put into her first port of call, which was Vancouver, British Columbia. It was a beautiful ride up the Strait to the City. Pine forests boldly pushed their way down to the deep blue indigo waters and the city stood on the water's edge. Orth, Donna and the boys disembarked to visit the city and the surrounding parks. The ship's notices told how long they would remain in port, so the passengers could judge their time before they would have to hustle back up the gang ways.

After Vancouver, they headed southwest towards their next destination, Honolulu, Hawaii. The cold abrupt weather gradually became warmer as they headed toward the lower latitudes. The Orsova seemed to respond likewise as she knifed along at about twenty-two knots. On a British ship, one had to hold to tradition, as in England, one's existence is shackled with tradition. Good manners are expected and one never becomes impatient or rude. In fact, the British way is exasperatingly patient. It is considered "bad form" to lose one's temper on board ship as well as anywhere. At breakfast you could dress casually within decent bounds – a man wore a sports jacket, slacks and tie. Sometimes you could dispense with the tie, but you replaced it with a scarf or turtleneck. The noon meal was strictly informal and generally, about anything was tolerated – shorts, sandals, open-necked sports shirts, etc. The women always wore dresses or skirts and blouse. Orth surmised, however, if

SHIPBOARD LIFE IS SIMILAR TO LIVING IN A SMALL CITY........

any joker showed up in the First Class Dining Room in blue jeans or a swimming suit, the Dining Room Steward would hastily dispatch him. At evening meal, which the British term "Dinner", one dressed preferably in semi-formal attire, which meant white dinner jacket, however, you could get by with a dark colored business (lounge) suit, which Orth wore.

Both John and Bert wore ties, white shirts, and sports coats to dinner. Second Class passengers had a separate dining room and their quarters were below, in the depths of the hull. Steel doors separated Second from First Class and signs were posted in conspicuous places saying "First Class Passengers Only – No Entry."

There was a definite snobbish attitude amongst the First Class Passengers. Orth even felt it in himself. He would later learn that to feel yourself better than anyone else because of money or social position, race, religion and so forth, is not Christian and God would look with extreme disfavor upon you. "Love your neighbor as yourself," is the message of Christ. But now Orth was still a "nominal or back bench Christian". He had yet to feel that tremendous change that occurs when one is truly born again in the Spirit as well as the flesh. As one author admitted, "Discovering the Truth of Christ is sort of like grabbing a live wire!"

The people seated at Orth's table were Australians, and this was beneficial because it gave him and his family an opportunity to see some of the characteristics of the "Aussie". They had a distinct twangy sound as they spoke, sort of like British, but more like you stretched your vowels out like a rubber band, then let it go. A's sounded like I's, so you heard "Mite" instead of "Mate", and r's were outlawed, so "Park" became "Pak". They tried to behave like the English, but would be enraged to have you tell them that. The men swill so much beer it makes Niagara Falls look like a faucet leak. The ladies are reserved and seem contented to sit and listen to the men rant on about Australian "footie" (football, that resembles soccer) or how East Calgoolie did against South Dalkeith in the Cricket finals.

The Aussies are a loveable lot, friendly, not cautious like the British. Men are "blokes", and there is a profusion of the word "bloody" in their vocabulary, which Orth discovered is a swear word, but when he tried to discover its origin, he was met with blank answers.

Shipboard life is similar to a small city. The Orsova had about two thousand people on board (the author begs forgiveness if this figure is inaccurate) about evenly divided between first and second class. The ship published a daily paper that showed the news, schedule of social events and so forth. So perhaps it would be Friday and the paper would tell you there is a dance scheduled in the Ballroom at 1900 hours, dress to be formal or dark lounge suit, then the afternoon would be Cricket on the "A" deck, and so forth. On Sundays they held Church Services, non-denominational in the Ballroom. Orth would not normally have attended, however, Bert had been a regular attender at the local Lutheran Church Sunday School and in deference to little Bert, he went to services on board ship. Donna and John remained in the cabin. Orth would recall later how the scriptures recite how age does not matter when it comes to doing your job as a Christian Disciple. The young as well as the old all have a commission to work for Christ, to bring others to know Jesus, Our Lord, through deeds, words and example. Little Bertram Orth Volzenkoff was an example to his Dad. So they sat in the gathered congregation in the Ballroom, Orth with little Bert by his side, almost like Christ sits with His Father in Heaven.

They had a small service, hymns, etc. and then the ship's Chaplain, a retired Church of England Pastor, gave a sermon. The Chaplain's name was Reverend Alec Applebee, a tall elderly gentleman who held your attention and respect by his very stature and bearing. He spoke softly, yet his voice penetrated one's soul. He was not your Bible bashing, fist pounding evangelist, yet he was convincing. With eyes deep set and huge bushy eyebrows, he spoke about the Seventeenth Century English Preacher and author, John Bunyan. "Pilgrim's Progress is a book widely acclaimed, yet seldom read – often quoted, and read in parts by many," he said. Then he went on to explain in a humorous way the kernels of wisdom and delight that Bunyan used to bring the Gospel of Christ to the reader that had been fortunate enough to be feasted by its pages. Orth was inspired. He had read bits and pieces of the book, now he had a spark that motivated him to return to that volume.

"Why cannot other ecclesiastics use the type of message that Alec Applebee, or John Bunyan use to get their points across about Christ! Why must the majority of preachers, pastors and so forth feel that they have to stand upon a high altar, ensconced in flowing robes and with a voice couched in theological morbidity burst forth with words of esoteric humdrum that toss a damp rag over the story of Christ?" Orth mumbled to himself. "Men who have been educated at a seminary seem to become instantly defensive once you ask them questions about the Gospel of Christ. They give one the impression that they <u>have</u> the answers, and you are expected to <u>believe</u> it," he further mused. "The enormous simplicity of the Gospel of Christ has been turned into a manufacturing plant of sanctimonious mummery, ostentatious displays of piety, reams of man made rules and regulations pumped out by the theologians, popes and what have you. It makes one want to rush out of a denominational church and leap towards the hills yelling frantically, 'Lord, Christ save me from this straight jacket. Come tell me on a lonely hillside like you did in the hills of Galilee and Judea, because your Church has been turned into an ice cream social club,'" Orth thinks to himself.

He frequently met with Reverend Alec on board ship, in the Lounge, the barber shop, or walking the deck for exercise. Alec was Oxford educated, a don, yet he had a simple sincerity about himself that Orth enjoyed. He authored several books and gave one to Orth entitled, "Further Adventures of a Church Mouse." It was a small treatise filled with cartoons and stories about a mouse that lived in churches along his journey through England. Each little story bore a point of Christ's message of love, respect for your neighbor and so on. Alec would stride along the decks of the ship, his tall, gaunt frame leaning into the wind and taking gigantic strides as if he were in a hurry to cross the commons of Oxford between lectures.

It was night time when the ship entered Honolulu Harbor. She would be there overnight and depart the following day at 1400 hours. The Volzenkoffs decided to disembark for several hours in the evening then for a short stroll the following day. It was exciting to see the Aloha Tower all lit up. It shone like a torch as they walked down the gang plank after supper. They walked about and felt unsteady because they were used to the ship's motion and had not been on land long enough to receive their "land legs". Orth glanced back at the Orsova. She was a blaze of lights as she stood proud along the shore, a truly gallant old Lady of the Sea. Built in 1954, she was ready to be soon "retired from service", a polite way, the Captain said, of going into the scrap heap. At the termination of this round the world trip, she would be turned over to the salvage people in Southampton, England, and sailed back to Hong Kong to undergo the degrading spectacle of the hammers and welding torches, perhaps once again to emerge, like a Phoenix, as a shining new super cruise liner, or worse, as a snappy Japanese sports sedan.

As they walked along the main streets of Honolulu, Donna and Orth both decided to return to the ship. Inwardly Orth yearned for the comfort of the ship, rather than roaming aimlessly about the glitzy streets of this laboriously boorish tourist haven. They stayed on board until the tired but elegant Lady Orsova edged her 23,000 tons towards the mouth of the harbor while on shore a band played a Hawaiian farewell song and flower leis were tossed from passengers into the sea, which is supposed to symbolize that you shall return to the Island Paradise soon, and bless the populace with your enthusiasm to spend lots of dollars on useless and frivolous activities and trinkets. The hotels will also bid you farewell and wave their traditional Hawaiian flag of love, "Come Back Soon – We Accept Visa and MasterCard."

The Captain set his course south - south west towards the Fijian Islands, a part of the British Commonwealth. It was very warm now and the Orsova would soon pass over the International Date Line, about 180 degrees, dividing east and west. The regions to the east are one day earlier than the west. So, if you traveled on an airplane, which departed on 12 December 1970 at 10:00 a.m., from Japan, it is possible if you traveled fast enough to land at Honolulu a day before you departed. Confusing? Of course! The author admits to always getting it incorrect, and just shrugs his aged shoulders and stoically thinks, "What bloody difference does it make?"

Passing the Date Line is a momentous occasion and demands the attention of all non-seafaring land-lubbers. If you have not passed over the Date Line previously, then on board ship, the ship's Captain is duty bound to insure that the mythical King of the Sea, Neptune is satiated. The First Class passengers assembled about the pool at about 1100 hours and the area was bedecked with decorations of a festive tone. One crew member was dressed as Neptune and sat on a contrived throne. He had attendants about him who proceeded to dunk those who had yet to pass over the Date Line. It was a happy time and all took the ceremonies in the best spirit. All of the Volzenkoffs were spared the dunking, however, all received their Certificate from the Captain showing they had passed the accepting ritual of Neptune. After the festivities, the stewards served a sumptuous buffet luncheon under a canopy on the after deck, adjacent to the pool. The Volzenkoffs wore shorts and light attire, as it was now evident that the haughty Orsova had penetrated deep into the South Pacific, the land of the Tropics; 23 degrees north or south of the Equator.

CHAPTER XX

> *As he journeyed he came near Damascus, and suddenly a light shone around him from heaven. Then he fell to the ground, and heard a voice saying to him, "Saul, Saul, why are you persecuting Me?" And he said, "Who are you, Lord?" Then the Lord said, "I am Jesus, whom you are persecuting. It is hard for you to kick against the goads." So he, trembling and astonished, said, "Lord, what do you want me to do?" Then the Lord said to him, "Arise and go into the city, and you will be told what you must do."*
>
> Acts 9:3-6

Orth would be like Paul as he recounted in the Bible. His life would be completely changed by a stroke from Heaven as he lived in Australia. Why are some people changed suddenly into Christians like Paul? Why has God, the Father of Jesus Christ selected certain people on His Own, while others muddle along during their lives – never experiencing that tremendous feeling? Many try to explain, few truly find the answer. Best to admit that God alone decides and we should not fret nor worry about it. There are many unanswered questions that buzz about one's brain like a beehive, and Jesus Christ tells us not to be troubled as there are many things that will be revealed to us later…now we are not capable of fully comprehending them. Our Christian lifetime journey holds many exciting things to be discovered just around the next corner – hold on! The road will be bumpy and twisting – but what a marvelous ride we will have as the

Holy Spirit is our traveling companion and guide. Ah! Yes! A jolly-good journey towards our Master in Heaven – Christ, our eldest Brother, who sits in counsel with His Father.

The ship Orsova plies the South Pacific heading for Fiji.

"Could I see what the Engine Room looks like?" Orth inquires of one of the officers.

"Of course, there are several other passengers interested, so I shall arrange a tour and advise you by message," the Purser replied. The Purser is an officer in charge of the bookkeeping of the ship. On the Orsova, he was a corpulent, round-faced man who appeared to be choked by his white collared uniform. He wore glasses and had a reddish complexion, sort of like Santa Claus.

The message arrived the following day – that those passengers interested in visiting the ship's engine room should assemble on "B" Deck at the Life Boat Station Twelve.

Orth and Bert assembled with several others. They were briefed by an Engineering Officer, who wore white coveralls and an officer's cap, from appearance the officer wore little else, and for a reason. He explained that in the Engine Room, the temperature can well reach above 150 degrees Fahrenheit – and may feel above that because of the humidity.

Down they climbed; the ladder (never "stairs" on a ship) was extremely steep and you had to grasp the railing. An experienced black gang sailor could descend the ladder in seconds by grasping the hand rails and leaving his feet – just sort of slide feet first down like on a slide. Expecting to see a black oily abyss – Orth was surprised. The Engine Room was as clean as an Austrian bakery – the brass fittings shone bright, what didn't shine was painted white. The decks (not floors as a lubber would say) were black metal and they were bright as a Nazi Gestapo Mercedes. But, it was beastly hot! The Engineering Officer had been typically British by avoiding extremes or exuberance with describing something.

The ship was powered by twin steam turbines which were heated by diesel oil. The boilers were side by side and fed live steam under enormous pressure through small jets that forced large pistons to turn the crankshaft. The noise was terrific. The visitors moved along as the officer attempted to explain the workings of various valves and fittings. He was virtually yelling as Orth and the others nodded in a nondescript manner, which was more politeness than understanding. There was a jungle of valves, gauges and pipes going here and there. All were clean and looked well-greased. The drive shaft to the dual aft propellers was a gigantic piece of steel whirling about. Then came the terminus – the bilge.

The very bottom of the ship had a modicum of sea water sloshing about that the officer explained was of little consequence and resulted from leaks that are inevitable in the steel plates of the hull. When the tour was ended the group once again gained the access hatch far above the heat and noise. All gulped the fresh sea air as they exited.

* * *

It is Wednesday in Milwaukee, as Orth drives Whitey into the parking lot near Frederick's. He has done his shopping and laundry and is now ready for a nice meal at his favorite eating establishment. He locks Whitey, grasps his old battered brief case and heads down north Fourth Street. He passes Juneau Avenue and notices how busy the town seems in the fall season. It's nearing Thanksgiving and the air is vitalized with the coming holidays.

"Hello, Doctor Volzenkoff," Otto chides as he meets Orth coming in.

"Why so formal, Otto?" Orth asks.

"Well, it's just that I feel good today and I wanted to show you the respect you are due," Otto says.

"I'm nothing, Otto, just a tired old man who was stupid enough to become a Ph.D.", Orth adds, as he continues towards his usual table.

"You're always so self-effacing, Ortie – not like these loud beer swilling bozos that come in here," Otto remarks.

He sits down and pulls out several pages of written material and reads them – making corrections and notes as he scans the pages.

Bertha walks up with a pot of coffee.

"Same, Ortie?"

"Oh…Hi, Bertha – yes, the usual," Orth replies. He continues reading the pages, but manages to glance up occasionally to notice the gang mingling about the bar. There were Eddie and Barney talking, several men in their middle ages in business suits, and the usual set of young types who worked in the banks and other corporate offices nearby. Being Wednesday, the German Band would show up later on and there would be dancing.

"What are you working on?" Bertha asks as she brings Orth his supper.

"It's another book, Bertha – I'm having trouble finding time to work on it, and I just brought this chapter in to look it over before I take it to my typist." Orth thinks to himself how writing has to be done with dedication – one has to be consumed with the idea – always looking for ideas – new thoughts and characters.

Orth's first treatise was a book on systems analysis that was published by Street and Sons, Inc., Chicago, Illinois. It sold well and is still used as a textbook by many colleges and universities. It is not a large volume; Orth wanted to keep it small as he felt too many texts are too verbose. However, he did use freely illustrations and flow-charts, his axiom being – "A picture is worth a thousand words."

A volume on management and leadership was our hero's second book. This was necessarily a rather large work – over five hundred pages. He delved into the subject with intense vigor and devoted more time to it now being in a retired status. It was broad in nature and commenced with questions dating from the pre-Roman epoch up to contemporary days. Again, his publisher was Street and Sons, who lamented the fact that such a well-researched treatise was not as well received on the market as expected. Orth was puzzled, but soon realized that his book was unpopular because it demanded a great deal from the reader. It was <u>not</u> an easy essay to digest because he had to be factual and philosophical. The topic could not be handled in a light manner as a pulp fiction piece of trash that was popular today. The lazy, casual reader today did not desire to tax his brain. He sought after things of the occult, sex or violence. Things that satisfied his base desires. Of course, other works that were popular were the "How-To" compositions that excited the miniscule brains of many. Orth presently desired to bring more religion into his work – and that is very unpopular in the present days. Mention Jesus Christ openly today and you were immediately labeled a "Jesus Freak" – a "Religious Fanatic" and one who would be targeted by the American Civil Liberties Union as a dangerous subversive who should be locked away in Auschwitz guarded by the SS with Doberman Pinscher watch dogs.

Now, our hero is working on a composition that can best be described as an autobiographical novel. A story about his own life, but using fictional characters and to some degree, places and events. He wanted to have it be fictional because in this manner he could have more liberties to use his imagination. He gathers notes as he reads and travels and uses them in his manuscript – and he expands upon them. If he meets an interesting taxi driver, waitress, or Christian along his journeys, he inserts them – and molds them into interesting people, much as a sculptor molds his subject. He writes the manuscript out in long hand upon legal tablets using his notes as he goes, that have been arranged into chapter groupings. He does not edit his work, or strive to rewrite to perfect certain errors in syntax or structure. "What I put down stays, except for punctuation or spelling errors," Orth once told a colleague.

Upon completion, he drives to Milwaukee and delivers it to a charming southern lady from Tennessee, Ann Roustone, who types the written manuscript and corrects as she goes, places it on a computer disk. She then returns the original typewritten pages plus the handwritten to Orth via the mail. Ann is a perceptive young lady, attractive and with a pleasant personality. She often gives Orth advice about the direction of the book – Orth admitting "It's nice of you to say that, Ann. I need the female point of view in those mushy, romantic scenes."

Barney Blitzgreez and Eddie Aiteanwealer notice Orth sitting by himself and they amble over and sit down with him for a short time.

"Who do you think will make it into the World Series, Ortie?" Eddie asks in his usual bass voice.

Orth looks at Eddie for a moment, replying finally, "The seventeenth century mathematician and philosopher, Rene Descartes once said, 'All problems can be solved using mathematics, then with an algebraic equation.' Now... let's see, if I can recall my baseball days in Oesterich, there are a few essential statistics that tell how successful a team is:

1. Batting Average
2. Fielding Average
3. Win-Loss Record
4. Runs Batted In
5. On Base Percentage
6. Pitching-Percentage of Wins
7. Stolen Bases - Number
8. Number of Runs Scored

...there could be more, but that's a start. If we set these down in a columnar format like this," Orth pulls out a sheet of paper from the battered old leather briefcase, and starts his calculations. Eddie shifts his bulky-corpulent frame about on his chair, muttering, "Damn, Ortie! You're always so school like, you almost sound like a person speaking in a foreign language."

"Shut up, Eddie," Barney exclaims, "let him explain it – go get yourself another beer, the Band is about to play and you can get one of those office chicks to polka with you."

Eddie stares bleary-eyed, remaining seated, saying, "I'll hang around, maybe I can win some money on Ortie's answer."

The following is our hero's computation:

1990
World's Series Probability
New York Yankees vs. Los Angeles Dodgers

	Team	
Attribute [1=Best, 0=Worst]	X	Y
Team Batting Average	1	0
Team Fielding Average	1	0
Won-Loss Record	0	1
Runs Batted In	1	0
On Base Percentage	0	1
Pitching Percentage	0	1
Number Stolen Bases	1	0
Number of Runs Scored	1	0
Total	5	3

n=5+3=8

P(E)=m/n

m=Success
n=Total Probability

Game Number Best of Seven Games	X	Y	Winner on Percentage
1	5/8	3/8	X
2	4/7	3/7	X
3*	3/6	3/6	Y
4	3/5	2/5	X
5*	2/4	2/4	Y
6#	2/3	1/3	X

* On a draw - a 50/50 probability exists - therefore Orth concedes to the underdog....

\# X wins four games - best out of seven.

X = Yankees

Y = Dodgers

His calculations complete, he hands them to Barney, who examines them, then hands them to Eddie, who folds them up and places the pages in his plaid shirt pocket. Eddie walks back to the bar, where Otto is busily working and arguing with a waitress. Eddie stops to talk with his long-term protagonist, Archie Airehorn. This ends as expected in exchanged heated words, but fortunately, no confrontation developed.

Orth departs the restaurant bidding goodbye to Barney, and walks to Whitey. This evening is choir practice at church, so he drives to the Choir Room where Bernadette Lore is arranging music scores. Other members are there also. It is the fall season and Bernadette usually starts practice on a Christmas cantata. Practice ends at eight-thirty and Orth drives to Homeport. Upon entering the rear door and greeting Mutnik, he hears the phone ringing and hastens into his study to answer it.

"Orth Volzenkoff," he answers as is his custom.

"Hiyah, Ortie, it's Libby," she says in a demure low tone, adding, "Danny's having a birthday party and we both would like you to come."

"I would be pleased…six?…fine…should I bring anything?…Okay…I'll see you then," and he replaces the receiver.

Libby sits on the edge of the bed her hands on her lap…she lied…<u>she</u> wanted Orth to come, but dreamt up the excuse that Danny did, too. Actually, Danny had not been consulted, but she knew he would not mind, as he thought highly of Orth – not as an adult, but like a friend or big brother.

There were about ten or twelve people at the party. Libby had worked an early shift at Zippo's and came back to the apartment barely before Orth pulled in. She still had her waitress uniform on and looked attractive to Orth. The uniform was starched and showed just enough of her firm breasts to excite any red-blooded male, including Orth.

"I've got to go and change," she said to Orth as he was helping to get things ready in the kitchen. "Would you be a dear and set the table? We'll eat buffet style," and with that Libby departed and Orth fumbled about putting paper plates out and the punch and things.

"Happy Birthday to you"…they sang in the living room before adjourning to the dining room.

"Ortie, would you say a blessing on the food?" Libby asks.

Orth is moderately surprised, inwardly he *knows* there has been a complete change in her.

"Father in Heaven, we here assembled do humbly thank Thee for this

"WHO DO YOU THINK WILL MAKE IT INTO THE WORLD SERIES?", EDDIE ASKS ORTH—BARNEY LOOKS ON......

food that Thou has so graciously provided. And we pray for the companionship of the Holy Spirit, that He may comfort and guide us in our efforts to live worthwhile Christian lives. Bless Daniel Luther Zimmerman on this his twelfth birthday that he may find warmth, peace and happiness through faith in Jesus Christ, Your Son. Now, Father we pray for forgiveness and we freely admit being unworthy of your love, mercy and clemency. Have patience with us and instill in our empty hearts a burning desire to manifest our love of you by indeed loving those about us as we love ourselves. In the Holy name of Jesus Christ, our Redeemer we ask and thank Thee... Amen, and Amen."

All were silent after this prayer, except Libby, who added her "Amen". She thanked Orth for the blessing, and he noted that her eyes were moist! "Yes!" Orth thought to himself, "she is truly one of us now, Father, and I do thank You!"

Danny had his friends there, also Mr. and Mrs. Thompson, the Grandparents from Arizona. They all filed about the serving table and retired to the small living room to eat and chat. The younger children went with Danny into his bedroom. Libby sat next to Orth on the couch. The conversation was measured, Norman and Adelaide were friendly, yet reserved as German people naturally are.

"I'm, err glad you're here, Mr. Volzenkoff," Norman stumbled out, "and want to thank you for helping Danny and Catherine."

"I suppose in His own way God led me to Libby - err, I mean Catherine," Orth said. Libby drew nearer to Orth and clasped his hand.

"And, I'm glad he is here, too, Dad, he has been the one bright spark in my lonely, wretched life since Joe left us," Libby adds.

They talk for a long while. Danny and the others went across to the park to toss a football Danny had received as a birthday gift.

"I was in the Army, too, Mr. Volzenkoff," Norman states. Orth urges him to dispense with formalities and call him "Orth" or "Ortie" as he is known to his friends.

Norman then goes on to tell of his experience as an infantry soldier in France during World War II.

"I was a young bank clerk with the First Wisconsin Bank in Madison when the Army drafted me – I was eighteen – boy! Was that a long time ago, right Adel?" as Norman glances at his wife, who is unusually quiet and sits upright and fidgets with her coffee cup and dish of cake and ice cream. Adel has a kind, courteous manner, not pretentious, as one might say, "comfortably polite."

"The Army is a breeding ground for stupidity – oppose it and you are locked up, insulted or silenced. I hated it, but you had to go. I was in the 83rd Infantry Division and we went into France several weeks after 'D' Day. We had it relatively easy. I was a Company Clerk. Nobody is civilized in war, education, reason and wisdom are buried by gunpowder. Our Company saw combat and there is no training that can ready you for the confusion and fear. You had to move fast, if you hesitated, you were likely to have your ass chewed up by a Kraut machine pistol. It's kind of like hunting. You're stealthful, quiet, patient and then move quick when the chance comes," Norm continues.

Orth sits quietly enjoying the warmth and closeness of Libby. She fidgets her fingers in his large boney hands and he feels empty in his stomach. "My God, how I like her! Am I bloody falling in love?" he thinks to himself.

"Yes...well, the most ignorant of all people are those who express an opinion on combat when they have never fought in a war," Orth tells Norman, adding, "just as men in love are half-mad, so are men in war. They are out of their senses from fear – they rage on eager to kill."

"Why all this talk about war...let's talk about something else!" Libby concludes.

They talk on about things of little consequence and Orth begs to be excused. Libby walks him to Whitey. They pause to watch Danny and the others playing football in the park across the street. Danny stops to wave at Orth and Libby – and they wave back. Libby grasps both of Orth's hands saying in a coyish manner, "see you again soon?"

Orth looks into her blue eyes searching for words to express his feelings, but repressing any outward display of emotions, "I'll phone you…I've got to get some things done."

Libby kisses him on the cheek and they part. Orth turns Whitey about to head for home and Libby pauses on the front lawn and waves goodbye.

* * *

The Orsova slows from her usual speed of twenty-three knots to barely a crawl as she nears Fiji. The smell of land and burning hemp are odious after the fresh warm South Pacific ocean breezes. Orth and Bert lean on the railing and can just see a glimmer of a sliver of land in the distance. No tugboats are used because the tides are almost nil being so close to the Equator – and the channel is wide and deep into Suva, to capital.

As the ship nudges up to the long wharf one can view the flood of trinket and gee-gaw vendors standing ready to tempt the unwary greenhorns from the ship with their wares. The town is a swarm of people – multi-racial and ethnic churning about like a nest of angry wasps.

The Volzenkoffs make their way through the throng to find a local bus. The market place is difficult for a writer to describe. There is no visible order to things – just a mumbo-jumbo, helter-skelter disarray of shacks, tents, tables, umbrellas, lean-tos and what-have-you's where the vendors vie their products, fruit, produce and livestock. The meats and produce are displayed on open tables or on the ground where they provide ample joy and sustenance for the voracious and abundant fly population.

Orth heard that the local buses are a "must" for a visitor because of their local color and quaintness. The buses run about in the town, setting their own schedule. Orth, Donna and the boys locate one and hop aboard. Now – this is an experience!

There are no windows, only the driver's windshield. You do not pay to ride, the government operates them out of tax dollars. Everything is good to go on the bus. The Volzenkoffs discovered an assortment of pigs, chickens, dogs, people, etc. The "seats" were benches placed fore and aft, no side seats, so the Volzenkoffs just had to stand amid the mess and hold onto straps that hung from the roof like willow branches. The smell was horrid, it stank like a barnyard mixed with body odor. So, the old wreck went "ka-puta-ka-puta, chugga-cough" along struggling with the weight. The driver tried looking official, but failed in the attempt. He wore a visor cap that was two sizes too small, a white short sleeved shirt unbuttoned to the waist, shorts and sandals. The noise and confusion behind him did not bother him in the least. Orth and the family had enough of this after several hundred feet and they abandoned the colorful carriage at the next stop. Hailing a taxi, they made their way to the King Edward VI Hotel, which they learned about from the shipboard chatter as being a majestic old edifice that wreaked of old British tradition and culture.

The taxi driver was a talkative Indian who explained that since the British granted independence to Fiji, there has been a power struggle between those of the Indian race, the Japanese and the Native Fijians, as to who should govern. The Japanese and Indians were said to have the intellectual and cultural minds and also hold the majority of the money. The Fijians oppose the haughty attitude of the Asians and Europeans and feel that the Archipelago belongs to the native population. And so the struggle continued.

The King Edward VI Hotel was a large imposing structure and seemed incongruous to the surroundings. There was a large winding palm lined road leading up to the main entrance. The building was painted pink and had long awnings stretched out to the automobile entrance, plus an enormous red carpet that started at the main entrance stairs and kept going into the Lobby. The Lobby was overly large with marble columns, huge urns filled with plants, wonderful Oriental rugs and other accouterments expected to be found in a royal palace. The lofty ceiling had rotating fans that reminded one of a Humphrey Bogart movie filmed in Malta. One felt small in this Hotel and expected bugles to sound at any minute to announce the arrival of some prince or duke.

Back on board, to enjoy dinner (lunch) which was again served outside, poolside, because of the tropical climate. And, a real treat was forthcoming. The Fijian Royal Police Band performed for the passengers. They danced and played their native instruments, drums, bugles and so forth. To add to the distinguishing quality of the show, the Band was attired in their dress uniforms of dark blue coat, brass buttons, high stiff collar, red sashes, and long white skirts. They wore no shoes, but heavy leather sandals with no socks. All of the Band were of one size – very tall, well over six feet and in top physical condition. They smiled and laughed as they played and danced. A truly memorable event for all.

About 1400 the ship loosed her heavy howsers and slowly edged her way into the main channel. Passengers tossed coins into the water and young lads, who were waiting along side, dove into the turquoise clear water after them. The depth must have been well over forty feet, they swam like seals, darting down deep, then careening up to the surface wearing a bright white smile to indicate success. Orth learned from one of the ship's officers, that the Fiji port of call was not a social-economic event, but was necessary to replenish the ship's supply of fuel oil. Huge storage bunkers were kept at Suva by the P & O Lines for that purpose.

The course was set for New Zealand, almost 180 degrees south. Orth walks "A" Deck daily – about four miles if you walk around it eight times. He and the boys also swim in the pool, but it is so small one cannot seriously swim laps to get a decent workout. One day he joined a group playing cricket in the stadium, the uppermost deck where there were several tennis courts and several shuffle board courts. Cricket was strange to Orth – the method of throwing the ball, batting and so forth held no resemblance to baseball, other than the ball was round. He took his "at-bats". A large red haired ship's officer was bowling, which meant he ran a short distance and threw the ball in an awkward overhanded manner. Orth let several go by. Then the big, burly chap let loose of one that caught Orth squarely on the knee – the one that had been severely wounded in Korea. He buckled and fell. His leg swelled up and he was in pain for several days. So…that ended Orth's brief and unsuccessful attempt at cricket.

New Zealand was a Port-of-Call only to disembark some passengers. The Orsova docked at Wellington only for several hours. The Volzenkoffs got off to stretch their legs and partake of a milkshake, because they had heard that this member of the Commonwealth was famous for its dairy products. It was a disappointment – the milkshakes were watery thin. If you asked for a thick shake the sales girl would think you were an escapee from the loony-bin. The cost was amazingly cheap…U.S. 12 cents. Back on board the motherly Orsova…the family were now headed for their final destination.

CHAPTER XXI

The Bible contains the mind of God, the state of man...It contains light to direct you, food to support you, and comfort to cheer you. It is the traveler's map, the pilgrim's staff, the pilot's compass, the soldier's sword, and the Christian's charter. Here Paradise is restored, Heaven opened, and the gates of hell disclosed.

Preface, The Gideons

Somewhere God was directing the Volzenkoffs. Perhaps it was faithful Mother Bertha or Frederick or even Uncle Humphrey. Orth would later realize the power of the Holy Spirit and prayers. Anyway, now the family was blessed on their life's journey – this segment in a far distant land. A mysterious land – mostly desolate waste, but in many ways a haven – a shelter, apart from the Western contamination. Australia is about two-thirds desert. The fertile soils lie along the western and eastern coasts. It is a new land in the sense that it became known to the Occidentals in the eighteenth century – like the United States. The evidence of England is obvious to the casual observer, she is now a member of the Commonwealth. A Governor General holds office – appointed by the English Monarch – and is a position that is basically a gift requiring little of the holder other than holding forth in uniform at the formal ceremonies required of the post. The capital is Canberra (emphasis on the "Can") where Parliament meets. The structure of politics follows that of Britain.

The gallant, weary, proud old lady Orsova slowly pokes her nose into Sydney Harbor accompanied by several tugs. The day is bright – a shining September morning. The ship is elbowed against the wharf as the sun brings his warm bright beams onto the Orsova's after deck. The Volzenkoffs are excited to step ashore and greet the new land. A package of mail is delivered to Orth by the Purser and he and the family adjourn to the after deck to enjoy the fresh air and peruse the letters. Aunt Evelyn had been nice enough to act as a collecting point for the post – and she had forwarded the package. Orth thought about Evelyn and Dr. James – such loving and generous friends they have been, and they shall forever be remembered by Orth during his life's journey.

Orth telephones the President of the Australian Society of Accountants and invites him and his wife to lunch (dinner) on board ship. He graciously accepts. However, before noontime, the Volzenkoffs have time to disembark to visit Sydney after passing through an immigration checkpoint set up inside the dining room. The sun gives way to an occasional spring shower – the air is bright and crisp. The reader must recall that we are now in the Southern Hemisphere – so everything is topsy-turvy. Fall is spring, summer is winter and so forth. Even the black widow spider's red spot is reversed from bottom to topside. The family takes a harbor ferry cruise getting off at Torango Park where there is a zoo the boys had a desire to visit.

The City of Sydney is a gem – a beautiful place (excepting parts that have become dark holes of the Philistines). The harbor is one of the most picturesque Orth has ever viewed – and classes it above San Francisco.

The family visits the zoo where, upon visiting the reptile exhibit, Bert stares down a large lizard. He simply stood there intent upon staring into the lizard's eyes to see which one would blink first. Bert was the victor.

Back to the ship to ready for their guests, Mr. and Mrs. Graham Greensleeve. Orth thought it may help his professional desires to establish an early relationship with the accounting fraternity in Australia. Therefore, he invited Graham and his wife, Hazel, to the ship. They were pleasant guests, but highly reserved – almost aloof – indifferent, at the edge of being rude. Graham was from New Zealand (a "Kiwi"). He intimated that the "Yanks" were tolerated in Australia, but not too warmly thought of, especially after being defeated so often in tennis and the challenge of the America's Cup. Well, after a decidedly dour luncheon, the Greensleeves were led to the gangway and the Volzenkoffs retired once again to the casual friendliness of the shipboard life.

The Orsova departed Sydney late in the afternoon and reached open sea about sundown – setting her course virtually due south towards the Island of

Tasmania. The seas were violent – the winds high and the temperature continued to descend as they aimed toward the Australian Bight and the notorious "Roaring 40's". The Volzenkoffs would later learn that these oceans are among the most fickle and turbulent in the world. The ship dug her bows deep into the icy chill waters then raised up abruptly as if to say, "no, thank you, the water's a bit cold for my liking." Then after rising high above the water level – the bows would once again come crashing down – while the stern of the ship would rise up and vibrate with enormous force. In their small cabin, the Volzenkoffs could hear the loud bangs and clanks as the Orsova struggled under the mountainous seas – her engines churning wildly to counteract the huge waves and headwinds. Sleeping was difficult – the crew added large nylon lines along the passage ways and decks for added handholds for the passengers and crew. The Dining Room was noticeably absent of its usual crowd, many being overcome by sea-sickness. Donna became highly ill and retired to her bunk for most of the journey from Sydney to Perth, Western Australia. Because the toilets were outside the cabin, she found it necessary to deposit the contents of what was in her stomach into the wash basin and using a pencil, she forced those large bits of regurgitation down into the drain pipe. She was mortified to admit this to Orth and the boys who found it absolutely hilarious, which did not add a bit to mitigate her discomfort.

Now...a word has to be said about Room Stewards aboard passenger ships. Each cabin is assigned a Room Steward. They are part of the crew and are specially trained to handle the needs of his charges. They bring you coffee, biscuits, fruit and juice in the morning before you go to the Dining Room. They also do the same thing before you retire for the night. Of course, they are also responsible to insure that your cabin is kept clean and tidy. Ralph was the Room Steward for the Volzenkoff's cabin. As Stewards go, Ralph would no doubt rank in the lowest percentile as far as overall efficiency was concerned. Ralph was small and had a weasel like appearance and personality. He was not of the London or Oxfordshire ilk and spoke with a cockney brogue. If it could be left until tomorrow – Ralph would, for certain, elect tomorrow. At times, he did not bother cleaning the cabin, and often did not show up with coffee or tea in the mornings and night. His appearance was one that gave the impression that he had just gotten out of bed a few minutes beforehand, collar opened, a day's growth on his beard – trousers wrinkled and so forth.

On one occasion Orth discovered Ralph in one of the passageways with his arms about a female steward and kissing her. Now...one does not have to be a Scotland Yard genius to deduce that Ralph may have taken ample use of spare cabins to carry on his shipboard romances, and that his Don Juan escapades took priority over his more menial duties. It is customary to tip your Steward ten-percent of your fare at the completion of your journey. This thought really nettled Orth and Donna, who felt like handing him a hand grenade (pin pulled) instead of any money. But, they had a change of heart and left an envelope on one of the cabin bunks at the termination of the journey with a nominal $50.00, and they were even repulsed at leaving that!

The ship's next port of call was Adelaide, the capital of South Australia. It was a welcome relief to travel up the long river channel to the city after the battering the Roaring Forties had dealt the ship. However, the stop was brief – merely a matter of hours – just to disembark a few passengers. Now the ship was practically deserted. The last and final stop, in a commercial way, would be Perth, the capital of Western Australia and final destination for the Volzenkoffs for five years. After Perth Orth was informed that the ship would be sailed to Southampton, England – void of passengers, to be turned over to salvagers who would sail the gallant old lady to a shipyard in Asia to be banged and torched to pieces. Now this is noteworthy. The part of the journey from Adelaide to Perth was used by the crew to dump a profusion of furniture and equipment not used into the sea. As Orth would walk the decks morning and evening, he would notice deck chairs, tables and other items falling from the upper decks. The ocean between 40 degrees and 50 degrees south should be littered with old ship furniture and hardware.

Again, as the Orsova, now demeaned by some of the passengers with the ignoble title of "Worsova", departed Adelaide and gained the main ocean; the Roaring Forties once again placed their tight grip upon the ship and she struggled – yet did not complain. She was a British ship and as a Brit, she would accept all adversities with indifference, bite the upper lip, and stand tall and proud – fighting the high winds and mountainous waves.

Early in the morning, 30 September 1973, the Orsova slipped past a small island – her engines slowed from the normal throb, and crawled into port. Tugs and a pilot boat came out to greet the ship. The Volzenkoffs were charged with excitement, getting up early they hugged the railing straining to get a first glimpse of their adopted homeland. After the small squat island (later they discovered to be Rottnest – a small offshore clump used as a recreation and vacation spot) they saw a low, yellow orange line on the horizon that would soon become the greater Perth area. They hastened below to pack and call at the appointed location in the dining room to pass another passport check. They entered the line with their baggage and the official at the makeshift desk examined the document and Visa picked up a rubber stamp and went "ka-plop-ka-plop" with it on the papers. He glanced up and smiled at the Volzenkoffs and said, "welcome to Western Australia." It sounded nice to their ears. They then proceeded to the baggage collection point in a shed on the wharf where they would retrieve the baggage they had placed in the cargo area. Now here they were, not having the foggiest idea where to go to find living quarters until they could locate a house.

Now comes the rented car story. Orth rented a compact car and they struggled to get all the bags in and on top of the vehicle. They managed, then started out of the parking lot. Australia, like Britain and some other countries drive on the left hand side. The United States, like Germany, Austria and other lands use the right side. So, our hero starts out of the lot at a normal pace until he reaches the street and is shocked into the reality that he is facing traffic head-on. With enraged Aussie drivers yelling at him, horns blaring, and Donna and the boys exclaiming loudly, Orth suddenly realizes his misfortune and hastily corrects the situation. They drive along Canning Highway looking for a friendly sign that might display, "Holiday Inn", "Travel Lodge", or some such signal to let them know that rooms are available. However, in Australia, at this date no such animals exist, and motels are more of a novelty than a necessity. On the outskirts of town they do discover a "motel". It is a brick structure of about six units. The Volzenkoffs check in and discover that the room price is astonishingly steep. Not to worry, they accept the fact that this is an adventure full of surprises. After several days of scouting about town they rent a house in the Applecross District – south of the Canning River. They discovered the house by inquiring at the ANZ (Australia-New Zealand Bank). An officer at the Main Office assisted them. The Canning River is not truly a "river", but is more like a tidal lagoon that is roughly twenty miles long that empties into the Indian Ocean at the port City of Perth called Fremantle. The Canning River about Perth is shallow – averaging twenty feet or so, then becoming quite shallow as you head east. Yachting (anything with a sail in Australia is termed a "yacht") in Australia is extremely popular. The Perth City environs are replete with yacht and sailing clubs, each with their own tradition and pride that they hold dearly second only to their love of Aussie beer.

The house was in a neat and tidy neighborhood. The structure was small, but sturdily constructed of double brick, inside and out. Painted white and with the ubiquitous red tile roof that are typical of Perth and Australia, it was a quaint place, nicely furnished. The toilet was outside – another trait of the Aussies who call them "loo", as is the British and French way. So you wash and bathed inside the house, but you did "your duty" running outside in your briefs and bedroom slippers – shivering as you contemplate life, having a healthy defecation. Some of the newer Australian houses have indoor loos, considered a luxury akin to the Roman Baths. All in all, the Australian houses are smaller, but constructed better than the American ones that are roomier, but built to withstand little more than a puff from a sparrow. The landlady was a shrewish type old scarecrow that sat stiffly upright in a wooden chair in the living room and explained to the Volzenkoffs the "rules of the road" as far as the house was concerned. Orth signed the lease, which was reasonable, and the shrew departed with her milquetoast husband trailing behind her flowing black coat and dress.

"Enough of this renting stuff," Orth thought to himself. So...he contacted an "Estate" agent, which is a Real Estate Agent. The salesman assigned to them was a middle aged, heavy set swarthy chap from India. He was talkative and drove the Volzenkoffs all about looking at various houses; all the time keeping up a running account of his experiences since arriving in Australia – his opinions concerning the Aussies and so forth. No house they looked at suited them. While Orth was driving about Applecross he happened upon a white house on the corner of Kintail Road – number 44, that had a "For Sale" sign stuck in the front lawn. He stopped and inquired. The owner showed him through and Orth was struck with the thought that this is the place for his family.

Donna agreed. The price was right, ($14,000) so Orth wrote the owner a check and the transaction was terminated through a local bank who acted as escrow agent. The Merced farm had sold for $30,000, so Orth had the cash to complete the purchase without any hassle about a mortgage or deed of trust. The house had small rooms, but arranged so that they had ample room. Three bedrooms meant both John and Bert had their own, and Orth and Donna had the Master bedroom. The dwelling was "L" shaped, with the lounge or living room on the bottom. Orth purchased a new Toyota yellow sedan and they began to settle in.

Bert and John were enrolled in Middle School and Donna began to understand the methodology of the Australian way of managing a house. There was no lawn mowing. You naturally had a gardener come and do it for you. It was customarily so and the price was ludicrously low. Orth arranged to have the house repainted from a dull grey to a bright white and he added attractive yellow and white awnings that blended nicely with the green shutters.

Orth learned through the Australian Society of Accountants to which he had been admitted as an "Associate", by virtue of his being a U.S.A. Certified Public Accountant – a reciprocity arrangement that there was a local manufacturer of building materials that was looking for a systems analyst, and internal auditor. Orth talked to the owner, a young Jewish man, and was hired the following day. The job went very well and the owner was quite happy with the results of Orth's thoroughness. However, the duration was short lived. Somehow, the Dean of the Commerce Department at the University had received word that Orth was a recent arrival and held the academic and professional talents and qualifications that would satisfy his requirements to fill a position as lecturer in Management Accounting and Systems Analysis. Orth was telephoned and he accepted the position. It meant a considerable increase in revenue and portended to demand more of his intellect and imagination. He regretted having to inform the owner of the Ajax Building Materials Company because he had been extremely pleasant to work with and Orth liked him as a friend. He had accepted everything Orth had submitted to him with gratitude and without question as to the wisdom of installing necessary changes. At parting he shook Orth's hand and bid him well at the University.

* * *

Mrs. Jessica Broadstreet and her husband, Harry lived next door to the Volzenkoffs when they had rented the house on Tweedale Road in Applecross. The Aussies <u>are</u> friendly. The Broadstreets invited the Volzenkoffs over for "tea", which is sort of an American coffee break, at about 3 p.m., where light refreshments are served and gossip is the entertainment – or how the cricket finals will come out. This is the habit of the Aussie, when newcomers arrive, they invite them in as a warm and friendly gesture to get acquainted. Has this ever happened to you in the U.S.A., my esteemed reader?

Jessica was a tall, slender, silver-haired lady in her mid-fifties. She had a long pleasant face with a Prussian-like square jaw. Harry was short and wiry and was what one may term "typical Aussie". He was non-pretentious and as comfortable as an old pair of slippers.

They talked and soon Jessica seized the opportunity to invite the Volzen-

"HELLO, I'M ALF KOENIG, THE METHODIST MINISTER HERE IN APPLECROSS".......

koffs to the neighborhood Methodist Church. Orth accepted and thought it well from a social point of view, not for any religious theological reason. Orth still was not a Christian in the strict sense. Oh, yes, he had his brief encounters with Christianity, but he still was a far distance from being "converted", or as the term is used, "born again". Church to him was something that others went to, not him. His "religion" was of the world, his life and education had been based upon pragmatics. Facts that could be seen – proven. Material things that can be bought, tasted, handled. Things that were transcendental, supernatural, spiritual were okay for the weirdoes – the way-outs, the religious freaks, and those of that ilk, but not for Orth Schilling Volzenkoff, who started battling life on his own at age seventeen. Yes, he would go to the Methodist Church, but strictly for the social, fashionable, friendly aspects, not for the theological value.

A day passed after the Volzenkoffs enjoyed tea at the Broadstreets when they heard the front door bell ring in the late afternoon at the rented house on Tweedale. Donna answered it, and who did she see? The doorway was almost blackened by his bulk.

"Hello, I'm Alf Koenig, the Methodist minister here in Applecross." Donna ushered him to an armchair where he settled, consuming the entire seat. Alfred was not fat or corpulent, he was just big. He was dressed in a black suit with his white clerical collar fighting against the flesh of his thick neck. When Orth entered the room, he thought the Day of Judgement had arrived. They shook hands and Alf sat there with his huge hands clasped across his chest. They engaged in small talk and Alf concluded with an invitation to church. Orth thought, "Well, if this man thinks there is a chance for old wretched Ortie, I damn well will go."

The Methodist Church was a small brick edifice situated on a corner. The congregation was small also. There was a five member choir who made up for their lack of numbers by the excellent tone and force of their voices. The Volzenkoffs occupied seats in the rear. Orth was noticeably uneasy. He had not entered a Church since his days in Oesterich and thought to himself, "the walls shall tremble and fall on me any minute!" All went well. The choir sang, Michael P. Oxford, the Church Clerk ("Clark") presented the announcements, Alf preached and performed the necessary ecclesiastical ceremonies and that was that. The congregation assembled on the lawn to exchange greetings on a bright and sunny Western Australian morning. Orth felt happy – the people were warm and friendly.

In a few days Jessica Broadstreet called upon Orth and asked him to be the youth leader. He was flabbergasted! Him, of all people! Well, he liked Jessica and he thought, "what the heck – I'll do it." The Youth Group was comprised of teenagers, and there were about twelve of them. He had fun meeting with them Sunday afternoons at 3 p.m. The group assembled, read from the Bible, had a sack lunch, played games, then disbanded. The sessions usually lasted about an hour. Orth was still clumsy with the Bible and theology – a "babe-in-the-woods" as it were. Jessica was there to help. She stated that soon there would be a Youth Conference for the District, and it would be held in the country in a lodge about twenty miles from the City, in a south easterly direction. The Conference would be termed a "Retreat", and the young adults from the District would attend, accompanied with several adult counselors.

The lodge was a large wooden structure with sufficient rooms for classes, sleeping, living, a large dining hall and kitchen. The problem was the hot water and heating, which was done by an ancient wood furnace – a giant monster that had a voracious appetite. The black monster had to be fed by wood chopped outside then hauled inside and dumped into the cavernous mouth. So, who should go the duties of wood chopping? That was the whole problem. A roster was formed, but when those whose names came up, managed to find unique methods to escape detection. Thus, usually the slack had to be taken up by the adult leaders. Up at 5 a.m. to "bang-crunch-bang-crunch", the ax against the concrete hard Aussie wood. The showers were boiling hot (shower room, just one large bin, boys followed the girls) until the wood gave out. The same with the heat. The rooms were cozy and warm in the day and evening and bitterly cold in the morning. Anyway, it was a happy outing, there was a joyful atmosphere, jokes were made of the uncomfortable items, who cared? All was fun, the Holy Spirit made certain of that; "Where two or three are gathered together in My Name I shall be there," Lord Jesus assured.

The meals were done by some of the men, who served up basic Australian victuals, spaghetti and bread for breakfast, sausages and mashed potatoes for lunch, meat-kidney pie, etc., for supper and so forth.

Class sessions were held in the afternoon. A clergyman usually presented the lesson and the youth carried their Bibles to class. Orth would cower in the rear, being ignorant of the Scriptures, it was deep water that he would rather not venture. Well, lo and behold, on one such session, he was summoned to read an opening passage from the Bible – John 3:16, one of the most familiar passages known in the Gospels. Well, Orth came forward and the Clergyman asked him what version of the Bible he preferred – the King James Version, the Revised King James Version, the Paraphrased New English Edition...and so forth.

"What?" Orth thought to himself, "I always thought there was only one – what's with all these others?"

"Oh, the King James Version will be okay," he finally replied. The next problem our hero faced would be to locate the passage. After an embarrassed pause, he retreated to one of his student and asked him to help him find it.

"Matthew, Mark, Luke and John, Mr. Volzenkoff," Michael, the young student replied.

"How stupid I am," Orth thought, "I'm supposed to be <u>their</u> leader and teacher and I don't know the first thing about the Bible!"

He stumbled though the passage, mortified at his ineptitude. Closing the Bible, he retreated once more to the rear of the room. Something suddenly happened to him. He felt "different". Things around him all at once were of little consequence. As he sat through the remaining minutes of that meeting, he felt as if his old brain had been removed and a new one inserted that had been fashioned by the Hand of God and handed to him by the Holy Spirit. Now he <u>knew</u>! Christ is real – actual, fact! All the hocus-pocus stuff about religion had been cast away. The clouds were whisked off, he now "saw" Christianity the same as Saint Paul had nineteen hundred years earlier.

"Good heavens, I am 'born again' as the phrase goes," he ponders.

Who can adequately explain the experience? It just happens, as if Christ grabs you by the seat of your trousers and dispatches you into the pool of Siloam to be healed of your wretched worldliness – you come out of the waters shaking and dripping wet to see Christ as your Friend, as your Salvation, not ever again merely a name, but a whole and real Son of God the Father. Not a figurative nothingness, but a live elder Brother to you. Someone you can learn about – read about – talk to, share your thoughts. Someone who is absolute, never changing, that is Christ Jesus. He <u>is</u> there and the Bible is His Word!

After this experience Orth is inflamed with a desire, insatiable, to read and study the Bible. He assembles John and Bert about the dining room table and take turns reading paragraphs, completing a chapter a night, from beginning, (Genesis) to the end (Revelations). Donna abstains from this enterprise. She is still not convinced of the verity of Christianity and remarks to Orth in a cold, indifferent manner, "the Bible to me is just a book."

* * *

Orth was appointed a lecturer at the University of Western Australia. His task was to design a course on Systems Analysis and to assist tutoring students on Management Accounting. The University is situated in Nedlands, a pleasant, expensive neighborhood of Perth, lying north of the Canning River. It is a beautiful campus commanded over by a large, tall massive campanile. As one walks the paths of the older part, one would be reminded of the beautiful buildings of older Austria or Germany. The new buildings lay south of the main older ones, and the Department of Commerce was housed in one of those newer. It was a two-story structure, and Orth occupied a small office on the second floor. The Dean was a young man in his mid-thirties that had received his Ph.D. in economics from the University of Chicago. He was astute and bright. Orth liked him.

The semester had not yet started when Orth joined the staff. He had time to design a course syllabus – arrange for textbooks and help with the registration of students, who were about 80% Asian, from Malaysia, Singapore, China and so forth. He would discover that the Asian students were more intent on performing well, and serious about their studies than the Australians, because their education was a great economic sacrifice for their benefactors back home and the competition to go abroad to study was extremely intense.

CHAPTER XXII

For the Lord gives wisdom; from His mouth come knowledge and understanding; He stores up sound wisdom for the upright; He is a shield to those who walk uprightly.

Proverbs 2:6-7

A whole new realm of understanding opened for Orth as he and his sons studied the Bible after supper. They sat at the dining table and feasted upon the words of the Lord. Orth could not gain sufficient to satisfy his appetite. He read and struggled to understand. The Holy Spirit, his instructor and tutor, was finding it difficult to contain his enthusiasm. He was feeding him as fast as was prudent within the bounds of standards set in Heaven by the Father and His Son, Jesus Christ.

Life at the University was progressing well. Classes commenced and Orth lectured to as many as two hundred at a time. The tutorials were much smaller, usually about thirty or so. John and Bert were enjoying their school. They had more activities and homework than that of the U.S.A., but they were adjusting rapidly. Donna located a position at a school for the handicapped. She worked with children who had speech problems. Orth joins the Royal Kings Park Tennis Club, and the South Perth Yacht Club – only a few blocks from the home on Tweedale. Orth's tennis skills were only a rung above horrible, and he soon corralled the tennis coach at the University to give him lessons. The coach agreed and Orth made rapid progress so that his game became more respectable, about on the "C" level. He had a good serve and ground strokes, but lacked the required speed on his feet to pose much of a threat against skilled players. Additionally, being at the net and volleying were, for him, as frightening as combat in Korea. He had the form, but simply could not see the ball well enough to collect a fitting set of strokes at the net.

The Tennis Club was located in Kings Park, a large reserve occupying many acres close to the center of Perth. The Club is a spacious edifice with perhaps twenty grass courts including a center court and pavilion. It had a club house, including a restaurant and bar (the Aussies could not exist without this). Orth applied and was accepted. The fee was nominal considering the beautiful amenities. You wore white at the club, which had its traditions. Saturday and Sundays the members assembled to play doubles. It was a social affair not expected to be one of exerted energy. At three, play was tacitly ended and you made your way to the Tea Room under the Pavilion for a cup of tea and biscuits (cookies). Orth made many friends there – and worthwhile contacts. He managed his schedule at University so that he could play singles on Wednesday afternoons. His game improved, but he still had difficulty winning. He simply could not tolerate prosperity.

Next – the Yacht Club. Through a friend he had at the Methodist Church who was gracious enough to act as his Sponsor, Orth applied for membership in the South of Perth Yacht Club. He was accepted and ceremoniously proclaimed at a formal supper party. The Commodore presided and the event was impressive. Orth had sailed in San Francisco with Les Masterson (Chapter VI) at the Saint Francis Yacht Club and had sailed a small lateen rigged dinghy locally around Merced, California, so he was not a green horn. Additionally, he had purchased a fourteen foot dory in Perth that he sailed on the Canning River with John and Bert. He placed a notice on the Club Bulletin Board for a crew position on a racing yacht. In a few days he received a phone call from Bryan Beardsly, a Geologist, and owner of a 28-foot sloop berthed at the Club. He asked Orth if he would like to be the sheet-hand on his yacht during the racing season.

"Yup," Orth answered, and so it went.

The yacht season in Perth commences about the early part of November and ends in April some time. Races are held generally every Saturday, with special races on odd days like Wednesday. On race days the waters around Perth are boiling with sailboats as all the Yacht Clubs about Perth are sponsoring races for several divisions of large to dinghy size boats. The courses vary to try to void confusion, which is nearly impossible because of the number of boats competing.

Australians are serious sailors, almost enjoying it more than their grog. On race days Orth saw little of what was going on about him as he whirled away at the wench when tacks were changed and was constantly adjusting the sheets to compensate for wind shifts or the demands of Bryan (the "Skipper"). There were two other crew members – a forward hand that was responsible for setting the spinnaker and sail changes, and the main sheet tender, who was more of a jack-of-all-trades and food handler.

Orth remained with Bryan, as sheet hand until he departed Perth. He learned a great deal. Bryan knew boats and sailing. He was a toughened salt who reacted fast in emergencies and remained calm during crises. Bryan had built the yacht. Around the Club she was considered a "pig". She never had placed in a race during the five years Orth crewed on her, except the one time that he was given the helm and she took first place in a race from Fremantle to Ocean Beach, a race of about sixteen miles on Cockburn Sound on the Indian Ocean. Orth would recall that day. Bryan and the others were so elated that they commenced to raise the tankards of Aussie beer to the high at the terminus of the race at Ocean Beach. That would be okay if they were home... but, the problem was that they still had to sail home and up the Canning River to Perth.

Bryan and the others were beyond sobriety when Orth, who had abstained, convinced them that they ought to be casting off for home as it was now dark and it would be a long journey home. Well, they finally had their last prosit and poured themselves on board, casting off in a casual manner, the Skipper announced that they would use the engine all the way home. This meant that only one had to be on watch – and guess who? Orth would have the honors of conning the vessel home alone...the others silently slipped below into the cabin to find a soft bunk and bedtime. All would be well...however, it was a very dark night and the channel lights of red and green are difficult to see at times. Besides, in Australia, the navigation lights are reversed from those of the Northern Hemisphere. In the Southern Hemisphere, when you are returning from sea, the red lights are on the port (left) side of the ship and the green lights are to be kept to the starboard. Just the reverse in the Northern Hemisphere. It was a warm, long and sleepy journey for Orth. He nodded off several times, being lulled to sleep by the monotonous, "chug-a-chug-a-chug" of the diesel engine. Orth thought he had things pretty well under control, but he had a lapse of memory and ran a little out of the main channel, keeping a red light to his starboard side. The problem was it <u>should</u> have been on the <u>port</u>.

The yacht slowed with several bumps on the bottom, then came to an abrupt halt. Bryan bolted from his bunk and his drunken stupor to topsides glanced about and exclaimed, "What are you doing way over here!"

Orth, in a somewhat sleepy, dazed condition answered, "I thought I was in the channel!"

Bryan, in his always forgiving and understanding manner said, "naw, mate, the channel is way over there by that red light."

Bryan and the others jumped over the side and began attempting to push the boat off the shoal. The attempt failed. Bryan issued commands to hoist the sails and cleat them windward so that the boat would heal over thus lessening the hold the sand had on the keel. The boat came off the shoal and started off sailing on her own. But before this, while all were in the water, Orth felt a body float by his legs and thought immediately, shark! And he yelled, but just a few seconds later, a seal surfaced and barked…Orth was embarrassed, but laughed with the others. What else was one to think? It was pitch coal dark, and of course, one's imagination runs rampant in these cases, thinking the worst.

Now, the yacht managed to vacate herself from her not appreciated grip of the muddy bottom and moved off swiftly with nobody on board! Bryan ordered Orth to hastily get on board. He grabbed hold of a trailing line and with a total effort managed to just haul himself on board – and exhaustingly turn the boat about to retrieve the others still treading sea water and yelling exclamations to Orth as to what he should do, and not to leave them all night out in the middle of the Bay on a narrow spit of shoal dept of sand.

Orth was successful in positioning the yacht and all personnel were retrieved. They motored back to the Yacht Club without further incident other than being exhausted and fatigued. Orth remained on the crew until he departed Australia in November of 1977.

Life was enjoyable in Australia for the family, but as time wore on, they became more homesick for their homeland. Orth would meet with visiting academics and men who worked in the petroleum industry from the U.S.A. and pry information from them about conditions and so forth. The University asked him to write a textbook on Systems Analysis, because they thought, and Orth agreed, that the available texts coming from the States were inadequate and dealt too heavily upon the computer side of systems, which ignored the vast arena of data assembling and input. So Orth was given more free time to write. He completed the text in one year and it was quickly adopted by the University as its standard reference.

Orth had been on the staff five years and he noticed that he had been passed over several times for promotion to Senior Lecturer. He became mildly concerned. Of course, he did realize that the Australians would naturally prefer their own to a foreigner. So, he endeavored to philosophically accept the fact that he has been stagnated and would think about what course to pursue in the future. He also noticed that if he were to persist as an academician, he would need to have a doctorate.

The family would often discuss matters over the dining room table. The tenor of conversation seemed to have settled to a course pertaining to a return to the United States. Donna also felt an urge to return, and both John and Bert were excited about the prospects. Orth mailed out numberless inquiry letters to universities in the U.S.A. asking for application details into doctoral programs in the faculty of business or management. Replies came filtering back and he applied to at least fifteen schools hoping to get at least several likely possibilities. He was accepted at two universities, Tulane in New Orleans, and the University of Missouri in Columbia, Missouri. He and Donna made plans to move back to the U.S.A.

Both boys were active in the Sea Scouts and the author desires to describe a rather humorous incident that happened to John. The Methodist Church had appointed a British Chartered Accountant, Michael P. Oxford, as Clerk. Michael was the epitome of the staid, true-blue English Accountant. He walked with his head held in an unusually high manner – and his steps were as though he were in a King's processional down the aisle at Westminster Abbey. Each Sunday Michael would march down the aisle of the little Methodist Church and punctiliously cry out, "and now the announcements." This amused Orth and Michael became a favorite topic of the Volzenkoffs for a jovial discussion over the dinner table. Actually, the Oxfords became quite good friends. The two families met frequently and enjoyed teas, picnics and other social visits. Mrs. Oxford, Millicent, was a perfect match for Michael. She was demure and reserved, when she had guests she enjoyed putting out her finest dinnerware that she brought from England. Her conversation was measured and her manners were proper, yet not prudish. There were three children, who also attended the Methodist Church, two daughters, Jennifer and Pamela, and a son, Peter, who was in the middle, age-wise, and was a school chum and fellow Sea Scout with John and Bert.

THE FAMILY WOULD OFTEN DISCUSS MATTERS OVER THE DINING ROOM TABLE....

Bert and Peter had decided to build a raft and sail it across the Canning River, from the South of Perth Yacht Club to the opposite shore, not a great distance, about a quarter of a mile, but wide enough for these two adventurers. They toiled away building the monstrosity at the Sea Scout Boat Shed and Orth put it on his boat trailer and hauled it to the launching site – the beach near the Yacht Club. The boys decided to cast off on a Sunday after Church. Millicent and Donna packed picnic baskets and the two families adjourned to the ill-fated location. Orth viewed the beastly craft and immediately had grave doubts as to its seaworthiness. However, he mused, "the boys deserve to try out their planned epic, even if it is doomed to failure, besides, they probably will not even get out far enough for the water to be over their heads."

After the picnic lunch, all was made in readiness for the undaunted, fearless mariners to launch and cast off for the world beyond the horizon. Both families assembled on shore. It went well for the first few yards, then as the distance from the shore increased, the raft decided to become several smaller parts...The boys had no means to paddle and the poles they had did not now reach the bottom. Soon, the raft tipped and both boys plunged into the water. They were about two to three hundred yards from shore now. They yelled and splashed about. Bert was an excellent swimmer, but it was apparent that Peter lacked the nominal skills. Orth shed his shoes and dove in with his clothes on to go to their aid. He was a few feet from reaching them when a large diesel power cruiser from the Yacht Club came upon the scene.

The skipper called, "need some help, Bert?"

Whereupon both boys were hauled on board and taken to a Yacht Club wharf. Orth thanked the skipper and swam back to shore. The whole episode was made slightly more dangerous because the Canning River was the habitat of numberless large jelly fish who had the ability to sting and paralyze a person's arms or legs if they brushed against the fish's tentacles. Plus, it was widely held that Great White Sharks frequently swam in from the Indian Ocean to the warm shallows of the Canning River seeking tasty morsels. Thus the Great Raft Debacle ends.

Orth submitted his resignation to the University and began to make arrangements to move back to the United States. He went to a travel agent and received information on airplane and ship travel. The family met over the dining room table and made a decision. They would fly from Perth, Australia to Frankfurt, Germany, staying there several days, then travel to Paris, spending two or three days, thence by train travel to the coast of France. They would traverse the English Channel by ship to England – and devote some time there seeing the sights about London. Finally, they would depart England on the Queen Elizabeth, II, a majestic passenger liner operated by Cunard, and land in New York on or about the middle of December, 1977. They held a grandiose garage sale prior to departure and arranged to sell the house. Orth packed the items they decided to keep and shipped them by freighter. The Oxfords drove them to the airport and saw them off accompanied by many other friends. Orth was nervous and kept fidgeting about making certain of passports, traveler's checks, tickets and so forth. He had a family to think of now, not like the old days when he could just pop onto a plane or train and not worry about the many details of carting a family on a long journey.

At about noontime, they boarded a Singapore Airlines flight to Bangkok. Upon landing in Bangkok, they had to change planes to a larger Boeing 747 Jumbo Jet that would take them to Frankfurt, Germany. The airport at Bangkok had a small passenger terminal for the number of people waiting. The Volzenkoffs elbowed their way into the crowd endeavoring to locate the boarding gate for their connecting flight. The small terminal was a din of chattering people conversing in all sorts of foreign tongues, and many were smoking which added to the stench of the already fetid air. But, soon they boarded the large jet and were whisked away toward Europe, arriving in Frankfurt in the morning, not knowing where to stay. Orth inquired at an information booth and obtained a room at a hotel near the center of town. After one night, they moved to a cheaper pension. Donna and Orth agreed they must conserve their cash if Orth is going to pursue his doctorate. The family visited various places about the city for several days then boarded a train for Paris. Any movement of the family meant hauling large suitcases, so they had to plan their moves... However, Orth usually ended up toting several of the boys' bags in addition to his own.

Paris was a disappointment. Large, confused and untidy. They obtained quarters in the "red-light" district, which irritated Orth, as he had asked the information desk at the train depot for a moderately priced hotel nearby. Well, upon hiking up numberless flights of narrow stairs they discovered their room to be a virtual hovel, a wretched mess. Disgusted, Orth said to himself, "I'll be damned if my family is going to spend a night in this run-down dirty dump!"

So, they hastily checked out, and made their way back to the train depot. Onto the train to the coast of France, thence onto a ship from Dunkirk to Dover, England. It was a desperate move, but all agreed that Paris was not a place for a family with scruples.

They traveled all night, hustling bags about, finally exhausted, they sat on board the ship as it churned across the Channel. At about six in the morning the family hastened to the dining room on board and ordered breakfast. Orth would recall, "those fried eggs, toast and coffee tasted like the best I had ever been served."

Of course his opinion was tainted because of his tired exasperated condition. The ship landed at Dover, whereupon the Volzenkoffs trudged off to a train that would take them to Victoria Station, London. Donna had an address to a pension, a bed-and-breakfast, establishment in London that was provided to her by her ex-boss in Perth, a jolly rotund white haired Ph.D., who had taken a liking to her and regretted her departure.

Upon arrival at London, they boarded a taxi. Now, if you have not ridden a London taxicab, you have not experienced a special joy! They are large black Austins, and they are box-like in appearance – going "put-a-put-put" as if their engines would chortle along forever, never missing a beat. And the taxis are clean and neat, the drivers well groomed and decent. Well, our adventurers arrived at the address, whereupon the taxi driver announced that it was too early in the morning – and that the Landlady would not allow the Volzenkoffs in until nine a.m. It is now about eight a.m. What to do?

The cheerful cab driver offers a friendly solution. He offers to drive the family about London, without charge, until the lodging house is opened.

"Marvelous!" condescends Orth, and they enjoy the drive about the City as the "Cabbie" points out various places of interest. Soon, the time is ripe to return to the Hotel. The family heart warmingly thank the cabby who waves them a "goodbye", and they enter the Pension. It is located near Hyde Park, a respectable location. The room is large and clean. The toilet and bath are shared, down the hall. Breakfast is served downstairs in a tidy small dining room between eight and ten in the morning. Fine. Orth is pleased. The landlady is courteous and the accommodations are decent for the price.

After unpacking, they begin to tour London. The subway trains are fast and efficient. The Volzenkoffs spend several days at this location and enjoy seeing Buckingham Palace, Westminster Abbey and Museums. In the evenings at the Hotel, Orth would study the Bible with John and Bert while Donna would busy herself with other endeavors. Orth would frequently play chess with Bert, who was somewhat of a young genius, and often defeated his Dad.

The family departed from London for Salisbury in Wiltshire to view Stonehenge. They packed up and found their way to the train. It was a short journey and they located a moderately priced Hotel near the town center. Orth was disappointed with Stonehenge for some inexplicable reason. He had mentally pictured something much more impressive, and what he viewed, was in his own mind, "a heap of stone monoliths placed there a few hundred years earlier by some scholars as a hoax or as an expression of art."

After Salisbury, the Volzenkoffs once more tugged away with their baggage and by train journey to Southampton, a gigantic port city where they prepared to board the Queen Elizabeth II, which to all was the apex of their journey.

Unless you have ridden on a passenger liner, it is difficult to describe the thrill and joy of shipboard life. There is a magic to it. The Queen Elizabeth II is a large, luxurious ship designed and staffed to pamper the traveler. The family occupied quarters in the second-class section, however, the quality of the accommodations exceeded those that they experienced on the P & O Liner, Orsova, when they traveled to the Pacific. Because it was the slow season, November, they enjoyed the extra freedom from crowds and had double the number of dining room stewards. The ship departed Southampton for LeHavre, France in the afternoon, arriving in France to embark more passengers for the transatlantic journey. The ship put into France at about midnight, staying only briefly, then put out to sea to cross south of the Lizard in England. Here they encountered extremely heavy seas and the Queen was buffeted severely. All 66,000 tons of her groaned under the pounding of the North Atlantic.

It was difficult sleeping in the cabin under those conditions. Donna became seasick along with John. Bert and Orth were rustled about, but managed to avoid any discomfort.

They awoke the following morning and made their way to breakfast. During breakfast they learned from a bulletin that was placed on the table that the ship had slipped an anchor and that the anchor had swung down and punctured and small hole in the bow. The hole was leaking water, but the ship's pumps were able to stay ahead of the in-surging water. However, to lessen any possible further damage to the bow section, the Captain announced that they had to reduce speed ten knots, and therefore, they would be several days late arriving in the United States. Additionally, the ship would put into Boston Harbor rather than New York, because of the necessity to secure repair facilities. These circumstances did not trouble the family, they would adjust. So, they settled into a shipboard life once again. Orth met daily with the boys in the cabin to read the Bible together and pray. He was committed to teach his sons Christianity.

People so often deny the truth out of ignorance, and Orth now *knew* the Truth! People deny God and His Son Christ Jesus just like some professors in Italy during the seventeenth century denied the existence of facts concerning the solar system and details about the sun, stars and the moon. Galileo was persecuted and ridiculed when he attempted to prove his theories by telescope. People remained ignorant, blinded by stupid obedience to Aristotle's ancient incorrect hypotheses. Orth wanted his sons to taste the Truth, he wanted his sons to know Jesus Christ, the redeemer of mankind.

Orth would swim in the ship's swimming pool and work out in the gymnasium. He was always concerned about keeping in reasonably sound physical condition. In the afternoons he and Bert would play chess. John remained closer to Donna, which Orth didn't mind, hoping that he would alter his behavior later in life and enjoy more time with his Dad. Orth would walk the decks doing about three or four miles in the morning and evening. He liked the sea, and the Atlantic in November had a real bite as the winds would swirl down upon the ship. Nature is an intelligible minister appointed to lead us. The powerful oceans lead one to God, being a revelation of Him in one aspect of His personality – His power and wisdom, brought to our comprehension by the Holy Spirit (our Teacher). The Spirit shows us the Divinity of God in

Christ, it is our means of rising up to a knowledge of God in His holiness and love – and of man in his duty and destiny to serve our Master. Orth ponders continually now upon the character of God and of philosophical and theological questions. He marvels at the whole new realm of thought opened to him by his conversion in Australia. He has gained an unquenchable thirst to learn of the Church of Christ. The early Church – the Reformation, that period of time wherein God tenderly placed the trust of the Gospel of His Son Christ into the hands of a few courageous and faithful noble humble beings. The sixteenth century – the dawning of the great Protestant movement. So much to do, so few moments to achieve. But Orth concludes that if Christ decides to use him, he will wait upon the Lord. He will cast his bread upon the waters. He will struggle and do the tasks set before him as they occur and try not to be fretful nor worrisome.

CHAPTER XXIII

Now we look forward with confidence to our heavenly bodies, realizing that every moment we spend in these earthly bodies is time spent away from our eternal home in heaven with Jesus. We know these things are true by believing, not by seeing. And we are not afraid, but are quite content to die, for then we will be at home with the Lord. So our aim is to please him always in everything we do, whether we are here in this body or away from this body and with him in heaven.

2 Corinthians 5:6-9

Orth would meet death again soon when his beloved Donna departs the earth while they are living in Missouri. But that is getting ahead of the Orth story.

The Queen Elizabeth II eases into Boston inner harbor in the morning. It is chilly on deck as it is now late November, and New England is bone-jarring cold for the Volzenkoffs who have been pampered by the mild Mediterranean climate of Perth, Australia. The family disembarks and is met in the terminal with a mass of passengers, many confused and boisterous. Orth hails a taxicab. The driver is a huge obese man who seems unimpressed with an opportunity for business. He labors out of his long oversize vehicle, opens the trunk lid and motions the family to deposit their luggage into the recesses. The family enters the cab and as the driver lowers his layers of blubber into the front seat, the taxi takes on a decided list to the port side. Orth tells the driver to take them to a Howard Johnson Motel, the address and location he had obtained from a friendly fellow passenger as a place of reasonable price and worthwhile location.

They check into the motel and Orth is stifled by the heat in the room. He mumbles to himself, "the U.S. is a nation of excesses, too much noise, money, earthly luxuries, fat taxicab drivers, and fast food joints." He supposes it is endemic to those who have traveled abroad, coming home to see the wretchedness of their homeland. A reverse culture shock as it were. Thus the Volzenkoffs are again introduced to their birthplace. America – founded by Puritans, forged by stalwart Christians, now a wasteland of confused souls seeking their illusory philosopher's stone. Religion to many now is compromises between Christian moral values and success in business, profession, military, academia or what have you. The "comfortable" Christian places success in worldly things above God.

Orth purchases a large Oldsmobile station wagon from a local new car dealer, paying him $1000 cash. The vehicle is five years old, but in excellent mechanical condition. So, the family checks out of the motel and begin their long journey to Missouri. They stop at various places along the way, Washington, D.C., and of course, Wisconsin to visit with Donna's parents and Orth's brother, Fritz, before heading south to Columbia, Missouri. Orth rents a motel room in Columbia until they are able to locate a house. With the help of a real estate agent that was referred to them at the University, they locate a nice two-story house west of the center of town and Orth settles the deal with cash obtained when he sold the house in Perth.

Soon the household goods and other personal items arrive from Australia by ship and once again the Volzenkoffs settle in attempting to establish a peaceful and meaningful routine. John and Bert are enrolled in High School and instead of being placed in a class behind their years, because of the time lost in travel, they are advanced an entire year because of their superior training provided by the Australian school system. This was a profound message to Orth which told him how sad the United States educational system had become since he had attended school.

Orth is enrolled into the doctoral program soon after his credentials had been submitted, and after scoring high on the Graduate Records Examination (GRE). All of this was academic as he had already been accepted, but the administrative wheels of academia grind slowly at a consternating pace.

> ORTH'S DOCTORAL FACULTY ADVISOR WAS DR. SAUL HENTLIFF— A JEWISH PROFESSOR— THEY BECAME GOOD FRIENDS....

His faculty advisor in the Graduate School of Business is Saul Hentliff, a Jewish professor who had obtained his Ph.D. from the University of California. Orth likes Professor Hentliff. He is a small man with a large oversized bald cranium, deep-set dark eyes and a hawk-like nose. His glasses sit on the edge of his nose and he is constantly pushing them back. When he sits at his desk, he is so small that his feet do not touch the floor as he swivels about. Dr. Hentliff is a neat and preppie dresser. His rhetorical style is casual but exhibits a deep and keen intellectual mind. He leans back in his chair and informs Orth at their first meeting, "the measure of a person's intellect is the time it takes after he opens his mouth to the time he convinces you that he is a fool...Listen intently, Mr. Volzenkoff, speak with measured accuracy and with truth and facts. Use few words, treat words as pearls to be of value, not to be cast about in a careless manner."

Orth is assigned several classes to teach while he attends sessions on research and some classes at the graduate level on investments, managerial problems, statistical analysis and so forth. The classes he is assigned to teach are undergraduate courses in accounting and systems analysis. He formulates his dissertation plan and submits the proposal to Dr. Hentliff, who thinks it has scholarly merit. The work is entitled "Risk Measurement and Evaluation in Bank Audits".

The Dissertation Committee meets in a lecture hall where the seats are along the north and south side of the room, either ends are open. In the center of the large room is a long library table and at one end is a long table where the Committee was seated. Orth was the only person seated at the library table in the center. An audience of faculty and graduate students sat in the side seats. Copies of the Proposal had been previously submitted to the Committee for their perusal. Dr. Hentliff was seated in one of the Committee seats – the Chairman, Dean of the Graduate School, Dr. Phillip Graham, sat in the center. The hall was quiet as a morgue. Orth thought his swallowing could be heard a mile away.

Dr. Graham, after a long intentional pause, opened by saying, "Mr. Volzenkoff, I have looked over your proposal, and we are assembled to hear your comments as to the scholarly merits of this research. You have forty-five minutes to try to convince myself and the other members of this body that your proposal is a worthy endeavor for a candidate for a doctoral degree – or that it lacks the necessary depth of an intellectual pursuit and can be counted as a somewhat shallow attempt to perform research upon a topic seen wanting as far as being of benefit to this University, mankind in general and the area of finance which you have chosen as an arena of interest...you may proceed."

Orth was frightfully nervous after that opening. He paused then went into the fight to defend his ideas. He argued, he submitted facts, he toiled and sweated for the full forty-five minutes. Then it was over. Silence.

Then Dr. Graham tersely said, "we shall let you know."

As Orth gathered his materials from the table and stuffed them into his briefcase, several came down and offered him encouragement. Dr. Hentliff also walked up to Orth and uttered, "don't give up yet, Mr. Volzenkoff, there is still hope."

Eventually he received word from the Dean that his proposal would be accepted given several modifications were made. These were not serious – and Orth was elated at the thought that his research now may begin in earnest. It took him until April 1975 to complete his work. It was a monumental task. He dug up files from various governmental agencies, took a trip to Washington, D.C., to dig up data on banking crimes in the Library of Congress and did extensive reading on his topic. His office at home was cluttered with cardboard boxes of data and information. There were numberless pages and files on mathematical calculations and statistics. Dr. Hentliff typed up the final manuscript for a fee and Orth assembled it and submitted it to the Dissertation Committee for approval. Dr. Hentliff worked right along with Orth as he wrote. The time was now that he must formally defend his work before the Dean and the Committee.

All went well – Orth was surprised! He had perceived that Dean Graham did not necessarily like him. Perhaps it was because Orth was older than Dr. Graham and had been through a great deal more. Orth – an Army combat veteran, CPA, MBA, serving in Australia as a faculty member of a noteworthy university. Who knows?

People are self-centered by nature – their motives are selfish – therefore there will be a factious spirit – always present and seditious; dissenting persons – evil by nature. God alone can save one from evil. Anyway, it was done now and Donna rejoiced along with the boys.

Donna did not look well these last several months of 1974, and it carried into 1975. Orth was worried, she had lost so much weight. She always was so quiet, never complaining and doing her wifely chores without a whimper. Orth almost had to pry information out of her. One evening after supper and the boys were in their separate bedrooms studying, he edges up to Donna as she is washing the dishes. He places his arm around her and says, "Hiyah, beautiful, how about you and I going out to some remote spot and neck?" She turns and places her tear-sodden face into Orth's chest and reaches around his neck with both arms.

"I'm not going to be with you very much longer, my dearest."

They stay embraced saying nothing for several moments; Orth seems to know intuitively that something is dreadfully wrong with his sweetheart's health.

"Can you tell me?" he quietly utters.

"I've taken some tests at the University Hospital...they concluded that I have cancer of the uterus...I have to go back Friday for more tests and X-rays," Donna tearfully forces out. "I've thought about dying and you and the boys – I'm just so happy we have had such a wonderful time while it has lasted," Donna concludes.

They retire to the parlor and sit alone thinking, when both John and Bert enter. They talk to Orth and Donna who avoid the topic about her health. Her condition deteriorated rapidly and she was considered a terminal case. Any surgical procedure the doctors thought would only be detrimental to the little strength she had remaining. Donna retired to bed at home where she was attended to by a nurse. However, as her condition worsened, she was moved to the Cancer Research Center of the University. The boys and Orth visited constantly. She always managed to smile right up to the time that the Lord called her home.

Orth was stunned over the loss of his cherished wife, but his faith bolstered him. John and Bert wept fervently and Orth met with them constantly at the dining room table to read the Bible and hold prayer sessions. Orth would find himself absently glancing over to the stove and sink expecting to see Donna standing there – showing him a smile over her shoulder. Donna was buried in her home town of Cockhan, Wisconsin, under a large oak tree. Many of the Sregor's were there. Orth and the boys had accompanied the casket from Missouri to Wisconsin.

After several weeks, Karen, Donna's sister came to visit Orth and stayed for a month. She was a blessing to Orth, because she cleaned the house and prepared the necessary meals for he and the boys. Orth was simply overwhelmed. Because of his teaching schedule at the university, and household chores – he lacked the time and energy. June came, and Orth attended the commencement exercises held in Jesse Auditorium where his Doctoral degree was conferred upon him. Somehow, he felt Donna was with him – as he walked upon the stage to receive his Ph.D. diploma – he seemed to feel Donna's hand in his, saying in a soft, sweet voice, "I knew you could do it, you big galoot – will love you till eternity."

Orth shed tears as he departed the Auditorium with John and Bertram by his side.

Now that he had his doctorate, it was time for Orth to seek a teaching job of a permanent nature. He sent forth many applications to various universities that were seeking to have positions filled for the fall semester of 1975.

He waited and waited but no replies came. Then a stroke of luck came from an unexpected quarter. Dr. Hentliff and he were discussing a project that one of the students was working upon. The student was Francis (Frank) Fogelmeyer, from Salt Lake City, Utah. Frank was working on his MBA, Master of Business Administration Degree and was currently involved in writing a paper on bank frauds for his class on business ethics. Somehow, the topic got around to Orth's trying to locate a teaching position at a university or college. Frank commented that his father was Dean of Faculty in the School of Business Administration at the University of Utah, and suggested that Orth send him a resume as his father was always lamenting the fact that he had difficulty in staffing because of budget limitations. Qualified professors were always seeking a better paying job elsewhere at a university of better name. Enough. Orth wasted no time and sent his qualifications to Utah. The reply was almost instantaneous!

Dr. J. Finchley Folgelmeyer telephoned him after several days and requested that he come immediately for an interview and tour of the campus. Orth informed Dr. Hentliff, and departed from the Kansas City Airport for Salt Lake City. The University of Utah sits under the shadow of surrounding mountains. It was not a particularly pretty campus. Orth chatted with Dr. Folgelmeyer and several other academicians. He walked the campus, situated within the city limits, and decided to accept the starting salary and title of Associate Professor of Finance and Accounting. He took the return flight back to Columbia, Missouri and announced his decision to John, Bert and Karen. It was now in the middle of summer and the Volzenkoff family made ready to move to Salt Lake City, Utah.

The house was sold and Orth and the boys traveled to Utah. The furniture was shipped by a moving company. Karen bid them "goodbye", as she had to return to her job in Cleveland.

Orth was successful in locating a fine home in Salt Lake City close to the University, in the avenues. Both John and Bert were enrolled in High School where they were now in their senior year. The semester commenced at the University of Utah and Orth was assigned to teach twelve contact hours – which consisted of three classes of four credit hours each.

The years rolled by and both boys were attending university. John enrolled at the University of Missouri, Columbia, and Bert enrolled at Southern Methodist, but transferred to the University of Missouri after one year.

Both John and Bert desired to attend Missouri for sound reasons. They had applied there and were accepted. They also learned that substantial scholarships would be available and many of their friends in Columbia would be going there. Additionally, they preferred Columbia to Salt Lake City because it was a smaller city and not as "Mormanized". Both boys had been reared by Orth in the Methodist tradition, had been baptized Methodists and they desired to remain so. In fact, Bert was so enthusiastic about John Wesley and his plight and courage as a pioneer Christian hero that he entered Southern Methodist University in Dallas, Texas. However, he transferred to Missouri after one year, as he could not tolerate Texas and Dallas – and felt more at home in Columbia, Missouri.

The boys would come home to visit their father at semester breaks and holidays. Bert was the student – John was struggling. Bert was majoring in Nursing and doing well. John declared a major in archeology. Orth re-entered the Army Reserves to finish his time until retirement at age 60. He was now forty-eight years old. Soon the Army promoted him to Chief Master Sergeant (E-9) the highest enlisted rank. He held this rank until he departed the Army in 1989.

Orth liked to sail and he purchased a twenty-one foot "Victory" that was advertised in the Salt Lake Tribune. He rented a slip at the Great Salt Lake Marina and he would sail on the weekends and occasionally on hot summer evenings. The University would hold "mixers" at the Officers Club at Fort Douglas, an Army Post adjacent to the campus. One evening he attended one of the socials just for an opportunity to meet the female of the species again. He had not had anything to do with the femme sole after the death of Donna, and he felt himself becoming a detestable hermit or monk. A band played at these gatherings and the participants would enjoy a cocktail between dances.

"Hi, I'm Nancy."

Orth looked up from the table he had seated himself in the corner, and had been carrying on a light conversation with several other male academics. He rises and answers, "Sorry, were you addressing me?"

"Yes, of course, would you like to dance?"

Orth stammers for an answer, then weakly says, "why, er, yes." He excuses himself from the others at the table and he and Nancy step out upon the crowded floor, where the band is playing a waltz. Bertha had taught her son well as Orth and Nancy cut a trim couple dancing with style and grace.

"You dance well," she said.

"Thanks – you, too," Orth replied.

As the music ended Nancy invited Orth over to her table where another couple were seated. After introductions, the other couple excused themselves and departed. Nancy and Orth remained at the table and began to converse in light conversation.

Nancy Baum Steinmann, was the young lady's name. She was a Ph.D. candidate in the College of Health Sciences, age twenty-five, a very bright and intelligent woman, Orth perceived. She was of medium height, dark hair and a full figure tending toward the plump side. She was employed as a Teaching Assistant while she worked on her doctorate. She had a good sense of humor and laughed heartily when Orth would utter something flippant or funny. Orth enjoyed her company and they met often and dated regularly. Orth would go over to her apartment on occasions and Nancy would prepare a delicious supper which delighted him because he was not a cook and his meals were monotonous and in want of variety.

Religion was irritating to Nancy. She was Jewish – from an orthodox family, but she could not be bothered with worshipping as a Hebrew, in fact, she admitted to being hostile to anything Jewish in the traditional sense. Orth strived to teach her Christianity but her mind was immovable. Anyway, Orth enjoyed her company because she was one of the few females that he had ever encountered who had a poignant mind, and intellect with wisdom. They used to go sailing together out on the Great Salt Lake. Nancy enjoyed the water and used to take her dog with her on the boat with Orth.

"Are you one of those dreadful Mormons?" Nancy asked one evening after supper.

"You have to be jolly-well not serious to ask such a ridiculous question as that! Of course not," Orth replies vehemently.

"Just curious," she replies.

They then discuss the Salt Lake City area and the Mormon church, or as it is formally known, "The Church of Jesus Christ of Latter Day Saints."

"I'm a Methodist, have been since my conversion in Australia some nine years ago," Orth explains. "The Mormon missionaries come to visit me from time to time, and we go through a series of exercises in frustration – they trying to convince me of their opinions on theology and I trying to convince them of the errors in their ways of thinking," Orth says.

"I know," Nancy continues, "they talk to me and I simply show them the door – this town wreaks with their sanctimonious mummery – their pious attitudes and so forth. I just cannot stomach such provincialism," she concludes.

"Let me show you something," Orth says. He asks Nancy for several sheets of paper and starts to write while explaining his viewpoints as he progresses.

"The Bible warns us about False Prophets in Matthew Chapter 24, and The Second Epistle of Peter, and I believe in the ideas of John Wesley, who set down some thoughts on how you can ascertain if what a particular sect says is truth or not." And this is what our hero writes down for Nancy's edification:

False Prophets –
According to John Wesley's Twenty-Seventh Sermon

1. They will have a fair appearance – they will give the impression of impeccable cleanfulness.

2. They will interpret the Bible in their own meaning to try to convince their listeners. They will twist and turn words in a cunning and artful deception.

3. They deny Christ by placing obstacles between you and the Lord. They appoint officials who sit in judgment – yet the Bible tells us that forgiveness comes only from Jesus.

4. They profess to be sent of God – that their way is the only way to heaven. Yet the Bible tells us the Christ is the way to salvation and He only holds the keys to eternal life – no man made code or institution.

5. They will tell you that God only communicates the truth to their appointed leaders – yet the Bible tells you that Christ is with us always and speaks to us through His Holy Spirit.

6. They will tell you a great success story of their sect – how many have joined. This is the false way – the broad way to falsehood. Christ is not a popularity contest – few will trod the unpopular narrow path. You must be singular – truth is the narrow way.

7. The way to heaven is lowliness, mourning and meekness. Sects that are proud of their growth – their programs, their good deeds are not lowly – are not meek. Church leaders who sit in plush red chairs – enjoy luxurious offices – ride in expensive automobiles and so forth are not meek nor lowly. To mourn is to regret your wretched sins. Church leaders who hold themselves above others as sinless are not being mournful.

8. They teach that their "church" has the proper authority received from God or his appointed. They stress they hold a direct line from the Apostolic

succession. However, there is nothing in the Bible that states that this will happen. The Bible stresses that all Christians are 'Priests unto God' - and are children of Abraham.

9. They "say" that they are "kind to their neighbors", but their actions prove otherwise. They do not acknowledge that righteous deeds done by others outside their sect are worthy of God's blessings – contrarily they count them as naught.

10. They come in the meek and mild manner – professing to be useful – to do good – to watch over your soul – to educate you in the ways to eternal life.

11. Any person or organization that places themselves between you and God are denying the gift of the Holy Spirit as your companion that Christ promised, when he ascended to Heaven after His resurrection! They deny the blood of the Savior!

12. The Bible teaches us that we are a "church" within ourselves, which means, we decide our destiny with the help of the Holy Ghost. No worldly organization has the right to dictate our actions, our salvation is up to us. Either you are with Christ or against Him.

13. They come appearing to be religious – making God a liar by giving their own ideas to replace or distort the Bible.

14. They appear to love you – to rescue you from error or mischievous doctrines.

15. "Ye shall know them by their fruits," our Master says. And what are their fruits? Large expensive buildings and accoutrements. Money rules. You can become important in their organization if you donate enough money. They say one thing, but do another. They deny your privilege to think for yourself. With them it is "You follow this line, or else we toss you out on your buttocks."

16. They will tell you "God has spoken to them or to their organization..."

"You need not have written a book on the subject," Nancy asserts.

"Well, I want you to see for yourself, and the next time a Mormon challenges your belief...use these notes," Orth says.

"I don't have any belief," Nancy confesses.

Orth feels sadness for her. So many parents scrape together their hard earned dollars to send their children to college, expecting them to receive an education. But alas! At college the young fertile minds are taught by atheists, in many cases, to ignore the Bible as being old-fashioned. Colleges now days seem palaces for the pragmatists – the materialist who ridicule Christ – who mock the God of Abraham, Isaac and Jacob as being superstitious nonsense. Most universities and colleges today worship Kant, Nietzche, Dewey, etc. But the "Truth" is Christ! Men shall come and go, but the Truth remains – and that undeniable Truth is a word manifested in flesh who lived before the earth was formed and He lives today, and he will live forever.

CHAPTER XXIV

Oh, remember how short you have made man's life span. Is it an empty, futile life your give the sons of men? No man can live forever. All will die. Who can rescue his life from the power of the grave?

Psalms 89: 47-48

Our hero is promoted to Assistant Professor. And time marches forward toward his 58th birthday. John and Bert graduate from college. John acquired a bachelor's degree in archeology and Bert a bachelor of science degree in nursing. Bert obtained a decent position with the Veteran's Administration – in a hospital in Portland, Oregon and John had continued difficulty locating any kind of employment that suited him and bounced about from job to job.

John married a young woman from Connecticut who attended the University of Utah and had a position with the City Library system in Salt Lake City. She was a Mormon. Her name was Emily Klankfort and she was corpulent. Bert married a young nurse he had met in Nursing School, Amie Dingfelt and they both moved to Vancouver, Washington. Amie was a lively girl. On several occasions Orth flew out to visit Bert and he enjoyed the robust spirit of Amie. She was an excellent cook and pampered Orth with her delicious delicacies, especially her own concoction of pound cake. Bert and his dad enjoyed chess, tennis and sailing together. John's interests were toward the performing arts and a deep seated, almost obsessive fascination toward the civil war.

The University had an early retirement program which interested Orth. He felt that he had become stagnant, he needed time away from the cloistered life of academia. He wanted to write – to do research, and the schedule he had did not allow such activities. Therefore, he sat down and planned a retirement budget. He concluded that if he moved to a less expensive area, and with his University and Army retirement, he could live quite comfortably. In addition, in a few more years, he would qualify for Social Security at age 62. He would do it.

He applied for early retirement and he departed the University on the fifteenth of May 1988. The University gave him a retirement luncheon in the faculty Dining Room on the top floor of the Harris Student Union Building. Nancy Steinmann was there along with some of Orth's other friends and cronies. At the conclusion, all bid our hero a fond farewell accompanied with the usual trite and hackneyed phrases commonplace upon such gatherings. Nancy walked with him to his car and they embraced and kissed each other goodbye. Orth drove home. He felt empty, lonely. He would miss the campus life where youth seemed to permeate his aging bones. He thought to himself how he must learn to live alone, but yet he is never alone, because Christ said He would send the Holy Spirit to be his companion. And who was it? Yes, Galileo said, "I am not alone! The truth is with me. And truth can defeat the whole of Rome." Of a certainty – and it did! Christ's chosen defeated the legions of Rome by example – coming forth from the catacombs to be living martyrs. Witnesses to the world that Christ died – and rose to be the Master of mankind universally and eternally. "I AM the Way, the Truth and the Life," the Lord said. Man's natural inclination is to reject the truth..."Don't confuse me with the facts," is the way of the world.

He drives home and starts to think about where he should move to now that he is retiring.

"Why not back to Wisconsin?" Nancy suggests over the phone.

Orth phones Fritz, and learns that there are many places available and suggests that he contact their old neighbor, Eddie Burran, who has decided to move into town from his farm which is seven miles from New Hesse. New Hesse is approximately twenty-seven miles north west of Milwaukee. He phones Mr. Burran and learns that an adjoining farmer had purchased his farm, but the house and the surrounding few acres and barns had been excluded from the sale and Eddie would be happy to have Orth consider the purchase.

Orth called up Delta Airlines and flew to Milwaukee the next weekend to look over the old Burran homestead. He rented a car and drove to New Hesse. The house was well maintained and large. Sufficient for Orth to have his library and plenty of additional space for an office and other living accommodations. He agreed with Mr. Burran upon a most amicable purchase price and the purchase was consummated. A bank in New Hesse handled the escrow.

It took Orth several weeks to move out of his Salt Lake City home. A buyer was rapidly located, in fact he was an addition to the academic staff at the University and was happy with Orth's house being so close to the campus and in one of the most desirable locations of the City.

"I'm going to call her "Home Port", in informed Fritz during a visit.

"You are crazy, Orth" Fritz retorted, being his usual irascible self.

Orth busily worked upon Home Port, moving in his library arranging furniture and building needed bookshelves and shelves to lodge his many volumes and papers. Generally, then dear reader, this brings us to the point of our journey wherein we find our hero comfortably living with his trusted dog, Mutnik, in his rustic rural abode, as a retired, musty old university professor. He has his books and memories. He has written several books and is currently writing his memoirs from a wealth of descriptive notebooks he has energetically maintained. His literary desires are to bring for Christ in his life in such a manner as to spark hope and joy to others who may stumble upon his works. Orth is adamant in his attempt to refute the words of worldly atheistic scholars, like John Dewey, who have deceived gullible masses by discrediting Jesus and rejecting God. Saint Paul said it sagaciously and shrewdly when he said, "The wisdom of man is dross and base next to that of God."

* * * * * * * *

"I have a couple of tickets to a concert by the Milwaukee Symphony on Saturday – can you make it?" Orth asks Libby over the phone on a Monday evening.

"Love to Ortie," she replies.

"Pick you up at six – that will give us time for supper at Frederick's before the concert, which starts at eight – Elein Hall. I'll phone Otto for a table – Saturday is usually fairly crowded especially at concert night," Orth continues.

They chat for a while and they hang up.

Orth thinks more of Libby these days and even ponders thoughts of a matrimonial alliance. "Good grief," he thinks to himself. "I wonder how it would be after all these years, having a female about the house." He hums to himself as he putters about the kitchen – the tune from "My Fair Lady"...

> *"I've grown accustomed to her face...she almost makes the day begin...her smiles, her frowns...her ups – her downs..."*

"Well," he thinks, "if God wills it – it will happen."

Saturday arrives and Orth takes a shower and readies himself to drive in to pick up Libby for the concert. He arrives at the apartment – Libby greets him and he sits in the living room while she puts the finishing touches upon her attire and other female duties. Danny comes in from outdoors and they chat briefly.

"Are you going to hear Beethoven?" Danny asks.

"To tell you the truth I have not learned what the Orchestra has planned. There is a guest conductor, Michael Tilson-Thomas from the Philadelphia Symphony Orchestra, and I'm sure that the music will be most enjoyable and entertaining, why do you ask, Danny?" Orth answers.

"Well...we are studying Beethoven in our music appreciation class...I really enjoy his Fifth Symphony. It's real cool," Danny replies.

"I'm glad for you, Danny. Good music is an art that can enlighten and be a soothing experience," Orth says.

"Ya...most of the other kids in the class think the classics suck. I don't care, I just enjoy the sounds and stuff," Danny states.

"Don't try to pay too much attention to what others think – or what the crowds are doing, Danny. Be yourself. It is natural for young people to be impetuous, fiery-tempered, irrational, over emotional, frivolous and visionary. I know. I was there once," Orth counsels as Libby enters with her coat draped over her arm.

"Will you be all right, dear?" she asks Danny.

"Don't worry, Mom. Bob Munchen is coming over and we are going to play chess, talk and watch the Brewers on TV."

"Well...we should be home sometime around eleven – is that right, Ortie?" Libby eyes Orth and he nods agreement.

Orth and Libby drive to Frederick's. Few words were exchanged as they drove. Orth was thinking about Libby and Libby was thinking of Orth.

"She is so much younger than I...I wonder how she would feel being wedded to such an old antique as I?" he thought.

"He is so educated and cultured. How could I ever expect to make him happy?" Libby thought.

Otto was behind the Bar, talking to customers as Orth and Libby entered. He waved, smiled and exclaimed, "Hiyah, Ortie...Who's that charming young chick you have with you?"

Libby felt embarrassed – both smiled and said hello to Otto, then headed for the Dining Area. Bertha, the waitress showed them to a table close to the old stained glass leaded window facing the sidewalk. Some of the usual crowd were at the Bar and they came by to greet Orth and Libby. Eddie Aiteanwealer and Archie Airehorn came in together and after sitting at the bar for a short while came to greet them.

"Well, this is a cozy couple," Eddie mockingly commented, adding, "I haven't seen you around for a long time, Libby. Where have you been hiding out?" Archie returned to the bar.

Libby answered quietly, "My life has changed, Eddie. It's a long story."

They talked about the usual light matters, then Eddie joins his companions at the Bar.

"What a waste," Libby comments about Eddie.

"Eddie is not lost, Libby. Perhaps he will discover he has a potential. Christ never discarded anyone and He is the beginning of life and wisdom. Christ did not toss me out on the trash heap of society. I struggled – thought I had an education and a good life after college and so forth," Orth says.

Bertha brings their supper. "What to drink, Libby?"

"Coffee, and you, Ortie?"

"Coffee for me also, Bertha."

"The mind is a marvelous thing, isn't it, Ortie," Libby observes.

Orth pauses a moment. "An ego is easily flattered by intellect. The person becomes self-righteous–he avoids reality by thinking mankind can solve all his problems. He eliminates God as a philosophic value. Eddie is at this stage. He is no intellectual giant, yet he thinks mankind can solve his woes. Satan grows quite well in the fertile soil of pride in intellect. Eddie and Archie and others who are non-Christians turn to the government – to social workers – to astrologers – to psychologists to solve their problems. Their philosophy of humanism is reinforced by ministers or others who remove Christ and God from their messages. God is present in our lives. He is close to us, He (the Holy Spirit) urges us to come into His arms – yet His invitation is too often sadly refused.

He is often rejected – and people run hither and yon for help," Orth reflects.

"I've lost so much ground – but, I've found out one thing. My mind has changed, Ortie. I'm reading the Bible with Danny – maybe it's you, maybe it's going to the Church in New Hesse. My college education at Wisconsin seemed to lead me away from religion, Ortie. You know how it goes – the campus lifestyle is all party – going out on dates and stuff like that. I went to the Lutheran Church as a youngster, but religion seemed so distant – so mechanical," Libby remarks.

Orth nods. They continue to talk along philosophic lines.

"I suppose you may say that $x + y =$ the 'whole' person, Libby, 'x' being the materialist part of a person and 'y' being the spiritual, transcendental part. Some people wander along life's journey never discovering 'y'. Others are fortunate to unearth Christ and God therefore becoming a 'whole' person. Thomas Carlyle wrote about the 'Everlasting Yes', when he found God amongst nature, Libby," Orth reflects.

They finish supper and walk the short distance to Elein Hall for the concert, holding hands like newlyweds. Libby enjoys the warm, strong feelings of Orth's large bony touch. He likes the soft feminine palms of Libby. The theatre was almost full and their seats were superb – center section – Row G, seats 15 and 16. Some were seated in the row as they excused themselves to settle in their location. The Milwaukee's Symphony Orchestra is a fine accumulation of professional musicians and the music selection for this evening's performance included Tchaikovsky's Piano Concerto No. 1 in B-flat Minor, Opus 23 and Beethoven's Ninth Symphony in D Minor, Opus 125, Ode to Joy.

The performance ended at slightly after ten and they walked back to the parking lot enjoying the warm early autumn evening. Orth was keenly aware now that his attraction to Libby was more than a casual friendship. He felt strongly toward her, almost more emotionally than he had experienced toward any woman before, even his departed cherished wife, Donna. He would not admit to this – but there it was. His nose sensed her perfume which was not overly pungent, just simply divinely womanish.

Orth unlocked the passenger side and opened the door for her. She turned abruptly and embraced Orth, they kissed warmly then drove to the restaurant near Libby's apartment where they ordered coffee and apple pie. They spoke little, but searched each other's eyes. They seemed to know that they both shared the same amount of profound love for each other. The pie and coffee came and they both ate and drank thinking little else as they did so except about their affections.

Orth drives Libby to her apartment. They sit and talk for a while.

"Would you consider living with an old war horse like me?"

Libby looks into Orth's thoughtful and sad blue eyes and says nothing for several moments."

"You're so intellectual and cultured, Ortie – and I'm such a blockhead with a shaded past – I don't know," she replies.

"I do <u>know</u>, Libby. I would consider it a blessing if you would say 'yes'."

"I want you to be happy, my dearest. I'm not much – my life has been a hell hole," Libby laments.

"We will let the Lord direct our lives from here on out, Libby," Orth reflects.

"Well, for starters…I guess we had best go in and break the news to Danny. I know he will be happy," she concludes.

They go into the apartment. Danny is listening to a baseball game on the radio in his room and Orth and Libby join him and announce their betrothal. Danny throws his arms around Orth, then hugs his mother.

Orth requests they go into the living room and have a prayer circle. They kneel and join hands, while Orth prays:

> "Our Heavenly Father, we, your children humbly gather together at thy feet to thank Thee for blessing us so enormously and for being so gracious to us continually – unworthy as we are. Father, Thou knowest all things, and we here declare our intention of becoming a family in Thy sight – that Thy will be done in our lives – as Husband and Wife, as Parents and son. Bless our union Our Father, that it may be one in love and harmony with Thy heart, that it may be a marriage till death takes us back into Thy Holy presence – And, that we may continue in union even beyond the grave if it be Thy pleasure. Father, we ask these things and seek Your guidance and wisdom through the Holy Spirit – and we pray these things in the Everlasting name of Jesus The Christ, Thy Holy Son and our Master and Redeemer. Amen and Amen

They rise. Danny and Libby exhibit tearful eyes, and Orth promises Libby that he will drop by tomorrow, Sunday, to pick them up for church in New

Hesse. Also, after church, they will have an opportunity to meet with Mike Wilinda, the Pastor, to make arrangements for the wedding ceremony. Orth departs and commences his drive back to Homeport. He laughs to himself, "how will John and Bert react, I wonder, when I inform them that they will have a new mother not ten years older than they are, well, God knows best."

* * *

It is seven thirty Sunday morning when Libby is aroused by the doorbell. She slips into her robe and opens the door to discover Pastor Mike Wilinda standing there – the hallway light showing his bright white clerical collar. His countenance is sad and his eyes reflect compassion. Fear grips Libby's heart – she has a premonition that something dreadful has happened. Danny joins them in the living room.

"Prepare yourselves...The Lord has taken Orth," Mike silently speaks.

Libby sits stunned – she presses her hands to her eyes and lowers her head to her lap not saying anything, just weeping uncontrollably. Mike and Danny wrap their arms around her.

"He was the most wonderful man I have ever met...I don't know how I will..." She stops, but tears continue to flow. After several minutes, Libby gains sufficient composure for Reverend Wilinda to explain what happened.

"It was a large grain truck, Orth was on his way home last night when on one of the country roads leading to his home, he noticed a car pulled off the road with the lights on – the car was being driven by a young woman with several young children with her. They had a flat tire and no jack or other tools to change it to the spare. Orth stopped to help...it was near midnight or one in the morning. The grain truck swerved to avoid an on-coming car and when he did so, he struck Orth. He was taken to Saint Joseph's Hospital in North Milwaukee where his condition was listed as critical. The Hospital phoned me and I spent most of the night there while they worked on Orth. He was badly hurt, managed to tell a nurse to phone me and that I was to inform you," Mike stated.

The funeral for Orth Shilling Volzenkoff was held at the Memorial Gardens Cemetery in Oesterich on Tuesday, the fourth of October 1993. A Color Guard came from Fort MacArthur and presented the flag that had draped the casket to John. Libby stayed a long while after the service. Danny was driven home by Reverend Mike.

THE FUNERAL FOR ORTH SCHILLING VOLZENKOFF WAS HELD AT THE MEMORIAL GARDENS CEMETARY IN OESTERICH WISCONSIN.....

She stood, head bowed weeping and wringing her hands. Catherine Irene Zimmermann.

John and Bert stood at a short distance behind her then they walked up and put their arms about her and led her to Bert's car. Bert drove her home. The Lord knows how devoted her love was for Orth. She would remain as his sweetheart now and forever.

Libby as always at the cemetery on Sundays and special days to place flowers on Orth's grave. She would stand there, with Danny, sometimes. They seemed to feel that Orth was there with them.

> *And we are not afraid, but are quite content to die, for then we will be at home with the Lord. So our aim is to please Him always in everything we do, whether we are here in this body or away from this body and with Him in Heaven.*
>
> 2 Corinthians 5:8-9

EPILOGUE

Orth was the yeast to ferment many souls he met along life's journey. Libby became a devout Christian. She taught Sunday School – helped constantly with Methodist Church activities and reared Danny in the ways of the Lord. She never remarried preferring to save her love for her departed beloved Orth. Robert Scapegrace became a Methodist preacher – having his own congregation in Des Plains, Wisconsin. Fritz Otto, Orth's brother remained a bachelor and converted to Catholicism. Eddie Aiteanwealer met a Seventh Day Adventist girl and they were married. He is now a missionary for that church and will not touch any alcoholic beverage.

Barnabus Blitzgreez attends church where Libby teaches Sunday School in Green Bend. He still enjoys his tankards at Frederick's however – but Libby has hopes he will discover the happiness of Christ.

Orth's faithful dog Mutnik was taken in by Libby, but died of old age and a broken heart soon thereafter. He was a one-man dog and seemed lost when his Master departed. Orth's rich Uncle Humphrey fell upon bad times. Through a series of bad investments he ended up almost destitute and passed away shortly after he wife, Mae, in a small apartment on the south side of Milwaukee. Nancy Steinmann married a Muslim mathematics teacher in Salt Lake City. She and her husband later joined the Central United Methodist Church in the central part of the City.

Both of Orth's sons, John and Bert, remained steadfast Christians and members of local Methodist congregations. And many other comments could be related to the efficacy of Orth's words of Gospel teaching, for example, his tireless work with youth groups and his relentless witnessing for Christ during his travels. But the Lord knows of all of our efforts and I am certain that the indestructible soul of Orth Schilling Volzenkoff will go on working for his Master in heaven.

—M.B.
1999, New Haven, Connecticut

LIST OF CHARACTERS

Not sequential.

Orth Schilling Volzenkoff. Our hero.

Eddie Aiteanwealer. Tavern patron at Frederick's, a truck driver.

Barnabus Blitzgreez. Friend and drinking companion of Eddie Aiteanwealer.

Libby Latouche. [Catherine Irene Zimmermann]. Friend and Sweetheart of Orth's.

Bertha Mueller. Waitress at Frederick's.

Archie Airehorn. Friend, and sometime antagonist of Eddie Aiteanwealer.

Paul Worthy. Police officer in Milwaukee, friend of our hero.

Frederick Hauptman. Deceased owner and founder of Frederick's Tavern in Milwaukee.

Otto Lufthaven. Tavern manager and present owner of Frederick's.

Robert (Bob) Scapegrace. Gang leader who attacked and injured Orth in a Milwaukee parking lot. Became involved with illegal drugs, etc., later became converted to Christianity and a minister for the Methodist Church.

Alfred Worthy Scapegrace. Attorney and father of Robert (see above).

Mrs. Mary Ann Scapegrace. Mother of Robert (see above).

Doctor Allworth L. Fairweather. Physician who attended Orth after his encounter with Bob Scapegrace's gang.

Kim Lok Song. North Korean sergeant who spared Orth's live on the Korean battlefront because of his Christian moral convictions.

Fritz Otto Volzenkoff. Orth's older brother and constant antagonist and critic.

Frederick Haupt Volzenkoff. Our hero's father.

Albert Haupt von Volzenkoff. Orth's paternal grandfather from Darmstadt, Germany.

Ida Anna Holtzmeyer. Orth's grandmother, divorced from Albert Haupt von Volzenkoff.

Bertha Mae Schilling. Orth's mother.

Humphrey Aldo Schilling. Orth's wealthy uncle.

Mae Winfield Goldstein Schilling. Uncle Humphrey's wife.

John Galileo. Orth's American Legion battery partner and high school chum.

Robert (Bob) O'Kelley. Negro buddy of Orth's during high school days.

Eddie Burran. Elderly gentleman living close to the Volzenkoff farm who used to drive Fritz and Orth to Sunday School.

Bessie Ordway. Elderly woman living close to the Volzenkoff dairy farm near Oesterich who used to drive Fritz and Orth to Sunday School.

Olaf Larson. School mate of our hero who played end on the high school football team.

Gus Hakeem. Football player at Notkot High School.

Ernie Swartz. Football coach at Oesterich High School.

Declan Angow. High school chum and fellow football player.

Doctor Bullins. Physician who operated upon Orth while he was in his teen years, to remove a cyst.

Louie Gonzalo. High school friend who played baseball on teams with Orth.

Ida Tross. High school algebra teacher.

Larry Parkinson. Oesterich High School baseball coach.

Francis Hutchinson. High School chemistry teacher.

Jim Brancis. Assistant football coach, Oesterich High School.

Mr. Schultz. Principal, Oesterich High School.

Joe "Atomic" Gariotta. High school friend.

Donna Lue Sregor. Deceased wife of our hero.

Horace Philpot. Captain, U.S. Army Company Commander, 24th Infantry Division.

Terry Smith. First Sergeant, U.S.A., Orth's Company in Japan, 24th Infantry Division, see Chapter III.

Bruce Namyah. Jewish buddy in the Army – see Chapter VI.

Les Masterson. Elderly gentleman that Orth sailed with, see Chapter VI.

Evelyn Lovejoy. Friend of Grandmother Ida's.

Mr. Flowers. Personnel Officer with the Wisconsin State Bank.

Marvin Florin. Friend of Orth's that resided at the Y.M.C.A. in Milwaukee.

Charles "Swede" Swenson. Friend of Orth's that resided at the Y.M.C.A. in Milwaukee, worked as a gas station attendant - Atlantic Richfield.

Malvina. First girl Orth kissed – see Chapter VII.

Ursala. Swede Swenson's girl friend.

Paul Semirg. Methodist minister at New Hesse.

Tom Tolliver. Buddy of Orth's in the Army – basic training and later in the 24th Infantry Division.

Nancy Steinmann. Jewish lady and friend at the University of Utah.

Robert Stimson "Chopsticks" Chang. Buddy of Orth's in the Army – see Chapter X.

Michael Roosevelt Chang. Father of Robert Chang.

Bernadette Lore. Choir director, New Hesse Methodist Church – see Chapter XI.

John Schilling Volzenkoff. Eldest son of our hero.

Emily Klankfort. Wife of John Volzenkoff.

Bertram Orth Volzenkoff. Second son of our hero.

Amie Dingfeldt. Wife of Bertram Volzenkoff.

Van Ibsen. First Sergeant I Corps Artillery Headquarters Battery.

Ronald Dilbert. Captain, U.S. Army, Commanding Officer Headquarters Battery, I Corps Artillery.

William A. Snowbert. Second Lieutenant, U. S. Army, Fire Support Section – see Chapter XII.

Joe "Rosie" Rosales. Corporal Radio Operator – see Chapter XII.

Steve Iverson. Sergeant, FSE, Orth's friend in time of need – see Chapter XII.

Marvin Funkweiler. Captain, U.S. Army, Orth's shift chief in the FSE Element – see Chapter XII.

W. Herbert "Shoe" Schuler. Brigadier General, U.S. Army, Commander I

Corps Artillery – see Chapter XII.

Regnald Arnold-Berkmister. Captain, British Artillery Officer – see Chapter XII.

Horace K. Scholder. Captain, Chaplain – Disciplinary Barracks, Japan – see Chapter XIV.

Abraham S. Rapaport. Lawyer, U.S. Army, assigned to defend our hero – see Chapter XIV.

Michael Paul Wilinda. Methodist Minister who replaced the Rev. Paul Seming – see Chapter XV, has wife Linda and two daughters, Roxanne and Bethany.

Albert Casebolt. First Sergeant, Finance School Company – see Chapter XV.

Tina Lovelace. Choir Director, Fort Leonard Wood – see Chapter XVI.

Lawrence P. Worth. Lieutenant Colonel, U.S. Army, Finance Officer – see Chapter XVI.

"Pops". Ticket agent – see Chapter XV.

Dr. Leonard V. Rasher, Ph.D. Professor of Finance, San Francisco State University – see Chapter XVII.

Paul Nippep. Corporal, Finance, U.S. Army, friend of our hero.

Richard "Rick" Jaggar. Chum of Orth's at Wells Fargo Bank – see Chapter XVII. Rick's girlfriend – Tina Whitecastle.

Fernando Gonzalo. CPA friend of Orth's who worked for Main, LaFrenz & Co. – see Chapter XVII.

Bill Tellborg. Old dairy farmer, wife was Ethel – see Chapter XVIII.

Svend Peterson. Dairy farmer – rented land from Orth in Hilmar – see Chapter XVIII.

Dr. James Colling Wilberforce. Wife Evelyn May Sregor. Donna's aunt. Family of six children – see Chapter XVIII.

Judy Wilberforce. Niece of Dr. Wilberforce.

Ardenello & Jarvis. CPA firm, Stockton, California, Partners - Bill Ardenello and James Jarvis.

Reverend Alec Applebee. Ship's chaplain on the S.S. Orsova – see Chapter XIX.

Mrs. Ann Roustone. Our hero's typist – see Chapter XX.

Graham Greensleeve. President, Australian Society of Accountants – wife, Hazel – see Chapter XXI.

Jessica Broadstreet. Neighbor in Australia who led Orth to his Christian conversion, husband is Harry.

Reverend Alfred "Alf" Koenig. Methodist minister in Australia that helped lead Orth to his conversion.

Michael P. Oxford. Friend of the Volzenkoff's in Australia, wife Millicent, son Peter and daughters Jennifer and Pamela.

Bryan Beardsly. Australian geologist and yachtsman.

Dr. J. Finchley Folgelmeyer, Ph.D., Dean School of Business – see Chapter XXIII.

Francis Folgelmeyer. Son of Dr. Folgelmeyer – see above.